INSIDIOUS ASSASSINS

INSIDIOUS ASSASSINS

EDITED BY WELDON BURGE

Smart Rhino Publications
www.smartrhino.com

These are works of fiction. All of the characters, organizations, places, and events portrayed in these stories are either products of the authors' imaginations or used fictitiously. Any resemblance to actual persons (living or dead), events, or locales is purely coincidental.

First Edition

DEDICATION

For my parents, Clark and Doris Burge.
They raised five quiet yet audacious children.

CONTENTS

ACKNOWLEDGMENTS

Thanks go to Whitney Cook for her striking cover illustration, to Scott Medina for designing the cover, and to Terri Gillespie for her excellent proofreading skills.

I must also point out here that, although most of the stories are original to this volume, a number are reprints. Jack Ketchum's tale, "Those Rockports Won't Get You into Heaven," was previously published in his collection *Closing Time*. "Labyrinth," by James Dorr, first appeared in the March 1997 issue of *Tomorrow SF*. Joe Lansdale's story, "Best-Seller Guaranteed," was initially published in *Espionage Magazine*, and later appeared in *Best-Sellers Guaranteed*, a collection of Lansdale's short stories published by Ace Books.

INTRODUCTION: THE ALLURE OF THE INSIDIOUS

BY WELDON BURGE

In 1913, a novel was published introducing one of the first true super-villains in popular fiction. The title of the book was *The Insidious Dr. Fu-Manchu*. The book by Arthur Sarsfield Ward—better known by his pseudonym Sax Rohmer—was the first of 13 novels, numerous short stories, and eventually many feature-length movies.

Bent on world domination, Fu-Manchu was the epitome of "insidious"—a criminal mastermind with unlimited cunning, a giant intellect, and a talent for monstrous cruelty. Killing to reach his goals was never even questioned, and his use of exotic poisons unknown to traditional science was legendary.

What I find interesting is that Fu-Manchu, the arch-villain, is far more memorable than his heroic adversary, Nayland Smith. Why is this? In the films based on the books, Fu-Manchu was played by venerable actors like Boris Karloff, Christopher Lee, and Warner Oland. Now, name me even one actor who portrayed Nayland Smith. No? Why is the hero of these tales far less interesting than his evil counterpart? Why do we find insidious characters so appealing?

Now consider Walter White, the antihero of the TV series *Breaking Bad*. Here we have a high school chemistry teacher, diagnosed with inoperable lung cancer, who turns to producing and selling crystal meth to assure his family's financial future. We can easily label Walter as "insidious" as he turns to murder, betrayal, and multiple criminal acts to obtain his goal. He is a heinous, despicable character. Yet, largely because of Walter's popularity, the *Breaking Bad* series ran for five seasons and became one of the top-rated and most-watched cable shows ever, winning numerous awards.

1

Clearly, there is a peculiar allure of insidious characters—and especially assassins, hit men, and their ilk. Perhaps we find their uncomplicated moral codes and brutal efficiency appealing. These characters care little about ethics—and perhaps that alone, that freedom from guilt, is exactly why we love them. Perhaps, deep down, we wish we could be like them. And perhaps, by reading stories with such characters, we can vicariously experience that thrill.

With this fascination with evil characters in mind, Smart Rhino Publications decided to publish this anthology, *Insidious Assassins*. The book contains 24 stories by some of the best horror, suspense, science fiction, and fantasy authors writing today. Here you will meet some truly insidious characters, characters you may find yourself applauding when you know you shouldn't. I hope you'll find their stories not only entertaining, but in many ways thought-provoking.

If Sax Rohmer were still with us, I think he would be proud of the following collection of stories. I know I am.

Enjoy (and don't feel guilty about it)!

THOSE ROCKPORTS WON'T GET YOU INTO HEAVEN

BY JACK KETCHUM

The place was going all to hell—not that you'd necessarily notice unless you worked there. The floor was mopped and the glasses fairly clean. The bottles were dusted and the bar wiped down, but then I took care of that.

But the owner had two other restaurants on the same block and kept swapping bottles back and forth between them. So you never knew when you came in after the day shift what would be on the shelves. You'd have plenty of Dewars one day and the next day maybe a quarter of a bottle. It also meant that you'd find a liter of peach brandy or port wine getting overly chummy with the single-malts. The wines kept changing according to whoever threw him the best deal that week, and half the time there was no beer on tap whatsoever.

Waiters, busboys, hostesses—everybody was owed back pay. Myself included, half the time.

It was March and one of the coldest, longest goddamn winters on record and the heat was off again. Had been all week. All we had between us and runny noses was a single space heater looking lonely

3

and pathetic behind the hostess station. Customers ate their *taramasalata* and *souvlakia* with their coats on.

There weren't many of them. You don't associate Greek cuisine with frozen tundra.

It was six o'clock Thursday evening and of my dwindling group of regulars not a single one had shown up. I couldn't blame them. They were all wised up to the heating situation. We had more waiters and busboys than customers. Two couples and a party of four in the restaurant and that was that.

I was going fucking broke here.

Not a tip on the bar in two hours.

I polished bottles. It's a bartender thing. You got nothing to do, you polish bottles.

When the guy walked in with his kid trailing along behind him the first thing I thought was Westchester. Either that or Connecticut. I don't know why because plenty of guys around here are partial to Ralph Lauren and Rockports and outfit their kids in L.L. Bean. But there was something vaguely displaced about him. That's the best I can do. He didn't belong here.

You get so you kind of sense this shit.

They walked directly to the bar but neither one sat down. The kid maybe fourteen I guessed and taking his cue from dad.

"Glass of white wine," he said.

"Sure. We've got pinot grigio, chardonnay, and two Greek wines—Santorini and Kouros. Both very nice. What can I get for you?"

"Whatever."

"Would you care to taste one?"

"No, that's okay. Give me the Santorini."

"You got it."

Like I say, you just get a sense about these things. The guy was *wrong* somehow. Wound so fucking tight he was practically ready to give off sparks should he start to do any *un*winding, and you probably didn't want to see that.

You're not supposed to have an underage kid with you at a bar in New York City but most of the time we look the other way and most of the time the guy will order his kid a Coke or something and we look the other way on that, too. This guy didn't. And of course I didn't offer.

I poured the wine and he drained off half of it in one swallow.

"I used to come in here all the time," he said. Not to me but to his kid.

Though he wasn't *looking* at his kid.

His eyes were all over the place. The rows of bottles behind me, the murals on the wall, the ceiling, the tables and chairs in the restaurant. But I had the feeling he wasn't really seeing much of it. Like he was scanning but not exactly *tracking*. Except when he turned to look out the plate-glass windows to the street beyond. That seemed to focus him. He drank some more.

"It's changed hands, hell, maybe a dozen times since then. This was way before I met your mother."

The kid was looking at him. He still wasn't looking back. Or at me either for that matter. He kept scanning. As though he were expecting something to jump out of the clay amphorae or the floral arrangements. That and turning back to the window and the street.

"Not really, sir," I said. "You must be thinking of another place. A lot of turnaround on the Avenue but not here. It's been the Santorini for about ten years now and before that it was a Mexican restaurant, Sombrero, from about the mid-fifties on. So unless you're a whole lot older than you look ..."

"Really?"

"That's right."

"Damn. I could have sworn ..."

He was trying to act as cool and casual as the clothes he had on but I could feel him flash and burn suddenly all the same. He didn't like me correcting him in front of his kid. Tough shit, I thought. Fuck you. Snap judgments are part of my stock in trade and I hadn't liked him from the minute he walked in. He made an attempt at a save.

"I used to live around here. Long time ago. Early seventies."

"Really? Where was that?"

"Seventy-first, just off the park."

"Nice over there. And pretty pricey these days. So where are you folks now?"

"We're out in Rye."

5

Westchester, I thought. Gotcha.

He turned back to the street again. I noticed that his son was staring at me and I thought, Jesus, if this guy looked displaced his kid looked absolutely *lost*. He had big brown eyes as bright and clear as a doe's, and the eyes seemed to want to make contact with me. For just a second there I let them.

It could have just been me but it felt like he was looking at me as though I were some kind of crazy lifeline. It wasn't a look I was used to. Not after two divorces and fifteen years bartending.

"I'll have another," the guy said.

I poured it for him and watched him gulp it down.

"We don't get over this way much anymore," he said. "Hardly at all. His mother's across the street shopping."

His mother, I thought. Not my wife but his mother. That was interesting.

And I figured I had it now—pretty much all of a piece. What I had here in front of me was one stone alky sneaking a couple of nervous quick ones while the little wife wasn't looking. Dragging his kid into a bar while she was out spending all that hard-earned money he was probably making by managing *other* people's hard-earned money so he could afford the house in Rye, the Rockports, and the Ralph Lauren and L.L. Bean.

I wondered exactly where she was spending it. Betsy Johnson, Intermix and Lucky Brand Dungarees I figured would be way too young for anybody he'd be married to, and I doubted she'd be bothering with the plates and soaps or scented candles over at Details. That left either L'Occitane if she was into perfume or Hummel Jewelers.

My bet was on the jewelers.

My other bet was that there was great big trouble in paradise.

And I was thinking this when I heard the *pop pop pop* from down the street.

The kid heard it too.

"What was that?" he said. He turned to the windows.

The guy shrugged and drained his wine. "Backfire, probably. I'll have one more, thanks." He set the glass down.

Only it wasn't backfire. I knew that right away.

6

When my first wife Helen and I lived in New Jersey, we'd now and then get slightly loaded afternoons and take her little Colt Pony and my .22 rimfire semiauto out to the fields behind our house and plunk some cans and bottles. The Colt made pretty much the same sound.

Ordinarily, I'd have been out in the street by now.

Instead, I poured him the wine.

This time the guy sipped slowly. Seemed calmer all of a sudden. I revised my thinking big time about him being just another alky. His eyes stopped skittering over the walls and settled on the bar in front of him.

"Dad?" the kid said.

"Uh-huh."

"Shouldn't we go see how mom's doing?"

"She's shopping. She's doing fine. She loves shopping."

"Yeah, but ..."

And now it was the kid's eyes that were darting all over the place.

"We don't want to rush her, do we? I'll just finish my wine here. Then we'll go see what she's up to."

I got that look from the kid again. The look seemed to say *do something, say something*, and I considered it for a moment.

The phone on the wall decided for me.

By the time I finished noting down the take-out order—Greek salad, mixed cold appetizers, calamari, roasted quail, and two cans of *Sprite* for godsakes—the woman's name, address, and phone number, the guy was reaching for his wallet. His hands were shaking. His face was flushed.

"What's the damage?"

"That's twenty-four dollars, sir."

He fished out a ten and a twenty and downed the last of his wine.

"Keep the change," he said.

Nice tip, I thought. You don't see twenty-five percent much. Maybe the bar at the Plaza, but not in this place. I figured he wanted me to remember him.

I figured I would remember him. Vividly.

The kid turned back to look at me once as he followed his father out the door. It was possible that I might have seen a flash of anger or maybe a kind of panic there but I could have been imagining that. You couldn't be sure.

I rang up the wine and cleared his glass and wiped down the bar. He'd spilled a little.

There were a few ways to play this. First, I could be straight about it and report exactly what I saw. *All* of what I saw. Not just his being there but the high-wire tension going slack as shoestrings once the shots went off and then all nervous again when he was about to leave. The way the kid kept looking at me. Or just for fun I could try to fuck the guy over royally and completely by saying gee, I really didn't remember him at all to tell the truth. Though that might not work if his kid said otherwise. Finally, I could find out who he was and shake him down for a whole lot more than twenty-five percent in maybe a day or so.

Hell, I already knew where he lived.

But I pretty much knew what I was going to do.

As I say, I've had two divorces and know what a bitch they can be. And I'm no big fan of married women in general, either.

But my daughter by my second wife was just about this kid's age. Maybe a bit younger.

I wondered who he'd hired. How much he'd paid. If they'd actually hit the jewelry store just for show or only the woman inside it.

I polished bottles—it's a bartender thing—and waited for the gawkers and the sirens and New York's finest to come on in.

Thanks to Matt Long.

DEAD BILL

BY SHAUN MEEKS

"Why do they call you Dead Bill?" Justin asked.

"One name's as good as the next." Bill said with a smirk. He took a sip of his beer, and then put his glass back down. "I guess the name probably has to do with how many times people have killed me. Luckily, a little killin' doesn't do much to me these days."

Justin looked at him, amused but curious. The guy looked like someone who belonged in a cowboy movie, one of those old black-and-white jobs with John Wayne or Roy Rogers. He wasn't dirty like some of the homeless people that were outside the bar on a regular basis, but he had an air of dustiness around him, as though a cloud of hardtop would puff off of him if you clapped his back.

When Justin had come in and seen Dead Bill at the bar, he hadn't thought anything of him right away. Dead Bill just sat there, nursed a beer, ate free pretzels, and looked just like any other barfly. But when Justin took a good look at him, saw the way he was dressed and the black cowboy hat next to him on the empty stool, he knew he had to talk to the guy.

Justin loved the weird people he ran into at bars around the city. Sure, there were other places he could meet the strange and unusual, but people at bars tended to wanted to talk, to tell their stories. And some of the stories he'd heard had been so good, so unique, they had to be told.

That's why he'd started his blog in the first place. He'd speak to people he met, ones that seemed like they had a decent story to tell. Some of them rattled on and on for hours, went from one story to the next, then retreaded over the same ground again and again. Justin would sit and listen to it all. He didn't interrupt much, nor did he ever mention it if they repeated themselves. He just listened, then went home and edited everything down to something interesting and marketable. Once he felt it was good enough, he'd post it online for people to read.

He called the blog *The Secret World Under Our Noses* and, within a month, the site received nearly three-hundred-thousand hits a week. It became so popular that the *New York Times* picked it up. Millions read his postings. He knew there were so many strange and interesting people in the city that he'd be in business forever—as long as he could keep hunting down the good tales.

When he pulled up next to the city cowboy, he hoped it would be good. He switched on the tape recorder hidden in his shirt pocket and then introduced himself. The man turned, gave him a nod, and then went back to his beer. Justin was worried that he'd be hard to crack, but a moment later the man turned back and said his name was Dead Bill. Justin was sure the story he'd get from the man would be the best to date.

"What do you mean by that? The thing about how you've been killed so many times."

"You're a curious sort, aren't you?" Dead Bill asked and downed the last of his beer. "Maybe you should order me a drink if you're going to try to get all intimate with my brain."

"Sure." Justin said and called the bartender over. "Can we get another beer for him, and just water for me?"

"Water?" Dead Bill scoffed and slapped Justin on the back. He shook his head and looked around the bar as if to see how many others heard the dumb words leave the kids mouth. "Look here, kid, if you want to sit with me and ask me questions, you're gonna need to man up and get something with more balls than a glass of water. Water is for plants and dogs, and you don't look like neither. Jack, get this boy same as I'm having."

10

"No problem, Bill." The bartender said and put two beers down.

"Now, kid, why you wanna know all this anyway? You some sort of cop? A reporter? What is it? I mean, I don't mind tellin' you. Hell, I love to talk. I think I've a voice as sweet as sugar, but I'm wondering. Not many people come in here with the curiosity you have."

Justin wasn't sure if he should tell him the truth. The man might seal his lips and walk away without as much as a whisper of "have a nice day," but there was no good way to lie about it. He usually told people what he did, and that made them want to talk even more. One thing he'd learned in all his time doing the blog was most people want to have their stories—even the mundane ones—out for others to read or hear; as though it was a way to leave something about them behind. So, Justin explained about the blog and hoped the old cowboy wouldn't mind. As he told him, Dead Bill smiled brightly and nodded.

"Well, hell then. That's as good a reason as any, I guess. Might be good advertisin' for me too."

"How so?" Justin asked.

"Well, I offer a service, you see. It's part of the reason I'm called Dead Bill. You might not know this, but some people just need to get things off their chest. They can do that with a priest, with a hooker. A few people might write in a journal, or just beat their kids to get these things out. But some people need to come see me and get into a little murder. You'd be amazed at how gettin' your hands all warm with blood can heal a soul. That's what I offer them. A person they can kill guilt-free. Me. No worries of goin' to jail or havin' their souls condemned to Hell. It's not a thing many, if any, can offer."

"Wait," Justin said, not sure he understood the old cowboy. "You mean you let people kill you? I take it this is some virtual version of murder. Like a video game thing or something acted out like those murder mystery weekends, right? They don't actually kill you?"

"Didn't I tell you my name is Dead Bill, son? I've been shot, stabbed, decapitated, disemboweled, exsanguinated, electrocuted, dismembered, and drowned. People have ways they want to kill someone and I let them use me. I have a talent for being killed and wakin' up right as rain the next day." The old cowboy said it so easily, believable and nonchalant, that Justin started to think the guy might not even know he was full of crap.

11

"That makes no sense. There's no way someone could kill you and you're still here." Justin said, and immediately thought about just getting out of there. If the old kook planned to tell him something so farfetched that there be no way for him to use the story, he figured he should just move on and find someone else to talk to.

Yet, there was a part of him, the child inside maybe, that wanted to believe the fantastic story, to hear him out. He briefly looked around the bar, looked for other marks that might give him a better story, but it looked like slim pickings. So he stayed in his seat and let the man that called himself Dead Bill finish his story.

"There's plenty in this world that makes no sense and ain't right, son. But it is what it is. When I was twenty, I was shot twice by some druggie that decided to rob a liquor store. He got all twitchy at the end, decided he didn't want witnesses, and I took a round of buckshot to my chest. I saw the room get all dark, felt my body go as cold as a lake in January, and then saw that light everyone talks about. Not sure if it was heaven or not, because I never found out. As soon as I started to move toward that warm light, things got dark again. That's when I woke up the next day to see the sun shinin' and hear the birds singin'. Not a scar on me. And I wasn't in a hospital or still in the liquor store. I was in my old comfy bed in my small but cozy house.

"Months later, I got hit by a car that lost control and took out a group of people on a sidewalk. I saw it comin', wanted to get out of the way. But it was like one of those dreams where your legs are frozen in place. The metal hit flesh and I went to that dark place again. And yet, I woke up from that too.

"Then I had an idea that death might not want me. For whatever reason, death wanted nothing to do with yours truly, or so I figured. Not sure why really. I've never been a particularly bad person, even went to church on the regular as a tike. But it was all I could think of, so I put the old theory to the test.

"I don't believe in suicide, but decided to kill myself a few times and test out this death thing. I woke up the next day after each one and felt great. Now my momma didn't raise no fool, so I knew I had a special gift here. A little somethin' God had blessed me with and I needed to make the best of it. The only question was—how? And after a few days of ponderin' the possibilities, I came up with somethin' I thought was great; and it would earn me a few bucks too. It wasn't

12

anything criminal, mind you, but a way to help out people live out that darkness that lives in them. It's not an easy thing to admit, I know at first it was hard to find clients that would, but I think that we all have a little killin' in our hearts. Otherwise normal people, moms, dads, teachers, you name it, have thoughts of murder from time to time. Lots of people have a dark streak, kid, and I'm here to help them get it out."

Justin, who hadn't had any alcohol since he left college four years before, grabbed the beer and chugged half of it down. It was cold and bitter, but he hoped it would help a bit to make sense of the whole situation. He was with a man that looked like a cowboy from an old movie, who carried himself with such strange confidence and had just told him the craziest, most unbelievable story he had heard since he had started doing his blog. He was so glad that he had stuck around and let the old coot tell his tale, because it was amazing, even if it was utterly impossible. Here was Dead Bill, a man that found he couldn't die, and had decided to use the gift to hire himself out to be murdered for money, only to wake up the next day without a scratch. To Justin, the old guy was pretty much saying he was immortal, could be a superhero if he wanted, yet instead he had become a businessman and sold people the chance to take the life of a human with no consequences.

This is going to make me famous!

"Have you had a lot of clients?" Justin asked.

"A fair amount. I usually have one or two a month. Been doin' this for about fifteen years, so you do the math."

"And how much do they pay?"

"Depends on their station in life. I ain't going to make a single mom of two pay the same amount to kill me as I would some high-priced lawyer or doc. I have a heart, you know. Better to see what they can do and take it from there."

"You get single moms hiring you?" Justin asked as he tried to wrap his head around someone like his own mother hiring a man to murder. It was absurd.

Dead Bill laughed and ordered another beer on the kid's tab. "Son, mothers bite down more urges to kill than anyone else in the world. They have to deal with their snot-nosed little brats, husbands that think workin' all day absolves them from raisin' a child, teachers and other parents that tell them they're doing their job wrong, and their own family that can only nitpick about how they're rearin' their own spawn. So yeah, I get a lot of moms doin' all sorts of evil to me. They do have a mean streak in them too. Creative little bitches."

The bartender had lingered there and began to nod when Dead Bill told him that. "Hell, even I paid Dead Bill here once. You might be surprised, but this job can push someone over the edge too. So many idiots come through that door every day and nine out of ten make me angry enough to kill."

Justin watched him walk away and felt that there was instant credibility with that statement. There was no reason for the bartender to lie, to jump in and say something like that. Justin saw the green of money and heard the echoes of fame ringing in his ears.

"So how do people find you?" Justin asked as he tried to hide his elation at how great the story was.

"Word gets around and they just do. I don't usually ask how someone finds me, but if you are puttin' up this blog I will give you my website address and it will be easier for more people to find me."

"You have a website?"

"These days, everyone has a website. A businessman with no website usually goes out of business right quick. I might look like some dim cowpoke, but I ain't ignorant, kid. I'm a modern hillbilly."

Justin knew what he said about websites was true. Everything was digital and had to be faster than fast. Blink for one second and the world forgets all about you. Becoming yesterday's news is as easy as taking a nap. Even with his own blog, there's always a chance someone else would write a better, more interesting one using pretty much the same formula as he did and people would just move on. Fast times for fast people.

But he wanted to make a mark. He'd always been on the lookout for bigger, crazier stories in the bars so he'd be able keep people reading and coming back to him. He was sure that Dead Bill would be his blockbuster. But for it to be a real hit, he knew he had to ask the right questions. As Dead Bill spoke, Justin thought about how he could make the story a multipiece set. He'd start big and then leave the readers hanging and begging for more. So the questions he asked had to be targeted and he knew he couldn't shy away from things. Nothing should be sacred.

"Does it hurt when you die? Do you feel the pain when you're getting shot or stabbed?"

"That's the one bad thing about it all. Getting shot hurts. Gettin' stabbed or skinned alive is not pleasant, but those things are nothin' compared to that moment when my body shuts down and pushes me into the darkness of death." Dead Bill paused there. He stared off into space and seemed lost for a second, as though the terrible memory was too much. Justin reached over and put his hand on the old man's forearm. The man was thin, but muscular; his skin had the texture or cracked leather, and looked like it too. These were details Justin knew he would need to remember and add later to his notes.

"You okay?" he asked the dusty cowboy.

"Sure, kid. I'm fine. It's just sometimes the memory of that pain can be something like a wall I need to get over. Damn, the cold I feel then is so vivid in my mind that I think I can feel it now, and it's a hard thing to get past. There's a moment, usually before I wake up, where the pain and the cold leaves me and there is such a sense of peace, total calm, and I feel like it's a place I want to be. But then my eyes open and I'm back in my apartment with just the memories of it all. I guess that's the downside. Never getting to feel the peace and calm for very long. But what can you do? Bitchin' about it ain't going to turn water into wine, right?"

"Have you ever denied someone? Was there ever a person whose idea seemed so over the top that you backed off, or at least wanted too?"

"Never. The customer's always right. That's my business motto, as it should be. Sure, there were some people that needed to know that there is a difference between killin' and torture. I don't allow that twisted shit where people get to spend hours messin' with me. Even the ones that dismembered me had to kill me straight out first, and then they can do the other stuff. I'm not lookin' to spend hours feelin' the bad part of it."

"You ever worried about people, you know ..."

"What? Let me guess, the whole sex thing?" Dead Bill said with a raised eyebrow and a sly smile on his face.

"Yeah," Justin said, and felt a little uncomfortable with the question. But he knew it had to be asked. Readers would want to know these things.

"Never. I make them all sign contracts and then the whole thing is videotaped. Never had someone do anything like that before. After all, I ain't the prettiest dame at the ball. My clients may be twisted a bit in wantin' to kill me, but they ain't so twisted as to want to saddle up on this buckaroo."

"Wait," Justin said, and felt excited. "You have them on video? All the killings?"

"Yeah. I usually give the client one and keep one for myself. Nothing I'd put on YouTube or anything, but I like to show new clients examples of what they can do. And I do like to make sure there's no real funny business going on when I'm all vulnerable."

"Could I see one?" Justin asked. He hesitated a bit because he wasn't sure how bad they'd be—but how could he not try? It wasn't something you saw every day. And it would also be hard proof that what the cowboy told him was legit, that he wasn't a complete nut. Even with the confirmation from the bartender, he still had doubt, and the videos would eliminate that completely.

"You ain't gonna get to post the videos on your blog, or record them. There's privacy to consider. My clients pay to have their dirty and violent secrets kept."

"Of course. I would never think of it. But to see them would make the blog even better. I could mention them only in the vaguest way, and say that I saw proof, firsthand, of what the process is like."

"Sure then. Why the heck not? How about one for the road though?" Dead Bill said and nodded to his empty beer bottle.

Justin happily ordered another beer for Dead Bill. Then the two of them left the bar and headed to the old cowboy's place. On the way there, Justin tried to picture where the man would live. In his mind, he saw a bachelor apartment in a less-than-perfect part of town, decorated with neon beer signs, posters of Dolly Parton, and a horseshoe over the door. He thought about a small, portable stereo set on milk crates with CDs by Travis Tritt, Hank Williams, and Bill Monroe.

When they stopped at an old industrial building that had been turned into loft space, he was surprised. They took the elevator to the

16

top floor and what Justin found there was not anything close to his expectation.

The place looked classier than the man who lived there. Expensive furniture, state-of-the-art entertainment system, and tasteful paintings filled the stylish interior. As they walked in, Dead Bill turned to Justin and saw the look on his face.

"Not what you were expectin'?" Dead Bill said with a smile.

"Not really. Very modern."

"I might have a cowboy in my heart, but I do love the comforts the city offers. Let's go over here."

Dead Bill led Justin over to the computer, pulled a chair out for him, and motioned for him to sit. As he did, the old cowboy turned the computer on and scrolled through video files in his hard drive until he found what he wanted.

"This is a good one to start with, to give you an idea of what I do."

Dead Bill hit play and stood behind Justin. At first there was just darkness, but soon the camera focused and on the screen was a dimly lit room with an empty chair in the middle of it, and nothing else.

"Now, no tapin' this," Dead Bill said, and Justin nodded. He would record it all in his memory. "Give it a second and it'll start."

Justin waited with nervous excitement. He'd reported so many great stories with his blogs over time, but nothing would be as amazing as what he would write up for Dead Bill. He thought that it would be so good that the *Times* might even move him from resident blogger to something with a little more panache to it. It might even be something that paid better than his normal rate, and then he'd be able to live somewhere as nice as Dead Bill's loft.

Someone moved in front of the camera on the video. The person walked toward the chair and Justin took a deep breath as he watched the man sit down and face forward. He expected it to be Dead Bill, but it wasn't. It was a man in a bad suit, with thinning hair. He looked familiar, but not so much that Justin could put a name to the face.

"First off, I want to thank Dead Bill for this opportunity." The man in the chair said and there was a wheeze in his speech, as though he had just run up a flight of stairs. "It's not every day someone gets to do this. So Bill, thank you."

"No problem," the old cowboy said from behind Justin, as though the guy on the video screen could hear him.

"I guess we should just get things rolling. There's no time like the present, right Justin?"

"What the fuck?" Justin said, and felt confused that the man in the video had said his name. But the feeling of confusion left him as he felt a belt wrap around his throat and squeeze. It choked him, made him gasp and struggle to breathe, but it was only tight enough to hold him still, not strangle the breath from him—yet.

"Sit still, kid," Dead Bill said, pulling tighter on the belt. "Calm down or I'll put you down. Your friend here has something to say to you."

Justin stopped his struggles and felt the belt loosen a bit. He gasped, his throat already felt as though it was on fire, but he needed to think, to make sense of what was going on. He heard the man on the screen laugh and looked over at the monitor. When he did, he saw his mistake. He'd been so anxious to see the videos that Dead Bill described that he didn't even notice it was a webcam feed, meant to look like a video. It was a live feed, and the man in the chair watched him with a smile.

"There, there, Justin. Just calm down a second, okay? I have a few things to say to you before we do anything else."

"Fuck you," Justin gurgled out. When he did, the belt tightened.

"Show some respect, kid!" Dead Bill growled, and then loosened the belt again.

"No worries. No worries at all," the man said. "Justin here just likes to spew shit without any thoughts. Isn't that right? Don't answer that. It's more of a rhetorical question. But the real questions start now. Do you know who I am?"

"No."

"You sure? Think hard on that."

Even when the man got up, walked toward the webcam, and gave Justin a good look at his face, there was nothing but a vague familiarity. He had no idea who he was, or what the hell was going on.

"No." He grunted and half expected the belt to be tightened again, but it wasn't.

"I feel a little insulted, Justin. I really do. After all, you talked to me for nearly three hours one night, bought me some drinks, and then fucked me like I was a two-dollar hooker. That help?"

"No."

"We met at the Silver Dollar and you came up to me. Maybe I looked funny to you, strange or just pathetic enough to spill out the details of my life that were juicy enough for your stupid fucking blog. You told the world my name, who I was, and that I was cheating on my wife with a priest. You told everyone and I lost everything I had. Everything, because of you."

Oh shit! Justin thought.

"I think I see a spark there, like you know. So, who am I?" the man in the chair asked.

"Darren Duffy."

"Ah, now you remember! That's good. Did you know what your stupid little blog did to me? Did you ever think that you were destroying people when you aired their dirty laundry in a public forum and got rich off it? Or were you just like, fuck it?"

"I didn't know."

"Nor did you care. You just go around and do these things without a thought in the world. My wife took off with our kids. I got fired from my job. My family disowned me. Even the priest left me, although he killed himself to hide his own shame and self-loathing. I lost everything that meant anything to me, just so you could write your little blog.

"And now, here we are. I knew you would come, too. I knew that when Dead Bill told you that story you would just eat it up. You'd be so captivated by your own potential fame, greed being the dirty whore that powers your mind, so you'd buy into it, no questions asked. I paid the bartender too, just to add to the mysticism of it all. But, seriously, a guy that gets paid to be murdered over and over again? Are you so stupid you would buy into a story like that?"

"He was convincing."

"And I have no classical trainin'. Go figure." Dead Bill laughed.

"Well, Dead Bill is his name, and although he doesn't get paid for people to murder him, he does get paid quite well to murder other people. And you are other people. I'm just glad that I'm going to get to watch. Now, Bill, I leave it to you."

19

"Please! Mr. Duffy, please don't do this. I will do anything! Just please don't kill me."

"I'm not going to kill you. He is."

"What can I do to make this right? Money? I can do that. I can even write a blog and say I lied about it all. If you want that, I can do that."

"No, Justin. You can't put a broke mirror back together. You'll always see the cracks. You can only do one thing for me ... and that's die."

Justin tried to plead again, but the belt tightened. The leather dug deep into his neck. Behind him, Dead Bill grunted from the force he exerted. Justin's hands flew up, fought to breach the space between neck and belt, but there was no use. He tried to breathe in, his lungs on fire from lack of oxygen, and dots of blinding light exploded in front of his eyes as he began to suffocate.

The pain was terrible.

Panic and fear of what was to come made him struggle, but Dead Bill was too strong and too experienced on serving out death. The pain pushed through in waves, his body throbbed with it. Tears poured down his face and he wasn't sure he would be able to take it anymore, thought that his suffering would be eternal.

But, as he thought that, he blinked and then the room dimmed. He felt calm. Pain began to bleed away from him as the light and sounds of the room left him. The darkness called out and seemed so much better than the loft, than the pain of the chair he had sat in. His name was being whispered, soft and sweet, and he knew that the dark he had feared as a child wasn't as bad as he thought.

He embraced the darkness and let go of everything that he once thought mattered. As the belt squeezed tighter, his body felt free for the first time in his life.

WORSE WAYS

BY MEGHAN ARCURI

Liv scrolled through the email on her phone and opened the latest message from her boss.

Subject: **Your probation.**

Shit.

Like she needed to be reminded. The body of the email stated the same trash he'd said before she left on this trip. You messed up with the last client, blah blah blah. You need to shape up or you won't move up, blah blah blah. You have promise. Don't waste your talent.

Blah blah blah.

So he sent her to a self-help conference. She and her colleagues traveled all over to do jobs. But self-help conferences were torture.

p.s. If you mess up on this assignment, these self-help conferences will be all yours. Permanently.

Double shit.

The thought of spending her time in smelly hotels listening to Guy Smiley-types peddle crap did not appeal.

Liv entered the Grand Ballroom for the main event and took her seat. She didn't bother to check out the attendees. She'd been to enough of these babies to know the players: housewives with extra padding, men in ill-fitting suits, young people hoping to become the

21

next guest speaker. All yearning for something to improve their lives, just a little.

Good luck with that.

Her cell phone vibrated. Another email. This time from Mary, a co-worker.

Subject: **The Big Apple.**

Just took my first bite and, boy, was it delicious. Wish you were here. How's the self-help industry?? ;) m

"Brat."

The woman next to her with a fanny pack gave her a look.

"Sorry," she said to Fanny Pack.

The New York City trip had been hers. And Mary was supposed to be here. That kiss-ass. She always found a way to get on the boss's good side. Not that Liv tried to get on his bad side. She just always seemed to be there.

The emcee wrapped his little spiel and introduced Bill Williamson, the self-help guru.

Williamson walked to the microphone, his gait full of a confidence that bordered on cockiness. Late fifties, maybe sixty. Salt-and-pepper hair. Tall. Striking. He started speaking. A rich, deep baritone. No wonder these people paid the ridiculous entry fee.

Her phone vibrated again. A text from her boss: **He's your client.**

Dammit.

She wanted to scream.

First, she'd been put on probation. Then Mary took her New York City trip. And now her boss wanted her to target the guest speaker?

Shit. Shit. And triple shit.

She rolled her eyes. She'd been given some doozies before, but this one was too much. The seminar lasted all weekend. Most workshops featured this guy. And the place crawled with people who loved him.

Her phone vibrated again.

Another text: **Just kidding. How was your hissy fit?? He's not yours. Beth's mtng him between 6:45 and 7:15.**

Liv texted: **Two jobs at one convention?**

He replied: **Your guy's at the end of your row. Meet him between 6:30 and 7:00.**

Liv checked her watch: 4:00. *Plenty of time.*

She found the man in question. Twenty-something, light hair, skinny but not scrawny. Wore khakis and a button-down shirt. She smiled. She could totally do this.

Another vibration. The boss: I'm pulling for you. But don't make it a repeat of last time.

Her reply: That guy totally deserved the fat lip.

After a second: Livvie ...

She shook her head and wrote: I'll do better this time.

Liv didn't anticipate trouble. This guy was attractive, but not her type. And nothing about his look or clothes bugged her, so she had that going for her. That last guy, Fat Lip, wore an Elmo shirt and banana slippers. And he was forty. Plus, he did a lot of whining and crying. Who wouldn't wanna smack him?

When her new client turned toward her, she let her stare linger too long, batted her eyelashes, and turned away. She may not want to bed him in actuality, but she could pretend with the best of them.

5:00.

Mr. Guru had completed his presentation and the breakout groups were next. Her client would attend one, but even if it ran long, she'd be able to deal with him by 6:30.

After more purposeful eye contact, she left for the lobby. As she pretended to check her voicemail, he approached. She held up a finger and waited, touched the screen of her phone, and pocketed the device.

"Not buying the seminar?" he said.

She gave him a playful look. "Not really."

He held out his hand to her. "Roger."

She took it with a light squeeze. "Liv."

"So which group are you going to?"

"The one led by Glen."

"Who's Glen?" He checked his program. "Which one is that?"

"Glenlivet. It's the one in the bar."

"Oh, I see." He laughed. "Mind if I join you after? I really want to check out the one called *Embracing Change*."

Sweet Jesus.

"Sounds interesting," she said.

"Definitely. Especially since I can be a little stubborn."

"I'm pretty sure I'll be hungry by the time that's over. Why don't you come up to my room and we'll order room service? My treat."

He seemed surprised at first, but then a big smile spread across his face.

"That sounds great. See you a little after six."

She gave him her room number.

Study up. You're going to embrace a big change real soon.

At the bar, Liv sipped her scotch and checked her phone.

5:30.

"You didn't do the breakout groups, did you?"

Not Roger's voice. Bill Williamson's.

Shit.

She did a quick scan for Beth, but didn't see her.

I'm sure she has it under control.

"Nope."

"Why not?"

She held up her glass. "I was thirsty."

"Me, too." He waved to the bartender. "Glenlivet neat, please."

"Nice choice," she said, pointing to her near-empty glass.

"Make it two."

He sat on the barstool next to hers.

"Bill Williamson."

"Liv."

"You didn't find the presentation helpful either, did you, Liv?"

"How could you tell?"

"Eye rolls are usually pretty good indicators."

"Oh. Yeah. Sorry about that."

He gave her a thoughtful look. "You don't seem sorry."

Liv's attitude had cost her opportunities for advancement. But she didn't care. She did her job well. Usually. And if she had to deal with some tsk-tsking from the powers that be, then fine. This guy would fit right in with them.

"Well, I guess I'm not."

He stared at her.

"Sorry," she said.

"Sorry for not being sorry?" He laughed. "That's priceless."

"You're not upset?" she said.

"Not at all."

Wow.

"I get scolded at my job for my attitude."

"I like it. It's refreshing. I love helping people, but sometimes it's nice to be around someone who isn't so ..."

"Needy?"

"Yes. Don't tell anyone I said that."

"No prob."

Maybe he's not an uptight idiot.

"Why bother coming, then?"

"My boss sent me."

"Ah. An information gatherer. I get a lot of those. Taking back tricks to bolster teamwork and office morale?"

"Something like that."

After more small talk about self-help, he said, "Listen. I'm going to have to be visible for dinner, but maybe afterward we could meet up? In my room? We could go over the general ideas you missed. Then you won't go back to your office empty-handed."

Oooo. He's hitting on me.

Under different circumstances she'd go for it, but he was a client. Beth's client. And Liv had no desire to interfere with anyone else's work. He'd be gone by that time anyway.

"I'm sorry," she said. "It sounds like fun. Truly. But maybe some other time."

The bartender set the bill on the bar. As Bill reached for it, she put her hand on his. "I'll get this one. Well, my company will, anyway."

"Thank you."

"Please bill this to room 202," she told the bartender.

"I guess I'll see you in the ballroom for dinner, then?"

"I guess."

25

He shook his head. "I thought we established that I like your honesty."

She shrugged.

"You're leaving tonight, aren't you?"

She looked at the clock again: 5:55.

"In about an hour."

"Well, it was a pleasure to meet you, Liv. Even if it was only for a short time."

She liked this guy. He seemed genuine. Smart. Not what she'd expected.

"The pleasure was mine." She shook his hand. "Good luck with the rest of the weekend."

Not that you'll make it that far.

She headed to her room. She had enough time to pack her bag, shower, and change out of her skirt and blouse. No sense in being uncomfortable for the Roger gig.

6:28.

Roger still hadn't arrived.

Where is he?

She put on her yoga pants and tank top. So much comfier.

Heavy footsteps and muffled voices sounded outside her door. She poked her head out. Three paramedics pushed a gurney toward the elevator. They shouted things like "not breathing," "heart failure," and "CPR."

Beth must have dealt with Bill. A little early, though. I thought they were meeting between 6:45 and 7:15.

Then she saw the patient's face. A young man.

The emcee. The guy who had introduced Williamson.

What the hell? Only two jobs at this convention.

Her phone vibrated on the nightstand.

A text from the boss: **Beth messed up. Wrong guy. I sent her home.**

She replied: **What???**

He wrote: **Deal with Williamson. Finish Roger, then find Bill. Not much time. Don't miss the window.**

26

She threw her phone on the bed.

Beth got the wrong guy?

"What a goddamned idiot."

6:35.

Already five minutes into Roger's window and still no sign of him. Maybe he forgot? And she had no idea where he'd be.

Ten minutes until Bill's window, but she knew exactly where he'd be: finishing dinner. In the ballroom. In front of hundreds of people.

"Dammit!"

She grabbed her phone and key, and yanked open the door.

Roger faced her.

"Hi. Sorry I'm a little late. There was some commotion in the lobby. Paramedics. Ambulance. The emcee had a heart attack, or something."

Thank Christ.

"I'm so glad you're here," she said, guiding him into the room.

"I'm happy to be here."

Only a few minutes until Bill's window. She didn't have time to waste.

"Can I get you something to drink before we order? I'm afraid I only have bottled water and Coke."

He sat on the bed. "Water sounds great."

She gave him a bottle of water from the mini-fridge. He took a sip.

"Crazy about the emcee," said Roger.

"Totally."

Stupid Beth.

Sweat formed on Roger's forehead. Pain crossed his face. He closed his eyes and put his head in his hands.

Showtime.

While his eyes were closed, she prepared herself and went to work. Within minutes, she finished the job and stepped away from him.

Roger's body slumped to the floor, a heap of lifeless humanity. His water bottle fell next to him, its contents pooling on the carpet.

"Thank God," she said.

6:43.

Now to deal with Bill.

How could she get him out of that crowded ballroom in time to finish the job?

27

A knock at the door.

Shit.

She checked to see if Roger's body was visible from the entrance. It wasn't, so she opened the door.

Bill Williamson.

What luck.

"I had a change of heart about trying to convince you. There were some points I should have made down at the bar. I was hoping you'd give me another chance."

Liv gave him the warmest smile she could muster. "Can you wait right here one second, please?"

"Sure."

She closed the door and hustled to Roger's body. She threw out his water bottle, dragged his body across the room, and stuffed it in the closet. Not dignified, but time was not on her side.

"Sorry about that," she said, letting Bill in the room.

"No problem."

He sat on the desk chair, turning it to face her.

She could relax now. He was here, with her. And his window had just opened. She had the entire half hour to finish the job.

"You have five minutes to make your case," she said, sitting on the bed.

"And if I don't?"

"Then it's back to your room. Alone."

You'll be dead, too, but that's a whole other issue.

"Then let me get right to it."

He offered data. She listened, asking pointed questions. He was engaging. Charming. He even made her laugh.

But she still had a job to do.

When he finished, she said nothing for a minute, pretending to process his information. Then she stood and walked to the mini-fridge.

"You should have a drink before you go."

"Before I go? I didn't convince you?"

"Not really," she said. "I've got water and Coke. Which will it be?"

"I didn't convince you."

"You made some good points, and I can see where you're coming from, but mostly I think it's a load of bull."

"I don't believe you," he said, standing.

"It's true."

He hadn't convinced her of the benefits of self-help. Maybe another time he would have. But not now. She'd had a long day, and she wanted to go home.

"Well?" she said.

"Well, what?"

"Water or Coke?"

"Coke. Please."

She poured the drink and handed him the glass.

He set it aside and stepped toward her.

"I just need to ..."

His hand slipped to the back of her neck. He pulled her into a kiss. She let him.

Then she pulled back and said, "Listen, I—"

But he didn't let her finish, finding her mouth again with his. Using his tongue. Playing with hers.

His hands moved down the sides of her body, before resting on her hips.

She hadn't done this in a while. And it felt good. To hell with that, it felt amazing.

She opened her eyes to peek at the clock: 6:52.

More than enough time. Might as well enjoy myself a little.

Through the kiss he said, "Is this okay?"

She put her arms around his neck and jumped onto him, her legs wrapping around his waist.

He laid her on the bed.

Rubbing a finger over her lips, he said, "You are a beautiful woman, Liv. Irreverent and funny. I noticed you the moment I walked out on that stage and haven't stopped thinking about you since."

"You can turn off the charm now. This is a done deal."

"I'm serious."

She put her lips on his.

He slid his fingers under her shirt. She loved the feel of his warm hands on her bare skin. He pulled off her pants and smiled, seeming to appreciate her decision to forego underwear.

His hands wandered over her naked body. Followed by his mouth.

He took his time. She closed her eyes. Within minutes, her body tensed, her back arched, and she let out a small gasp of air.

That felt way better than I remembered.

She took a second to recover, then sat up and helped him remove his clothes. She pushed him onto his back and straddled him.

Time to return the favor.

They lay in silence.

Then she heard a creak, followed by thumping.

"What the hell?" said Bill, sitting up, looking in the direction of the closet.

Shit!

Roger's dead body lay over the threshold.

Should have checked the latch.

"Who the hell is that? Is he ..." Bill ran over to the body. "He's dead. He's freakin' dead!"

"Ummm ..."

"You've got a dead guy in your closet and all you can say is 'umm'?"

"That's Roger."

His name? Really, Liv? That's the best you can do?

"Did you do this?"

"Well ..."

"Holy shit!" He grabbed his pants and fell over trying to pull them on. He righted himself, secured his pants, and backed toward the door. "What are you, some sort of assassin?"

Sort of.

7:04.

He seemed so full of fear, panic. Her heart sank. She liked this guy. Maybe she should tell him the truth. His time was almost up, anyway.

"You're not going to believe what I have to say."

"Tell me what the hell is going on."

He did say he liked my honesty.

"Fine. I'm a Taker," she said, getting off of the bed and walking toward him.

"Excuse me?"

"A Taker."

"What exactly are you taking?"

"You'd probably call it a soul."

"Okay," he said, reaching for the doorknob. "I'm usually a pretty good read of people. But I was way off with you. You're fucking crazy."

He can't leave. Not now.

"Bill, please. Don't go." She grabbed his arm. Her hand glowed. She felt his heartbeat slow, his tense body relax.

He returned to the bed and sat. "What did you just do to me?"

"Part of my job is to calm the body and mind."

"So that you can more easily kill me?"

"I'm not going to kill you."

"But you said you're taking my soul."

"It's really more of an essence. And I deal with it after your body starts to die."

"So, what, is the Angel of Death going to join us to do the actual deed?"

"Angel?" She sighed. "I forgot how humans like to oversimplify everything."

She sat next to him.

"I don't have time to explain it all to you. Bottom line? Your body's gonna die. Your essence is inside, and I need to take it."

"Because you're a Taker?"

"You got it."

"I can't believe I'm still listening to this."

"The sex probably helped."

"Probably. And you have quite an imagination."

"I do. But I'm not making this up."

She held up her hand and let it glow again.

"Okay. I'll play. Why are you taking my soul—I mean, essence?"

"Nice," she said. "I got a text from the boss and he said your time's up."

"The boss?"

"Yup."

"Would that be God?"

"Again with the oversimplifying. I thought we were making some headway."

"So he's not God?"

"Sometimes he acts like he is."

Her phone vibrated.

She smiled. "That's probably him right now."

"He sends texts?"

"Gotta keep up with the times."

"So, what are you going to do?"

"Well, you're scheduled to die right about now."

"Oh really. How?"

"I don't know for sure. Something natural—a heart attack, brain aneurysm, something like that. Basically, your body's going to fail."

"Then what?"

"Then I take your essence."

"Where? To Heaven?"

She laughed. "So it can go play in the puffy white clouds with the angels and their halos? I suppose you think there's fire and brimstone, too. Guy with a goatee. Pitchfork. Little red horns?"

"We're talking about my death and you're mocking me?"

"I see your point. Sorry."

"It's okay," he said. "So what exactly happens to my essence?"

"It has to go to Containment to get cleansed and nourished. Honestly, though, it's a good thing you showed up when you did."

"Why?"

"There's a half-hour window when a person starts to die. As a Taker, I need to be near you during that half hour, preferably alone. If you'd died somewhere away from me, your essence would have been trapped in your body. Would have become corrupted. Damaged. And if I don't get it out within that half hour, the damage is irreversible."

"That doesn't make any sense. Tons of people die every day. Car accidents, plane crashes, drive-by shootings. Those people aren't alone."

"That stuff's for Level Two and Level Three Takers. I'm only a Level One. I just deal with solitary deaths."

"Solitary deaths? Level Two? What are you even talking about?"

"I haven't studied for those qualifying exams yet, so I can't tell you much more than that."

He ran a hand through his thick hair. "This is unbelievable."

7:07.

"Look, any minute now, you'll start to feel off. And I'll change into my regular form."

"This isn't your regular form?"

"No. This is what I looked like before I died."

"You were so young."

"Yeah, but I've been a Taker for a while now."

"Can I see it?"

"My other form?"

"Yes."

"Would it help to convince you?"

"It might."

She shouldn't show him. The boss would not approve. But he kind of put her in this crappy situation. And, at the end of the day, she'd be going home with two successful jobs.

Why the hell not?

She stood. Putting her arms over her head, she transformed into a white, wispy apparition. Both humanoid and ghostlike, it sort of reminded her of dry ice. Her head took the shape of the one in Munch's painting, *The Scream*, but without the horrified expression. Amorphous, wing-like appendages rose from her back, but they weren't functional. She loved this form. She'd always found it beautiful. Haunting, but beautiful.

Amid the ethereal beauty, one part of her attracted more attention than the others: her left hand. Silver, razor-like claws protruded from the tips of her thumb and forefinger. Solid in form, they stood in stark contrast to the rest of her diaphanous figure.

She returned to her human form.

"Are you convinced?"

"I'll say."

"What'd you think?"

"Stunning. But ..."

"The claws?"

"Yes."

"If I were human, I'd call them my STDs."

"Excuse me?"

"STDs. You know, Soul Trimming Doo-dads. They help me sever your essence from your body."

He said nothing.

"You went frigid for a sec, didn't you? Right when you saw them?"

"Yes."

"That was your essence. Totally recognized those bad boys for what they are."

"How does it work?"

"Right after your body begins to fail, I change forms, enter your body and cut out your essence."

"Sounds painful."

"You're pretty much dead anyway, remember?"

"You're very cavalier about all of this."

"I guess. Kind of like anyone who does something often enough. Fisherman doesn't think twice about gutting a fish. Gynecologist doesn't get all crazy about seeing a va-jay-jay."

He laughed, then stopped. "Am I really going to be the cliché?"

"Which one?"

"The old guy who dies having sex in a hotel room?"

"I guess so. But it's better than the one where you wake up next to some dead prostitute. Like *The Godfather*. Or was it *The Godfather 2*?"

"Seriously?"

"Yeah. Which was it?"

"You're going to kill me and we're debating *Godfather* vs. *Godfather 2*."

"I told you. I'm not going to kill you. I'm going to take your essence."

"Splitting hairs, aren't you?"

"Not really. Killing you would be a grisly, ugly affair. I don't do blood. Your time's up. Your essence has to be returned. And I'm taking it from this world to the next. Consider me your inter-world guide."

"It was *The Godfather 2*," he said.

"You sure?"

"Prostitute? Politician? That's Vegas. Much of *The Godfather 2* took place in Vegas."

"And what happens in—"

"Please. Don't."

"Sorry."

"So what now?"

7:10.

She put her hand on his chest. An irregular heartbeat. The process had begun.

"I think we have a few more minutes."

He sat forward, fear on his face. "Can you do that glowy thing again, please?"

She let her hand glow over his heart.

He lay back on the bed. "That's much better."

"Good. Now that you're more relaxed, I can help out with any last minute requests." She slid her other hand up his leg toward his zipper.

"Well, if you're offering."

He cupped her face in his hands and gave her a kiss.

She pulled away. "After that, well ..."

"I'm dead."

"Pretty much."

"Definitely going to die?"

"Yes."

"But before that, I get to make love again to the most beautiful woman I've ever seen?"

"Really?"

"Really."

"Thanks. But that about sums it up."

"Well, I can certainly think of worse ways to go."

"Oh, believe me," she said. "I can, too." And she covered his mouth with hers.

She closed the door to Bill's room. Getting him back there was kind of a bitch. Same with Roger. But she couldn't leave two dead bodies in her room. As she walked down the hallway, her phone vibrated. Another text.

From the boss.

You had sex with the guy?

No One of Consequence

By Christine Morgan

It was during a natural lull in the after-dinner conversation that the drawing room door opened to admit, in a rustle of brocade and scented powder, Great-Aunt Gertrude with her immense silver-point Persian cradled in her arms.

"I don't mean to be a bother," she said, "but there appears to be a dead man floating in the swan-pond."

This pronouncement produced, as might be expected, a considerable disruption. Miss Caroline Eldridge struck a discordant jangle of notes on the pianoforte. Lord Fitz-Hughes choked and coughed out a sputter of brandy. Cards fluttered across the table as the players sprang up from their after-dinner bridge game.

"You know," the elderly dame said, stroking the cat between his pewter-colored ears, "I *did* think it was odd, seeing somebody like that. I was on my way downstairs and happened to glance out, and—well, I did think it was odd."

They paid her no mind in the general rush for the windows that followed. Ladies in satin and men in smart black jackets crowded together, jostling indecorously for position. Their voices formed a hectic babble, within which cries of 'who is it?' and 'oh my God!' predominated.

"My first impression was, of course, that he might be swimming for some reason," she went on. "Though goodness knows I've never seen anyone swimming in the swan-pond before, by day let alone moonlight. Then I noticed the rather peculiar face-down way of his floating, and the fact he didn't move at all, or lift his head to breathe, and—"

Lady Fitz-Hughes staggered back with a hand pressed to her brow. She fell half-swooning onto a sofa, surrounded by a bevy of solicitous daughters-in-law. Salts and air were called for, and a glass of cold water.

The men, meanwhile, reversed their course from the window. They streamed into the hall, debating in excited tones their plan of action, whether someone should go fetch the doctor from the village, call the police, and so forth. The disruption had become a full-blown uproar.

"Such a fuss," Great-Aunt Gertrude said to Leopold, whose magnificent silver-banded plume of a tail flicked at the noise and activity. "I'm sure it's nothing, no one of consequence." Yet she, along with those ladies not occupied tending their hostess, moved in the wake of the throng.

Within moments, the great front doors flung open, spilling light down the broad stone steps. Lanterns were brought. Servants flooded from every corner—maids and footmen who'd been clearing the dining room, the butler, valets, the housekeeper and cook, even the kitchen-drudge popping her head out of the scullery.

Between the upper gallery railings peeped a host of little faces, the various children of the family and guests, like inmates of some mahogany prison. Sir Geoffrey barked orders to the nannies to keep them in the nursery until further notice. This was done, albeit over bleats and wails of protest.

Soon, most of the household stood outside, the ladies and female servants gathered on the eastern slope of lawn overlooking the pond. They murmured and whispered their anxiety to one another, fanned themselves, and held delicate handkerchiefs at the ready.

Lady Fitz-Hughes, recovered enough to join them, bemoaned this rude ruination of their hitherto quite agreeable evening. She despaired whatever in the world their esteemed guests must think, to which she was offered much polite assurance that the incident could hardly be held against her as any sort of blight upon Woadcastle's hospitality.

The gentlemen and senior male servants, meanwhile, clustered at the pond's edge as the younger footmen, gardener and groom's lad waded into the shallows. Their shoes sank deep into soft, spongy black muck, eliciting grimaces and squishy, squelching sounds. A green layer of algae some inches below the surface that, by day, gave the pond a most picturesque opacity, adhered to their pant-legs in a scummy manner the laundresses would no doubt find difficult to contend with.

"Does anyone recognize him?"

"Not from here, I don't."

"Not from this angle, either. Hardly a chap's best."

"Isn't one of the staff, is it?"

"Certainly not, m'lord."

"By the look of his clothes, I'd say he's no gentleman."

"That's a cert. From the village, do you reckon?"

"Must be, or traveling through."

A long pole-hook was fetched from the gardener's shed. It took some fiddling, and one unfortunate clonk to the drifting man's head, but finally they snagged his waterlogged clothing and haul him within reach. The footmen took hold of limp arms and legs and carried the body ashore.

"You might want to stay back," Lord Fitz-Hughes said to the women. By his expression, he wished he himself could do the same. By his expression, he also wished he could sit down, and perhaps finish that stiff slug of brandy.

His advice was, for the most part, hardly necessary. Only Rebecca, Sir Geoffrey's stepdaughter, had inclination enough toward the morbid and ghoulish to attempt a closer look.

The servants set the man down on the grass and rolled him over. His hands flopped out pallid and wet by his sides. His head lolled. Pond-water trickled from his gaping mouth. A lily frond lay pasted across his cheek.

Gasps, small shrieks of horror, and little outcries greeted this glimpse of his slack, blue-gray face in the moonlight. Lady Fitz-Hughes swooned again and two other ladies followed suit. Eyes were averted, mouths daintily covered, pearls clutched. Some of the men shared grim looks. Others had to turn away. Old Bennings, the butler, tottered and pressed a palsied hand to his chest. Lord Stafford's valet was sick all down his shirtfront.

He was, most decidedly and most definitely, dead.

He was also, most decidedly and most definitely, a complete stranger.

Sleep would be a rare and much-belated business that night, if in fact it arrived at all. For any of them besides the children, that was. They, at least, succumbed to a reasonable bedtime ... if perhaps generously helped along by cups of hot chocolate laced with a tincture of something from a brown bottle the governess kept in a locked cupboard for just such occasions.

Well, perhaps not just *such* occasions. It wasn't every day, after all, that anything so noteworthy as a *death* took place at Woadcastle. The last one had been, oh, ages ago, the preceding autumn, that regrettable hunting accident with the poor Earl of Falloway. It had very much put a damper on the whole month. Of course, there had also been the matter of the actress a few years previously, the one young George found so fascinating, but her suicide had put quite the tragic end to their star-crossed love affair. Everything worked out for the best eventually, with George going on to a far more suitable engagement, though they all agreed it had been a most shocking breach of hospitality by the actress. The stains would not come out of the porcelain; the entire bathtub had to be replaced.

These topics were uppermost on the minds of the Fitz-Hugheses and their houseguests, not to mention the servants. The temptation among the adults to seek a similar insomnia remedy as had wafted the children away to dreamland was not inconsiderable, but none of them wanted to be the first to make such a medicinal request. They contented themselves for the time being, therefore, with brandy, whiskey, and other spirits.

Besides, the doctor had been summoned from the village, and the police were on their way, and nobody wanted to miss any further developments.

"This isn't going to turn into another of those garish murder-mystery affairs, is it?" inquired Great-Aunt Gertrude, comfortably ensconced in a chair with Leopold curled on her lap. The cat's pale-sapphire eyes glimmered under drowsy half-lids.

"What, you mean with some inspector nosing about?" said William Stafford, Lord Stafford's brother. He threw back his third or fourth drink at a gulp, insulting to such a fine vintage of scotch whisky.

"Oh, I do hope not," fretted Lady Fitz-Hughes. "All that asking of impertinent questions—"

At that, several more of them chimed worriedly in.

"Not to mention making accusations and sinister assumptions about motives!"

"Insisting no one's permitted to leave the estate, and so on?"

"Digging for secrets and scandals—"

"So uncouth. Not to mention inconvenient."

"A man has *died!*" cried Louisa, Henry's wife of a few months, silencing the rest. "Doesn't that matter rather more than our inconvenience?"

"Well, my dear, it's far too late for *him* to be troubled by it," Gertrude said. "Why should the rest of us be put out?"

"We don't know it's murder!" Lady Fitz-Hughes wrung her many-ringed hands. "We don't even know who the man is yet, let alone how he died. Let's resolve that before we go leaping to any melodramatic conclusions!"

"Melodramatic?" echoed her husband. "Oh, I say."

Their eldest son, Roddy, chuckled. "Besides, if this were one of those murder-mystery affairs Auntie mentioned, shouldn't it be Father as the victim?"

"To be sure," said Roger, Roddy's younger brother by only a matter of minutes. He grinned a wicked grin at the blustering reaction of Lord Fitz-Hughes. "He would have had to bring us all here to discuss changing his will, and then be found dead—"

"Several times over," said Roddy. "Shot, stabbed, cracked on the head, *and* poisoned."

"*Then* pushed down the grand stairs for good measure."

Just like that, they were off to the races, exchanging rapid-fire remarks as their wives—they'd married sisters, of course, Lord Stafford's cousins—heaved identical sighs of chagrin.

"With the will then gone missing, and none of us knowing what it had said."

"Everyone a suspect—"

"You having learned you'd been disinherited and furious about it—"

"Because he blamed me for something you'd done, disguising yourself, easy enough as my twin—"

"With some long-hidden bastard popping out of the woodwork."

"I've half a mind to disinherit you both on the spot," Lord Fitz-Hughes declared.

"Capital!" Edmund tugged on his jacket lapels. "That's me next in line, then!"

"Rubbish it is," said Elizabeth, who was Roddy's wife. "I won't see my son passed over for the likes of you."

"What's wrong with Edmund?" Caroline favored him with a smile. "I find him quite charming."

Edmund preened. Rebecca muttered what might have been, "You *would*," but in so low a tone only those nearest to her heard.

Elizabeth glared icicles at Caroline. "Oh, of course you do, now that he stands to inherit and reduce my children to paupers!"

"What about mine?" added Adelaide, Elizabeth's sister. "How will Roger and I find good husbands for our girls? They'll need a fortune to back their prospects more than ever, with their father disgraced and a suspect in his own father's murder!"

"Need I remind you all," grumbled Lord Fitz-Hughes, refilling his drink, "that I am *not*, in fact, dead?"

"Weather's all wrong for it, anyway, of course ..." Roddy went on, glancing out the window.

"Absolutely," said Roger. "Should be the proverbial dark and stormy night."

"Indeed. We'd lose the electric at a crucial moment."

"You see?" Lord Stafford shook his head. "Told you it was a mistake to rely too much on these modern williwags."

"That's when the next shot would ring out," said Roddy.

"Another murder, the killer eliminating someone who'd gotten too close to solving the crime."

"At that rate, half the household could be dead by dawn."

"More, if dinner had been poisoned."

"Or the brandy." Roddy raised his in a toast.

Great-Aunt Gertrude, who had been watching the interplay with the avid attention of a spectator at a tennis match, spoke up. "I thought, in those dime-novel situations, it was always the butler that did it."

"The butler?"

"Good God, old Bennings?"

"Given how he shakes, the safest place to stand would be wherever he was aiming—"

"Would you all *stop!*" Lady Fitz-Hughes, in her extremity of emotion, went so far as to make a throw-pillow live up to its name, hurling the small embroidered cushion across the drawing room.

"Careful!" Roger caught it. "This might be the murder weapon itself!"

"He was suffocated as well?" asked Roddy.

The others, however, had the decency to be more duly chastened. A moment of polite silence passed, one for which idle chatter seemed discouraged. The awareness gradually returned to them that, murder-mystery fancies aside, a man was dead. A stranger, yes. Not a gentleman of quality—not a gentleman at all, judging by his attire. Not one of the household or visiting servants. Not one of the villagers that anyone could recognize, or a local tenant farmer. He was no one, really.

No one in particular, no one important, no one of consequence.

But still and all, a person. Some parents' son, possibly someone's brother, some woman's husband, some child's father.

"Perhaps it was an accident," Sir Geoffrey suggested, breaking that long moment of silence. "Perhaps the wind blew his hat into the pond, and he was trying to retrieve it, when he had a cramp."

"Perhaps a swan struck him," Henry said.

Edmund nodded. "They can do real damage, you know. Strength of their wings and all. They don't look it, of course. They look so regal, gliding about the way they do, but I wouldn't cross one."

"Met a bloke once whose arm was snapped in three places by a swan." Major Eldridge, Caroline's uncle, puffed on his pipe. No one had the heart to dispatch him to the smoking room at the end of the hall, him being a war hero and all, requiring a cane just to move about. "Vicious brutes, swans."

Louisa touched her fingertips to her brow. "I can't bear to think one of our swans might be a murderer!"

"Oh, for heaven's sake!" exclaimed Lady Stafford. "Listen to yourselves! How ridiculous you sound!"

"Or he might have done it himself, drowned himself," Edmund said. "Suicide, don't you know."

"In *our* pond?" said Lady Fitz-Hughes. "What kind of man would *do* that?"

"Well, but, Mother, I'm only saying, a man so deranged as to be suicidal wouldn't necessarily be bound by concerns of whose pond he chose. Not in the right mind, hey-what? Taken leave of the wit and wisdom."

"Nonsense. There is still such a thing as common decency."

"You do remember the actress—"

"Yes, but she was American."

"The moon's full," Rebecca said, nodding toward the white orb visible in the dark star-sprinkled firmament through the drawing-room window. "Suppose a werewolf got him?"

"A what?"

"A werewolf?"

"Are you daft?"

"Gracious!" Gertrude pursed her lips, stroking Leopold's back. "It's like living in the penny dreadfuls."

"Besides," said the Major, "if it was a werewolf, he'd be right torn up, wouldn't he? Throat laid open, gutted, eaten on—"

"Major!" several voices pleaded at once.

"No, the Major's onto it, he is," said Edmund. "Any sort of wild animal had done this—"

"Barring a swan," Louisa said.

Henry rounded on his young bride. "Would you forget the damnable swan!"

"Fine, fine, only *you* brought it up in the first place, the idea of murderous swans!"

"Not murderous, only ..." He broke off. "Are we having our first fight?"

"Oh! Yes, I rather think we are!"

"Our first fight! Oh, darling!"

"Darling!"

They clasped hands and gazed at one another with lovestruck adoration.

"As I was *saying*," Edmund continued, raising his voice and giving an exaggerated roll of the eyes, "we'd be knee-deep in entrails, blood from hell to Christmas."

"Edmund Chamberlain Hubert Fitz-Hughes!"

"Sorry, Mother. Ladies. Sorry." Stammering and blushing, he rubbed the nape of his neck.

It was hard to say which proved the more comical in the next instant—the cliché of the doorbell, or Edmund's pantomime of relief at the cliché of the doorbell.

Shortly thereafter, Bennings—who, to be fair, *was* on the far side of ancient; none of those present, even Gertrude, could recall the butler as a young man—tottered in with his usual unctuous discretion. "M'lords," he said. "M'ladies. Doctor Lenk has finished examining the, ah, deceased."

"Well, for heaven's sake, man!" said Lord Fitz-Hughes. "Don't bandy about ... who is he? How did he come to be floating in our pond?"

"I believe the doctor would be better able to—"

"Yes, yes, show him in!" Lady Fitz-Hughes dabbed at her brow. "I honestly don't know how much more strain I can be expected to endure for one night."

Bennings, again with unctuous discretion, cleared his throat. "The police have also arrived, m'lady."

"Oh, God!"

"So it is murder!"

"What do they say?"

"Are they going to shoot the swans?"

"Here, now, that's hardly sporting."

"I agree. If anyone's going to shoot those honking, black-banded blackguards, it should be done properly."

"Show in the doctor, Mr. Bennings," Lord Fitz-Hughes said. "And the police captain, when they've done ... whatever it is they do."

The butler performed what, in earlier years, would have been an unctuously discreet inclination of the head. As it was, however, with time and palsy doing their work, it proved more of an impression of a nearsighted pigeon attempting to peck for seed. He stepped back into the hall and, moments later, ushered in the village doctor.

Doctor Lenk looked as if he'd been roused from a deep slumber, and no doubt had been. He blinked around the well-lighted drawing room at the well-dressed gentlemen in their dinner jackets and the well-dressed ladies in their evening gowns and jewels. If Bennings was the nearsighted pigeon of this nursery fable, Lenk was an owl, unceremoniously thrust into the midst of a gathering of songbirds.

He flinched from the barrage of questions peppering him like birdshot from all corners, clutched his sensible black doctor's bag to his stout frame, and wet his dry lips with a nervous little pink tongue.

"*Was* it the swans?" Louisa's clear voice rang in an opportune lull. She and Henry had mended their differences and sat side by side on a velvet settee, his right knee pressed to her left and her gloved hands clasped in his.

At this, Doctor Lenk blinked again, goggled, and said, "Beg pardon, mum?"

"Never mind that," Sir Geoffrey said from the mantle. "What can you tell us? What's going on?"

"Yes, please do, by all means, make your report," urged Gertrude. "It's far past Leopold's bedtime." On her lap, as if to second her remark, the Persian yawned to expose sharp, pearl-white teeth.

"Blimey, Auntie," Roddy said. "You could send him up. It isn't as if the police will want to question the cat."

"Send him up? Alone?" She gave her great-nephew an affronted look.

"Alone, nothing," said Roger. "Ring for … what's-his-name. Bloody cat's got his own valet, might as well earn his keep."

"I'll have you know that Clarence very much earns his keep," Gertrude informed him. "He takes excellent care of my Leopold."

Rebecca leaned toward Edmund. "Her cat has a valet?"

"Oh, yes. Damned animal lives better than most anyone else in the house. I wouldn't mind sleeping half the day on silk pillows, eating from crystal dishes, and someone to brush my hair on demand."

"That *is* how you live, you ungrateful gadabout," his father said.

"What about tummy-rubs, then? He has tummy-rubs at his beck and call, hey-what?"

Caroline tittered. "Well, then, Eddie, maybe you should get married."

46

"Would it trouble everyone unduly," began Lady Fitz-Hughes, with one of those sorts of tight smiles that would send sailors scurrying to batten down all hatches, "to let the doctor have his say?"

When he did, however, it turned out to be far less than enlightening. All that Lenk could tell them with certainty was that the man was dead, which obviously anyone with even a fraction of brain would have known. He showed no evident injuries or signs of violence or a struggle. For anything else, they would have to wait on a more thorough medical investigation.

"That's it?" Lord Fitz-Hughes said. "That's all you can tell us?"

"I'm not sure what else I could tell you."

"Who he is, for starters!"

"Doctor," interrupted a crisp baritone from the doorway. "Why don't you leave that ... to me."

All eyes in the drawing room, even the pale-sapphire ones of Leopold the cat, turned to behold a tall man in a dark coat, returning their startled looks with a narrow, sharp, and flinty gaze.

The local constable, their village peacekeeper, lingered in the hallway, deferentially behind this striking new arrival. To carry on with the earlier descriptive bird motif, Constable Potter was more of the waddling gander, if ganders were possessed of muttonchops and made excessive use of moustache wax.

As for the striking new arrival, with his chiseled profile, sharp gaze, and erect carriage? An eagle, a peregrine falcon, a hunting-hawk.

"Isn't that Inspector Braithley of Scotland Yard?" whispered Caroline.

"Why, yes," Gertrude said. "I do believe so."

"He's famous! His picture's been in the papers!"

"Our own Sherlock Holmes." Edmund tugged at his collar. "What was it you were saying earlier, Auntie, about those murder-mystery affairs and whodunits?"

"I seem to recall saying that I hoped this wouldn't turn into one."

"We should all hope so, too," said Roddy. "God, King, and Country help whoever *that* chap decides to twig for the crime."

"You were joking about it not twenty minutes ago," Roger said.

"So were you!"

"And you both should have known better," Elizabeth said, eliciting a fervent nod from her sister.

"Was there a crime, though?" Louisa clasped Henry's hands even tighter.

"Must be, if he's here," he said. "But don't worry, my darling. None of us have done anything wrong."

"Which won't matter a fart in church if he takes it otherwise into his head—"

"Roddy!"

"What? It won't. You know how these genius detectives operate. They make up their minds and that's that, and they find the evidence to suit."

"They can hardly find evidence if there's none to be found," said Henry.

Roger and Roddy gave him the kind of lofty, pitying, you-poor-fool kind of looks that only elder brothers can manage. Meanwhile, Old Bennings the butler stammered a mortified apology to Lord and Lady Fitz-Hughes, something to the effect of the inspector had not given him time to make a proper announcement but insisted on going right in. This was waved off, and Bennings retreated, though of course not so far as to altogether leave earshot.

Sir Geoffrey and Lord Stafford seemed acquainted enough with all parties to handle the necessary introductions, though it quickly became apparent that Inspector Braithley was not one for idle chitchat and social niceties.

"Oh, but he's much more handsome in person, don't you think?" Caroline said.

"I think you've been tossed over," Rebecca said to Edmund.

"I'd only barely been tossed on in the first place."

"But what in the world is he doing here?" William Stafford wondered aloud. "He can't have come all the way out from London already, just tonight."

"He must be working some top-secret, exciting case!"

"Here?" said several of them together, equally askance.

"At Woadcastle?"

"Or the village? What could have happened there? Someone steal the vicar's pig again?"

48

"Scotland Yard's scraping the barrel if that's the state of things."

"He married one of the Durham girls, didn't he?" asked Gertrude. Leopold curled on her lap, setting his chin on his forepaws, and rumbled a low but steady purr. "I do think he did. Evelyn, the one with the red hair. Such a nice young lady. Quiet, pretty, mild. I know her mother."

Caroline's face fell. "He's married, then?"

"Lucky you," said Rebecca, the words dripping sarcasm. "You might still have a shot."

"Shot?" cried Lady Stafford. "He was shot?"

"Who's been shot?"

"Someone's been shot?"

"We might have heard a gun—"

"Nobody's been shot!" Lord Fitz-Hughes struck the edge of a table with his heavy signet ring, the ring that surely would have been used to seal the envelope for his rewritten new will, if matters had gone the way matters such as this were traditionally supposed to.

"Then would someone mind terribly explaining what *is* going on?" Gertrude soothed Leopold, who had twitched to full wakefulness at the loud rap of the ring on mahogany, hooking his claws into thick brocade. "There, there, don't snag my dress; my maid will have fits."

"If I may," said Inspector Braithley, moving to a spot that commanded the center of attention. The surrounding lamps managed simultaneously to highlight his features in a dramatic fashion and cast an imposing shadow.

"Oh, quite," murmured most of the Fitz-Hughes ladies, as Lady Stafford snapped open her fan and Caroline seemed to be having trouble drawing sufficient breath.

It wasn't that he was a particularly handsome man in the classical sense. But, the cut of his cheekbones, the set of his jaw, the backswept sleek and shining hair once he'd removed his hat, and those piercing eyes combined for a most riveting effect.

"To begin," he continued, with a cool glance at William Stafford, "I have not, in fact, come all the way out from London tonight."

The glance shifted to Gertrude's aged countenance.

"My wife and I, yes, Evelyn, were over at Durham House in Wilmingtonshire, visiting her family."

"Dear me," she said. "I do hope Lady Durham is in good health."

"Excellent."

"You will give her my regards, won't you?"

"Certainly." Next, the glance moved—cooling several further degrees as it did so—to Roddy. "And I assure you that if there has been a crime, it is my intention to determine the responsible party based on evidence, rather than take it into my head to *twig* anyone for it."

Roddy was by no means the only one to flush scarlet at the realization that the Inspector had overheard their every word. He was, however, the one to go the reddest ... although Caroline was a close second.

"A local policeman, one of your Constable Potter's men, knew of my presence at Durham House and wired me there."

"Surprised the stuffing out of me, it did," Potter said. "I had nothing of it until he showed up, else I would've sent word."

"Wired you?" asked Sir Geoffrey. "Whatever for?"

"I can't imagine why something like this should require an emergency telegram to interrupt your visit," Lady Fitz-Hughes added. "We don't even know who the man in the pond is."

"As it happens," Braithley said, "the man in the pond had in his possession and on his person certain papers. Documents possibly pertaining to a complex and highly confidential case with which I am currently involved."

This revelation, with its implied deliciousness of secrecy and intrigue, thrilled through the drawing room. Anticipation had them, if not on the literal edges of their seats, at the very least figuratively hanging on his every word.

"My, isn't it exciting?" whispered Lady Stafford to the Major.

He harrumphed. "A spy ring, no doubt."

"The nature of the case being, as I've stated, complex and highly confidential," Braithley said, "you'll pardon me, Major Eldridge, if I do not respond."

"Spies?" Lord Fitz-Hughes looked thunderstruck. "Here? What in God's green earth would spies be doing *here*?"

"I'd guess it's political," Edmund said.

"Again, why *here*? We've nothing to do with politics."

"There was that fellow, the union agitator—"

"We've nothing to do with unions, either!"

"No, but, I mean to say, the way he died, that could have been political too."

"Who's this, then, that died?" Louisa asked Henry. "When?"

"Months ago," Henry said. "Well before the wedding."

"You never told me!"

"Why would I? And he died in a tavern brawl, that's what I heard. Nothing political about that."

Lord Stafford uttered a disdainful snort. "Any union agitator mouthing off in a public house about his cause deserves anything he gets."

"We seem," said Braithley, his right eye suffering a brief twitch of irritation, "to have drifted somewhat from the matter at hand."

"Indeed, yes." Lord Fitz-Hughes cast about a stern glower. "My apologies, Inspector. Please do go on."

"The papers in this man's possession were water-damaged from his immersion, the ink badly smeared and smudged. The post-marks enabled the policeman to recognize their significance, but it will take some time to dry and decipher them and reach a conclusion."

Lady Fitz-Hughes latched onto this. "You'll stay here, of course," she said. "For the night, and for as long as is needed. Bennings?"

"Yes, m'lady?"

"Tell Mrs. Harte to have the ..." Her pause as she performed a quick headcount of her guests and compared that to the available rooms was incremental, but seemed eternal. "... the Spruce Room made up for the Inspector."

"Very good, m'lady."

"And reasonable accommodations for any other officers, staff or personnel. Inspector, you'll have full use of the study, the library, anything else you require."

"That is both kind and generous, Lady Fitz-Hughes. I do appreciate such a gesture, and on such short, unexpected notice."

"Nonsense," Lord Fitz-Hughes said. "Whatever we can do to help. Upsetting to us all, yes, but, a man has died and ..."

"... and that rather matters more than our inconvenience," finished Louisa, not without a hint of smugness at reiterating her earlier point.

"I will need to request," Inspector Braithley said, "that no one leave the estate until we've finished the investigation."

"No one would dream of it," Gertrude assured him.

51

The rest of the night, not that there was much left of it before dawn began to color the eastern horizon, passed in a blur of activity.

Outside, Constable Potter's men scoured the grounds for clues, poking into hedges and under bushes, dredging the swan-pond, trampling the gardens, tracking mud, and generally making nuisances of themselves.

Inside, below stairs, the kitchen bustled as the cook and her assistants put together an early breakfast, ran trays of sandwiches and tea out to the policemen, and did what they could to keep the body and soul of Woadcastle together. Housemaids and footmen rushed about their duties, changing linens, sweeping up, seeing everything was in order.

Inspector Braithley set himself up in Lord Fitz-Hughes' study, alternating telephone calls with interviews of the family, servants, and guests. A mortuary wagon arrived and took the body to Doctor Lenk's little hospital in the village for further examination.

Rampant gossip was the lifeblood of the day. Might they be called upon to testify in court? When none of them knew anything? Would it be in the newspapers? How much of a scandal could they be facing?

To the great relief of Louisa, the swans were soon cleared of suspicion. They had been safely shut up in their swan-cote for the night, and the dead man bore no injuries consistent with being battered by powerful wings.

He had also, came the news by way of the gossip grapevine, been drunk. Very drunk. Very, *very* drunk indeed. No one in the village recognized him either, and he had not taken on such a skinful at any of the local pubs.

Who he was, where he'd come from, where he'd been headed, and why remained unanswered questions, much to Inspector Braithley's frustration. The man's clothes and calluses marked him as a common laborer, possibly a vagrant or a veteran or both. He had no money on him, no identification of any kind.

More and more, it seemed apparent that he must have made a drunken stumble-blunder into the pond. There, perhaps unable to swim or simply too impaired to do so, he'd drowned. A stupid and senseless accident, but an accident nonetheless.

Except, of course, for the matter of that sodden, ink-smeared papers he'd been carrying. Papers which, despite great care and attention in handling, proved all but illegible.

Had he been delivering a message? From and to whom? Did the post-marks have actual significance to Braithley's case, or was it some sort of strange coincidence? In his line of work, he was not much of a believer in coincidence ... but, try as he might, he could find no connection.

Two more days passed, during which the other policemen finished up. The restriction against anyone leaving Woadcastle was lifted, allowing the Staffords and Eldriges and those Fitz-Hugheses who had other residences of their own to depart. They all did so with an odd mix of relief and reluctance, and only after obtaining sworn promises from their friends to share any new developments.

Inspector Braithley lingered to press on with his investigation. He proved, in his working capacity, something less than an ideal guest ... not one for idle after-dinner chitchat, or billiards, or bridge. The offer was extended to invite his wife to come over from Durham House to join him, but he refused, limiting his communication with her to brief telephone calls.

Lord Fitz-Hughes and Sir Geoffrey seemed to find his company agreeable enough, terse though it was. The initial blush and flutter his chiseled profile had occasioned among the ladies did wane somewhat at his continued reserve and coolness of manner. The Fitz-Hughes sons, Edmund and Roddy in particular, suffered a certain awkwardness in his presence.

All in all, however, it went tolerably well and without further incident.

Until it was that, one night in the dining room, the Inspector suddenly uttered a gasp, interrupting a discussion between Lady Fitz-Hughes and her daughters-in-law.

"Gracious," said Great-Aunt Gertrude.

"Inspector?"

He commenced coughing, thumping a curled fist against his breastbone while attempting to quell the outburst of concern with an apologetic waving of the other hand.

"Inspector, are you all right?"

"Something down the wrong way, no doubt."

"Whatever is the matter?"

Rather than clearing his breathing, the fit worsened into a whistling wheeze. His face went the most alarming shade of red, deepening toward burgundy. His eyes watered, his mouth gaped, and in a sudden surge of movement he lunged from his chair with such force that it overturned.

"Oh, my God!"

"I don't think he can breathe."

"Give him a glass of water."

"Clap him on the back."

"Have him bend over and breathe into a bag."

"That's for hiccups, you fool."

"Well, someone do something!"

"He must've caught a bone in his throat!"

"It's a roulade; there's no bones in it!"

"Well, he's caught something, no bones about it!"

"I said clap him on the—"

"I'm clapping, I'm clapping! I clap much harder, I'll knock him over!"

The Inspector lurched away from the helpful clapping. He bumped into the table hard enough to make the dishes jump. Several wine glasses tipped with a crash and a splash. Those few of the ladies who had not yet risen to their feet did so with cries of alarm.

"He's choking!"

"Look at his face!"

The face in question had gone from burgundy to a purple-verging-on-plum. He clawed at his neck, which strained and bulged. His lips, and his rudely protruding tongue, seemed to be swelling before their eyes as if inflated by a bellows.

"Get the doctor!"

"Give him some air!"

"He can't breathe!"

"That's why he needs air!"

"But he can't bloody breathe!"

"Open his windpipe!"

"With what, a dinner knife?"

Footmen and housemaids rushed to and fro. Old Bennings, the butler, had to steady himself on the back of a chair. The family dithered about in frantic helplessness.

Inspector Braithley staggered a few steps, both hands clamped to his neck. His watering eyes rolled madly in their sockets, exposing vein-burst whites. His shins struck the jutting legs of his own overturned chair and he went down with thrashing, bucking convulsions.

Some days later, Gertrude Fitz-Hughes arranged to have herself driven out to Wilmingtonshire to pay a condolence call at Durham House. She found the place subdued, as was proper for a time of mourning, but was still warmly received by Lady Durham.

A lovely afternoon tea was laid out for them in a corner parlor overlooking the garden. Gertrude duly admired the china and silver, and how well the flowers were doing. Inquiries were made after mutual acquaintances, the weather was discussed, the polite small-talk was done.

Gertrude also spoke with effusive appreciation that, amid the delicacies, a dish of flaked whitefish, a portion of cold salmon mousse, and a tiny pot of caviar were sent up for the pleasure and privilege of Leopold. Who was, as a gesture of respect, wearing a collar of black velvet dusted with diamond chip.

Soon enough, the servants went on their way and left the ladies in genteel privacy to enjoy their tea, and the conversation was able to turn to more personal matters.

"How *is* your Evelyn?" asked Gertrude, spooning a selection of delicacies onto a saucer.

"Well, it's been a terrible shock to her, as you might imagine. A man his age, so fit and healthy ... if he'd fallen in the line of duty, that would be one thing, but ... like this, so sudden, so unexpected."

"Yes, very." The dryness of her tone was not lost on her hostess.

Lady Durham forced a pained smile as she poured. "I suppose I needn't talk on *that* point, should I? After all, it must have been a shock to everyone. I'm so sorry for Lady Fitz-Hughes. Is she well?"

"Rather shaken, of course. It was something of a scene."

"I can only imagine."

"She's gotten it into her head now, I'm afraid, that Woadcastle is bad luck, or some such nonsense. Wouldn't go so far as to say cursed, of course, let alone haunted—Sir Geoffrey's stepdaughter was kind enough to put forth those options; morbid girl—but Lady Fitz-Hughes does worry it will give the house a difficult reputation."

"Hardly surprising, after what happened with the Earl of Falloway."

"Fortunately, his widow doesn't hold it against us."

"I understand they'd not been on the best of terms, anyway."

"Oh, you know how these things go." Gertrude glanced around approvingly at the furnishings. "I must say, I love what you've done with this room. The new wallpapering brightens it so."

"You mean," said Lady Durham, stirring her tea, "that the old stuff was atrocious, and I'd be the last to argue. I'm thinking we'll redo Evelyn's suite next. It might help her feel better, particularly now that she'll be spending more time here."

"Has that all been decided?"

"Well, there's no reason for her to keep the Watson Street house now, is there? And I'll be glad to have her home. I don't believe she was very happy in London."

"The poor girl. I remember her as being so lively before she married. So sweet and vivacious in those days."

"Marriage can change a person." Lady Durham went to the mantle, where there stood several small, framed photographs arranged in progression. The change in Evelyn, from rosy-cheeked bright smiles to a wan, withdrawn reserve, was slight ... but it was there to be seen by the discerning eye.

"For better or for worse, as they say," said Gertrude. "Or so I've been told."

"And not all husbands are created equal, are they? Not all marriages are the same from within as they might appear from without. Sometimes, years can go by before even one's nearest and dearest realize the whole truth."

"I do hope she won't face too much trouble in the settling of the Inspector's affairs."

"No, I don't expect so." Turning from the mantle, Lady Durham sat again at the tea-table. "He was very organized. Meticulous and thorough. I'm sure it must have annoyed him dreadfully, dying in the midst of such a baffling, unsolved case."

"He certainly kept to himself, didn't he?" Gertrude helped herself to another dainty scoop of jellied salad. "Close to the vest, as I believe the young people call it."

"And impressed upon Evelyn to do the same. Most firmly. I doubt she had a soul to confide in; he worried she would spill a vital secret or some clue or another. Even so simple a detail as that matter of the postmark, for instance."

"As if anything so small as that could do any damage." She tutted and fed Leopold a morsel of fish.

"Why, even his personal physician was unaware of that dangerous mango allergy," Lady Durham went on. "His own *wife* wouldn't have known, had he not fallen ill in her company on that trip to India."

"Indeed ... speaking of something so small doing such damage ... who would have suspected that even the tiniest amount could cause a fatal reaction?"

They paused for a quiet moment to reflect upon the fickle and capricious nature of life.

"What I do wonder, though," said Lady Durham, stirring her tea, "is ... who *was* the man in the swan-pond? The one upon whom those post-marked papers were found."

"Just some drunkard, some vagrant, they tell me," Gertrude said. "No one of consequence. These cakes are superb, by the way. Do give my compliments to your cook."

"Oh, I certainly shall. You must try the scones as well. A new recipe. Which reminds me, I heard there was a most interesting pork roulade served at Woadcastle the other evening. With an apricot and bread-crumb filling?"

"Normally, yes, but I understand certain substitutions can be made to spice it up. With, oh, say, a nice fruit chutney, for example."

"That does sound exotic. More tea?"

"Yes, thank you."

She refilled the cups, musing. "And that man ... no one of consequence, you say?"

"Quite."

"So, then, there won't be any additional charge?"

Gertrude reached across the table and patted the other woman's hand, Leopold purring in her lap as she did so. "My dear Lady Durham, don't be silly. Our arranged-upon fee will more than suffice."

AND THE HITS JUST KEEP ON COMIN'

BY DOUG RINALDI

The old man set down the sundried bones on the small stone altar. He pounded the worn and battered mallet down upon them in a controlled rage and didn't stop until nothing but dust remained. *"With these bones, I now do crush!"*

He swept the mound of bone dust with his craggy hand into a small burlap bag and turned back to the ancient symbol he had scrawled in chalk onto the cold wooden floor. In the four corners surrounding the sigil, the ceremonial black wax of the candles melted and dripped, hardening into a pile around the candlestick bases, securing them in place. The man drew another circle in the center of the symbol in the powder before reaching into the satchel and pulling out a dusty photograph.

"There has been unfairness done to me ... I summon the elements ... I invoke them ... I conjure them to do my bidding!" He chanted in his native tongue as he placed the photo of a man in the center of the bone dust circle. Then, reaching into the satchel again, he retrieved a bound locket of hair. *"I call upon the Ancient Ones from the great abyss to do my bidding!"* On

top of the photograph, he placed the hair, before grabbing one of the candles, letting the wax drip to seal the pieces into one effigy.

Behind him, a young boy rang a bell three times.

The old man pulled a crude blade from the floor beside him and sliced his left palm open. With the blood dripping from his wound, he extinguished the four flames around the sigil while chanting. *"The four watchtowers shall lay their eyes and minds ... there shall be guilt and fear and bad blood ... there shall be submission and no pity."* Each candle sizzled, releasing their final plume after he read each line.

"Bones of anger, bones to dust, full of fury, revenge is just ... I scatter these bones, these bones of rage ... take thine enemy, bring him pain ... I see thine enemy before me now ... I bind him, crush him, bring him down," the old man recited while dumping the remains of the dust onto the effigy. *"With these bones I have crushed, make thine enemy turn to dust ... torment, fire, out of control ... With this hex I curse your soul."*

He raised his bleeding hand over the pile, letting the blood flow freely to mix with the dust to create a ruddy sludge. In a sudden blaze, the candles reignited, casting dancing shadows over the room. *"I point the threefold law against thee ... against thee it shall be ... threefold, a hundredfold, is the cost for my anger and pain. Thou shalt be blinded by the fear, blinded by the pain, blinded by me ... bound by me ... cursed by me ... So mote it be!"*

The candles flickered out and the room fell completely silent and still.

"What the hell are you talking about? I'm the epitome of perfect health!"

"Are you absolutely sure about that, Mr. Wright?"

"Of course I'm sure. Healthy mind, healthy body. And please don't call me Mr. Wright. Every time you do that I think my father's in the room."

"Very well, Jacob. You've always been our best asset, yet ... you seem ... off lately."

"Bull! I'm on the top of my game," Jacob blurted before taking a sip of his drink.

"Tell that to our Haitian clients. They are none too pleased with us at the moment."

"Screw them. The job got done, didn't it? So what if it lacked some of my usual finesse. They were gonna kill that other guy anyways. I did them a favor. Was just a matter of time." Jacob poured the rest of the bitter liquor into his mouth. "Shit happens."

"Yes, you are probably right. Apparently shit does happen. Please realize that your actions, whether just or not, have deadly repercussions in our industry. The quality of your work is the unseen face of this organization. Your *finesse*, as you put it, is an equally important part of our business model."

"With all due respect, spare me the lecture, alright? Do you have another job for me or not?"

"Of course we do. It's a two for one for a new client. It's yours as long as you don't plan on mucking this one up as well."

"Like I said, chief, top of my game."

The "buy-one-get-one-free" gimmick usually didn't pay well in this line of work.

In an effort to bring in more prospective clients, the bigwigs upstairs at The Collective sometimes rolled out these bargain hits. Jacob hated when they screwed with his paydays, but in light of his screw-up down in Haiti, he sucked it up and took the job with a smile. Being the consummate professional, he always talked a big game but never downright disrespected or challenged the bosses. Just wasn't good for business, or breathing.

Nestled in his meager safe house in town, he laid out all the files from the dossier on his kitchen table. He slowly sipped away at his three fingers of scotch, the good stuff, aged three times longer than he'd been alive, given to him years ago for a job well done, a job that put The Collective in the murder-for-hire arena.

The clients had printed out vague notes, explaining how each hit should go down. The first needed to be from a distance, preferably in public with plenty of witnesses. The second needed to feel personal, no witnesses, just a brutal mess that would send a precise message.

The client left the details up to him. As long as he met those two nonnegotiable terms, he had free reign. Explosion or sniper shot, garrote or blade, he had ultimate say in his victims' demise. And he liked it that way.

He studied the information, the photos, and the files. He didn't care who they were or what they had done to be put on his list; they remained faceless and he remained detached. That's how he did the job and, to be successful, objectification was key. His brain worked over the details, building the schematics of the kills in his mind. After he had set everything to memory, he tossed the dossier into the sink and doused it all with the remainder of scotch from his glass. He lit a match and tossed it in, setting the file aflame.

As he watched the paper smolder, he felt half-guilty for wasting such expensive hooch. *Fuck it*, he conceded, *I hate scotch anyway*.

Jacob had decided that killing the first mark in public would be a solid way to start the day. It had been months since he got a chance to play with his Dragunov SVD. Lightweight and durable, the sniper rifle was a Russian masterpiece. His plan went off flawlessly, as he knew it would. Lunchtime in the city would give you some goddamn witnesses—witnesses covered in brains, but witnesses nonetheless.

He knew the second half of the job would be a little trickier—up close and personal. With timing and opportunity being essential, he chose the only logical option to make sure he met his client's strict demand—a hammer.

So, in the hallway closet he waited, with hammer in hand, for the next poor soul on his list to get home. As much as killing didn't bother him, he never really liked the messy ones. Just the mere thought of ruining his clothes and shoes on some chump's blood and guts gave him anxiety, never mind the chance of it getting into his mouth. Thankfully, he always had a set of scrubs and booties at the ready to go along with his gloves and face mask.

Keys jingled in the lock.

The doorknob turned and the hinges squealed.

Time to work.

The mark entered his home, mail and a bag of groceries in his hands. He walked right by Jacob's hiding spot; shadows momentarily blocked the light shining through the breaks in the door. Jacob slowed his breathing, timing it with the creaks of the man's footfalls on the hardwood floor. He gripped the weapon tight in one hand and slowly turned the doorknob with the other.

Out in the open now, Jacob stalked the man who stood at his kitchen counter, thumbing through his mail. Poor guy had no idea what was about to happen. As much as Jacob disliked getting this close to his kills for pure sanitary reasons, he still enjoyed seeing that final look of disbelief in his victims' eyes before the strike. And that almost made ruining some clothes worth it ... almost.

"Psst."

Jacob slept soundly on his twin-size mattress with his head squished against the soft pillow. The deeds of the day behind him, he rested without a care in the world, satisfied with a job well done.

A noise roused him—a bell chiming. He sat up and wiped the sleep from his eyes. In the dark of the bedroom, he saw nothing. The bell chimed again. This time he could tell it came from nearby, but he still couldn't pinpoint exactly where.

He reached for the lamp on the nightstand but grabbed nothing but air. Confused, he swung his legs off the side of the bed to get up. When his feet touched carpet, he grew concerned. Not only could he not find his lamp, his hardwood floor somehow grew a rug during the night. Knowing full well, at this point, that his gun would not be where he kept it, he felt for it anyway. "What in the hell?"

A bell rang again, the third time.

Jacob didn't scare easily; still, uneasiness crept across the back of his neck. He got up and started walking slowly in the direction he thought the sound came from. As he bumped into the doorframe, inhaling sharply from the sudden pain, he found the light switch and flicked it on. Incandescence chased the darkness away and Jacob stood frozen.

He wasn't in his apartment.

Someone started pounding against the front door so hard he thought the banging was in his head. Jacob steadied himself to gather his senses. He looked out into the hallway. At one end he saw the front door that someone still mercilessly beat upon and at the other he saw the familiar kitchen that he used as his office earlier in the day when he bludgeoned a man to death with a hammer.

"What the—"

He crept to the front door, feeling naked without a weapon. In the center of the cheap board door, he saw a peephole just below his eye level. Thankful that the pounding seemed to stop for at least a moment, he put his eye up to the cold, fish-eyed lens. Standing on the other side, a man in a bloody three-piece suit with a head that looked like an M-80 went off in it reeled back and slammed both fists violently onto the door.

Over and over, banging and pounding on the front door.

Jacob's head snapped back into his pillow as if someone just cold-cocked him; his eyes jolted open from the incessant pounding on his front door. The fright sweats broke out, exuding cool perspiration all over his body. His eyes watered as he reached for his gun under his pillow. With the weapon gripped tightly, he just stared up at the ceiling unsure about what was happening.

The banging persisted.

Someone's at the door, asshole. Snap out of it!

He sat there and collected himself. When his feet touched the familiar coolness of his hardwood floor, he knew that he had been dreaming. *A nightmare was more like it.*

The knocking tested his patience. "Hold on, for Christ's sake!" he yelled. "I'm coming." Still in a bit of a daze, he kept the gun primed as he opened the door as far as the chain would let him.

"Hello, Mr. Wright."

Jacob sighed in relief and undid the chain lock. "Jesus Christ, man! You scared the crappola out of me. I was having—" He paused, details of the dream flooding back into his memory, the man with coleslaw for a head and the American flag pin on his lapel that he now remembered seeing through his scope the day before. "—the weirdest dream. "Do you have any idea what time it is?" Jacob asked as he gestured the man to enter.

"I know, Mr. Wright," the man started. "It's very ear—"

"No, really. What time is it? My brain is still in a fog."

"It's five o'clock in the morning, Mr. Wright."

"Ugh. That's too early to be alive," Jacob said between yawns. "And what did I say about that mister crap?"

"Apologies," the man said. "But it couldn't wait until a more reasonable hour. We have an issue to discuss."

"Okay, great. But I'm gonna need some coffee first. Want some?"

"No thank you, Jacob."

"Suit yourself," he said with a shrug.

"I'll just begin, if you don't mind," the man insisted. "I have a very busy day ahead of me in light of this new situation brought to my attention."

"Alright, no problem." Jacob fiddled with his fancy coffee machine before turning around. "Go ahead. Shoot."

The man groaned before he began, not once moving from his spot on Jacob's floor. "It appears that you left a job unfinished, Mr. Wright."

"Bullshit!" Jacob blurted. "That guy's face looked like a bowl of Spaghetti-O's after I shot it."

"Not him," the man started. "The other job. The one in the Village that needed to look personal."

"With all due respect, that's impossible, sir."

"Yet, the fact remains. He was seen late last night walking down the main strip. A little worse for wear, but alive and walking, nonetheless."

Jacob, caught off guard at the revelation, put his palms to his face and slowly shook his head. He stretched and opened his eyes wide as if to retune himself. "There's gotta be a mistake. He was deader than ... dead ... when I left him on his kitchen floor with about ten extra holes in his head. Are you pos—"

The man unceremoniously pulled out a high-resolution photo of the target and handed it to Jacob, who studied it in dismay. "Yep. That's him," Jacob admitted, almost embarrassed. "He looks like some bad hamburger helper, but that is him."

"As if I would come all the way over here at this ridiculous hour if I were wrong," the man spat. "Upstairs is not very impressed with you at the moment, and I mirror their sentiments."

"I guess that's understandable."

"This needs to be addressed immediately, Jacob," the man said. "That is, if you enjoy your current position and the livelihood afforded you by The Collective."

"Yes, sir. I do. And I'll get right on it."

"Final chance to win back their trust," explained the man. "Don't make me regret sticking my neck out for you."

He stood at the counter, contemplating his predicament as he sipped on his third cup of coffee. Yet, the prior night's dream gnawed at his guts. Jacob didn't dream much, if at all, let alone about work or his targets.

"I need to get my shit together," he announced as he stared ahead in a daze. With a big sigh to calm himself, he dropped the mug into the sink and headed to his bedroom to get ready for the long day ahead. At the mirror over his dresser, he looked at his reflection, studying it for any signs of coming apart at the seams. "This is the last thing I need," he said through another round of yawns and stretches, still exhausted from his troubled sleep.

He had upset the bosses; not something you do—bad for business. Getting back into their good graces was paramount. "Snap out of it, buddy," he grunted as he slapped his face a couple of times to psych himself up.

Not only an expert marksman, Jacob also excelled at tracking people, a talent he honed after many years of black-ops work overseas in "The Sandbox." Therefore, he figured tracking a man whose face looked like someone took a brick to a cantaloupe should be like a jaunt through a meadow.

He started with the hospitals and struck out. Not one person reported a case even remotely resembling the target. Outside the man's apartment building, Jacob watched from a safe distance as police cordoned off the area and stood at attention by the entrance. Detectives shuffled in and out of the complex, obviously confused by the grisly scene with a missing dead body.

His patience waned. He had until the end of the day to rectify the situation or else he'd end up a free agent with a target on his own back. *Think, think, think!*

He decided to backtrack to where witnesses had last seen the mark. The main strip of town was a big area and had its good and not-so-good sections. A guy all banged up as that might stand a chance of hiding out in the shadier parts of town. Up and down each filthy alleyway, Jacob looked for any signs that his target had been around. Witnesses. Bloodstains. His *body*.

Still no dice. "Where would I go if I was a half-dead, bloodied mess in a shirt and tie?"

As the day's light began to fade between the tall buildings, the town's more unique and unsavory residents seemed to ooze from the cracks in the pavement. Jacob continued his search, determined to finish the job he thought he finished once already. Up ahead, a woman strutted forward along the sidewalk. Definitely out of place around these parts, her uptown fashion sense and sparkly jewelry immediately caught the attention of the neighborhood dregs. She met Jacob's gaze and kept it there. From a distance, she seemed well put together and ready for action, but as she got closer, he noticed dirt stains on her arms and legs. Her hair that he thought she had pulled back into a bun was actually matted to her head, her outfit disheveled on her frame.

She smiled at Jacob as she approached, her smirk nothing more than a mouthful of rotting teeth and gums. Jacob tried not to maintain eye contact, but couldn't help himself—she looked like a damned walking corpse. He grimaced as she licked her dry, cracked lips, her tongue darting out like a bloated slug.

Then he noticed the deep gash around her neck, from when he garroted her about two months ago. Worms and maggots weaved through the breach in her throat, squirming between the desiccated folds of the laceration.

This is impossible!

Jacob never sugarcoated it to anyone. He was a monster and he never denied it, not even to himself. It was his detachment from his fellow humans, the desensitization he carried with him his whole life, that made him such an asset to The Collective. Since the beginning, it was what helped him carve out a fruitful and lucrative career in the murder-for-hire field, even before he hitched his star to the Machiavellian corporation. He had also seen some shit in his lifetime. Whether here in the states or across the ocean in the sandstorm of enemy territory, he had seen *and* done more than his fair share of primal evil.

But ... this business before him was just absolutely ridiculous.

People on the street pointed at her, gawked as if she were a sideshow attraction, but they sure got out of her way in a hurry, not wanting anything she might be selling. Oblivious to the spectators, she reached out toward Jacob, who, still staring in disbelief, reached for his gun. She hissed at him through her putrid scowl and then lunged.

"Fuck this!" Jacob blurted just before firing three rounds, center mass, into the woman's chest. The street cleared of all witnesses as if the sound of gunfire made them evaporate back into whatever hole they called home. The woman dropped to the sidewalk with a meaty thud. No blood spilled out of the wounds, just a fetid stink that made his eyes water.

He saw something on the back of her neck, a small flower tattoo that he recalled from their previous encounter. *Yup, that's her, alright.* He slid his gun back into its holster, looking around nervously before booking it down an alley.

Jacob paced in front of his building, trying to release his anxious energy. He did his best to keep his voice to a whisper as he talked into his phone. "I don't care what you say. This is impossible! She was like a walking friggin' corpse and she had the smell to prove it."

"Let's not get carried away, Jacob," said the man on the other end. "Discussions about the reanimated corpses of the people that you've already received payment for killing is not going to help your case any."

"Listen to me, asshole," he spat into the receiver, immediately regretting his choice of words. "I know how this sounds, but I know what I saw." He left out the part about the maggots writhing around her opened throat. "I don't know how or why, but someone is seriously fucking with me."

"Mr. Wright, do I have to remind you that you're on a timetable here? Time is running out and you still have a job to finish. All this nonsense you're spouting is making me regret my decision to continue soliciting your services."

"You don't understand," Jacob said, almost pleaded. "Something is wrong. I just need some time to—"

"No!" the man boomed. "Finish the job now and maybe you'll still have a life to retire to. Is that understood, Mr. Wright?"

"Unquestionably."

"Good." *Click.*

All Jacob wanted to do was take a long, hot bath and let the insanity of the day disappear. He tried to remind himself that none of it was real. *Couldn't be.* If someone wanted him dead, had gone to such lengths as to make him think dead people were after him, he most certainly was going to make their success as difficult as possible.

He slid his key into the lock and shuffled right down the hall to his secret room behind the wall in his bedroom. "Now where did I leave my vest?" he asked himself as he rummaged through totes and shelves of all sorts of tactical gear. "I seriously need to clean this place. Looks like a goddamn Army & Navy store threw up in ... ah, there you are." He lifted the Kevlar up to the light, admiring the craftsmanship that saved his butt multiple times, as demonstrated by the dents left by some not so stray bullets.

With his determination renewed, he slipped on the vest and grabbed a new gun strap lined with reserve clips, just in case things spun even more toward the absurd. Jacob backed out of the handmade doorway in the wall and slid the fake panel back into place. Something tickled his sixth sense, the same reliable sense that had saved him on many a prior occasion. It rarely belied him.

Someone whispered.

Jacob whirled around and pulled his gun out in one fluid motion. He saw no one, yet he didn't relax his aim as he surveyed the empty bedroom over the barrel's sight. Seconds passed as he stood on alert. Finally satisfied by the silence, he lowered his aim and holstered his piece.

He checked his alarm clock as he walked by the nightstand. "Christ! Running out of time."

A faint metallic, sickly sweet smell crinkled his nose as he neared the door to the hallway, giving him pause. His cell phone burst to life in his pocket and startled him dizzy. After a couple of rings, he grabbed it. "Restricted number?" Against better judgment, he answered the call. "Hello?"

"Hello, Mr. Wright." A man's voice, thick with a Creole accent. *"I hope this evening finds you well and that I'm not,"* he started, only pausing to chuckle, *"interrupting anything."*

"Who is this?" Jacob asked. "How'd you get this number?"

"Relax, Mr. Wright. No reason to get excited. I take it you received my message?"

"What message? What are you talking about?"

"Oh, I am sure you know." His voice brimmed with confidence. *"Have any bad dreams lately?"*

Jacob's aggravation grew to exponential heights. "How did you know about ... who are you?" Incredulous, he stared at the phone before placing it back to his ear. "Listen, fella, I have no frickin' idea who you are or what you want, but you are fucking with the wrong son-of-a-bitch!"

"The dream was the first of many things I have planned for you, as I'm sure you are intently aware." He chuckled, again. Jacob could feel the man's twisted coolness emanate through his phone. *"Things are going to get much more interesting for you this night, Mr. Wright. Soon you will understand and feel my wrath, my pain."*

"Eat me!" Jacob shouted. "You got some brass balls, buddy. I don't have time for this!"

As he was about to hang up, Jacob heard the man laugh, clearly amused. *"Farewell, Mr. Wright. My son, Nicolas, wishes you safe travels on your journey. You remember Nicolas, don't you?"*

Jacob's face dropped; color drained from his complexion. His head spun, whipping up ghosts of the recent past.

"He wants you to know that he will be there to greet you in the Afterlife!" The man continued to snicker.

"Then I guess I'll see him in Hell!" Jacob pitched his phone across the bedroom. It smashed into a mirror and exploded, raining fragments everywhere.

Images flashed through his mind: the nightmare with no head in his dream, the woman he had strangled to death in her office late one night, the face of Nicolas when the bullet ricocheted and sliced through his carotid.

That wasn't my fault, his inner voice screamed. *He was gonna be as good as dead soon anyway!*

Jacob, for the first time in years, began to panic. He was well aware that he no longer had time on his side, regardless of the job's outcome. "Calm down," he told himself. "Screw that voodoo horseshit." He pulled his gun, reflexively checking the clip, and headed out of the bedroom. "Let's get this show on the road."

At the threshold that separated his safe haven from the lunacy befalling the world outside, Jacob took a deep breath and caught another whiff of that same coppery scent that had bombarded him earlier. He yanked the door open.

Two hands reached for Jacob's face and throat, intent on inflicting maximum damage. The nail of a crooked finger raked across his face, digging out a hunk of cheek with it. Jacob stumbled backward, losing his gun before slamming into the wall. The force of the blow knocked him into a coat rack and the hanging picture on the wall behind it. He fought to remain conscious after his brain collided with the inside of his skull from his abrupt impact with the laminate floor.

Everything started crashing down around Jacob. Sanity no longer spun out of control; instead, it quickly rose to the surface like the dirtied water of a clogged latrine, threatening to overwhelm him. And here he was—without his plunger.

With a cursed glint in his one good eye, Mr. Hammer-Smashed-Face lunged again. Jacob—with the determined, albeit sudden, wherewithal of a man in mortal danger—snatched a broken arm of the fallen coat rack and thrust it between the third and fourth rib, puncturing the half-faceless man's lung before imbedding it with a sickeningly wet *squish* into his heart. That seemed to halt his forward momentum and he fell flat on top of Jacob like a sack of beef innards.

Jacob gagged at the awful stench that oozed out of the wound. "Get the fuck off me!" he blurted as he shoved the man's motionless corpse away with a mighty heave. "That's the second time I've killed you. You asshole!" Whether the reanimated cretin had been breathing prior to having his lung ventilated, Jacob didn't know. Jacob just stared as black sludge poured from the breach—*glub, glub, glub*—it's wretched, oily appearance matched only by its revolting stink.

He gave the corpse one last, solid kick for prosperity before scooping up his firearm. "Piece of shit."

71

"Hey. Is everything o—?"

BANG!

Jacob realized his adrenaline pump was on overload. His nerves were tighter than razor wires. His neighbor from down the hall must've heard the commotion and, in her infinite nosiness, decided to check out the situation. Now, her elderly brains streaked across Jacob's front door, sliding down with the consistency of raspberry jam.

"Why'd you make me do that? You stupid, nosy old bitch," yelled Jacob as he holstered his gun and leapt over the reservoir of blackened sludge pooling on his floor. He already knew that Mrs. Fitzgibbons was gone, but he felt for a pulse regardless. While she was an annoying little snooper, she didn't need to have her skull aerated in such a manner. Soon, all the noise and gunfire would rouse the other inhabitants of the apartment complex. *Shit's getting even deeper!*

As Jacob knelt before Mrs. Fitzgibbons's corpse, he heard the distinct sounds of locks disengaging and door chains sliding off their guards. *Fuck!* He bolted down the hallway as all the doors opened in unison. He would have to forsake his abode and all his possessions, knowing that he could never step foot back inside this building. He was through ... done. No more jobs with The Collective and no more freedom if the police caught up to him.

All the opening doors were a blur as Jacob made his hasty escape. He didn't recall this hallway to the elevator being so long. Every time he turned a corner, he found nothing but more opening doors and the deadpan faces of his neighbors. In chilling unison, they all opened their mouths and spoke, their collective voice saying the same thing, "*Feel my wrath ... feel my pain.*"

Right away, Jacob recognized the voice as the father of the man he accidently killed while on the job in Haiti, Nicolas In time, all the doors of the ever-expanding hallway opened and filled with the gaping and whitewashed eyes of his neighbors as they repeated Jacob's tormentor's mantra like a broken record.

The hallway branched off to the right and Jacob kicked his pace up a notch, hoping that the exit to his current metric ass-ton of problems would be around the corner. He did his best to ignore the thunderous voice that filled the hall and vibrated inside his skull. All they did as he raced by them was glower while repeating the same thing. As he zoomed by one open door, he launched a right hook into one fellow citizen's pale face to no reaction whatsoever, despite the resounding crack of the man's head smashing into the doorjamb.

Yet, he had the corner in his sights. *Almost there—!*

No sooner than the thought popped into Jacob's head, the ragged, moldy corpse of Nicolas turned the corner before him —all the way from Haiti. Everything switched to half-speed as Jacob's face contorted into a grimace with a side order of what-the-fuck.

Feel my wrath … feel my pain … feel my wrath … feel my pain

To Jacob's utter dismay, the undead behemoth of a man lurched forward, looming like a mountain, his shadow engulfing the hit man's puny form. Nicolas opened his mouth, *"Feel my wrath … feel my pain."*

Jacob's eyes watered and his vision wavered. "Oh my Christ! Stop saying that!" He scrambled backward, the treads of his shoes gaining traction in the cheap carpeting, clambering to his feet. Now that he faced the opposite direction, he noticed that Mr. Bullet-To-The-Head and Miss Garroted-Zombified-Bitch had joined the soirée. Behind them was the mindless throng of his neighbors, their cold eyes now blackened and dead.

Feel my wrath … feel my pain … feel my wrath … feel my pain

The chant was getting too much to bear. Each one of them repeated the words in the Haitian man's voice—all except the guy he shot in the face. He sounded like a quasi-catatonic slurping soup from a spoon.

Nicolas shambled closer. Jacob could still see his mortal wound on the young Haitian's neck amid the rancid decay and vermin crawling all over his mottled flesh. "I'm sorry," shouted Jacob. "It was just a goddamn accident!" Nicolas kept coming. Jacob pressed up against the wall in between the incoming gang of walking nightmares. "I didn't … mean it … I was," he stammered, unable to piece together a full sentence.

What Jacob knew as reality had evaporated. All that it left in its wake was this numbing sense of defeat and lunacy. He began to sob as he slid down the length of the wall into a broken pile of a man—once strong, logical, and capable, now just a quivering heap of jelly.

They advanced on Jacob, crowding around him like gawkers at a crime scene. With a sharp inhale, he threw his head skyward, eyes clenched tight and beseeching the heavens. "I'm so sorry," he screamed over the droning of the mob, apologetic for the first time in his life. As his returning victims hovered over him—including Nicolas, his ultimate mistake—Jacob yanked his gun from his holster and pressed the cold barrel against his temple. With a vice grip on the weapon, he forced himself to look up at Nicolas.

"*With these bones I have crushed, make thine enemy turn to dust ... torment, fire, out of control ... With this hex I curse your soul,*" chanted Nicolas in his father's voice.

"Fuck it!" Jacob responded, hoping, in the end, for a sweet release as he pulled the trigger.

Click.

Empty.

Nicolas smiled, maggots swimming through his gaping grin, as the horde converged upon Jacob, piling on to his screaming form with teeth and fingers ripe for rendering his flesh into dust. Nicolas's reawakened corpse stood over the bloody maelstrom of ripping skin, pleased.

Feel my wrath ... feel my pain.

THE NIGHT GORDON WAS SET FREE

BY BILLIE SUE MOSIMAN

My name is Gordon and I know what I want. They just won't let me be myself because they're afraid. They've taken me to psychiatrists since I was seven years old (going on eight years now) and they were told I was special. The real words they kept using were psychotic and psychopath. I prefer *special*. Fucking psychiatrists. What do they know?

Due to my special interests, I tend to get into trouble. I shrug that off. Trouble is in the eye of the beholder. It seems like fun to me, what they call trouble. Fuck them. Sorry, but that's what I think about everything and everyone in the world—fuck 'em. If that's all you ever know of me, it's enough.

When I burned down the pool house, they hired guardians. Dad said to Mom, "That's it, we need help." They got two big, burly, gangrene-spirited, thick-necked morons to live with us in our house, sleeping next to my room. Like I couldn't shake them. Combined, their IQs don't add up to mine. I just keep my *fun* more secret, that's all.

I was all ready to step up my game when Mr. Brandywyne came to me on the sly. It was like a sign from God. Mark Brandywyne is an old family friend, almost as rich as my own parents—and trust me when I say my folks are rich as Croesus. If you don't know who Croesus was then you're too dumb to deal with me.

Brandywyne comes to all our parties with his young new wife, Sally. She always looks sour. Like she swallowed a sour ball candy and is about to throw up. He was over that day of the proposal; when it happened, my parents were away from the house. I soon found out he was there to speak to me, not the folks. He walked with me to the pool to sit under the cabana, in the shade, both of us wearing sunglasses in the Southern California noon sun. My guardians stood at the French doors watching, but out of earshot. Most of the time they seem more like ghosts than men. Ghosts that lurk around the perimeter of my life. When they think I'm getting close to doing something ... odd ... they shake a finger at me and frown, letting me know they're watching. I hate them. I was thinking of poisoning their lemonade.

That day Brandywyne said, "Gordon, I've known you since you were born. It occurs to me you possess a skill set I have need of."

"You ended that sentence with a preposition," I said, giving him a grin. He was the kind of guy I could play with that way. He'd never treated me like a kid.

"You're smart, too, I know how you scored off the chart."

"You flatter me, Grasshopper."

"Gordon, let's be serious. What is it you want most?"

"Can I name anything?"

"Anything." He picked at a tiny bit of dark lint on his white slacks. I studied him a moment. He had something up his sleeve. He wanted something big.

Now was my time, that's what I thought. No one had ever asked me what I wanted. Everyone assumed he knew what I needed and to hell with what I wanted. I was pretty sick of it.

"I want my freedom." There. Let's see what he'd make of that.

He sat staring ahead at the Olympic-sized swimming pool with the rock falls at the far end. "I can give you that," he said.

I turned to him and slid up my sunglasses. I squinted. "Mr. Brandywyne, I'm not someone you want to trifle with. Do you know what freedom means to me?"

"Tell me, Gordon. Tell me specifically what you want."

"I want out of this house. I want to be flown to another continent where I can disappear. I want ID stating that I'm eighteen so I can be

76

on my own. I want a bank account, a nice one so I don't have to work. I don't want any guardians or parents or trustees. I don't want anyone looking over my shoulder. And remember this—we're not friends. I have no friends."

Mr. Brandywyne sat still for long moments. Finally he turned to me, took his sunglasses off and looked me in the eye. "I can guarantee that."

"You can help me disappear?"

My gaze widened in surprise. Who would really give me my desires? He had to be as warped as a sickle moon. Give a fifteen-year-old kid a passport faked to make me older? Give me a fat bank account in a new country, and true, real freedom to live life the way I wanted? We were talking heaven.

It was a no-brainer. "What do you want me to do?" I asked. "I'm up for it. But I have to see everything before I start. The passport, the bank account, the flight ticket. I'll want you to get me away from these ... these baboons." I waved my hand in the air indicating the two baby-sitters standing behind us. "I mean it. I want proof you'll keep your word."

He nodded. "I figured you wouldn't trust me. I'll bring it all to you within the week. When it's time, I'll take you to the airport myself."

"First, tell me what *you* want."

"I want you to kill my wife. Then I want you to disappear."

Gordon agreed to my plan the way I hoped he would. Even at fifteen I saw the potential in the boy. If I tried divorcing Sally, she would take me to the cleaners. She said she would and I believed her.

Oh, in the beginning it was wonderful. She was young, lithe, and smart. She professed to love me. I was an old fool, just like all old fools. Her beauty blinded me. The long, tan legs; the thick, luscious hair; those succulent lips. And she could play chess. Not only play it, she could beat me at it. She was all I'd ever wanted, or so I thought.

Not long after I put a ring on her finger she began to change. She grew temperamental and sometimes she mocked me, pursing those red lips and repeating something I said to her in a hateful, gravelly voice. She began to go off on her own, not coming home until late at night, without explanation. She began to spend money like it grew on the trees.

I tried talking to her, loving her, giving her everything she wanted, and the more I gave, the more she took.

I couldn't kill her and risk prison time. I couldn't divorce her. I needed Gordon. Love had long vanished and I saw the relationship for what it was—an old, balding man, lonely, desperate for companionship, who fell for a femme fatale, a women bent on breaking me and leaving me penniless.

I began to study her routine and decided Gordon would have to come in the early morning, after two a.m., and bludgeon her in the bed. She was only predictable when asleep. I never knew when she was going or coming. While she slept, deep in the night, I'd leave our bed and wait in the living room while upstairs Gordon took care of the problem. Could he slip the men who hovered over him? I knew Gordon could do anything. Gordon was an assassin. He was born to kill. Even his parents didn't know it went that deep, but I knew. I could see it in his eyes from a young age. In the depths of his soul the boy was as conscienceless as a pit viper. It was a wonder he hadn't already murdered his parents in their sleep. I think they hired the two guards for their own peace of mind more than to keep Gordon under control. Who could sleep at night with a boy like that in the house?

I knew what Gordon was because I'd seen it before a couple of times. Once in the Army. A guy in our platoon had those eyes, those dead pools without feeling. One day he caught our sergeant alone in the latrine and, because he hated him, broke his neck. We all knew he'd done it, though the investigator never figured it out.

Another time I met a child of the devil. Not really, she was just born evil. But for all I know there really is a devil and she was the spawn of it. She had those eyes. She tortured animals, she laughed at pain and the distress of others, she stalked people, and by the time she was ten she'd killed a playmate while playing in a kiddie pool. Held her head under until she drowned. The worst ones are the ones born bad.

Gordon was like that—capable of anything. He was my only hope. He wanted his freedom. And so did I.

It's occurred to me that I'm not any better than Gordon and the others like him. I just don't want to get my hands dirty. I hire it out.

Mr. Brandywyne brought me all the documents on a day in late April. I was alone at home again, except for the baby-sitters. We sat by the pool and he handed over a folder. Inside I found my passport. My name was Peter now and I was eighteen years old. I found an ATM card in my new name and he told me I could check the account. An open-ended flight ticket was in an envelope, one-way, first-class, to Spain. I had a new Social Security card in the new name and a driver's license. I was legit. A brand-new person.

I gave him a thumbs up and folded closed the sheaf of documents. I'd check the bank account online as soon as he left.

"Okay," I said. "When and where and how?"

"My house, Friday night. My bedroom. I'll be downstairs to let you in. Afterward I'll make it look like a break-in. When you get there I'll leave, go to a bar, have a beer. That's my alibi. Wait half a hour so I can get there and be seen."

"How you want it done?"

"Use a baseball bat. Bring it with you, wear gloves, leave it behind." He added, "You can do this? You won't freeze? Or change your mind?"

I shook my head, holding the folder so tightly my fingers were white. "A deal's a deal. Sally's gone on Friday night. Just like you want. So when will you take me to the airport?"

"There's a flight Saturday morning at 4:30 a.m. Wait for me at the house when you're done. When I finish the beer I'll be back for you. We'll disable the security and break the door lock. I'll just drop you at the airport and hurry back to call the police. You'll be free. We'll both be free."

"I'll ride my bike over. You'll have to take it in your car trunk and get rid of it."

"I can do that," he said.

He nodded, stood, and walked away. I sat looking at the pool and decided to get my swimsuit when I took the folder to my room to hide. I felt like getting in a celebratory lap.

Friday was fantastic. All day long I was like hot grease on a griddle. I was popping around the house like a kid, deliberately annoying the baby-sitters. They could hardly keep up with me. I couldn't wait for the night. I had the bat leaning on my bike and Mr. Brandywyne's house was only a mile away. We'd been there for dinner. He lived in a big stucco monstrosity at the end of a winding lane from the street. There were no gates and the lights were trained on the hedges near the front windows, leaving plenty of darkness. I had my folder ready. I had a small backpack with a few clothes and toiletries. I was beginning a whole new life and it was going to be mine, mine, all mine to spend the way I wanted.

At one o'clock in the morning I stood and picked up the backpack, stuffed the precious folder into it, and opened my bedroom door. The two baby-sitters were snoring in their rooms. I crept past them, past my folks' bedroom, and down the stairs, letting myself out quietly.

Taking the bat, I climbed on my bike and rode out into the gentle night. The houses were dark. The dogs were sleeping. Only one car passed and I ducked with my bike into a yard thick with trees and vines.

When I got to Brandywyne's he met me at the front door, stepping aside without a word. He pointed upstairs.

I walked softly, my heart beating in my ears. You might think I was playing a game, that I wasn't serious, that I hadn't killed before. You'd think wrong. My mother gave birth to a girl when I was seven. All that baby did was cry, for hell's sake. Cry, cry, cry. They said she died of SIDS, luckily for me. Not so. I put a pillow over her fat red face and suffocated her. Bye-bye, baby. The folks didn't even try having more babies after that. Maybe they suspected ...

When I was ten, I pushed a boy off a tree limb after school and he fell to his death. He said I was crazy. He never should have said that. Accident, I exclaimed! I wasn't even near him! That was when the psychiatrist visits went from once a week to three. I was shackled to the old, stupid geezer. If we hadn't been rich, they would have sent me to juvy or some mental institution.

Taking out Sally was child's play.

The house was supernaturally quiet. I could hear my breathing and held my breath until I had it under control. In the open door of the bedroom I stood looking at the bed, the woman sprawled there, and I cared no more for her than if she had been a four-legged bug. I remembered her red lips, how they turned down at the corner like she was bored enough to slit her own wrists. She wasn't having any fun anyway with her old, balding, rich husband.

As soon as I heard the front door snick shut and knew Mr. Brandywyne had left, I stood waiting, counting minutes, listening to the night beyond the windows. Palm leaves scraped the glass like skeletal fingers seeking a way inside. A car went by. A dog barked somewhere far off. It was a lonesome night and the only people in it were Sally and me.

I spent time thinking about being free. Being able to indulge whatever wicked fantasies that came to me. I knew I wasn't the only one in the world who couldn't be shackled. I knew there were others, lots of others who stepped right into the dark side and found a home. I might be special, but only because I knew exactly what I wanted.

When I judged Mr. Brandywyne had been gone long enough, I moved quickly through the dark room of shadows and brought down the bat hard on the sleeping figure's head. Blood and teeth spewed and I ducked, still swinging, swinging with all my strength, over and over and over.

The quiet fell like a shroud again and I could hear my labored breath. I had snot hanging from my nose and if I'd touched my forehead I would have felt sweat through my surgical gloves.

I dropped the bat to the floor and backed away. In the bathroom adjacent to the bedroom I washed up, taking the small towel with me in my backpack.

I felt nothing. Not even exhilaration. This wasn't my kind of killing. I would have preferred a machete.

I waited in the living room and soon saw the headlights. Brandywyne met me at the door with a tire iron. He locked and closed the door once we were outside, and then he jimmied it, busting the lock from the door frame.

"It's done?" he asked.

"Done."

"Take your bike to the car."

On the way to the airport, he said, "Good thing you wore black. Can't see the blood if there is any."

"I'm no amateur," I said.

Along the highway to the airport, he took an exit in a bad part of town. "What are you doing?" I asked. "This isn't the way to the airport."

"Dropping off your bike. Someone here will steal it first light."

"You're no amateur either," I said with admiration.

He parked on a street and took the bike from the trunk, standing it next to a hurricane fence by a desolate ballpark.

When he neared the airport I said, "Mr. Brandywyne, I think you should park and let me out by myself. If you let me out in the unloading zone, someone might remember you or the car."

He glanced at me. "Maybe you're right."

He drove into the parking garage and, as I'd hoped, chose a level with few cars. He opened his door to say goodbye or maybe shake my hand, the way I had hoped he would. That made it so much easier. I snagged the tire iron along with my backpack from the backseat, and then dropped the backpack on the passenger seat. When I got out, he was already around the back of the car to say something, but he never had time to speak. I brought the tire iron down on his bald head with a solid crack, and grinned as he went to his knees. His hands came up to his head; he lifted his face, blood streaming down his cheeks, his eyes wide and startled.

"Gordon!"

"Yes, Grasshopper, that's my name and you're the only one who knows it. Fuck you, okay?"

I swung the tire iron from the side, catching him in the temple, and he keeled over like a bag of cement. I leaned over him and saw the open, dead eyes before cleaning the weapon of my fingerprints, taking up the backpack from the front seat, and closing the car door.

I looked at my watch. I only had an hour to secure my boarding pass.

Walking to the service elevator, I could see the pink-shell dawn threatening the horizon over the city. I felt overwhelmed with joy.

Spain was going to be spectacular, I just knew it. I was so free. Finally, finally free.

ALMOST EVERYBODY WINS

BY LISA MANNETTI

"Sally's trance doings were always spoken of as her own, as if done by herself in a state of somnambulism. Sally's letters she regarded as her own trance vagaries and Sally's signature as a name used by herself."

—Morton Prince, *The Disassociation of a Personality*

"A person—like Sally—with aboulia may find it impossible to pick up something from a table, or to rise from a chair, though strongly desiring to do so."

—Morton Prince, *The Disassociation of a Personality*

"Chris was inclined to be boastful ... 'I made her do it. I make her do all sorts of things. She is a stupid chump.'"

—Morton Prince, *The Disassociation of a Personality*

Somebody or other, she thought, has said we often see life through a glass darkly—or maybe it was a veil. Shit, who knew? *All* that Christine knew was that this loser of a waiter was standing over them with a loaded gun and Sally Grimshaw sat frozen, slowly blinking, mouth hanging open like the dirty oven door she constantly thought about shoving her head inside, laying her flabby cheek against its cold blue enamel tongue, and then turning on the gas. As if death would

83

transmogrify her into some modern-day version of fucking Sylvia Plath. Sainthood. Accolades. Yeah, right. Sally's poetry earnings to date wouldn't feed a goddamn goldfish, for chrissakes.

Aboulia, or some crap-claptrap, Sally's current shrink Cleckley called her inability to move. Like the name of a condition mattered. What mattered now was getting them the hell out of there—alive and in one piece. No time to get Sally to act—even if this depressed waiter was in the same suicidal boat along with Sally and had signed the same ridiculous illegal contract with Mr. Vinny of the Lifespan Treatment center. No, not enough time to push Sally from her own side of the veil. *Not enough time—*

Christine bulled ahead—a dynamo, a NASA rocket with enough thrust, enough force to launch entire Himalayan mountains into outer space—at the same time she crammed Sally back down inside; now instead, thank God, she was the one who was out and in control.

Using her slightly weaker right arm, she shoved the hesitant waiter's gun hand aside—the .45 clattered to the floor, spinning. While the waiter's eyes followed it with the concentration of a big bettor who had his life's savings riding on 22 black on a Monte Carlo roulette wheel, Christine slammed Sally's gun into her left palm, got her itching fingers into position, aimed at his forehead and pulled the trigger. He shoulda bet on *red* coming up, she smirked at her own pun. Smoke drifted from the barrel, and Christine inhaled its bitter odor gratefully. *Sally* might have hated the target practice at the shooting range Mr. Vinny insisted on, but Christine loved it. At the same time the waiter's bleeding body fishtailed backward and slumped to the floor, Chris hightailed it, heading for the restaurant's front door.

Mr. Vinny was in for a little surprise. No, she amended, stuffing the gun inside Sally's worn tan leather handbag, a big surprise. Lifespan itself was so aptly named, its Catch-22 element made Christine inwardly dizzy. Imagine wanting to kill yourself, then being told you had to make a hit and you either signed the contract that would loose another suicide killer on your own ass, or Mr. Vinny and Co.—and plenty of 'Co.' at that (as Cate Blanchett said in Christine's favorite movie, *The Talented Mr. Ripley*) would bring Mom, Dad, little sis or the christforsaken family dog into Lifespan's green room for a little reorientation training—translation: knife wounds, broken, bleeding jaws, or the ever-popular blackjack therapy. And frigging Sally, that stupid chump, who practically couldn't sign a check for groceries, had agreed!

Sirens wailed in the distance, and behind her confusion and commotion were on the verge of spilling onto the sidewalk. Shedding Sally's wrinkled brown raincoat, but imitating her timid, hunched walk to appear more innocuous, Christine crossed the street. She hailed a passing cab and told the driver to take her uptown to the shabby Yorkville apartment Sally called home. Christine figured she had a little time to regroup; especially since—she glanced at the cheap chrome watch on the body's left wrist—it was now officially Christmas Eve. A big day for Italians. Or so Mr. Vinny had said, and Christine decided there was no reason to doubt him. In the meantime, she twisted the watchband over her hand and, chuckling, switched it to the right side. Unlike Chris, Sally was a righty—and Christine guessed the ex-Mafia man had probably taken note of that little factoid; but at least for now, she was in control and she had every intention of being comfortable over the next few days. Or better still, she thought, the next few decades.

Christine had been watching Sally—and intervening—since Sally was a kid, she reflected, adjusting the wadded up hem on the flapping mu-mu Sally laughably considered a dress, and settling against the taxi's lumpy upholstery. But Sally didn't know shit about what Christine thought *or* did. In the past, she often let Sally regain control when some situation arose that Chris didn't want to deal with. Like the failed exam years ago in freshman comp. (Sally was the bookworm, all that literary stuff bored the bejesus out of Christine); Sally had "come to" sputtering over the big red F on the first page of her essay test, her eyes misting with confusion and sorrow, while Christine went to the little interior space she privately called "the cove" and took a nap. She could watch Sally whenever she wanted, but naturally there were plenty of times she had no interest in what Sally was up to—watching some sappy movie like *You've Got Mail* or writing her stiff, gray poems about November fields and desolate cemeteries and weeping willows. Ugh.

She could—and often did—imitate Sally to perfection when it was necessary. Just now it would be necessary to pass herself off as old Sal' for Mr. Vinny the former hit man and Cleckley the shrink—especially the latter. Sally, she knew, had scheduled so many goddamn psych appointments over the dreaded holidays, it was practically in-patient

85

therapy. But that was okay—she could handle the fake scare tactics and muscle imposed by one, and the sheer monotony doled out by the other. After the first, it was going to be a New Year. Yes, indeedy, a new year *and* a new life. Sally was a wimp. Tough luck, Sal. Christine knew—and didn't care that she herself was what was politely called "not a very nice person."

The dented cab pulled up in front of Sally's crumbling building and Christine thought: *This might be the very last time I ask anyone to drop me at this piece-of-shit address.* She slammed the bright yellow taxi door behind her, and on the heels of that rising determination to grow and prosper, a very Sally Grimshaw-like reference spontaneously popped into her own mind: *Now, gods, stand up for bastards!—and bitches, too, while you're at it,* she revised.

Christine sat on Sally's narrow bed and pulled the ugly mu-mu over her head; she tossed it in the general direction of the straight wooden chair that sat in front of the scarified library table Sally used as a desk. She sucked in her stomach and pressed her breasts together. Sally thought *she* was fat—wrong. Just curvy, but Sally was too dumb to know better. She kicked off a pair of black loafers and looked at Sally's closet door, then up at the painted tin ceiling tiles briefly; but she was too tired tonight to climb on furniture and open up her secret stash space to retrieve a nightgown—one that didn't look like something a baggy grandmother wore in the dead of a Vermont winter.

Fucked up Eve White in the Joann Woodward flick was a sap just like Sally, whining when she came to and found a teapot broken or a new dress in the closet. Wouldn't you think after more than twenty friggin' years, a new goddamn dress with some beads or spangles wouldn't be a life-shattering shock for god's sake? The movie was dullsville, but one thing Chris learned was to hide her own select wardrobe well, and it was a happy day when she found the space in the ceiling behind a few of the looser tiles. The glamour dresses, high heeled shoes, and trendy accessories were all up there. Along with the monthly bank account statements that were in—*note*—her own name: Christine Sizemore. Sally Grimshaw scraped along financially, but over the last few years, with some judicious small-time finagling and plenty-big heaping doses of befuddlement conferred on Sally when necessary—say, every third check that arrived from Sally's parents—she, Christine, had saved up a tidy sum. By itself, it wouldn't be enough to get Chris where she wanted to be (moved away from the dump, out of the reach of Vinny and Cleckley and the Grimshaw brood alike) but she'd had the good fortune to win $18,000 in the lottery a few weeks ago. Still small potatoes, but enough potatoes to buy some good clothes and, most importantly, drinks at the upscale bars in the tonier hotels—like Bemelmans at the Carlisle on Madison Avenue—where it had been easier than she ever imagined possible to snag a rich Mr. Right—or in this case, a forty-something divorcee named Richard Morrison.

So screw the sultry nightgown, Christine thought, yawning and sliding under the covers. She was an adult and she could sleep naked, for god's sake. She smiled. There was a new black cocktail dress in the foot-high makeshift storage area behind the ceiling. Richard adored a very chic white faille she'd worn once or twice, telling her he just loved the way she'd been poured into it. Wait till he saw her in the daring little Isaac Mizrahi—he'd be gaga. On the verge of sleep, a small nagging voice spoke up: *You have to be more careful; you have to pay more attention!* Daydreaming in the cove about hot sex with Dick Morrison—and simultaneously tuning out Sally—had led directly to the meeting with Mr. Vinny, psych counselor un-extraordinaire. Chris had assumed old Sally G. was merely visiting another wigged out mental guru—no reason to tag along on *that* trip, she'd decided. "It was *one* time," she told the voice, "so shut up. Nothing to worry about," she muttered. "I'm in control."

The day after Christmas Sally had a scheduled appointment with her annoying shrink—in the bright and early. Well, the bright and early for old sad sack morose Sally, Christine thought, which was three p.m. When she had the body, she liked waking up early and eating a big breakfast—not the weak tea and bagel thins Sally munched half-heartedly. The thing was, *she* was supposed to meet Richard at 4:30 p.m. for early cocktails at the Bull and Bear—one of the three greatest bars in the world according to the *New York Times*—at the Waldorf on

Park and 50th—and the goddamn shrink's office was way downtown. Not even a taxi could get Christine home and to the hotel on time. And worse, what was she supposed to do about wardrobe? Show up in one of Sally's drab A-line skirts and a long-sleeved beige polo shirt? The girl ate like a sparrow—and worse in Christine's opinion, dressed like one, too.

She could skip Cleckley—or Cluckley, as she privately called him—and his droning, indefatigable natter; the problem was Mr. Vinny might've set some low-level stealth-meister to keep an eye out for Sally's ass. Even if a few years ago a female shrink had been knifed by a psycho right here in New York City, Christine didn't think Mr. Vinny would try for a hit in Cluckley's office arena. It would be better to show up—as if everything was normal. Chris groaned. Normal meant the ugly clothes, the cheap metal watch and PayLess shoes—and not enough time to doll up for her paramour. "Christ," she said. "I'm going to have to double-dress. Just like they do in prison movies. Well, this *is* a prison, Sally," she shouted. "You're my goddamn ball and chain. And I cannot fucking wait to break out." Christine got on the phone and—lucky break—rescheduled Sally's appointment for two p.m.

Leave the good bag with the receptionist, Christine reminded herself as she stepped from the cab in front of Cluckley's office building. It wasn't flashy—not like the tiny red-and-black Prada clutch stashed *inside* the tote—but it *was* a brown leather Ferragamo satchel (bought, like the Prada, for just a couple hundred on eBay) and she wouldn't be embarrassed to be seen by Dick carrying it. Christ, even my *pocketbook* has to double dress, she thought, pushing the elevator call button.

"How was your holiday, Sally?" Cleckley, shaved bald head gleaming, brown eyes atwinkle, sat across from her, one urbane ankle crossed on the other knee, a steno pad and pen in hand, poised to write.

Eyes down, keep both hands on the unravelling dirty tan handle of Sally's ancient purse, Christine instructed herself. *Fidget—but just a little.* "It was okay, Dr. Cleckley." Half-smile, half-grimace.

"Good." Pause. "Well, what did you do? Did you spend it alone or with family?"

What did I do, Doc? After I got on eBay and had to pay for overnight shipping just to keep this fucking appointment so my boyfriend wouldn't see me carrying a twenty-year-old Macy's purse and dressed like an extra in a film about the homeless, I sexted Richard on my hidden cell phone and he sent me a close-up of his cock with a red Christmas ribbon tied around it, and then he said it got him so hot he called me, and we went live—or as live as we could—over wireless, and we pretended we went down on each other while we both beat off. He loves the way my hair feels when it's dangling against his thighs. We couldn't hook up at his penthouse like we usually do. He had to spend Christmas, naturally, with his kid in Connecticut. And thank Jesus the little bastard went to bed early.

"I made a little turkey, Dr. Cleckley."

"Good, Sally. Excellent."

"Well, it was just a slice of a Butterball turkey half-breast, but I did thaw it and cook it, and I had mashed potatoes and gravy and peas and a pumpkin pie from the A&P."

"Well, that's better than two years ago when you spent the whole day in bed and last year when you couldn't even bring yourself to heat up the Swanson's frozen lasagna, isn't it?"

Nodding.

"And did you call your mother in Pennsylvania?"

I called Richard a hot piece of ass with a dick that drove me wild.

"Uh-huh."

"I can tell by your expression that the conversation went well."

"You bet!" *Watch it, Christine.* "I mean both of them got on the phone and I thanked them for the $500." *And just in time to cover what I had to spend on eBay, thank God.* "And here, Dr. Cleckley, I have a check for you for today's appointment and I'll make up the rest next week—"

"Just give it to the receptionist on your way out, Sally."

That went well, Christine thought, ducking into the ladies room on the first floor of Cleckley's building. It was too bad, but she was going to have to accidentally on purpose leave the bathroom key the receptionist had given her on the sink—wouldn't do at all to be seen dressed to the nines and wearing make-up when she was supposed to be draggy-ass Sally Grimshaw. Sally forgot everything anyway, so the key would be no big deal. *Except, of course,* the nagging voice Christine sometimes called MomGhost—the voice of Christmas-hell-past—spoke up: *If Sally locked the door she'd go right back up to the third floor and tell Cluckley's receptionist. She'd be all sheepish—a regular sheep—but she'd let Mrs. Davis know.*

"Too bad," Christine said, pulling off Sally's sweater and stuffing it into the worn purse.

"And didn't you notice," the voice chimed in. *"Didn't you see good old Hervey M. Cleckley, M.D., Ph.D., when you tried to hand him the check with your left hand, and looking at your wristwatch? Your Cartier tank watch on your right arm?"*

"Big deal. I'll tell him Sally inherited it from her Aunt Martha or her Aunt Asshole and auntie sent it for Christmas—so she could know Sally was enjoying it before auntie kicked the bucket."

"It's a big deal, all right, Christine. You just don't know it. Just like you don't know—because you almost never pay attention—Cleckley's been using hypnosis on Sally and he thinks there's another personality inside her—an alter—short for alternating personality. Not you—he doesn't know about you—"

"Shut up, Moms—okay? Just shut up."

Richard wasn't there when she got to the Bull and Bear. Christine sipped a brandy Alexander as slowly as she could, stirring the drink into a watery tan slush. An hour oozed by. She checked her watch for the umpteenth time, frowned at the dark, silent cell phone sitting on the wooden bar to her left. He was never late. She passed a damp, clammy hand across her forehead. No, it was still pretty early—by Wall Street standards—maybe he'd gotten held up at work. Why didn't he call? Maybe he was stuck in a meeting or in some out-of-the-way, subterranean spot where it might as well be the 19th century as far as wireless was concerned. Maybe he stopped to buy flowers or some other little surprise for her—just last week she'd been gushing over a modest sapphire bracelet in Tiffany's window while he'd been walking arm in arm with her, strolling past.

At the same time Christine reluctantly ordered her second drink (*Where the hell was he?*) and it arrived with a thump on the cocktail napkin, her cell phone buzzed and lit up neon blue. She jumped. "Hi, Richard," she shouted into the phone.

A voice that—for a moment—wasn't recognizable because Christine had been so sure it was the wavy-brown-haired, thoroughly smitten Morrison on the other end of the line, said calmly: "Sally, old sock; it appears we've still got some business to attend to—"

Her face went slack and she blinked once slowly.

The last thing Christine recalled was wondering where *Richard* was, and how in the hell *Mr. Vinny* had gotten hold of her private number.

Jane could have told her.

She had taken over, first as Sally when Mr. Vinny phoned, and then as Christine when Morrison finally showed up.

Jane Beauchamp was what Dr. Cleckley called the "organizing personality." True, unlike some cases the psychoanalytic community treated and wrote about, she'd only recently been "out," but she'd been around—carefully observing—years before Christine Sizemore even *existed.* Just like—speaking of *organization*—she could've told her alter that "Richard Morrison" was an alias for an ex-Mafioso; that the guy Christine naively thought had marriage on his mind was actually a plant from the Lifespan Treatment Center. Jane had cornered most of this inside dope from a spy-sized, miniature camcorder she found in his penthouse. "Big Al Moretti" was a part-time counselor whose moonlighting avocation harkened back to his glory days as muscle for the mob. And he enjoyed infiltrating the straights (otherwise known as Lifespan's clients) even more—as he told Vinny over anisette one night in the Brooklyn-based supper-club/*ristorante* called Roma! Roma! where most of their old cronies hung out. In his forties, brains had won over brawn; finesse was more fun than breaking fingers (or kneecaps or ribs).

"If it was good enough for those *capicolls* at the FBI—for friggin Joe Pistone to masquerade as Donnie "The Jewel Man" Brasco and to penetrate the Bonanno family—may the old man rest in peace," he said, crossing himself, drink in hand, "what the hell."

"When it comes to ideas—you know my motto," Vinny said. "Learn from everybody, but *steal* from the best."

"Yeah. And with the old man gone, it definitely don't get no better than the FBI—"

"Al, I told you a hundred times, you gotta stay in character even when you're not on the job. From what I read, Morrison is supposed to be an Ivy Leaguer—"

"Jeez, Vin, I'm sorry—"

"Just pretend you're like, say, Brando—and live the role even when you're off stage, okay?"

"*Marlon* Brando? Jeez, he was the size of the entire Sicilian town my grandparents were born in when he died." Vinny glared at him. "I see what you mean though, I mean he *was* the godfather—"

"He *was* a method actor,"

"Huh? Oh. Right. Like James Caan playing Sonny Corleone."

"Close enough," Vinny sighed, "just tape everything, *capisc*?"

"Sure, Vinny, sure ... no problem."

"*Salut,*" Vinny said, raising the small liqueur glass and signaling for another round.

But the twin to Moretti's miniature spy camera, Jane discovered, cost a whopping $2,400. Sure, she thought, what did *he* care? He was on expense account from Lifespan and his idea of playing the Morrison big shot-*pezzonovante* role (even when he was off the job, as Mr. Vinny admonished) was to buy only the very best.

Jane knew that Christine could make Sally forget certain things. Unlike Christine, Jane liked learning and she read up on how Eve Black actually made Eve White forget the pain and bruises and the very beatings themselves some drunk bestowed—even when she retreated and left an uncomprehending Eve White to bear it all in her place. Now Jane needed Christine to forget certain things—including the fact that she, Christine, now had time loss and memory lapses too.

Christine wasn't anywhere near what anyone over the age of fourteen would charitably call conscientious; Jane knew Christine's idea of fiscal responsibility was to occasionally check the account balance when she withdrew a larger-than-usual amount of cash from an ATM. She didn't really even keep track of how much was in savings because, after all, *Sally* had no idea either account existed. And Christine never opened the monthly statements—she just threw them in a plastic grocery bag inside her stash compartment. If she was even slightly adept at using Sally's old Toshiba netbook, Jane thought, Christine would have gone paperless.

Meanwhile Jane had needed to buy that spy camera; she meant to leave it in place for a day in Morrison's apartment while she watched all the footage on the original—not just the fleeting minutes she'd be able to view while Morrison (aka Moretti) showered after sex with Christine ... or, to be more precise, her, Jane—at least the last time. Jane giggled—was she a voyeur or just kinky? Was sex with Dick (as Christine thought of it—because she really only cared about landing a Mr. Rich) a threesome? A foursome if you counted Sally? Anyway, she consoled herself, she could return the camera, which would be brand-new—she doubted that Big Al's ego was so big he'd be unable to resist watching himself for *one* day. And that was all she needed, she reminded herself—one day to leave the dupe in place at the penthouse and watch the footage at home—as she plunked down the cash and took the receipt from the salesman at Hammacher Schlemmer on East 57th—scant blocks from the place on Park Christine's erstwhile fiancé was calling his home.

So Mr. Vinny likes to read, too, does he? Jane (whose surname, Beauchamp, was straight from the pages of famed psychiatrist Morton Prince) continued watching the digital images from Moretti's pilfered camcorder. She sat cross-legged on Sally's spinster-sized bed, a bowl of warm Paul Newman popcorn (to keep the Sally side of her happy) between her thighs and snugged against her crotch (to keep Christine happy and under wraps).

Moretti was sitting in Vinny's clients' hot seat and for the first five minutes they were shooting the breeze, but when Big Al had walked in Jane had gotten a good look at the mahogany desk: A Stephen King paperback—and well-thumbed at that—was cracked open, face down.

93

A second book—another King collection, in fact—lay on the edge of the head counselor's workspace and Al had been toying with it, till Vinny told him to cut it out. *Yep, Mr. Vinny liked to read—short stories, anyhow.*

That cleared up one mystery—she paused the camera footage she was viewing on Sally's Toshiba netbook and googled "Stephen King characters"—and there it was: Richard Morrison, the antihero in a story called "Quitters, Inc." She downloaded a Kindle App (reminding herself to delete her tracks later). And in two clicks—and less than one minute—she was at location 4333 (aka page 220 according to the mighty Amazon software she'd just installed), and she was reading.

Nice to know Mr. King had inspired good old Mr. Vinny. It looked to Jane as if the fictitious company King wrote about had been transformed—and upgraded—to become Lifespan Treatment Center where, instead of losing your cigarette jones, the company guarantee was your own suicide. *Clever.* Damn *clever. You have to stop underestimating him, or find yourself—that is, what's left of yourself—reposing for eternity in an urn on the Grimshaw mantel.*

Back in spy-camera land, Jane Beauchamp, third personality in a constellation of women known (mostly) to the world as Sally Grimshaw, avidly watched more captured footage.

"I tell you, Vincenzo, of all the put-up jobs I've done for you, bar none—even picking off the gun-shy suicides, blasting those *cafones* who don't have the goddamn decency to honor a signed contract for chrissakes—even *killin'* those sons-a-bitches—none of the jobs have been as much fun as putting the sausage to this Sally chick."

"Hey, that's good, *cumpar'*—you've got it. You've really got it down. Stayin' in character even when *we* talk—"

"—she's got a good sense of humor too. Instead of the Richard alias, she calls me Dick when we're makin' it, and she calls herself all the time—and this is really funny, Christine Sizemore. You get it, Sizemore?" Al puffed his chest out. But Jane could have told him that Christine's name was what Cleckley would have called "leakage." Christine had named herself because Jane had actually read *The Three*

Faces of Eve and looked the case up on the Internet. Christine Sizemore was Eve White's real name ...

"That's swell, Al. And I'm glad you're doing such a good job and you're so much into the part, you're even enjoying the balling, but I gotta get back to work—"

"Sure, Vin. And you get any more hot numbers who need the Richard Morrison treatment, you let *me* know first—"

"Numbers—hey. She bought into the lottery scam, no problem, right?"

"Sure. I sent her to Loopy Louie—to his deli over on 86th, and he gave her a fake scratch ticket. His garroting days are over, and the Loop gambles like a mad bastard. He was into for me *twenty* grand, so he got off cheap—"

"How much you think she's got left?"

"Hey, *paisan,* I already told ya. It was your idea about some of the suicides—the ones, that is," he grinned, "who wouldn't decide, with a little cash on hand, that life was suddenly worth *living*—and letting 'em score phony Lotto wins. And I told ya I'd split whatever's left with you fifty-fifty."

"Yeah, the Grimshaw broad, what could she spend? She owes on some shrink bills maybe, or the utilities ... whatever—the way she dresses, it's not like she's a shopaholic—"

"Man, she looks good dressed up, though—you oughta see—"

Another mystery cleared up, Jane thought, pausing the program. Christine's scratch ticket was fake, but the neighborhood guy she bought it from (and lots of tri-state small-delicatessen dealers did such a brisk cash-on-the-barrelhead lottery business that they paid directly if the winnings were under twenty-five thousand—it was in everybody's interest to bypass Uncle Sam and *his* tax agenda) owed Big Al Moretti who, apparently in addition to his other skills, was also a moneylender with interest rates that would send most people into instant cardiac arrest.

She fingered the built-in mouse pad and Big Al and Mr. Vinny popped up larger than life. Another few seconds played and Jane said:

"Another mystery cleared up, but oh my God, it's out of the frying pan and, oh shit, *directly* into the fire—"

"Take a look at this—" Big Al took off his spy gear and attached a short USB cable to Vinny's laptop, then to the duplicate featherweight spy camera that looked to Jane like a thumb-sized electric razor and could be worn—as Big Al had—clipped inside the placket of any ordinary shirt where what was visible to the beholder seemed like any ordinary button.

"What the hell you recording us for?" Vinny fumed, staring at the monitor.

"You said get everything—"

"Not us, you big lugoon—we know what *we say*—you're supposed to tape *her!*"

"Lemme fast forward—hang on—"

That camcorder footage was blank, of course, and for a second Jane was not only relieved but laughing at these two incompetents' antics. For a second. Then she heard Big Al say, "No worries, I got back up." And the next image she saw—because, in his anxiety over Vinny's impatience, he hadn't turned off her substitute spy cam and it was sitting on the desk recording—was a pair of expensive-looking sunglasses—its attached UB cable, the umbilical cord sharing hidden truths.

"Oh my God, those sunglasses," Jane whispered. She'd seen Big Al in Richard Morrison mode wearing them pushed up on top of his head—*like,* she sniffed with derision, aware of Christine's anger welling up, *like he thought he was goddamn George Clooney on the set of Monuments Men directing the movie*—and she'd naively figured the ex-mobster was making his idea of a fashion statement; but a pulse ticked in her throat at another memory: She'd also seen them lying, lenses facing outward, seemingly innocuously, on the custom-made mahogany bookshelf built into the elaborate headboard on Morrison's king-sized bed.

"Wide angle, too," Big Al said. "Check this out."

"Holy shit," Vinny said. "Grimshaw? That's Grimshaw doing a strip in that teensy black see-though chemise-thing?"

"Uh-huh ..."

"Something's wrong—that *can't* be her. Hey, does this thing have a zoom? Let me see her face better—"

"It's her—"

"It can't be ..." He turned quickly and rummaged a filing cabinet behind the desk and pulled a folder. "This is *Grimshaw*," Mr. Vinny said, smacking a large black and white glossy of Sally, who was sitting on the chair, her eyes squinted completely shut from the flash, her hands tightly gripping her pocketbook handle, her hair a dark greasy mop that brushed the top of the shoulders on the stained turtleneck sweater she was wearing. "See? Grimshaw looks like a schizo K-mart shopper on disability ... and *that* chick looks like she could hang out with Brad and Angelina—and hold her own."

"Huh ..."

"Something's wrong here," Vinny said. "Turn that thing off," he waved one hand over the laptop, the other, finger-scanning down the top sheet in Sally's file. "Yeah, here it is, I knew she wrote it down." He began punching buttons on his desk phone.

"What are you going to do?"

"I'm going to call her shrink—Cleckley his name is, and ask him for some information on Sally Grimshaw—strictly in confidence, of course—as one psychological counselor to another." He winked up at Al.

"No kidding, Doc," Vinny said.

Oh thank Jesus, Jane thought, Big Al had turned off the laptop, but the camera still running. He'd clipped the celebrity-style sunglasses into the V of his white Jeremy Argyle shirt, and her mind roiling, she heard an interior voice say: *Figures, the men's shirt store New York Magazine called the best in New York City is, what, a three-minute stroll from Little Italy? How convenient.* But, when she shook her head to clear it, she recognized that was pure defense on the part of her unconscious. It was way more important to pay attention to Mr. Vinny's end of the conversation.

"No kidding, Doc, and you're sure she has at least two—and possibly three personalities, huh?" Pause. "Sure, of course, I'm familiar with *Sybil* and uh, Dr. Wilbur."

"I saw that movie," Big Al chimed in. Vinny's jaw clenched with irritation and he flapped an arm irascibly at the ex-mobster to shut up.

"Yeah, but for her it's more like *Three Faces of Eve*, though, you think, huh?" Pause. Jane wished she could hear Cleckley's end of the conversation, but "Dr. Vincent" was using a tried-and-true mob gambit to give Sally's shrink the impression he was considering the older man's words ... listening closely. "And now, even without hypnosis, you noticed this other personality who, uh, erupted spontaneously was left-handed, but Sally is a righty. Right. Uh-huh. *And what else?*"

Vinny suddenly curled his palm over the receiver. "Excuse me, Doc. I'll be right back in one second." He punched the mute button. "What the hell are you doing?" Al was standing on the other side of the desk making the classic up-and-down hand gesture in the region of his crotch, then spinning about-face and doing the same thing with his other palm and fingers. "I just want to know which one I slept with, so I'm trying to figure out which hand the broad used to jerk me off—"

"Will ya just get the hell out of here, Al—" Vinny said. "Now!"

"Sorry, Doc. There was a slight interruption here from one of the, uh, the other counselors."

The wide-angle lens provided a partial glimpse of the big man's sulky retreat.

And then, unfortunately for Jane, the tape ended.

Earlier that day—the same late winter afternoon Jane had sat on Sally's unmade twin bed watching Moretti's spy cam—Dr. Cleckley discussed amalgamation and murder.

"In the case of the woman known as 'Sybil,'" he said, "Dr. Wilbur referred to the process as integration." He paused. "It brings up the real threat of permanent extinction—the death of the other alters, and that can be terrifying," his eyes locked on hers, "for everyone—even the personality that survives."

Jane had come dressed as herself to the one o'clock appointment: Sally's shoulder-length hairstyle, but recently shampooed and shining;

she sported Christine's tank watch on her left wrist, and wore her form-fitting black sheath, but Jane had added a black-velvet blazer. Dr. Cleckley had recognized her at once.

"No heart stops beating, no flesh decays, but it is—or can be—a death of sorts," he said. "That's why I prefer the term amalgamation, and all it implies."

"I wouldn't exist," Jane said.

"Technically, no. But we're agreed that neither Sally Grimshaw nor Christine Sizemore is fully functional—"

"Christine is a lot of fun," Jane said. "And Sally's very emotional, very sensitive."

"You wouldn't be Jane—not precisely—but you'd have their memories and the traits you find endearing in each of them. Think of it as a merger, a welding. Just like," he said, "today you're wearing a combination of their clothes and yours. Only, there wouldn't be any 'leakage,' those random thoughts that cross over—the ideas and emotions and actions would truly be a part of the new you," he smiled.

"And it's permanent, you say?"

"Absolutely—in the hypnotic state all three alters will fuse."

"What should I call myself?"

"Whatever you like," Dr. Cleckley said.

There was a huge crash. The front door to Sally Grimshaw's tawdry railroad-style apartment flew open. In the light of the fourth floor hallway's naked bulb, Christine S. Beauchamp could see the silhouettes of two tall figures. She sat very quietly, very still in the dark. After she'd seen what there was of Moretti's amateur camcorder footage, she'd guessed this would happen and she was ready.

"Empty," Big Al said.

"She's here, all right," Vinny said. "These old dumps always have those steel police bars that fit into slots on the floor—and it's not in place, so she's here."

They ran noisily through the living room, heavy shoes thudding against the wooden boards, guns drawn.

When they reached the threshold of the bedroom, she switched on the sun-bright Petzl headlamp she'd rushed out to buy on Third Avenue an hour ago, just before twilight.

Startled—wildly blinking—each man stopped and instinctively threw a hand up to shield his eyes from the glare.

In one swift, elegant movement she pivoted and, crouching low at the same time, fanned the trigger, firing rapidly. Then, lightning-quick, she switched the gun to her left hand and shot again. Both Lifespan Treatment counselors were dead. "'Think you used enough dynamite there, Butch?'" she laughed. "'You know what, Sundance, the rest of the world wears bifocals, but I've got vision.'

Back in early December when Sally signed the contract, Mr. Vinny had told her that between the guaranteed painless suicide Sally wanted so fervently, and the hit on the abusive husband his Italian-American lady client needed so desperately, Lifespan was providing satisfaction for everyone concerned: It was good business, it was the smart money. "Everybody wins," he'd grinned. *Correction*, she revised, *almost everybody wins.*

Mr. Vinny and Big Al Moretti lay dead and bleeding on the floor of the threadbare apartment one Sally Grimshaw had leased. Sally was gone, Christine was gone. Jane was gone now, too. From the ashes, only the woman who'd never existed and no one had ever met—Christine S. Beauchamp—lived to build another day.

FRIENDS FROM WAY BACK

BY DENNIS LAWSON

The apartment building smelled like curry. The air was so thick with it that I was afraid it was sticking to my clothes. I was patient enough to listen outside Jack's door for a few seconds. Someone was strumming an acoustic guitar inside. That was a good sign. There was a six-pack of Rolling Rock in my left hand and a bottle of Seagram's Seven in my right. I stuck the whiskey under my arm and knocked.

The strumming stopped, a few seconds passed. "How did you find me?" Jack asked from behind the door, probably watching me through the peephole.

"Nice to see you, too. Are you going to let me in?"

The door opened as far as the chain would allow. Jack was dressed in a tank top, camouflage shorts, and black sneakers. Around his neck, he was wearing a hemp necklace with a seashell. "Did Snyder send you?"

"I'm here to help you," I said in a low voice. "No one sent me. I'm sticking my neck out here and I'm already starting to regret it."

"Are you alone?"

"Yes."

He let me in.

I assumed the place had come furnished, since there was a couch, two chairs, a coffee table, and a long television stand complete with TV. Seemed like a lot of stuff to haul for a guy in hiding. Jack and his band rented a house together in Wilmington, but he'd been crashing down here by the University of Delaware in Newark since Rachel Prescott had gone into a coma. There wasn't much else: a boom box beside the television, some CDs, an empty pizza box, and a guitar on the floor. Nothing on the walls. And it was dark—the hall light was on, but the lights were off in the living room.

"I figured you could use a drink or two," I said. I stuck the beer and whiskey on the coffee table. A cigarette was smoldering in an ashtray. Beneath the smoky smell, that curry was leaching in. And Jack had the same body odor that he had when we were teenagers. I lit a cigarette to help keep those smells down.

"Any word on Rachel?" he asked.

It made sense that he didn't know. Her family was rich, and they were really stepping on the news coverage.

"She died this morning," I said.

"Holy shit." Jack sunk into one of the chairs and lit a fresh cigarette.

I popped two Rolling Rocks. I brought Jack one and then checked out the CDs. One was a Prong album I didn't recognize, so I put that one on.

"I remember these guys from high school," I said. "Music to break bones to."

Jack's face had gone white.

"Hey, sorry. I'm not trying to sound tough. You are in trouble, though. I guess you know that." I sat down on the couch and drank half of my beer in one gulp. I was sweating, and for some reason Jack didn't have the air cranked. I ground out my cigarette.

"I know Snyder wants the money I'm down," Jack said. "The money that Rachel didn't cover. He won't get it if I'm dead! My band is at the tipping point. We're going to be big, I can feel it. If he just gives me a little more time, he'll get his money and spades on top of it."

Jack wasn't just bullshitting me about the band. They had been on the verge of something back in the early 2000s. Then the little record label in Philly that had signed them went under, and Jack's band didn't get the rights back to their music. Took years. Everyone just kind of

102

moved on. A year ago, they got asked to reunite for a benefit show—this old punk promoter had MS and no money left. The band started writing new material and getting a lot of play on local radio. And the fans weren't just aging rockers like us. Rachel was only twenty-one.

"The problem is a lot bigger than the money," I said. "You've made too many people angry. There's the drugs you didn't pay for. And then there's the nighttime sessions with Betty."

He stood up and pointed at me. "Betty is into me. She doesn't charge for me."

"Jack, we're friends from way back, but if you try lying to me tonight, I will kill you. Now sit down and drink your beer and listen to me."

He sat down.

"And, no, Betty isn't into you. She's not into anyone as near as I can tell."

Betty is one of Snyder's ladies. She's a big girl with big assets, but she wears them smoothly like a pin-up from another decade. The faint wrinkles around her mouth add to the idea that she's from another time. She's gotten more gray-haired lawyers and bankers in Wilmington into honey traps than you could ever imagine. She'd look great on an album cover, I'd give her that.

"So on those two counts," I said, "Snyder is down money thanks to you. Now we add in Rachel. The Prescotts make plenty of legitimate money, but they're also in bed with Snyder. You've put Snyder in a jam with them. Because he's been letting their sweet little angel go to his hangouts, drink his booze, buy his drugs, and support the bad habits of this thirtysomething punk rocker she's so in love with. Think about how much pressure he's under, from them, to kill you."

Jack had finished his beer. He looked like he was about to cry into the bottle.

"Have some of the whiskey," I said. "I think you need it. Hell, let's both have some." I stood up and took a pull from the Seagram's bottle. Then I handed it to him. He did his from his chair. I took it back and gave him another bottle of beer.

"On the other hand," I said, sitting on the arm of the couch, "it's not exactly a secret that you're in debt to Snyder. If someone kills you, the police are going to be all over him. It's a headache. But that's where you're really in trouble. Because there are guys out there who aren't in with Snyder, and they want to be. And knocking you off cleanly could make any one of them a star."

"How do you know all of this?"

"My Uncle Dick visited me this morning." I didn't really call him that anymore—Dick wasn't related to me by blood—but that's how Jack would know him. My dad left when I was a little kid, and Dick dated my mom for a while. After he broke things off with her, he still helped me out here and there. He's a weird guy, but he's the closest thing to a dad I ever had. He's also a triggerman for Snyder. Jack had seen him around when we were teenagers.

"Why would he want to help me?"

"He doesn't. This is just between you and me. Dick laid all this out for me because he knows we're friends. He gives you around twenty-four hours. He can't go against Snyder, but if I happen to know this stuff and decide to help you, no one has to know. It's just one of those things if you get away."

"What do you mean?"

"I'll explain it in a second. Do you have shot glasses in here? Or any sort of glasses? I think we need another shot. At least I know I do. This is a big deal."

Jack went into the kitchen and came back with a couple of plastic cups, the tall ones with three indentations. I pointed to the coffee table for them, and then I poured whiskey into each one, a little bit past the first indentation. The Prong was ringing in my ears, and my throat was getting dry. I had a little more of my beer. Jack put his empty beer bottle down on the table.

We were standing close enough that I could smell his unwashed odor. I clinked cups with him, drained my shot, and sat back on the couch. He stayed on his feet and drank his slow.

I needed another second. So I decided to ask a question about something I was curious about.

"Before I tell you my plan, can I ask you something? Why would you sleep with Betty and then not take care of it? You knew that Snyder's people were having Rachel cover your debts. It was going to get back to her that you nailed another woman."

Jack rubbed his face, up and down. "That fucking Rachel. Goddamn!" He took one of the beer bottles off the coffee table and whizzed it at the wall. Broke into a thousand little pieces of green glass.

"Knock it off! The last thing we need is any attention."

"I know. Sorry. I know!" He started to pace around the room. "Listen, I feel terrible that she's dead. I do. But she made so many problems for me. She was supposed to be a groupie, but she acted like we were married ever since I first let her backstage. She was a lot of fun, but she wouldn't take a hint. I tried blowing her off, and she would just get all psycho on me. I should've just sat her down and told her it was over, I know I should've. But I was scared that she would sabotage us somehow. We're getting so close. She did a lot of our promotional stuff. She was actually a big help.

"I was thinking that maybe I'd just wait it out, and then dump her when we got our record deal. You know, the typical rock star move. But then I got impatient. I figured that if she heard about me and Betty, it would break her heart and get her to kind of just fade away."

"But instead she OD'd."

"Yup."

"You can't blame that on yourself. You didn't kill her."

"Try telling Snyder that. Or her family."

"I don't think that'll work. That's why I hatched this plan."

I laid it out for him. I wanted us to get in my car and leave, tonight. Now. Head down to North Carolina, where a friend of mine from college had some rental property. Stay out of sight for long enough that the pressure eases up on Snyder—maybe some people would credit him for the disappearance, but there wouldn't be any evidence. Let the grief pass by and then, when Jack did come back, he just wouldn't be a priority any more.

Jack didn't like it. I could tell right away. He lit a cigarette and shook his head. His hand was shaking, too.

"My band is too close," he said. "We're about to make it. I can't just run away now."

"What good is your band if you're dead? I'm not kidding here. You wake up in Delaware tomorrow morning, it's going to be the last morning you see. Because someone's gonna come gunning for you. And if they do, believe me, I won't give a shit. I'll know I tried, I offered to put my life on hold, and you didn't play ball. You got it?"

We heard a series of knocks outside. It wasn't at Jack's door, though. Probably a couple doors down. Jack went to the eyehole, and I

105

stood by the door. We heard a door open, and then a bunch of happy greetings.

Jack took a few steps and then crumpled into his chair. "That's the second time I almost had a heart attack today. Okay. Let's do it. I want out."

I told him that he shouldn't bring anything, just his wallet. He was fine with that, since all his good gear was up at the house in Wilmington. I also said no final phone calls or anything.

"But I do think you should leave a note," I added. "Leave it for your parents, just so they have something to hold onto when they don't hear from you for a while."

"What am I supposed to say?"

"I don't know. 'I love you and I will see you again someday.' Just so they know you're not dead."

He didn't seem all that convinced, but he was scared enough to listen to me. He had a notebook for lyrics and stuff, and he ripped a page out and crouched down at the coffee table. I think that's when the weight of what he was doing really hit him. He started to cry. It was embarrassing. But he managed to get the note written.

"Why don't you leave that necklace you're wearing, too? It's seems kind of distinct to me. One less thing that's identifiable."

He fingered it for a moment, like he would miss it or something, and then he took it off and put it on the note.

"So how are my parents going to get the note?"

"When you turn up missing, the police will make their way here eventually. That's when your parents will get it."

It was getting to him more and more. He went into the bathroom and threw up. I read the note—it was good—and turned the volume up on the boom box. And that's when I sent a text message to Dick.

I used the bathroom after Jack. "Ready?" I asked.

"Not really," he said.

I slid the chain off the door and opened it. Dick strode in with gloves on his hands and the noose all ready. I put on my gloves as well. Jack was barely able to get a sound out before the noose was around his neck. Jack struggled but it didn't do any good. Dick was just too strong for him. When Jack lost consciousness, Dick dragged him to the bathroom. He tossed the rope over the bathroom door and then hoisted Jack up.

"Hold the rope for a second," Dick said.

There was no time to hesitate. I grabbed the rope and pulled to keep Jack aloft. Dick tied the rope to the doorknob.

I followed Dick back into the hallway. Jack's face turned light blue, and his legs had these terrible spasms. Then he pissed himself and shit himself and it was over.

The icing on the cake was this little plastic stool in the kitchen. Dick placed it on its side near the bathroom door to suggest that Jack had stood on it before stepping off.

Then Dick went over to the coffee table and read the note. "Hey, this is great work, kid," he said. "I mean it. I'm really proud of you. I think this is the beginning of big things for you with Mr. Snyder."

THE REPO GIRL

BY PATRICK DERRICKSON

Pina guided her compact, black ship under the larger yacht and, finding the metallic panel concealing the landing gear, attached with magnetic clamps. Her glowing computer display confirmed a solid connection. A quick security scan confirmed she had not been detected. Pina made a mental note to thank Martino again for updating her cloaking device. The upgrades from the tech wizard of her company were usually a couple of years ahead of the commercial tech available for nonmilitary ships.

With a tap of her finger, the pilot's seat contracted and slid under the console. This gave her petite, meter-and-a-half frame a little more room to shimmy into her spacesuit. Pina's ship was usually used as local system racer. She had modified the Stiletto-class craft for getting in and out of tight spots. Pina owned *The Lucy*, paid in full from her five years of professional racing through the Alcon system. Missing the adrenaline rush of zipping through an asteroid course and dodging hurtling rocks of death, Pina pursued a different career that filled that need. And paid well. Very well.

Pina strapped her carbon-ceramic knife to her leg, in the gap near her midthigh. Unless she was frisked or examined closely, the camouflaged weapon would not be seen. She had only needed to unsheathe it once before, when a drunken shipowner confronted her. He had been lucky that day, only losing a finger. Pina would have gutted him if the port security officers hadn't arrived. When they attempted to arrest her for assault, she flashed her warrant and they backed off.

No one messed with the Teras Bounty and Repo Company.

When someone did try, it never ended well. A missing freighter filled with millions of credits worth of cargo would disappear without a trace. Or a tough-as-nails security chief, trying to gain support for a local office by investigating the business practices of Teras, died in a horrific accident. The long-term health and well-being of the people that opposed the Teras Company was historically quite short.

Pina attached the small energy stun-gun to her hip. More a deterrent than an actual weapon, it was powerful enough to subdue anyone who resisted. She had drawn it on several occasions, but had yet to fire it. Not that she wouldn't. Once her marks realized who pursued them, they knew to surrender. The gun's best feature was that it could only be fired by her. Martino had programmed her biometric signature into the grip and trigger. Anyone else who tried to shoot the weapon would find it useless. And if someone other than Pina pulled the trigger two times in succession, the gun would discharge its energy with enough force to render the person unconscious.

Pina pulled the diminutive helmet over her head, and heard the sigh of air as the helmet sealed itself to her suit. The cool wisps of oxygen tickled her face as her HUD, or Heads Up Display, activated. *The Lucy's* 10,000-kilometer scan indicated no other ships nearby.

Time to go to work.

She slipped out of *The Lucy* and pushed off, floating across the two-meter gap between the two ships. Grabbing the underside of *The Lady Jane,* Pina pulled herself to the airlock, and typed in the override code she had received from the yacht's manufacturer. The panel opened and she floated inside. The interior door slid open once the airlock had pressurized. The quiet hum of the environmental system greeted Pina, but she didn't remove her helmet.

She followed her HUD's directions to the only other person on the ship, and found him unconscious on the galley's table. Pina's scan showed him alive, pumped full of Cota, a popular but expensive psychedelic drug. Damn. His enormous bulk covered most of the eight-person table, and easily weighed one hundred eighty kilos. She wouldn't be able to lift him from the table and lock him in his cabin. She was strong for her size, but not that strong. An alarm pealed and the galley's display screen turned red as the proximity alert warned of an incoming ship. Pina's HUD lit up as her own ship's alert flashed. The ship would intercept *The Lady Jane* within ten minutes. Right on time. She silenced the irritating tone. Pina's hand reflexively went to her gun when the bloated man stirred, but relaxed when he did not waken. The man smacked his lips and saliva pooled under his reddened face. Pina shook her head in disgust. Stupid shit always happened when you lost control of yourself. She secured the man's hands and feet to the table with carbon zip-ties, and disengaged her suit's helmet.

The reek of body odor stung her eyes. Pina coughed and backed away, waving her hands to dispel the stench. Holding her breath, she backed out of the galley. Users addicted to Cota suffered memory loss and often ended up dead. Thoughts of finding her brother, slumped in a closet, a few days after their parents had died, surfaced from the dark recesses of her mind. Pina suppressed them as quickly as she could; it was not the time to think about other people's decisions. She needed to focus.

As she made her way to the bridge, she admired the sleek, modern layout and real wood textures of the ship. The designer of *The Lady Jane's* interior was a true artist. She settled into the luxuriously padded pilot's chair, feeling the cushion alter its form to match her body type. Pina smiled. It would be a fun ride home. Her fingers flew over the console as she prepped the ship for the return journey. The navigation system was state-of-the-art. Pina scrolled through hundreds of star maps. An elaborate map of her home system popped up on-screen. Each port and planet was exquisitely detailed, and the search function allowed her to find a specific good or service on any planet. This navigation feature itself cost more than her fee for completing this mission.

An emergency signal from the other ship blared around the roomy bridge. *The Rock Smasher* had activated its distress beacon. Interstellar law was clear: If a ship activated its emergency protocols, and you were in proximity to offer assistance, you were required to render whatever aid you could. Failure to do so would trigger criminal charges. On several occasions, captains of merchant ships ignored those beacons and, when people died because of their inaction, were charged and convicted of murder. Pina wouldn't ignore this emergency beacon. She was a *responsible* employee of the Teras Bounty and Repo Company, after all.

"*Rock Smasher*, this is *The Lady Jane*. I've received your distress signal. Do you require assistance?" Pina said.

"Oh, thank the gods. I thought I was going to die out here. Must be my lucky day," a man's voice replied.

Pina snorted. Lucky was not a word she would have used in this situation.

"What can I do for ya?"

"I have a hull breach. Flew too close the asteroid I was mining and hit the damned thing. Put a hole in the side right near the bridge."

A quick scan confirmed the breach, as well as the minerals in his hold. Only a third filled. Just enough to led credence to his story.

"You in a suit?"

"Yep, I always leave it on when mining. Never know. Glad I did, too, the way that rock gutted my ship."

"Long way from a refinery rig. You a freelancer?"

"Yeah. That a problem?"

Freelancers didn't belong to a mining company or guild. They gave up the security of controlled mining operations for the thrill of hitting it big on a random rock in a system. Some were successful, selling rare minerals for a huge profit. Neither group liked each other, but it generally wasn't a problem until someone decided to mine in the same area, or on the same rock. When that happened, the local security force was called in to either stop a fight, or clean up the remains of the loser.

"Nope, I don't have a problem with people making a living. As long as they don't hurt anyone, I don't give a shit what people do. What's your name?"

The man laughed. "Call me Rocky. That's my nickname in these parts."

"Okay, Rocky. Let's see about getting you something to fix that breach. Can you get here?"

"Yep. Suit thrusters are working fine."

"I'm going to open my airlock."

"Sounds good. Be over in five."

Pina jogged to the hold and activated the floodlights outside the airlock. Within moments, a ghostly figure floated into view. As the man got closer, Pina noticed he wore the identical model of spacesuit. Tension wormed its way into her neck. So, he had some surprises for her. She had a few too, if needed.

The inner door slid open and the man stepped out, his helmet disappearing behind him. He slowly raised his hands when he noticed the gun Pina pointed at him. He had a round face, with a scar running down the left side. Thin hair matted to his sweaty forehead. His stomach swelled from his suit like a balloon.

"What's this about, missy?"

"Can't be too careful. Never know what kind of people you might meet out here."

"You did scan my ship, correct? Saw the hull breach?"

"I did."

"Then why the gun? Do I look threatening to you?"

"Looks can be deceiving."

"Hey, the law says you have to give me aid. Are you going to help me, or shoot me? If you're gonna shoot me, I'd rather just go back to my ship and try to make it to the next port. I'd rather die on my ship than yours."

"You wouldn't make it."

"I wouldn't?" Rocky said.

"Nope. It's four hours to the next port. Your suit only holds two hours of air, and you have no environment on your ship. So that leaves you two hours without air. I don't know anyone who can go that long without air."

Rocky snorted, the corners of his mouth forming a condescending smile.

"You're a quick one. You own this ship?" he asked.

"Me? Nah, I couldn't afford something this nice. I'm just flying it."

"So you're just a pilot? You look a bit young." Rocky glanced around. "Where's the owner?"

"The truth? He's in his cabin, strung out on Cota."

"Cota?" Rocky said. "I guess if he can afford a ship like this, he can afford Cota. When's he going to come back down?"

"Couple hours, maybe."

"I'd hate to waste two hours waiting for him to come back to reality. Can you help me now?"

"I'm not leaving the ship, but I have something to fix the breach. There's a repair kit in the tall cabinet on the other side of the wall."

Pina gestured to the side of the room. Rocky's head moved enough so that he could see both Pina and the direction she indicated.

"Thanks, much appreciated. I'll reimburse you for the kit."

He reached for a bulge in his suit and stopped when Pina cleared her throat.

"What? Oh, I'm just getting my data pad."

"Slowly."

"Okay, okay. Sheesh."

Rocky reached into his pocket and withdrew a data pad. He held it up for her.

"See? Just a data pad. Now, what's your account ID so I can transfer the credits?"

"I'll input it if you don't mind," Pina said.

"Not at all. I don't take you for the trusting sort. Me either, been burned too many times. Anyway, I didn't catch your name?"

"You can call me Suzie."

"Suzie? I guess that fits ya."

"What does that mean?" Pina asked, and glowered at him.

"Whoa, slow down there, missy. I just mean that you look young, and you have a young-sounding name. That's all."

He had gotten under her skin too easily. She had to keep calm. Focused.

"Let's just get this over with."

Pina reached for the data pad, but kept her gun leveled at Rocky. He handed it over, and stepped back, hands upraised. She peered at the information on the screen, then looked up. The amount on the screen indicated a fifty percent markup over fair market value. She looked at him with raised eyebrows.

"What? You stopped and helped me. I thought I was going to die out here. Least thing I could do is to repay you in kind. If you accept the credits, just hit the Accept button and input your account ID."

She rested the data pad on the crook of the arm that held the gun and pressed Accept button.

Her finger sizzled as an electric charge surged through her body. She fell hard to the floor, her muscles twitching and burning as if on fire. A gloved hand snatched the data pad and pried the gun from her stiff fingers. Rocky loomed in her face.

"You shouldn't point a gun at someone if you don't plan to use it. People don't like that."

Rocky pulled zip-ties from a pocket and secured her hands and feet. Strong hands picked her up like a pillow and tossed her against the wall, knocking the wind out of her. He crouched in front of her, typed on his data pad, and jammed it in her face.

"This is a warrant for repossession for *The Lady Jane*. The owner, Jon Colby, has forfeited his right of ownership due to nonpayment. I guess we know where he's spending his money. My name is Rolf Kirby of the Teras Bounty and Repo Company. Any further obstruction from you will be considered a personal attack, and I will use extreme force to defend myself, as granted by interstellar law. Are we clear?"

Pina couldn't blink, much less respond to his question. But if daggers could fly from her eyes, he would have a nice plume of carbon steel sprouting from his face right now.

"I'll take your silence to mean you have no objections. The shock will wear off soon. Sit tight while I check on our host."

Rolf left the hold, but returned a couple minutes later, still holding her gun. He had a thoughtful look on his face, but didn't say anything. He crept toward the galley and returned with Colby slung over his shoulder. Rolf tossed the man in the airlock, and closed the door. He pressed a button on the control panel.

Colby was sucked out into space.

Pina stared at Rolf, swallowing down the panic that had started to rise. Rolf saluted the ejected man as he faded away into the darkness. He turned toward her, tapping his chin.

"Well, he wasn't in his cabin. What's really going on here. Trying to steal this ship?"

His pad beeped.

"Don't go anywhere, I'll be right back."

He realized his joke and cackled.

Pina twisted her body when he left. Muscle control had returned to her body when Rolf had returned with Colby. Her suit had absorbed most of the electrical discharge, but she had remained still, wanting to see what Rolf would do next. Killing the shipowner was not in Rolf's warrant. Pina had seen the orders, and Rolf had been instructed to return with the owner.

Pina rotated her arms until her hands were able to grasp the hidden knife. The sharp blade easily sliced through the plastic zip-ties. She freed her legs and stretched her tight muscles before sheathing the knife. Rolf wouldn't be easy to take down.

"I wondered how long it would take you free yourself," Rolf said from the doorway.

Pina started to turn when he told her to stop.

"Turn around slowly," he said.

She found herself looking down the barrel of her own gun. Pina smiled.

"Is something funny, Suzie?"

"Are you going to take your own advice, Rolf?"

"I might have to. You have blatantly interfered with this repossession. I feel my life is in danger."

"Oh, it is."

"Is that a threat, Suzie?"

Rolf flashed a smile, baring white teeth.

"I don't threaten, Rolf. Not in my nature."

"Your nature? Why are you here, Suzie?"

"I'm here to complete my job, Rolf."

"And what is that, exactly?"

"For one, bring back this ship."

"You're a repo? Huh. That explains why Colby was tied up. But it's weird that a bank would hire two different companies to repo the same ship."

"They didn't."

"They didn't what?"

"They didn't hire two different companies."

A confused look appeared on Rolf's face.

"What are you talking about?"

"My name's not really Suzie. I'm Pina Crespi, of the Teras Bounty and Repo Company. Just like you."

"Bullshit. Why would they send two of us after the same ship?"

"You've never heard of me?" Pina asked. She was slightly miffed.

"No. Should I have? I've been doing this for fifteen years. You *look* like you're fifteen."

"Whatever. My other task is to bring you in to answer questions relating to some missing funds. Now, if you don't mind, please put down the gun and allow me to secure you. Or, we can do it the hard way."

His face turned a nice shade of white. As she stepped toward Rolf, he squeezed the trigger of the gun. When nothing happened, she smiled.

"Last chance, Rolf."

He cocked his head and laughed. "Martino," he said.

Pina stopped. Rolf laughed at her again, and shook the gun in her direction.

"You'll have to do better than this," Rolf said.

Pina shrugged and took another step.

Rolf hurled the gun at Pina's head and she ducked. But the slight distraction was all he needed, and Rolf bounded to her side in two steps. He grabbed one of her arms, locking it behind her, and thrust his other arm under her chin. He squeezed, choking her. Pina's free arm scratched at his face. Rolf jerked her in the air, and Pina's vision darkened. She jammed her heel into the side of his knee. He grunted, but didn't release his grip. His arms slid down and locked her arms to her side to keep her from thrashing. Her fingers rested on the hilt of the knife, but couldn't grasp it.

"This isn't my first circus, little girl."

"Nor mine," she rasped.

She pressed the hilt of the knife.

Pina's suit shimmered. She slid out of Rolf's grip, and rolled several feet away, brandishing her knife. She owed Martino another drink. The suit's infrastructure allowed her to become frictionless. The cost of an entire mission fee, it had just proven its worth. Pina's chest heaved as she fought to regain control of her breathing. Blood oozed down Rolf's cheek where she had scratched him. He touched a finger to his face, and licked his finger.

"Impressive. But, you know I can't let you go. You'll have to die."

"We'll see," she said.

Rolf ran toward her.

She dove to her right, and her hand struck like a coiled snake. Rolf squealed in pain. Pina sprang upward, balanced on the balls of her feet, holding her knife toward Rolf. A sliver of red ran down the blade.

Rolf clutched his thigh where she had opened a six-inch gash. She had just missed his kneecap. Two inches lower, she would have severed tendons.

"You have a decision to make, Rolf. You can either give up now, or I'll slice you apart, piece-by-piece, until you beg me to end you. Your choice."

"You little bitch. You haven't beaten me yet," he said.

But judging from the way he limped and the amount of blood seeping down his leg, he wouldn't last much longer. She had to end this now. Pina sprinted across the hold toward Rolf, and, just before she reached him, dropped to the floor. She activated her suit again, and plowed into Rolf. He flew backward and struck the wall. His outstretched arm, trying to stop his momentum, snapped under the force. He howled.

Pina stood a couple meters away, now pointing her gun at him. All those self-defense classes her father forced her to take had been worth it. Of course, he couldn't have foreseen the way she now utilized those skills. A pang of regret inched forward, but was quickly flicked away. He didn't matter any more.

"Wait," Rolf rasped.

"For what?"

"I'll give you half of the credits I took if you let me go."

"Are you kidding me? You think I can be bribed?"

"It's 25 million credits."

"You stole 50 million credits from Teras," she said incredulously. Rolf nodded.

"You've got some confidence, dude, I'll give you that. But no, I don't want Teras coming after *me*. I'll just kill you and pick up my fee."

She pointed the gun at his head.

"Wait!"

"What now?" she asked.

"I'll give you all of it."

"All of it?"

"Everything that's left. I swear!"

She moved her head side to side as if contemplating the offer.

"Okay," she said.

"Okay?" Rolf asked.

"Yeah. What else do you want me to say?" she asked.

"You'll let me go?"

"I'll get you back on your ship. I don't care where you go after that."

He pulled out his data pad and handed it to her. Pina's eyes narrowed.

"You try that trick again, and I'll cut your eyes out first. Are we clear?"

Rolf nodded.

She took the data pad and scrolled through menus until she found his accounts. He gave her the password and pressed his thumb to the screen. Pina whistled.

"You weren't lying," she said.

She removed a data stick from her suit, and transferred most of the funds from the account. She took out another data stick, this one lined with red, and transferred the last 250,000 credits onto it. Pina was loyal to Teras, but she wasn't foolish enough to pass on taking some credits for a rainy day. She had to look after herself. No one else would. No one else she had cared about still lived.

"OK?" Rolf asked.

"Okay," Pina replied. "You're going to need help getting back to your ship."

Rolf raised his good arm, expecting Pina to help him up.

She shot him instead.

The energy beam knocked him unconscious. She holstered her gun, and grabbed the med kit from the wall. She applied the skin sealant to stop the bleeding on his leg, and then slapped on some med-patches to accelerate the healing. Pina dragged Rolf to the airlock and shut the door.

She headed toward the galley for something to eat. She was famished. Grabbing an energy drink and a prepackaged ham sandwich, she made her way back to the hold, admiring the purr of the ship's systems.

What a beautiful ship. While working for Teras paid well, she wouldn't make enough to ever afford this type of ship. Maybe if she had stayed in racing. But when her best friend and teammate Suzie had died in a freak training accident, she had needed a change in scenery. It still hurt to think about Suzie. But Pina had a job to finish, and it was getting late. By the time she returned to the hold, Rolf had awakened.

"What the hell?" he groaned.

"What?" Pina replied. "Do you think I was going to let you live?"

"You said if I gave you all the money, you would let me go."

"No, what I said is I would help you get back to your ship."

The wild look on his face disappeared, and his shoulders sagged.

"You're just like me," Rolf said.

"No, I'm not. I'm much smarter."

She pressed a button on the panel and the trapped air whooshed into space through the vent near the outer door. Rolf slammed against the outer wall and asphyxiated within seconds. Pina closed the vent and pulled on her helmet. Her HUD flicked on and flashed green. Her suit hadn't sustained any damaged during her fight with Rolf. On her way into the airlock, Pina grabbed a cable, hooked it onto Rolf's belt, and pulled him toward his ship. She tossed his data pad into space. Once onboard Rolf's ship, she positioned his body on the bridge, and opened the nearby med kit, scattering the supplies in the zero gravity. That was one of the reasons Teras liked her—she had a knack for making things look like accidents. Back on *The Lady Jane*, Pina set the autopilot for the return trip.

"Yo, boss," Pina said, when she opened the secure com-relay.

"Pina. Nice to hear from you. How is the job going?"

"On my way back. Job complete."

"Any problems?"

"I'm a little sore, but nothing that a day at the spa won't fix."

"Good to hear. Anything else?"

"Do I hear anticipation in your voice, boss?"

He laughed.

"Yes, I got access to the accounts before completing the job," Pina said.

"You did? Really?"

"Yeah, I was persuasive. Transferring now," Pina said. She inserted the data stick into the port and typed on the console.

"Confirmed receipt. Hold while I verify."

Pina sunk into the pilot's chair. She wondered how long it would take to save for one of these yachts. The autopilot beeped and she saw that it autocorrected the course to use a nearby planet's gravity to increase the ship's speed. That maneuver would shave seven hours off her return trip. Damn, what a ship.

"Pina? You've really outdone yourself this time. When we negotiated this contract, I didn't think you'd recover this much. A fifteen percent bonus on top of the remainder of your fee is going to make you a wealthy young lady. I'm worried that you might consider retiring."

The silence hung heavy in the air. While recovering almost fifty million credits was great, Teras didn't want to lose his best employee.

"Nah, I'm too young to retire. But I understand your concern. Tell you want. Give me ownership of *The Lady Jane*, you can keep the bonus."

"That ship is worth 20 million, Pina."

"You can keep the other half of my recovery fee, too."

The seconds crept by before Teras answered.

"You'll have to rename her."

"Thank you, boss!"

"Yeah, yeah, just don't tell anyone. I have a reputation to uphold. You gotta new name?"

"Yup. *The Suzie*."

"*The Suzie*? Seriously?"

"Uh huh."

Her console beeped. A message from the Teras Company had just been received. Pina opened the communication and scanned the ownership transfer documentation. A huge smile on her face, she accepted the terms of the transfer.

"What are you gonna do now, Pina?"

"I'm going on a vacation."

"Where to?"

"Not sure. But I'll be in touch."

She scrolled through the star maps, finally deciding on a planet known for warm, sandy beaches, cold drinks, and eye candy. It would take a week to arrive, but that was okay. She needed time to get to know her new ship.

LETTER FOR YOU

BY CARSON BUCKINGHAM

"Letter for you!"

"Oh, yeah? Great!" Cody jumped off the couch, his cartoon show forgotten.

"You know how I feel about this, Cody."

"But Mom ..."

"You know that your Aunt Marjorie and I don't get along. Yet she keeps sending you money and you keep accepting it. You're twelve years old now, Cody. I know you understand the concept of loyalty, and what you're doing is disloyal, knowing how I feel."

Cody hung his head.

Jeanette sighed. "How much did she send you this time?"

Her son tore open the envelope halfheartedly. His mother, once again, had beaten the childhood joy at receiving a letter into submission and had locked it in the attic. He knew things hadn't been easy for her after the divorce, but since it happened, it seemed like the whole world had become the enemy and you were either with Jeanette or against her. No compromise, no middle ground. He knew she worked long hours at the fertilizer plant in Houston in order to keep them going. He knew she was giving up her life to take the best care of him she could. There was no money to go anyplace or do anything fun. No extras, no

123

frills, just bare bones. The last movie he had been to was a year ago—the week before Dad handed Mom the divorce papers and moved out. Now they couldn't even afford Netflix.

So why did she have to take this away from him, too? It seemed like such a small thing.

Cody withdrew the twenty dollar bill and showed it to his mother. He didn't show her the other four still in the envelope.

"Can I keep it?"

"Yes, of course you can keep it. I just want this stopped. First it was a dollar or two, then five, then ten, and now this. I know that you've been short of pocket money since I had to cut your allowance down ..."

"Yeah, a dollar a week doesn't go too far," Cody said, and instantly regretted it.

Tears filled Jeanette's eyes. "I know, sweetie," she said softly. I wish I didn't have to do it. I stopped smoking and skipped lunch first. Cutting your allowance was the only other place I could save. We have to eat. We have to have a place to live. I have to have a car to get to and from work."

"But doesn't Dad give you money every week?"

"We still have a mortgage on this house, and what your father gives me barely covers the payment."

"Why don't we move someplace else that we can afford, then?"

"Because this is the house I grew up in. I was born here. Your father and I bought it from Aunt Marjorie after we got married. She wanted a bundle for it and we financed it through her, so she holds the mortgage."

"Is that why you don't like her?"

"No. It goes back much further than that. We never did get along—even as children. I was surprised when she agreed to sell us the old place. But I love it here, and I know you do, too."

"I s'pose."

"So what are you going to do with your twenty dollars?"

Cody held the money out. "You can have it, Mom. Maybe you can buy some lunches with it."

"Oh, Cody, you are a fine, fine son." She took the proffered bill. "We're all out of milk, bread, butter, and eggs, and I don't get paid for

124

two more days. I'll go to the store right now and pick them up so I can make some dinner tonight. Thank you, Cody. I love you."

"I love you, too, Mom. Drive carefully. Don't let the cash go to your head."

They both laughed, and then she was gone.

Besides, he still had the other eighty bucks.

Over a dinner of omelets, toast and a cupcake each, his mother said, "Sweetie, I know how much you look forward to the little extra money in the letters from Aunt Marjorie ..."

"But you want it stopped. I know."

"Yes, I do. We'll get through this rough patch, Cody. Please write back to her and let her know that I won't allow you to accept her money anymore. If she wants to write you letters, I can live with that. But no more money, pkay?"

"Okay, Mom. I'll let her know." Actually, he already had taken steps to have his mail redirected a week ago. He knew his mother was getting pissed about these letters, and this letter was the last one he expected to receive at his mother's house.

"Cody! Your father's here to pick you up for the weekend! Shake a leg," Jeanette called up the stairs.

"Coming!" Cody rounded the corner clattered down the stairs.

"You sound like an elephant. How can one little boy make so much noise?"

Cody smiled. "Practice. 'Bye, Mom. See ya Sunday night!"

She watched Cody dash down the slate walkway. *You'd think the bastard could at least come to the door for his own son.*

She turned away to face an empty house and an emptier weekend.

"Hey there, Slugger! How ya doin'?"

"Hey, Dad!" Cody swung his backpack into the rear seat of the BMW and leapt in after it.

"How about Tiffany?"

"Oh. Hey, Tiffany," he said with far less enthusiasm.

"Well hi there, Cody! I missed you all week!" she said.

Cody regarded her with what he hoped was an indifferent expression, then sat back in his seat and fastened his safety belt as the car backed out of the driveway. After the divorce, his dad had gone through a series of bimbos half his age. Let's see ... there was Madison, Brittany, Crystal, Bethany ... and those were just the ones Cody'd met. All with soap opera names. All without two brain cells to rub together. But they were all gorgeous. Guess if you're not a rock star, the second best chick magnet is "rich prosecutor." Plus, he'd moved three times in the last year—to bigger and more luxurious houses in newer, more exclusive neighborhoods each time.

Tiffany worried him, though.

She'd been hanging around for quite a while now—much longer than any of the others. Oh, and she fancied herself an artist on top of it. A double threat—no brains *or* talent. He could do better paintings by just shutting his eyes and throwing mud at a wall.

"Oh, hey, Cody ... there's a letter for you at my house." his father said.

"Great!"

"Oooooooh, does Cody have a girllllllllfriennnnnnnd?" Tiffany asked, in that nauseating way all adults ask children about such things. She put on a pout. "I thought *I* was your girlfriend."

"When Satan skates to work, maybe," he muttered. But she heard it, and so did his father.

Tiffany looked at his dad. "*Steeeeeevvvvvvve!*" she said, tears in her eyes.

Cody's father wrenched the steering wheel to the left and pulled off the road. The backs of his ears were bright red—never a good sign.

He turned in his seat. "I don't know where all this animosity comes from where Tiffany is concerned, but you'd better knock it off right now. I was going to let you know later, but now seems like a good time. Tiffany and I are getting married, an—"

"*What?* You're *marrying* her?"

"Yes." Tiffany wiggled her left hand at him that sported a diamond so large that it probably would have paid off the mortgage on his mother's house.

"And what is so wrong with Tiffany, may I ask?"

Rather than spend the next hour counting the ways, Cody opted for the time-saver. "She's not Mom."

"No, she's not," Steve sighed. "Your mother and I will not be getting back together, Cody. I've told you this time and time again. So you'd better get used to the idea and start being more respectful toward Tiffany. I insist on it. I won't have my wife treated poorly."

"It didn't stop you with Mom. And after she worked her butt off to put you through law school, too."

The slap across the face came at lightning speed. And it wasn't administered by his father.

Tiffany had hit him.

"Are you going to let her do that to me?" Cody shouted.

"Yes. Now sit down and shut up. Maya has dinner waiting at home," his father said.

"Who the hell is Maya?"

"The new cook, and don't cuss, Cody," Tiffany said with a triumphant sneer plastered across her perfect, surgically-balanced face.

Cody was dumbfounded. *I had to give Mom twenty dollars to buy food until she gets paid and he hires a cook? No doubt because this one can't boil water. Probably afraid she'd break a nail or something. Or would need a road map to the kitchen.*

"Got a butler, too?"

"That's enough, Cody."

He was quiet for the rest of the ride.

He didn't trust himself to speak.

He needed to think.

"Oh, here's your letter," his father said, handing it to him.

"Yeah, thanks."

"Is it from Aunt Marjorie?"

"Yeah."

"Well, her handwriting certainly has gone to hell."

"She's old, Dad."

"So why is she writing to you here?"

"I used to get them at home, but Mom doesn't like that Aunt Marjorie sends me money all the time. Thing is, Mom cut my allowance to a buck a week, and this is the only way I get pocket money. She told me to ask Aunt Marjorie to stop; but I figure if she sends it here, Mom won't know and everybody's happy."

"I had no idea that you and that nasty old relic were so close." His father gave him a tired smile. "But your mother always was tight with a buck. I'm surprised she didn't just curtail your allowance altogether. I'll give you some money, too, Slugger. And it's okay for Aunt Marjorie to send your letters here. I'll keep them for you. Just please, try to get along with Tiffany. She really is a nice person. Just give her a chance."

"Okay, Dad. I will."

After dinner, Cody excused himself to go meet some of the kids he'd gotten to know in the neighborhood. He was good at making friends wherever he went.

"Be home by the time the streetlights come on," Tiffany called.

"Okay." This time of year, that wouldn't be until around eight o'clock. He had plenty of time to schmooze.

"Heeeeeeey, it's the Codester!" a skinny kid with braces and glasses called.

"Oh, great! You're here! Finally!" said a girl about his age who was dressed all in black.

"Hey Jimmy. Hey Lorraine. Anything new?"

"Oh, yeah! Got a gig for yuh. Same 'Aunt Marjorie' deal as before?"

"Yep."

Jimmy handed him an envelope.

"Talk to me."

"Cody, Tiffany and I are going out tonight," his father said over Saturday morning breakfast.

"Maya's here, so I guess I don't need a sitter, right?"

"Maya doesn't live here. She goes home after she does the dinner washing up. She has a family of her own to look after."

"So who, then?"

"I found a flier under my windshield wiper during the week advertising baby-sitting services. I checked it out and I think we'll give her a try. Whaddya say?"

"Not like I have a choice. I don't know any of the sitters around here."

"It'll be fine—you'll see."

"I hope they work out better than all the other ones have."

His father's faced darkened from the memories. "Me, too. We certainly haven't had much luck with them, have we? Oh, and by the way, here's an allowance supplement. Don't tell your mother."

Cody turned the five dollar bill over in his hands. His old man could have easily given him four times that without batting an eye, but he smiled and said, "Gee, thanks Dad."

His father reached down and tousled his hair. "Anything for my boy," he said.

It was a good thing he had Aunt Marjorie to fall back on.

The sitter arrived at seven.

"Hello, I'm Stella Fyler—the baby-sitter," she said when Tiffany answered the door. She was an older, chubby woman, kind of grandmotherly. She spied Cody. "Oh, and is this my charge for the evening?" she asked.

Steve walked into the room. "Hello. Yes, this is my son, Cody. He's twelve. Say hello, Cody."

"Hi."

"Oh, we're going to get along just fine," Stella Fyler said. "You two go out and have a good time."

"My cell phone number is on the refrigerator dry erase board. Don't hesitate to call me if you need me. We should be home between one and two. He should be in bed no later than ten," Steve said.

"You do know that my rates double after midnight?"

"Yes. Not a problem." Tiffany said, stroking her new lynx coat.

"See you later, Slugger. Be good for the sitter, please."

"Yeah, okay. See you tomorrow."

Once they left, Stella regarded Cody with a look one might give to something that had just crawled out of a sewer pipe. "Let's get a few things straight, young man. It is still light out, so I expect that you will be outside with your friends until it gets dark. After that, you will come back and go straight to your room where you will read or, if you have one up there, watch television until bedtime. You will not bother me. I do not play board games or cards. I do not play videogames. I do not watch television with children and pretend to be interested in it. I do not converse with or read to children. I do not tuck children in. Are we clear?"

Cody had taken a step back during this tirade and regarded the woman with obvious shock. "Y-yes. I guess so ..."

"What?"

"I said, yes. We're clear."

"Wonderful. Now scat," she said, holding the door open while lighting a cigarette.

He left, but he didn't go far.

She watched him run off down the drive until he was lost to sight.

"God, I hate kids," she muttered. "Now, let's see what's what around here."

Cody, meanwhile, had come back to the house through the woods that surrounded it, and was watching Stella Fyler through the windows.

The first thing she did was make a beeline to the bar that his dad bought in Ireland, which he'd had flown over and reassembled in his living room. She ran her pudgy hand along its Connemara marble counter like a child trailing her hand in the water off the side of a rowboat. After a moment, she found what she was looking for and carefully took down the bottle of Glenmorangie Ealanta whisky, which his dad had once told him cost $170.00 and they only drank for *very* special occasions. He supposed they'd be toasting with it at the wedding.

That is, if there was any left.

The baby-sitter grabbed an eight-ounce tumbler in her meaty fist and filled it more than halfway with the expensive liquor ... which she proceeded to chug.

Cody had to chuckle. Dad would have an aneurysm if he saw anybody chugging *that* booze.

Next, she tottered to the fridge, pulled out some caviar and found some crackers in the pantry.

She polished that off in no time, while watching porn on TV.

Just as darkness began to descend and Cody realized he'd have to get his butt back inside pretty soon, Stella got up from the couch and walked to the back of the house.

Cody dashed around the house to see where she was going.

He finally found her rifling through the drawers in the master bedroom ... where she found jewelry, money, and a Rolex watch.

All of which she pocketed.

Cody ran back to the front door, and silently ducked into the house.

He tiptoed to the coffee table, took a look at her drink (she'd refilled the glass) and then went back and slammed the front door.

Sure enough, she came bustling out of the back of the house.

"Wha you doin' here?" she slurred.

"It's getting dark out. I came home."

"Yesh, well, gesh yoursel' somethin' t'eat 'n' geddouta my (burp) shight," she said, flopping down on the couch and taking a long swallow from her drink.

"No problem. I'll just heat up a couple of Hot Pockets and I'm history."

"S'right."

By the time the Hot Pockets were ready, Stella Fyler had passed out on the couch. Cody laid her down on her back

At about midnight, a frightened Cody put in a call to his dad's cell phone. "Dad, Dad, the baby-sitter isn't moving! I think there's something wrong. I don't even think she's breathing!"

"Oh, Jesus! All right son, I'm calling 911 now, so when the ambulance arrives, let the men in. We're coming home right now. Be brave, Cody."

By the time everything got sorted out, the final tally was this: Stella Fyler was dead, having aspirated her own vomit; the stolen goods were taken from the body and returned to Steve and Tiffany, and the body was removed.

Steve smelled the glass she'd been drinking from. "Oh, Christ, Tiff! She got the good stuff. He dashed to the bar only to discover an empty bottle. "Goddamn it!"

That was his dad for you. More worried about his pricey booze than having left his kid with a drunk. A dead drunk.

"I need a drink. And Tiff, could you get the caviar from the fridge?" Steve asked.

"Uh, you can forget about the caviar. She ate it."

"Oh, shit!" Then, finally remembering his son, he asked, "What did she make you for dinner?"

"Nothing. I made Hot Pockets. She was pretty drunk by then."

The next morning, there was a letter with Aunt Marjorie's return address on it lying in the middle of the porch. Steve found it when he went out to get the paper.

"Huh. Another letter for Cody from Aunt Marjorie. I must have dropped it when I brought in the mail yesterday." He didn't notice the lack of a stamp.

"Is he ... you know ... all right ... after last night? Should we take him to see somebody?" Tiffany asked while cutting into her Eggs Benedict.

"I'm keeping an eye on him. He hasn't asked to go home and doesn't seem outwardly upset anymore. I think I'll ask his mother if I can keep him here for a few more days, just to be sure," Steve said. "And thanks for your concern, love."

Tiffany put on a slightly pained smile. "I guess I'll call the Ramsleys and beg off dinner with them tonight, then."

"Oh, gosh, is that tonight?"

"Yes. But it's all right ..."

"No! They were going to evaluate your paintings. If they don't do it tonight, then you'll have to wait until they get back from Florence in October. They might change their minds between now and then."

"I agree, but what do you want to do about Cody? Do you think it's okay to go out?"

"I'll call his mother and see if she can take him back for tonight, and I'll ask her about having him all of next week. How does that sound?"

"Sounds fine."

"No answer."

"If we're not going to go, I need to give Beatrice Ramsley as much notice as possible. I don't want to make enemies of those two."

"What does she care? She's certainly not cooking the meal," Steve said.

"She cares, believe me. To her, a social blunder—even a minor one—is the end of the line with her. We can skip it, it's all right." Tiffany said, putting on the biggest puppy dog eyes she could.

"No, we'll go. Even if we have to get a sitter for a few hours."

"Is that really a good idea?"

"Let me talk to him and see." Steve kissed Tiffany on the nose, then went in search of his son.

He found him lying on his bed, reading a *book* of all things!

"Hey, Slugger. Another letter from Aunt Marjorie."

"Thanks, Dad." Cody stuffed the letter into his pocket without opening it.

"What are you reading?"

"Hardy Boys."

"How you doing?"

"I'm fine, why?"

"It's just that Tiff and I have to go out tonight, too. Plans made a long time ago. You up for another sitter for a few hours?"

"Sure, Dad."

"Thanks, son. The question is, who?"

"I heard from some of the kids that there's this high school girl who's really nice. She even has references, if you want them. Her name's Amy Hopper. After the kids heard about Mrs. Fyler, they gave me Amy's number, just in case." He pulled it out of his shirt pocket and held it out.

"Wonderful. I'll give her a call and get her references. If everything looks kosher, she'll be here with you tonight."

"Okay, Dad."

His father left the room and Cody went back to reading the book he had hidden behind the cover of the Hardy Boys novel. The Hardy Boys were pussies compared to what he was actually reading about. He pulled the lined pad out from behind his pillow and continued taking notes.

"He seems to be okay with a sitter. He even had a name and number with one that's pretty popular with the kids in the area. She'll be here at six."

"Perfect," Tiffany said. "But are you sure we're doing the right thing?" Tiffany asked, not really caring.

"Everything will be fine. He seems like his old self to me."

Like you would know, with all the attention you pay to me, Cody thought from his listening post at the top of the stairs. *Bet you don't even know what color my eyes are.*

"Cody! Letter for you!" Tiffany called.

"Oh, yeah? Great!"

"Is it from your Aunt Marjorie again?"

I knew it! She can't even read! "What can I say? She likes me, I guess."

"Do all her letters to you have money in them?"

"Yeah, mostly."

He father walked in and said, "Well, you enjoy it, Cody. 'Bout time somebody pried some cash out of that tight-fisted old bat."

Cody took his letter and ran back to the room his father had given him in his latest mansion. He closed and locked his door, pushed aside the antique Persian area rug, and levered up the loose floorboard beneath it. He opened the letter from Aunt Marjorie and dumped out the pile of tens and twenties, then grabbed his backpack and withdrew a thick envelope, opened it, and added the bills on the floor to the contents. He guessed the new total was nearly a thousand dollars, but didn't take the time to count it. Instead, he placed the envelope in the empty Lucite box he'd stowed beneath the floor the last time he was here, knowing that his mother would soon get on his case about Aunt Marjorie's gifts. With the box there (to keep his money from becoming a very expensive mouse nest), the space was now so small that it was difficult to remove the other important item that he'd already spent big bucks on that was already down there, and once again, reflected on how easy it was to get a homeless guy to buy something for you for the price of a fix. He finally managed to get it out and practiced a few times putting it back and taking it out until he could do it quickly and with only the merest whisper of noise. He replaced it, repositioned the floorboard, and then pushed the rug back into place.

Sooner or later, his mom would have found his cache and spoiled his surprise. Here, nobody would bother it.

He had big plans for that dough. He was going to buy his mother two weeks of vacation time.

"Cody! The baby-sitter's here! We're leaving now. Come on down!" his father called.

Cody took his time coming down the stairs. Glancing at Tiffany, he noticed that she was wearing a bracelet that would have put him through college. He could barely hide his disgust at the incredible waste of money on such an incredible waste of space.

His father noticed, though.

"Something on your mind?" he asked, with an edge on the question that would have shamed a Henkel knife.

"I was just thinking about Mom working at the fertilizer plant," Cody replied, staring pointedly at Tiffany's bracelet.

Tiffany laughed, and gazed lovingly at her gaudy jewelry. "Guess she's not in the right line of work."

"I guess not. But then again, there aren't any street corners near our house."

This time, his father slapped him so hard he bounced off the wall. "Get to your room and stay there."

Cody dashed from the room and pounded up the stairs, slamming the door to his room.

"What did he mean by that, Steve?" Tiffany asked.

Steve ignored her and said, "My cell number is on the refrigerator, Amy. I doubt you'll need it, because I don't expect him to be coming downstairs this evening."

"Have a nice time," Amy said.

"We'll be back by midnight, I think, but if we're going to be any later, we'll call."

"That's fine."

"God, I thought they'd *never* go!" Amy muttered. She opened up the freezer and after a little rummaging around, found the stash of microwave pizza, pulled one out, and popped it into the microwave. Then she walked into the living room and flopped down on the couch to wait.

Up in his room, Cody could smell the pizza cooking. His stomach growled. He hadn't had any supper before his father smacked him into the wall, and after twenty minutes or so, hunger finally won out over his previous resolution to remain in his room until he starved to death.

He walked down the hall to the stairway leading to the living room, then decided that he didn't want to chance those slippery wooden steps in his stocking feet. He returned to his room, donned his sneakers, then made his way downstairs.

"Aren't you supposed to be in your room?" Amy asked, through a mouthful of pizza.

"I haven't had dinner. I'll just heat up a pizza and go back up."

"There isn't any more."

"Are you kidding? There were four pizzas in the freezer!"

"Not anymore."

Cody ran around the corner into the kitchen to see four empty pizza boxes on the counter. The fat pig had eaten every single one!

"Well, I'll just take the last two pieces of chocolate cake then," he muttered.

Amy heard him. "No you won't."

In the sink was the empty cake plate.

Cody made himself a salami and cheese sandwich and poured a glass of milk. He also took a small glass bottle from the cupboard.

"All set?" Amy asked. "Good. Don't plan on coming down here again tonight, or I'll be letting your father know about it."

Cody returned to his room.

A couple of hours later, he opened his door, and slipped silently into the hall. He crept to the top of the stairs and saw that Amy was sound asleep, mouth open and snoring, on the couch in front of the television.

Perfect.

He pulled the stopper from the bottle he'd taken earlier, then , mission accomplished, he crept back to his room, stood in the doorway and screamed until he heard the sitter wake and rush to investigate.

He stepped inside his room and closed the door, still screaming.

She never made it to his room.

She slipped on the olive oil he'd spread over the top two steps and bounced back down the stairway.

When the silence continued unbroken, Cody left his room.

The baby-sitter was sprawled at the bottom of the stairs, her eyes staring at nothing. He slid down the banister, hopped off, and checked her pulse.

Nada.

He cleaned up the area at the top of the stairs and the bottoms of Amy's shoes thoroughly, replaced the bottle of imported olive oil in the cupboard, and took care of one more bit of business before he dialed 911. He didn't bother calling his father this time.

Steve and Tiffany pulled into the driveway behind a police and ambulance light show. They both jumped from the car, Steve pushing in ahead.

"What the hell is going on here?" he demanded.

"I'll have to ask you to stay back, sir," the patrolman said.

"Stay back, my ass! This is my house! What happened? Where's my son?"

"There's been an accident ..."

"*Where's. My. Son?*"

"Right here, Dad."

"Oh, Cody, thank God! Are you all right?"

"Yeah. But Amy's not."

Steve turned to the officer just as the gurney with the body bag on it was wheeled past. "Dead? She's *dead?*"

"I'm afraid so. Looks like she lost her footing on the stairs and fell. Broke her neck. Very unfortunate."

"Cody, why didn't you call me?" his father asked.

"I really didn't think you'd care," Cody replied.

"Oh, of course we care, Cody!" Tiffany piped up.

"Shut up, Tiffany! He's my son and I'll handle this!"

"How dare you speak to me like that! And after all I do to put up with your little brat!" Tiffany shouted. Then she hauled off and slapped Steve across the face.

And Steve slapped her back.

The officers stepped in and separated them.

Cody stood there watching, trembling, eyes wide. The cop put a protective arm around him. "That's quite the bruise you have on your cheek, young man," the officer said. "Where did that come from?"

Cody gave his father a stony look and said, "I fell out of bed last night."

He turned and went back into the house.

By the time all questions were answered, statements made, paperwork filled out, and the police departed, it was well after two in the morning. Steve and Tiffany, having made up, shuffled to the bar for a well-deserved nightcap and were surprised to find two Waterford

138

double shot glasses and a bottle of the second-best whisky (the best having been consumed by Stella Fyler) on a silver tray with a note that read, "Figured you'd be wanting this. I'm really, really sorry," and signed "Cody."

Steve smiled. "I guess he must have done this while we were filling out paperwork."

"Well, I don't mind telling you that a double shot is just what I need right now."

"Me, too." Steve poured, they clinked glasses and knocked back the shots. "Again?"

"Please."

They drank again.

"Does this taste funny to you?" Tiffany asked.

"After all that far-too-garlicy food at the Ramsleys, who knows how anything should taste?" Steve replied.

"Boy, that's for sure."

They both sat together on the couch. Cody moved from the shadows at the top of the stairs and returned to his room. He moved the rug, pulled up the floorboard, slipped on a pair of latex gloves and removed the item he'd been storing there ever since that homeless guy had bought it on his behalf.

A gun.

A gun that he'd registered online in his father's name.

He took it with him and sauntered back downstairs. He figured they'd both be pretty woozy by now from the handful of their prescription tranquilizers that he'd crushed up and mixed into to the whisky. He knew they'd pound it down ... too fast to really taste.

They were both semiconscious and regarded at him with glassy eyes.

"Hey, Dad and Tiff! Let's play a game, okay? This one's called 'Murder-Suicide.' I think we'll have Dad murder Tiff, and then off himself," Cody said, arranging his father's hand around the pistol. "I know you haven't changed your beneficiaries yet, 'cuz I found your latest will and insurance papers in your file upstairs."

"Why?" his father croaked, too sedated to move.

"Nobody fucks over my mother—not even you. She's working herself to death and you couldn't care less ... you and this worthless cunt!"

139

"How can you do this?"

"I wasn't sure I'd be able to, but no problem now. You should be proud of me, Dad. I'm probably history's first baby-sitter contract killer. Not only was it profitable, but it was great practice. Now let's get your finger on that trigger ..."

THE ROCK

BY JOSEPH BADAL

"Why in God's name would you bring that old lady down here? Look at her. Seventy years old. White hair, frumpy, face like a bloodhound. She's a grandmother. No record—not even a parking ticket." Lieutenant Kyle McIlroy blew out a loud breath. "Your typical cold-blooded killer, right?"

"Looks can be deceiving," Detective Sergeant Carl Baker said.

"You actually think she might know something about these murders? How's that possible? She's the perfect citizen."

"Could be the husband."

"Her husband's a vegetable. I mean, since their grandson was murdered, I hear he's been catatonic."

"I don't know, Lieutenant. I got a feeling."

"Hell, she just lost a grandson, Baker. You go easy on this one."

"Lieutenant, she could be the key to my investigation," Baker said. He held his gaze steady on the woman behind the one-way glass. "Three men killed in a two-month period. Cruz, Thomas, and Washington. Throats slit."

McIlroy huffed. "All three of those guys were convicted child molesters. Good riddance."

141

Baker turned his head toward McIlroy. "You can't possibly believe that. We can't have citizens take the law into their own hands."

"Yeah, yeah. I know. But what the hell do the Galantes have to do with any of the murders?"

"You said it yourself, Lou. They lost a grandson to one of the molesters. That's awfully strong motive."

"So they hired someone to kill Cruz? Maybe the others too?"

"Or killed them themselves."

McIlroy wagged a finger at Baker. "You've got to be kidding me."

"I tell you, Lou, I've got a feeling about this."

"You already said that. Don't you turn this into a witch-hunt. Keep an open mind."

"Sure, Lou. I always do."

"Uh-huh, just like with that guy you hauled down here last year. Turned out he just happened to resemble the real killer. Our attorney estimates that wrongful arrest will cost the city at least a hundred Gs."

Now Baker twisted fully toward McIlroy. "Come on, Lou. That guy was dirty and you know it."

"Yeah, Baker. He was dirty, but not for the crime you arrested him on. And where does it say cops can beat a confession out of a suspect? Even a guilty suspect."

"There was no evidence I ever touched the guy."

McIlroy now held Baker's gaze and leaned toward him. "I know you beat the guy," he rasped. "I just couldn't prove it."

Baker felt perspiration bead on his forehead. He turned back to the one-way glass. "Unless you've got something else, Lou, I'd better go talk to the lady."

"You be careful, Baker. You're already two strikes down."

Baker entered the room and flipped the camera switch between the door and the one-way glass.

The interrogation room was about eight feet square, with a metal table bolted to the concrete floor in the corner farthest from the door. A plastic chair was placed on each of the two open sides of the table. Spotlights hung in all four corners near the ten-foot-high ceiling. A tiny camera was fixed below the spotlight diagonally across from the table.

"Mrs. Galante, thanks for coming down here."

Susan Galante shot Baker a sour look. "Like I had a choice."

Baker shrugged. "Of course you had a choice. I appreciate your willingness to cooperate with the police." He smiled and paused a second. Then he said, "This interview will be recorded." He pointed up and to his left to indicate the camera. "I'll read you your rights and then we can start."

"My rights? Why? Am I a suspect in some crime?"

"No, no. Of course not. It's just a precaution."

Mrs. Galante snorted and waved her arms as though to indicate her agreement.

Baker read Mrs. Galante her rights, and then said his and her names and the time and date for the recording.

"How long will this take?" Mrs. Galante asked. "I don't want to leave Johnny alone for too long."

"Why's that, Mrs. Galante?"

She stared at Baker as though he was plain stupid.

"Come on, Mrs. Galante, I asked a reasonable question. Why can't your husband be left alone?"

The old woman seemed to sag a bit, as though the weight of the world was on her shoulders. "I told you when you called that Johnny is sick. The doctors say he is clinically depressed. He hardly eats; he can't sleep. He just stares out the window. I can't hardly communicate with him."

"And this happened right after your grandson was kidnapped?"

Mrs. Galante skewered Baker with a hateful look that surprised the cop. Just as Lieutenant McIlroy had described her, Baker thought the woman looked like the prototypical loving grandmother. He didn't think she had it in her to express so much vitriol in a look. But then he felt a surge of adrenaline. Maybe a person, even an old lady like Susan Galante, who had that much hate in her, could be involved with murder. He suppressed a smile. "You know—"

"Eric wasn't just kidnapped, Sergeant Baker," Mrs. Galante slowly said, venom in her voice. "He was abused, tortured, and killed."

For an instant, Baker thought steam might erupt from the woman's mouth. "I understand—"

"You don't understand a thing. If you did, you wouldn't waste your time questioning me. You'd be out on the street arresting perverts and murderers who prey on innocent children."

"We're trying to do just that, Mrs. Galante. But we can't have vigilantes break the law."

"What are you talking about?"

"Ricardo Cruz. We found his body three days ago in an abandoned shack out on the edge of town. He'd been dead for two months. Someone slit his throat and left him to bleed out." Baker watched for some reaction from the woman, but saw nothing.

"Who's Ricardo Cruz?"

Still no reaction. "We compared his DNA against DNA found on your ... grandson's body. It matched. Cruz was a sexual predator. We've already tied him to crimes from California to Pennsylvania."

For the first time, the woman smiled. Her face turned absolutely gleeful. She instantaneously looked ten years younger. "Good," she said after a long beat.

"That's murder, Mrs. Galante."

"That's God's justice, Sergeant."

"There's no mention of *God's justice* in the criminal laws of this state."

"Maybe there should be."

"There are others," Baker said.

"Others?"

"Two other men were murdered in the last sixty days. Their throats were slit just as Cruz's was."

"Were they criminals like Cruz?"

Baker just stared at Mrs. Galante for a long moment. "Yes," he finally said. "They were convicted child molesters, too."

She smiled again, her eyes closed. Her hands together as though in prayer. "God's justice," she repeated.

Baker sat back and slowed his breathing. He needed to take a different tack with this woman.

"Why don't you tell me about your husband? What sort of man is he?"

Mrs. Galante tilted her head to the side and frowned. "What do you care about what sort of man my husband is?"

Baker shrugged again. "Just interested."

She went quiet and looked up at the ceiling for a moment. "I'm not saying another word until you tell me why you brought me down here. What do the deaths of three monsters have to do with me?"

Baker tried to stare the old woman down but gave up after fifteen seconds. He needed to shock her. Maybe that would get her to crack.

"We found something under Ricardo Cruz's body."

She tilted her head and widened her eyes.

"What we found could tie directly to your husband."

The woman straightened her spine and glared. "And what might that be?"

"A challenge coin. A military challenge coin."

"What in the world is a challenge coin?"

Baker reached into a suit jacket pocket and pulled out a silver dollar-sized coin in a small, sealed plastic evidence bag. Its rim was brass-colored with black capital letters that read Military Assistance Command Vietnam. In the center of the coin was a red and yellow shield with a sword. He flipped over the bag and showed her the obverse side, with the words Duty, Honor, Country, and Proudly Served around the edge. In the center were a smaller version of the shield from the front side and a map of Vietnam. "Military types often carry them," he said. "When they go into a bar, one guy might slap down his military unit coin, challenging others to show their coins. If one guy doesn't have his, then he has to pay for drinks."

Mrs. Galante laughed. "You think my Johnny dropped some stupid coin next to Cruz after he murdered him? After he slit his throat? Then he somehow found his way home. My Johnny, who can't walk to the bathroom without help?" She sneered at Baker. "How old was this man, Cruz?"

"Thirty-two."

She laughed again. "Johnny Galante slit the throat of a guy less than half his age?"

"I checked. Your husband was in Special Forces assigned to MAC-V in Vietnam in 1971–72. As best as I could determine—because most of his military records had been redacted—he was involved with some sort of Black Ops over there." Baker paused and then added, "You know there was a group over there called Studies and Observations Group, made up of Army Special Forces personnel. SOG worked closely with CIA and South Vietnamese special operations forces. They did all sorts of things in Vietnam, from night raids on North Vietnamese radar installations to more mundane activities like funding and logistics." He stopped, took a breath. "You know what else they did, Mrs. Galante?"

She shook her head as though she couldn't believe what she had just heard.

"Assassinations. SOG personnel slipped into North Vietnam and slit the throats of North Vietnamese officials. According to one study, SOG achieved a 100–1 kill ratio."

"So, because my Johnny was in Special Forces, and because he served in Vietnam, and because some of his records are redacted, you've concluded he was an assassin with this group you call SOG. And from that you've decided he must be a killer? Because of what he *may have done* over forty years ago?"

"Maybe he was able to use skills he learned while in the Army to murder Cruz. Maybe the others, too."

"I have no idea about any of that. Johnny never told me a thing about what he did in Vietnam. But I'll tell you this much, my Johnny couldn't hurt a soul, let alone kill someone." She hesitated a beat and then asked, "How many men in Wynnfield served in Vietnam? How many were assigned to MAC-V? Could be a whole bunch of them live here."

"I have no idea. But I'm checking on that."

"And maybe the coin belonged to Cruz. Coulda got it from a friend. Maybe his father served in Vietnam."

Baker just stared.

Mrs. Galante slowly shook her head. Then she chuckled and said, "You workin' on the Kennedy assassination, Sergeant? How about Benghazi? Any other conspiracies?"

Baker felt his face turn hot. His blood pressure was on the rise. He was losing control of this interview. He forced a smile and spread his arms. "Come on, Mrs. Galante, give me a break. Tell me about your husband. Maybe you can help me eliminate him as a suspect."

She seemed to think about that for a minute. "You asked about Johnny. I'd be happy to tell you about my Johnny." She paused. "Maybe you could get me some water. This may take a little time."

Baker walked from the room, suddenly optimistic. He grabbed a bottle of water from a refrigerator, hustled back to the room, and handed her the bottle. He watched her struggle to twist off the bottle cap.

"I don't know why they make things so hard to open," she said. "Cans, bottles, especially those blister-pack things."

Baker took the bottle from her, removed the cap, and passed it back. She nodded her thanks, took a drink, and placed the bottle on the table.

"So, you want to know about John Galante?"

Susan Galante lowered her head and rubbed both hands over her face, as though to organize her thoughts. Then she lowered her hands and looked back at Baker. "John Galante was born in Philadelphia in 1944. His parents were Italian immigrants who raised their kids to tell the truth, love their country, work hard, and get an education. They had six children and every one of them earned a college degree. The three boys served in the military after college, and all of them volunteered to go to Vietnam. One of Johnny's sisters is a doctor, another a teacher, and the third is a nurse who also served in Vietnam."

"That's really more detail than I—"

"I'll tell my story the way it needs to be told. If you don't like the way I tell it, I can stop and leave."

Baker raised his hands in surrender.

"Johnny and I grew up in the same neighborhood in South Philadelphia. We were two years apart in high school. Our parents were friends. After Johnny and I dated for a while, his mother pulled me aside and told me something I've never forgotten. She said in her heavy Italian accent, 'I can see you love my boy. And I know how he feels about you. Johnny's my rock, and he'll be your rock, too. You'll always be able to count on him to do the right thing. But even rocks can be broken. He's strong but he's vulnerable. Every heartbreak can chip away pieces until there's nothing left. Don't ever break my Johnny's heart.'"

She looked at Baker, as though to make certain he was paying attention. After a long sigh, she said, "I saw the first piece of rock fall off Johnny when his older brother, Frankie, was killed in Vietnam. It was a huge loss for Johnny, but he was such a strong person, he could afford to lose a bit of himself.

"We married after college, after he returned from Vietnam, and eventually had two children. The kids were about ten when Johnny's parents both died, when their car was hit by a drunk driver in a pickup truck. That incident knocked more chunks off the rock that was Johnny. Even more chips fell off when the driver that killed his mother and father got off on probation. Didn't serve a single day in prison. But my Johnny got through that awful time. Sure, I could see something in his eyes that was different, but he's always been a strong man."

She drank some more water. "We've had a good life. Our children have been successful and we haven't had the major illnesses some families have suffered through. Really, the only major crisis we had was in 2008 when the economy went south and we lost our business in the crash. But Johnny was a rock through all of that, too. I could tell he lost a bit of himself then, because he felt the leadership of our country failed the people. You see, he was raised to believe in the greatness of America and he saw the crash as a failure of leadership. But, as always, even if some of his hard core sloughed off, there was still plenty of rock left."

Tears suddenly slid from Mrs. Galante's eyes. She took a tissue from her purse and dabbed her eyes.

"You want to take a break, ma'am?" Baker asked.

She stiffened and said, "I want to get this over with so I can go home." She patted her eyes again, put away the tissue. "We got through that. Johnny got a job. We paid off our debts. Now we've been able to put a little into savings. We thought life would be good again. Then ..."

"Your grandson?" Baker said.

"Yeah, our grandson, Eric, was murdered. And you guys couldn't find the maniac who did it."

"We had some leads, Mrs. Galante. We learned Ricardo Cruz was in town. We just didn't have enough evidence to bring him in."

"Evidence, procedure, laws. They're all there to protect the criminals. What or who protects the innocent?"

Baker hunched his shoulders. He didn't want to go down that road. "You were saying ..."

"When Eric was killed and no one was arrested, my rock, my Johnny, disintegrated. There was nothing left. Don't you see? John

148

Galante believed in goodness, kindness, hard work, love of country. He believed if you worked hard and always did right by others, everything would work out. He was raised to believe that. But his parents were wrong in one respect. They did him and his brothers and sisters a disservice. They never prepared them to be able to confront real evil. Johnny wasn't prepared for the evil that men like Ricardo Cruz represented. When Eric was killed, the evil of it broke him apart. It shattered my rock."

She swept a hand over her head to push back long white hairs that had fallen over her forehead. She sat there, slightly hunched, seemingly worn out.

"One more question, Mrs. Galante. Did your husband ever have one of these challenge coins?" He pointed at the coin on the table.

"I never once saw such a coin," she said, with strength in her voice and fire in her eyes.

Baker felt deflated. He'd wasted his time. And he'd taken a chance when he showed the woman the coin. He'd stupidly disclosed evidence in the hope she might tell him something, might crack.

"Okay, Mrs. Galante," he said. "You can go now."

She stood and wagged a finger at Baker. "Do your job, Sergeant. Haven't we been through enough?"

Baker stared at her as she exited the room. He felt depressed when he saw Lieutenant McIlroy escort the woman toward the street. McIlroy had probably watched the whole interview through the glass of the interrogation room. He'd seen him reveal evidence. And he'd seen him fail to get a damned thing out of Mrs. Galante.

Susan Galante drove home. As soon as she closed the front door behind her, she walked to the front window, and stared out at the street and the car parked in front of the neighbor's. Maybe one of Baker's men. Couldn't be certain. She closed the curtains, draining the room of all light. Then she crossed to where John Galante sat in a recliner, staring straight ahead.

"How ya feeling today, Johnny?"

He grunted.

"That Detective Baker thinks you might have killed Cruz. Two other guys, as well."

Susan was just able to see a small smile crack Johnny's rigid features.

"I heard a little boy was molested yesterday."

John just grunted again.

"The police are looking for a man named Milo Davis. He has a record of child molestations. Been in and out of prison a couple times. The bastards keep releasing him on good behavior. Can you believe that?"

John slowly shook his head.

"Your VFW buddy, Lieutenant McIlroy, told me when I left the station where he thinks Milo Davis might be. He stays with a friend in a two-room apartment in a basement on the west side of town." She paused and took in and let out a huge breath. "Probably planning his next assault."

Johnny cleared his throat. It sounded more like a growl.

"But you've got to be more careful this time," Susan said. "You dropped that damn Vietnam challenge coin when you did Cruz."

"Sorry about that, babe," Johnny said. "It won't happen again."

THE HANDMAIDEN'S TOUCH

BY DOUG BLAKESLEE

Nidaria scratched her neck, trying to quell a persistent itch now that her gill flaps were sealed. They'd dried out by the time the procession reached the outer edge of the goblin market. Her lungs, struggling to acclimate once again, labored to bring in air. The thin, orange tentacles that made up her "hair" hung limply down her back, swishing against her pale blue skin. She stumbled and found that her underwater grace did not follow her to land.

She hated the quiet pall that hung over the goblin market. Buildings built on broken dreams and shattered hopes along with brick, wood, and mortar loomed in desperate menace. Today they were empty and soulless, devoid of the purpose and meaning that drove commerce without pause.

Thousands of merchants should be hawking goods and wares at bargain prices. A memory that would never be missed, perhaps a strand or two of hair, or a future service. Voices—once raised to attract the unwary, the naive, the desperate, to tents of bright colors and waving pennants—were stilled and hidden. None dared to practice their deceptions, to lay honesty by the wayside in the name of business, trade, and profit.

Today, she walked amongst the stalls and tents in silence. Guards in armor of silver and gold lined the roads, stationed to ensure that none disrupted the peace, allowing the Fae lords and ladies to gather undisturbed for their ceremony. Today's visit was special for many reasons.

"Nidaria! Come along, there's no time to tarry or wait for you to pick yourself up," Brolga said. A green-scaled hand pointed to the marble tower. "I do not wish to be the last to arrive."

"Yes, mistress." She scampered to catch up, bowing her head at the gaze of disdain. Her footsteps fell heavily on the cobblestone surface, unsure and awkward. Snickers from the retinue that died under the same eyes. Brolga Dister, The Lady of the Waves. Mistress of the Deep Keenings. One of the six Fae Lords and Ladies that held sway over this part of Arcadia. Her mistress and liege. She pulled at the gown of seashells and coral, adjusting to relieve the chafe on her scaled body. Undine handmaidens dressed to complement their mistress, not for personal comfort.

"Have you been practicing your skills, lovely Nidaria? It is my duty to provide gifts to the others. It would be a shame if something were to happen to them." That comment drew looks of venom from the other Undines in the retinue.

"The gifts are prepared as per your instructions." She nodded toward the chest carried on the back of a giant salamander. This was the first time in her service to be assigned this honor, one that came with a heavy price. "You will be pleased at the mixture of glass and shells, mistress."

"After your last misstep, this is your last chance." The other handmaidens tittered and smiled.

Nidaria nodded and swallowed heavily. "I will not make the same mistake again, mistress. You will not be disappointed."

"If you do not please me, I will give you over to The Arkholt's Seneschal. He was quite keen to inquire if you would be joining us this time."

Nidaria shivered, remembering the thin creature of granite skin and onyx teeth, one of the twisted elves that served the Lord of the Screaming Touch. He was a scheming monster that reveled in violence and other, darker practices. "Please do not give me over to him, mistress."

"It's your punishment, should you displease me. You won't displease me, will you?"

"No, mistress." Her mistress knew her darkest secrets and would craft the most fitting punishments. She'd seen to the packing of the cargo and its placement on the mount. Every precaution was taken to ensure nothing went wrong. She spent hours fretting over the details, knowing that it would cost her much were they not to the standards of her mistress. All would go according to her plan.

Six doors were carved into the base of the tower—an entrance for each, marked with their personal sigils, otherwise unadorned. A meeting of equals, or so they tell each other. Fiction that each paid lip service to with smiles, courtesy, and knives in the dark. The tower rose over the market, a reminder of who held the real power, but contained a single room. No stairs to present an inconvenient climb or embarrassing stumble. A round table of ash dominated the center, six chairs spaced evenly around it, and room enough for a small retinue. Nothing fancy, pretentious, or given to airs.

Nidaria surveyed the other rulers. The Arkholt dressed in green leather, stained red and yellow. His face was hidden behind a mask of bone and teeth. In the back lurked his Seneschal, bare-chested and scarred. Yellusia Adcraft, the newly coronated Queen of the Winter Night, towered over the rest with her blue skin, four arms, and hooves. The Vulture Lord, Cathare, was decked out in a robe of feathers, a brilliant array of colors. A murder of crows hopped about behind him, silent and observant. Grandfather Tick's representative stood next to his empty chair. The brass and silver automaton's head moved side to side in a measured pace, unconcerned at the appraising looks from the others. Arriving last, The Flowering Princess of Dreams wore a gown of gossamer, lily petals, and thorns. Gnomes milled around, folding her train of woven reeds.

"Why does the Lord of Order and Brass fail to show once again?" Brolga said, her voice a gurgle of contempt.

"My lord sends his apologies. His other affairs demand his full attention. His wakening is upon us and his wroth knows few boundaries."

The Flowering Princess of Dreams smiled and waved a rose-colored hand. "A true lord would not let his realm fall to neglect and disrepair."

"Irrelevant," said the automaton. "He is capable enough to defend his own from assassins and thieves."

"He sent a representative. That is not against the accord," Cathare cawed.

"Can he leave his realm anymore? Perhaps he's too weak, despite his protests," The Arkholt's Seneschal said, his voice a rasping whisper. His master nodded.

"It is the letter of the agreement," the automaton droned. "A more pressing matter is The Arkholt's actions. He seeks to usurp my master's domain. I have proof of this perfidy. He assembles an army to invade and take advantage of my master's divided attention."

"Insolent thing! My master's ambition is one of preservation and security."

"Lies. Misdirection. Why do you gather hobgoblins and the minor nobles to your court? The wild and untamed ones. Those that hunger for blood, violence, and flesh."

The two representatives faced each other; accusations, denials, and rhetoric flung between them, as the other Fae listened and plotted.

Nidaria hovered at the edge of the circle, keeping her eyes down, and hands folded. Half-truths danced in her ears. Words masked in glamour and lined with deceit. She touched her mistress's hand.

"What proof can the Lord of Brass present?" Brolga said.

The panel in the automaton's chest slid open to reveal a tattered scrap of green leather. A dagger-like sigil was embossed in black and red on it. "This was retrieved off a trespassing hobgoblin."

"Planted evidence. A flimsy excuse to divert attention away from Grandfather Tick's weakness." The Seneschal pointed a knifelike finger at the automaton. "We shall not allow this accusation to go unanswered."

"Nor shall it," Brolga said. "As the designated host, I call for a vote to censure The Arkholt based upon the proof proved. My handmaiden will collect your tokens."

Nidaria moved between the Fae rulers at her mistress's command. She shied away from the Seneschal's leer, flinching as his hand brushed hers as she took the token. They were disks of silver with one side blank and the other marked. A single line to signal neutrality, a thorn for a vote to condemn, and a twisted vine to show support. It allowed an anonymous vote and none would use it to gain an advantage on their fellow nobles.

Vines crushed the automaton's head and wrenched off its limbs with a dazzling swiftness. Oil leaked from the broken form as the remains were cast aside. The Flowering Princess of Dreams smiled with a mouth of thorn-like teeth as her creations retreated into the floor.

The Seneschal glowered at the wreckage. "My master wishes to convey his appreciation for the swift action on his behalf."

"Baseless accusations are not to be tolerated," Brolga said. "Nidaria, retrieve the gifts you've prepared for my peers. I shall send Grandfather Tick's offering another time."

"Yes, mistress." She retreated to the crate and traced a hand along the edge. The wax seal melted away and she pushed the lid off. The vote sided with The Arkholt, as did the subsequent one against his accuser. Her mistress's designation of punishment happened without a word of debate. Fae alliances dissolved on a whim and the action today made a clear shift in power. There might soon only be five Fae of power and a realm carved up between them. Nidaria reached in to remove the first gift.

Spun glass figurines covered in thousands of tiny pearlescent shells. Hundreds of hours of work had gone into each unique piece of work. She turned to present the first one, the fabric of her sleeve catching on the lock hasp and pulling on the crate. It teetered for a second, then slid off the salamander's back. The lid caught her arm, sending the statuette to the stone floor to join the others. Shiny fragments of glass and shell glittered on the floor. Her heart sank.

"Mistress, I'm sorry. I didn't mean to." Tears streamed down her face as she cowered, knowing she'd lost her last chance and what fate awaited her. The other Undines covered their mouths in shock and surprise, to hide the smiles at their turn of good fortune.

"Fool of a girl!" A hand slapped her aside with rough coral knuckles. Brolga leaned over the mess, anger spreading across her face in an instant. "Useless girl! You've ruined our gifts!"

She rubbed the bruised area on her arm and sobbed, knowing her punishment. "I'm sorry, mistress. I can replace them. Please, give me another chance."

Snickers and shocked gasps rose from the retinue at her temerity.

"You've embarrassed me for the last time! I gave you a chance to redeem yourself and this is how you repay me? I'm disgraced in front of my peers."

"I'm sure that it's a mere accident," Akholt's Seneschal said. "My master takes no insult from such things. They happen to even the best of us."

"He is gracious, but she must be punished." Brolga pulled Nidaria off the floor, her breath heavy with the smell of salt. "I told you what would happen, did I not?"

"Yes, mistress." Her voice came out weak and distant. She found herself cast to the floor, slamming into the hard stone surface.

"She is yours, Lord Arkholt. Do with her as you see fit."

"My master is pleased and conveys that no further gift is needed." The Seneschal smiled at her. "I look forward to seeing how well you scream."

His malice and anticipation, a lust for violence and pain, hammered on Nidaria's mind. The stink of decay and blood overwhelmed her as he bent close and pulled her up with steel, dagger-like fingers.

He tapped on the dress of shell and coral. "Unsuitable clothing, but we shall not shame you further in this company."

Her former mistress flitted away to lecture her retinue over the disaster. One cast a glance of pity in her direction, but the other two stared with satisfaction and delight. The lesson of her downfall lost to them as they plotted to usurp the now-vacant position. Nidaria cast her head down, letting her limp hair dangle to cover the look of fear and dismay. She cringed as his touch, wanting to pull away, but daring not to.

Nidaria let out an involuntary whimper as she passed from the goblin market into the realm of her new lord. No sun lit the sky, just the gloom of dusk and a half-formed moon to illuminate the landscape. No breeze to disturb the stillness or provide relief from the oppressive air. A path of paving stones ran through the plain of stunted weeds and bushes, the surfaces worn smooth by the passage of feet and the cold wind. Crevices ripped jagged tears, plunging into unfathomable darkness. Standing stones rose from the ground; black granite monoliths and plinths that stabbed toward the low-hanging clouds. Rusted chains dangled off them. Many empty, flecked with blood. Others held leather-wrapped mummies dangling from their feet, fluids dripping off to pool at the base.

"Come along. My master wishes to return home with all speed," the Seneschal said. He pulled at the leash wrapped around her neck. A train of robed cultists followed them, treading along the path without sound, heads bowed, and mouthing a wordless prayer. In the gloom, a spire of silver and black thrust into the sky to disappear into the cloud cover.

Her dress hung in tatters, flecks of material fluttering away as she walked. Each step fractured her desiccated hair, shards of orange melting as they touched the surface of the ground. The leather collar bit into her neck—not enough to cut off her air, but making each breath a struggle. She tugged at edges, seeking to loosen it, to give her a small bit of relief.

He slashed at her hand with a finger, cutting deeply across the back. "It is forbidden to touch the collar. Suffer well and you will be rewarded. After we pass over the Bridge of Fossa, the way shall not be as easy."

"It hurts," she whined, stumbling as they reached a wooden bridge. Below, a river of reddish water raced, sweeping past boulders and over half-submerged bodies.

"Get up!" He yanked on the leash.

She choked and vomited, spewing forth a glamour-laced bile of blue and green, stinking of fish and salt. It splashed on the surface, oozing over the edge in a thin stream.

Drops fell on his boots, staining them with dark spots. "You dare soil my presence! Now I see why your mistress was so eager to rid herself of you. Weak and pathetic. Unable to withstand even the smallest privation. I should throw you over the edge."

A lash tore across her back, flaying the dress. She held back another wave of nausea and rivulets of blue blood snaked down her back. "No. I can serve you," she gasped.

"Pitiful creature, would you act as my plaything? You'd not survive more than an hour before your heart gave out. To think that I coveted such a weak thing."

Her feet left the ground as his fingers wrapped around her throat. He tilted her head to meet his gaze. Eyes of blue stared from behind the leather mask. Hard. Uncaring. Disdainful. "Please ..."

"You're too pretty to meet with an accident." The Seneschal threw her to the bridge's surface. "My master wishes you to survive for now. He feels you might be useful."

Nidaria choked and warm tears flowed down her cheeks. The collar loosened a fraction. Just enough to provide a respite. "Thank you, master."

"Do not thank me. I merely obey. You will find that he's done you no favor."

Walls of red-washed stone encircled the keep. Hobgoblins patrolled the ramparts—pig-like snouts sniffing and grunting, testing the air for danger—a low breed of hedge creatures well equipped for violence and little else. Larger creatures, backs humped like boars with wiry hair, shouted commands as the procession approached. Bricks peeled back to allow passage, and then returned to form a seamless barrier. Nidaria dropped to her knees, unable to stave off the exhaustion of the march. Sweat streaked her soot-covered hands and arms. She could only imagine the rest of her mirrored the same condition.

"General Nin, report!" the Seneschal said. None dared to crowd him, the hustle and bustle of the fort flowing around him like a river.

"We discovered three spies. Two await interrogation," Nin said, as he pushed his way through the crowd. He towered over his subordinates and the Seneschal—nine feet of wiry-furred, porcine muscle. Six tusks, two upper and four lower, jutted from his jaw.

"Two?"

"One perished trying to escape. An unavoidable accident. At least one of Grandfather Tick's minions provided some sport."

"No matter. Display the body until it rusts to nothing as a warning. Find out what the other two know, then dispose of them."

"As you wish." The general spared a glance at her. "A new prize for our master?"

"She's mine, though a more worthless handmaiden could not be found."

"Her face and body are fair enough. The troops could use a new camp follower."

The Seneschal stared at her and smiled thinly. "No, she would not provide them much pleasure. I have plans for her. Until then, she will serve in other ways."

Nidaria lowered her eyes. The soldiers would not have been gentle with her. Only the strong would survive more than a few nights and she had no such strength to resist. Whatever else he might do, she would live to see the end.

"Already she quakes with fear. Fetch the jailor and put her to work serving meals to the soldiers."

The walls of the underground stockade dripped with moisture wherever the moss failed to cover. Humid air stifled and strangled as she was led down flights of steps. Spiked bars of black stone sealed off the prison cells, the gaps between them almost too small for even her arm to pass through. Shapes huddled in the dark recesses, none stirring at her passage. Weak flames sparked and popped from sconces, spattering drops of oil on her as she passed.

"Here's your new home." The jailor, a whip-thin pig-man, shoved her into a cell and pressed a tarnished metal stud on the wall, sealing her in. "Meals are at dawn. You'll be expected to serve the others before eating. Too slow and no food for you."

She staggered to her feet as the jailor walked away, laughing to himself. A pile of rags in one corner and a foul-smelling bucket in the other were the furnishings of her new home. Each step brought a fresh reminder of her ruined feet as Nidaria rested against the bars. She leeched their cool touch, gathering and focusing minute bits of glamour. A small magic. One that would go unnoticed amid the squalor and filth. She gave it life and let it go. With a smile, she stumbled to the rags and fell, drifting off to sleep. Dreaming of the sea, the endless call of the depths, and the stinging lash.

Nidaria placed the bowls of soup in front of the officers, hurrying between the kitchen and the tables. Whitish vegetables, green starchy roots, and meat from no known animal floated to the top. They grunted and slobbered, pushing their snouts into the slimy broth, and licking the remnants with thick, pink tongues. Her own stomach roiled and growled at the smell, a putrid scent of rotted onions and waste. She had kept little down the first night, earning lashes from the jailor. Her back glistened with red welts and semidried blood.

The chef slopped a bowl on the counter. "Eat quickly. The sappers shall be here soon, then the high guard."

She said nothing, but lifted the soup to her lips, feeling the contents flow down her throat. A few bits of solid food to keep her alive. Her skin drew in the broth, struggling to heal against the dry heat of the realm. Just enough to survive and serve. The Seneschal had visited her once during this time, channeling his anger and frustration in the whipping. He stopped only when she lost consciousness.

Dwarf pig-men marched into the tent, broad and humpbacked with thick limbs, smelling of cordite and grease. She rose, along with the other slaves, to serve the next round of meals. The soldiers paid her little attention, talking in low grunts about the upcoming war, how they would take a new realm and how The Arkholt would gain an edge over the other Fae. That he would, in time, rule over all of Arcadia.

Nidaria no sooner set down the last bowl when the ground heaved and shook. A column of fire and smoke rose from the prison. Chunks of masonry tumbled through the air, crushing the unlucky and slow as they crashed down. Goblin bodies, flung by the explosion, windmilled into the stone wall of the fortress, leaving streaks of red as they slid to the base.

Shouts of confusion and anger. Bells clanged, sounding the alarm and rousting the troops. She lay under an overturned table, amidst the stunned and shocked sappers, covered by the spilled soup. Unnoticed and ignored in the confusion, she drew in a thin stream of glamour as the liquid absorbed into her skin. It concentrated in her core, masked behind a shroud of pain and weakness.

"How did that happen?" The Seneschal stormed about his chamber. His attendants fidgeted and sweated under his gaze. The jailor knelt on the ground and cradled his arm. Flesh, blackened and charred, flaked off with each movement. The smell of cooked pork dominated the room, masking his unwashed stink—a small favor to those present.

"The prisoner self-destructed when General Nin and his retinue arrived for the interrogation," the jailor said, grunting with pain. "A bomb hidden inside his chest."

"And you fools failed to find it! Now my best generals are dead. There's no one left to lead my army to war."

"What of you?" a robed cultist said, then clasped his hands to his mouth, horror filling his eyes. "Forgive me, my lord!"

"Me? Preposterous! My job is to oversee my lord's holding, not nursemaid troops. The temerity of the thought." The Seneschal lashed out his sword.

The cultist shrieked as the Seneschal's blade pierced his eye and then brain. He convulsed once, then lay still.

"I'm surrounded by idiots, fools, and incompetents!" The door creaked open and a goblin scurried in, clutching a scroll.

"Master, I bear word from The Arkholt."

He snatched the document and unfurled it. His anger faded, replaced with a gut-wrenching mix of fear, disbelief, and confusion. "We march at dawn, two days hence. My luck is cursed! Fate plagues me like a useless burden."

His attendants stood in place. Terror and panic washing over him at the news. Even the jailor, a creature of hatred and anger, cowered on the floor. Glamour flowed forth, whips of malice and rage, lashing out with barbed lethality. All his plotting and planning ruined. Useless, like his so-called prize.

The Seneschal took three deep breaths and stepped over the cultist's body. He motioned for the messenger and jailor to follow him.

"Come, we need to prepare. Go fetch the handmaiden, she's a cursed creature and I intend on ridding myself of her."

Each step of the army sounded like the pounding of a drum, heralding the coming of death. Doom. Doom. Doom. Sprites and gnomes. Trolls and ogres. Elves and dwarfs. A collection of great siege engines dragged behind shaggy beasts that some might charitably call animals, if you didn't look too closely at the lack of fur, tanned skin, and pained eyes. The column wound through the broken landscape, a snake of metal and malice, poised to strike at an unwary misstep.

"Come along, worthless one. You'll provide entertainment for my troops this evening," the Seneschal said, "and in the morning, your blood will soak the battlefield as an offering to fate."

Nidaria whimpered as she trotted alongside her new master's mount. The thing might have once been a horse as sculpted by a blind man. Legs with extra joints. A tail that forked into bone-like spikes. Two heads without eyes or mouth or ears. Jagged stone cut into the soles of her feet, leaving bloody prints on the path. The leash hung limply, dragging on the ground behind. A reminder that if she didn't keep up, it would be fastened to the mount. She would be dragged along. One of the camp followers had been left at the side of the path, broken and gasping out life from such a failure. She would not be a similar example.

A boar-commander trotted his Horse-Yet-Not alongside. "Seneschal. The sappers and the high guard have fallen to the wayside. Many are sick, a few have died."

"How? When?"

"Rust poisoning. I've seen it before. The gnomes are tending to those that can still move, the rest are unlikely to live past the hour."

"Saboteurs and murderers surround me! Grandfather Tick seeks to defeat us before we reach his realm. I will not be deterred. Place extra guards with the provisions."

"So it shall be," he grunted. "We approach the Bridge of Fossa."

"Send out the engineers and make sure it is safe to cross," the Seneschal said. "March the troops double-time when we are clear."

The boar-commander saluted and spurred his Horse-Yet-Not to the head of the column, winding a low blast from his war horn. Leather-clad dwarfs stomped past, clambering down and over the wooden bridge.

"My talents are wasted here. Grandfather Tick shall pay dearly for this inconvenience. Forced to lead common troops, not even the elites in The Arkholt's service."

An hour passed before the boar-commander returned. "We're safe to cross. The scouts are moving forward."

"Proceed and bring up the siege engines. Move in haste before our enemy is alerted."

The bridge vibrated as the troops marched across the span, flowing around the Seneschal as he paused in the middle to survey the movements. Ahead, the first soldiers spread out to guard against attack. Behind, siege machines rumbled forward, inching up the steep approach as the beasts struggled under their load. Nidaria closed her eyes and leaned against the Horse-Yet-Not. She spun a thread, dragging up the latent glamour from her bile that stained the bridge—a touch of terror and vertigo into the mount. The casting of a pebble on a slope of scree.

"What are you doing, girl?" The Seneschal's head whipped around, eyes blazing with fury.

"Boo," she whispered.

His mount reared up, screaming and howling in a warbling wail, pitching him off, and bolting over the troops.

A boom echoed as a bridge support splintered and broke. Over the horizon, lines of silver and brass men whirred and clicked into view. Immense cannons rolled forward. Clouds of steam billowing out as the boilers roared to life. Cast-iron barrels spit fire and smoke as they sent balls of brass through the air.

A voice rang out, over the sudden hush. "Ambush!"

Panic. Chaos. Hands pushed her to the railing as panicked soldiers scattered about, uncertain on which way to run. From the center of the span, the Seneschal struggled to his feet. Blood spilled from a cut on his scalp and one eye was now swollen shut, but the other focused on her.

"You. This is all your doing." His blade wavered in his unsteady grip.

163

"My mistress knows of your plans. She will not allow you to gain power over the sleeping lord." Two more cannonballs exploded at base of the bridge. It teetered and shook, planks falling into the water below.

A flicker of fear crossed his face. "How do you know of those plans?"

"You should treat your underlings better. The jailor is showing evidence of your perfidy to The Arkholt even as we speak." His blade, cold and rough, cut into her stomach, causing an acidic pain that danced and flayed at her nerves. Blue-tinted blood gushed out, flowing in a sticky wave to cover the Seneschal's blade.

"You'll not survive to gloat about it to your mistress."

"I will." She gripped his hand, releasing the thousands of stingers hidden in the flesh of her palm, to deliver the toxin into his system. "I empowered the prisoner to self-destruct. I poisoned your sappers and guard. You are the fool and weakling. None will know you were defeated by a handmaiden, but all will revile you for treachery."

He fell limply onto her, sending them crashing against the railing. Panic filled his one good eye, forced wide by the venom coursing through his system. His mouth moved in a silent plea. The wood underneath them, rotted and decayed from her bile, collapsed as a cannonball crashed through the remaining supports.

His disbelief hit her as the bridge collapsed beneath them. Nidaria turned her head and spit out the last of her glamour, a blue pearl that tumbled toward the dark waters. Darkness clouded her vision as she plunged into the river's cool embrace.

Nidaria knelt before her mistress and placed her palms on the sand. Her tentacle hair hung suspended in the water, lifted by the slight current that drifted over the ziggurat. The small strands would grow longer over time, until they once again formed a halo around her head. The brine stung at the welts and cuts that crossed her blue skin, incompletely healed from her regrowth. Her gill slits flapped open and closed to move life-giving fluid, once more sending her lungs into dormancy. "Mistress, it is done as you wished."

"Welcome home, lovely Nidaria." Atop of the dais, Brolga burbled with delight. "The Arkholt sent a message lamenting the death of my gift at the hands of a foul traitor. He offers an alliance against our mutual enemies."

"As you planned. Without The Seneschal, his army is in disarray."

"He accuses Grandfather Tick and the Princess of collusion in the destruction of his army. That the vote of censure was a sham." Her mistress leaned forward. "Did you alter the vote?"

"I swapped Cathare's marker and tipped the vote in favor of The Arkholt. The others believe that he abstained to curry favor with whomever won."

"How did you tip over the crate? My guards reported it to be securely fastened to the beast."

"They left the beast unguarded during the trip when called away to attend to business of a personal nature. Those jealous of my position did the rest." Her eyes rested on the simpering Undine handmaidens, laying at the feet of her mistress. Uncertainty and confusion radiated off them. "They saved me the effort. All I had to do was accidentally catch my sleeve on the chest."

"They shall be punished for disobeying my orders." Brolga laughed and clapped her hands. "I am pleased with the result. War is avoided, three of my enemies weakened, and balance restored once again. All because of a useless handmaiden who perished with a vile traitor."

"Yes, mistress. A loss that you'll need to replace," Nidaria said. "The Arkholt will still expect a gift from you."

"Do you have any suggestions on what would be appropriate?"

She looked at the three servants that cowered before her. "Yes, I have."

THE BITTER AND
THE SWEET

BY DB COREY

Madeline Brzezinski wouldn't watch a TV even if her mother owned one. She preferred the world of her books, of the heroes who swooped in to save the damsel in distress, or the magic boys who could summon great power to protect their friends from the monsters. Madeline preferred her books to her own life ... because in her life, the monsters were real.

Nine p.m. had come and gone according to the cracked plastic clock askew on the greasy kitchen wall. Her mother should be home by now. Madeline hovered near the living room window on her second-floor apartment looking for her mother's beat-up '99 Toyota. The tiny, two-bedroom Section-8 on South Amity Street sat in the worst part of Baltimore, and the disorder in the streets belonged to the night. She couldn't block it out. The building was old, built before air-conditioning came standard with construction and the windows were always open. She slept in her own room with peeling paint and a fan that pushed hot air around. It made a breeze and it seemed cooler, but on the nights when temperatures climbed to the top of the charts, she could sleep in her mom's room with the window air-conditioner, but not until her mother got home. Electricity was expensive.

Favoring her left leg, Madeline limped to her room to get her favorite book—the tale of a boy who could fly. The book was old and dog-eared, and she carried it to the window with the care afforded a Fabergé egg. Reading by the floodlights on the roof, she sometimes wished that *she* could fly. Then she too could go to Neverland and be part of the Lost Boys.

Peter was wrangling with his shadow by the time Madeline heard the tick-tick-tick of her mother's Toyota. Gray smoke poured from the tailpipe as she watched it pull to the curb. She marked the page with a bobby pin and saw her mother heave her large body from the car. Once relieved of the weight, the Toyota popped up like a cork under water. But then the passenger door opened; something unexpected, and Madeline couldn't imagine who could be with her mom.

Maybe she met someone nice, someone who would take them from this place to a nice house in the country. She loved the country, although she'd never been, except for in her imagination, seeded from the picture books at the recycling center down the street. But when a small man hauling a green trash bag stepped under the streetlight, terror seized her, and her water escaped down her leg.

"Are you finished now, Cole?" Hanna sniped. "Any dessert for you tonight? How about some coffee? Or maybe a fucking *espresso?*"

CIA Deputy-Director Preston Cole dabbed his lips with his napkin, and the grin that hid beneath continued into the perfect smile. "I thought you considered cursing against the Word of God," he said.

"Yeah. Well, God and I aren't doing so well right now."

"I can see." He signaled the waiter for the check.

"What do I have to do to get the information I want?" she asked.

"Hanna, I told you already. When we struck our deal, I said you had to have skin in the game. Well, this is it." He tossed a manila envelope across the table.

"What's this?"

"Your assignment. This guy Hoffer is a piece of shit. Rapes and hurts little girls. Just like you."

"I'm not a little girl."

"Like Molly, then."

Cole watched the anger smoldering in Hanna's eyes flare into intense rage. He knew his cavalier mention of her murdered sister could bring her across the table at him. It was a calculated move on his part, designed to get a read on her state of mind. He couldn't have an asset going off half-cocked when provoked.

She kept her place. She was a pro, and Cole knew she wouldn't kill him, at least not right then. She'd wait until she got what she needed ... *then* she'd kill him.

Cole smiled inwardly, "Very good, Hanna. I see your training is still intact. So here's the deal. I have the information you want, and you will get it as soon as you have something to lose as I do. This op is not what we call *sanctioned* by the Masters. I'm on my own. If you want your stuff, you have to do something for me first."

Hanna glared. "*What!*"

Cole nodded toward the envelope on the table in front of her. "I need to burn that when you're finished."

"This is murder, Cole."

"Yeah. I know. So what do you call your plans for Daemon Goode? A play date?"

"I won't do it."

"Yes you will ... or you'll never find your sister's killer. This is the skin I spoke of." Cole shifted in his chair and let the tension wane for a moment. "Look, Hanna. This animal raped his girlfriend's eight-year-old daughter, but first took the time to beat her to a pulp. He did three years of a ten-year stretch and now he's out on good behavior. My sources tell me he's been released into the custody of a court-appointed custodian due to overcrowding at the halfway house, but the custodian is on the take, and Hoffer's shacked up with his ex-girlfriend, living in the same rat hole as the little girl. As long as Hoffer shows up for his court-appointed job, no one will check on him. He'll drop off the radar." Cole took a minute to let it sink in.

"Madeline Brzezinski is the little girl's name. Remember it, because he'll probably beat her to death this time."

Hanna's anger faded. "The girlfriend took him back? Is she unbalanced?"

"Unwanted. She supports him and he fucks her. It's a pure symbiotic relationship. To be honest, I don't see how he even gets it up for her. She's not what you would call desirable. But who am I to criticize."

"I ... I've never killed anyone close up before."

"Up close, far away ... killing is killing. This will be good practice for when you find Goode. Besides, how will you feel if Hoffer hurts Madeline again, maybe kills her this time, knowing you could have done something to stop him? You won't get a wink of sleep if I know you. Think of it as doing the world a favor. Then, when you off this misfit, I'll give you Goode. You get to take out two pieces of shit for the price of one. Win-Win. Don't you see? Guys like this make a mockery of our laws, and the judicial system keeps putting them back among us."

"You're going rogue, aren't you, Cole?"

"I'm doing what's right. Now ... do you want Goode, or don't you?"

Hanna pursed her lips in thought, much like a chess player looking for a way out of check. Her blue eyes never left Cole, and her next move didn't take but a moment.

"... I'll need a weapon."

Madeline made herself small, as small as she possibly could; curled into a fetal position in the saggy corner of a threadbare sofa. The groan of old wooden steps grew ever louder as her mother hefted herself to the second floor. She had brought the monster home, just as she did over three years ago. Panic stole Madeline's breath as she experienced the beating all over again. She was only eight when the monster raped her.

Madeline heard her mother's labored breathing on the far side of the door—then the jingle of keys and the click of a lock. The door creaked open and Madeline's mother poked her head in. She didn't see Madeline at first and called her name before pushing the door its full travel. She stood in the doorway, filling the space with her girth, her yellow uniform soiled with coffee and soda and food. Some of the stains were older than others, and most were older than today. She called again.

"Madeline? Where you at?"

A small voice. "Here."

Her mother's face took on a sheepish look as she stepped into the sparse living room. She toggled a switch and the harsh glare of a bare ceiling bulb filled the room. She started toward Madeline without closing the door. Madeline cringed.

"*There* you are, girl! Couldn't see you in the dark."

Madeline said nothing.

"Madeline? I gotta talk 'bout somethin' really important with ya. I brought—"

"*Why'd* you bring him *back?*" Madeline's voice quivered and caught in her throat as she began to cry. "*Why?*" her voice pleading. "He *hurt* me, Mommy! He hurt me *bad*. Made me *bleed* down there." Madeline peered around her mother looking for the monster but couldn't see past her, so she pushed herself deeper into the sofa with every step her mother took toward her.

"Now Madeline, you shouldn't be talkin' that way. Simon told me he didn't mean it. That he's sorry. He was drunk an' didn't know what he was doin'. He said to me he'd never *ever* hurt you if he didn't get drunk."

"HE'S *ALWAYS* DRUNK! I *HATE* him! I don't *WANT* him here!"

"Now Madeline, what did I learn ya 'bout God an' forgivin' an' forgetin'?"

"Madeline lowered her voice to just above a whisper. "You took him back because no one else wants you. He hurts you too, Mommy. I know he does. I saw him."

Brenda Brzezinski bent over to sit and eased herself down beside her daughter with much effort. After she caught her breath, she looked at Madeline. "He don't hurt me 'lessen I deserves it. But he promised he ain't gonna hit me no more. That's more better, ain't it, Madeline? We ain't gotta worry 'bout gettin' beat up no more."

At that moment, Simon Hoffer stepped into the apartment, dropped his green Hefty bag full of dirty clothes, and walked over to Madeline. His oily blonde hair had receded while he was in jail, and the

171

few teeth he hadn't lost to meth had something green built up at the gum line. As he leaned toward her, her hands shot up to ward him off.

"*Heyyy* ... Madeline! What's that all about? I told your mom I was sorry 'bout hittin' her and that I ain't gonna hit her no more. That means you too. I learnt my lesson in jail. I ain't never gonna hit nobody no more. I promise."

"You hurt me ... down there ..."

Simon glanced to Madeline's crotch, a gaze he held a bit too long. "Goddamn it! I *said* I was sorry, *didn't I?*"

Madeline recoiled as the chill of fear touched her spine.

"Okay ... so I hurt you. So what's the big fuckin' deal? I didn't *mean* it, ya *hear?* I was crazy high on PCP. That shit fucks me up! I done swore *off* druggin' an' drinkin'. Ain't never gonna hurt you ever again."

Simon paused and lowered his voice to let the tension fade.

"So whadda ya say, Madeline? How 'bout we be friends again?" Simon thrust his hand toward her. Madeline screamed and bolted from the couch into her room.

When Brenda heard the door slam, she pulled Simon down to the space Madeline just left and kissed him on the lips. She smelled of BO and her pasty skin held a fine coating of sweat. Simon kept his lips pressed tight, the kiss short.

"She don't seem none too happy I'm here," he said, breaking the embrace.

"Aw, she'll be okay, baby. She's just gotta get use to the idea o' you bein' here again, that's all."

"Yeah, 'suppose so," Simon said. He looked to Madeline's closed door. "So, how old is she now?"

"Madeline? Eleven ... I think. Ain't really sure."

"Eleven." Hoffer smiled. "Them's some nice little titties she growed while I was gone."

Hanna felt a bit out of place, lounging in her new, oversized, brown-leather reading chair. Her quarters at Base Chapman in Afghanistan had no such luxuries. She watched something called *Big Brother* on her new flat-screen TV; a show where the men were all heavily tattooed and buff or milquetoast and nerdy, and the women were all California blondes, long-haired and large-breasted, who bent over for the camera at every turn. It seemed that Wednesday was not a good night for TV.

The sun set twenty minutes earlier and she had nothing to do but wait. Cole said to expect a UPS delivery, but didn't tell her what time to expect it; so she kept herself busy cleaning, something she was unaccustomed to doing, having never been burdened with it in Afghanistan. She had no rugs in her quarters, or drapes, or dishes ... or anything else domestic, except for the sheets from the base laundry. Now she had her own sheets—new and never used in any fashion.

She considered leaving a note on the door and going for a run, but Cole told her to receive the package personally. She understood why, so she waited. When the knock finally came, she had dozed off. A second knock and she was at the door. The fish-eye view through the peephole distorted the visitor like a funhouse mirror. A guy wearing a brown baseball cap waited patiently, so she opened the door.

The square-jawed, barrel-chested UPS man wore brown shorts to match the hat, and an oversized shirt that concealed the service weapon Hanna knew he carried.

He smiled. Hanna smiled back.

"Ms. Braver. Package for you."

"Thanks. You need to see some ID?"

The man chuckled and brushed it off as if she was joking. "You've been away too long, Ms. Braver. Cole said your operational parameters are inside." He smiled again, wished her a good night, and was down the stairway in a heartbeat. Hanna closed the door and picked up a steak knife from the kitchen on her way back to the big leather chair. She heard the truck pull away as she lowered the volume on *Big Brother*, and set the UPS shipping box on the matching ottoman before slitting the tape with care.

Inside was a smaller, plain white cardboard box with no markings. She cut the tape sealing it and found an envelope, which she set aside. Under the envelope, seated in a customized Styrofoam base, was a Ruger SR-22 with a threaded barrel, two fully loaded ten-round magazines with subsonic .22-caliber rounds, and a pair of rubberized grips—large and small. A five-inch sound suppressor was tucked into the corner of the box, and a CMR-201 laser sight attached under the muzzle.

Hanna smiled. Cole had filled her order to the letter, right down to the laser sighting system. She extracted the Ruger and racked the slide, handing it as if it were an extension of her arm. The Ruger was light. Fully loaded it was less than twenty ounces. The laser and suppressor added a bit more weight, but nothing to concern her. Broken down, the system was easily concealed.

She tested the laser to ensure it functioned and then turned to the envelope and sliced it open. Inside was a handwritten note.

Excellent choice of tools, but somehow, it didn't surprise me.
311 South Amity Street, Apt 200, Baltimore, MD.
You have one week.

Hanna put a lighter to the paper and let it burn away the writing before flushing the charred remnants down the toilet. She had just one week to locate and assassinate Hoffer. Cole provided the exact weapon she wanted; that was her only condition. If she was going to do this, she wanted a weapons system suited for the job. But there was more to killing than just pulling a trigger. There was planning involved, timing to consider—she checked her wallet and fingered the company credit card.

Simon climbed the stairs after work, tracking dirt and mud as he went. He'd been at this court-mandated job for a week and he was sick of it—the foreman telling him where to go, when to smoke, when to piss, what work needed doing, sending him here, sending him there. Construction was a dirty way to make a living, not to mention the ass he had to kiss. Simon preferred that someone support him.

The door to No. 200 was unlocked and he snorted with satisfaction when the doorknob twisted in his hand. He told Brenda that he'd better not ever find she had locked the door or he'd make her wish she hadn't. He walked in to find her occupying most of the small kitchen nook as she prepared his dinner. She wore her stained yellow waitress uniform as she was due in for the midshift at the diner. Madeline sat rigid on the sofa, unmoving, not reacting to Simon's presence, and pretending to read as hard as she could, wishing she could fly.

"Hey baby," Brenda called. "How was your day?"

"How do you fuckin' think it was?" Simon snarled. "It sucked! I ain't goin' back to that shithole no more."

"Honey, if you don't go back, they'll violate your parole an' stick you back in that jail."

That, to Simon, was tantamount to Brenda telling him what to do, giving him orders, and running his life—just like that foreman. He charged across the small living room and grabbed Brenda's upper arm hard enough that she cried out in pain. "You gonna *tell 'em*, bitch? *Huh?* You gonna tell 'em I ain't goin' to work?"

"Nooooo ... Noooo ... not me, baby. I ain't tellin' *nobody*. I *swear!*"

The fury in Simon's eyes was enough to divert any normal person's gaze. Brenda kept talking. That was what worked. That was what calmed him.

"I was just *remindin'* you, sweetie," she whimpered. "That's all, baby. You know I love you. Don't want you leavin' us again, that's all." She chose her words carefully so as not to imply she wanted him back behind bars, where she and Madeline would be safe from his special brand of crazy.

"Look baby ... I done made you your favorite soup. It'll be ready in a minute. I tasted it for you. It's just how you like it."

"I don't want no fuckin soup! Gimme some money. I'm goin' to the bar."

"I have the rent money, baby, but it's for the rent. Why don't ya stay home with us tonight, just till I goes to work. I gotta be in at 11:30. Madeline's goin' across the hall with her little black friend, Rona. We can spend a little time together before I goes in."

Simon's laugh cut like an insult. "I'd rather shovel a ditch full of *shit!* Where's the money?"

"But baby ..."

The slap of Simon's hand across Brenda's rotund face rolled down the stairway like a clap of thunder. Madeline screamed and ran into her room. Simon laughed again as her door slammed closed. "Like that will stop me if I want to get in! You little whore!" He turned to Brenda and his face went dark. "I ain't tellin' you again, bitch."

175

The public notice nailed to the side of Ty's Bar on Washington Street declared the date, time, and place of the public hearing that would decide its fate. The notice didn't say as much, but rumor had it that the liquor board was looking to close it down. The numerous complaints from the neighborhood finally had the board's attention.

Ty's was less of a bar and more of a combination drug den/whorehouse—a dump, much to the liking of Simon Hoffer. With shuffleboard and pool tables and pinball machines, not to mention a steady flow of hookers and drug dealers, it was not only desirable, it was close. The Pigtown bar sat just on the far side of Baltimore's B&O Railroad Museum; an easy five-block walk from Brenda's apartment. Once Simon had Brenda's rent money, he made a beeline for it.

After slamming down his eighth beer, he bought another for himself, and one for his friend Henry from work. He still had plenty of Brenda's money.

"What time is it, Henry?" Simon slurred.

"Henry lifted his head off the bar and stared at his watch for a long minute. 11:30. I think. I gotta get home. It's late."

"Wanna do some meth?"

"Maybe tomorrow."

"Let's get a whore."

"I gotta get home. The wife ..."

"Ya know, Henry, I think when I gets home tonight ... I'm gonna fuck that little Madeline again. You should see those nice little titties she growed for me when I was in jail. I know she growed 'em for me for when I got out. Like a welcome home present. I think she liked when I fucked her that first time, ya know?"

Henry said nothing, his attention riveted on the woman who just walked in the door.

"Henry?"

Henry just nodded toward the woman on the other side of the bar as she climbed onto a stool. Simon looked over bleary-eyed and forgot all about Madeline.

"Jesus Christ!" Simon blurted. "Where'd *that* come from? Hey! Bartender! Where'd *that* come from?"

Janis, a scrawny, stringy-haired brunette, walked over wiping her hands with a bar rag. "C'mon, Simon. Quit callin' me bartender for Christ's sake. You been comin' here for a fuckin' week an' you don't know my name by now? It's Janis!"

"Yeah. Sure. I know, Janet. So who's that?" and he pointed.

The new girl glanced up, but took no offense at his uncouth attention or his overexcitement.

"Don't know," Janis said. "She only been here once. Yesterday 'fore you came in. I think she's new meat."

The blonde placed an oversized imitation-leather handbag on the bar and gave the three of them a dull look. "I can hear you fuckers, ya know. Why don't that little blonde guy who's pointin' at me buy me a drink? I ain't got no money."

Henry took that moment to pass out and fall off his stool. Simon and Janis peered down at him. He'd puked up some of what he'd been drinking and pissed himself to boot.

"Fuck," Janis said. "Now I gotta clean up that mess. Just leave him there. It ain't like anybody's gonna trip over 'im. Ain't nobody here ... 'cept you two."

Simon looked at the blonde. "What ya drinkin'?"

"Come over here an' find out."

Simon grinned, picked up his beer and stumbled in her direction. Up close, drunk as he was, even Simon could see that she had troweled on too much makeup. Her hair went to her waist and her points pressed hard against her sheer white top. She sat cross-legged, wearing black knee-high boots and a short black leather skirt that barely covered her ass. Long runs traveled down both legs of black designer hose, and both knees had holes torn in them, sending Simon's mind to delightful imaginings.

"You a pro?" Simon asked, pulling up a stool.

"Depends."

"Depends? Depends on what?"

"You gonna buy me that drink or what?" She pulled out a cigarette, held it between her fingers, and waited. Simon finally took the hint, snatched a book of matches from a bowl, and tossed them on the bar in front of her.

"Asshole."

"Well, whadda ya fuckin' want? I got you a light, didn't I?"

"Get me a beer. Miller."

Janis was paying attention and laughing at the same time. She brought the Miller bottle over and copped two-bucks from Simon's cash. The blonde took a short pull.

"So ... ya never answered me," Simon pressed. "You a pro?"

The blonde looked him up and down. "You can't afford me."

"How do you know?"

She began to laugh. "I been in this business a long time. I can see you ain't got no money."

"I got money."

"Okay, bigshot. How much ya got? Ya got three hundred?"

"Three *hundred?* What's it made of? *Silk?*"

"That's my goin' rate for the night. I said you couldn't afford me."

"Simon fanned through his bills. "I got a hundred-ten here."

"Shit ... that don't even cover the room."

"Don't need no room. I got a room."

The blonde hit the beer again and then smirked. "An' I bet it's the fuckin' Ritz, ain't it."

"It's just a couple blocks from here. I got more money there too."

The blonde pondered her options. She turned to Simon and pressed her chest into him. "Here's the deal. I'm new in town. Tryin' to build a clientele, ya know? So I'm goin' to make you a special offer. Tonight only. I take what you got there on the bar, and what you got in that room o' yours, and when you're done, there ain't no seconds. I ain't stayin' all night suckin' your dick or nothin'. Straight fuck. That's it. You get me some decent referrals and I make you a better offer next time."

The pressure in Simon's pants became unbearable. "Girl, you got a deal."

Simon opened the door to No. 200 with the blonde still on the stairway, trailing him by several strides.

"You didn't tell me I hadda hike these fuckin' steps after that long-ass walk. I oughta charge you extra."

"You been bitchin' the whole way," he barked. "It ain't that damn far. You *look* in better shape, but I guess you ain't."

"Fuck you! I'm in all the shape *you* need."

Simon opened the door with the blonde on his heels and didn't bother to ease into the room. Even if Brenda were still there for some reason, Simon would throw her out to have this blonde. What was she gonna do? She enabled him. He raped her daughter and went to prison for it, and Brenda visited him the entire time he was behind bars, worked two jobs to pay his bills, and had conjugal relations with him in prison, all the while leaving Madeline in the apartment by herself. When he got out, she brought him home. He thought her pathetic. The woman *asked* for the misery he brought and wanted more, and misery was the one thing he was all too happy to provide.

The parents of Madeline's little friend, Rona, knew the whole story, and they were appalled to find Simon living back in the same apartment with Madeline. So they brought Madeline into their home, modest as it was. They had her there as often as they could—when Brenda worked and Simon was home—to offer her peace of mind and a semblance of protection.

But the protection they offered was paper-thin, much like the walls of their tenement. They were old, grandparent old, because they *were* Rona's grandparents. They took Rona in when her father disappeared and her mother—their daughter—found herself caught up with the wrong people. She was as bad as Brenda, so they took Rona as their own, something they didn't expect to do at their stage of life. Their daughter made no effort to get Rona back, so now they protected two children. But they could not withstand an assault from Simon, should he want Madeline, or Rona for that matter. He had made it known to all—he didn't care what color they were.

Simon closed the front door and went directly to the bedroom to turn on the A/C. "Wanna beer?" he called.

The blonde ignored him. "This place is a dump," she said. "You sure you got the money?"

Simon waved a wad of bills he rooted from the dresser drawer.

"I gotta piss," she said. "Where's the john?"

Simon pointed.

"Go get naked," she told him. "I'm gonna freshen up a little. That fuckin' hike made me sweat terrible."

Madeline woke at the sound of Simon's footfalls on the creaky old steps. He made no effort to stay quiet. Someone was with him, Madeline thought, but not her mother. She knew her mother's labored breathing, even through the walls. Maybe one of his friends. Maybe he was looking for her. Maybe they both were. Madeline began to cry to herself, terrified. She slipped off the couch to her knees and began to pray.

Please ...

Simon disappeared into Brenda's bedroom as the blonde closed the bathroom door behind her. He undressed as fast as he could, pulling at his clothes before turning off the only lamp in the room. The light from outside seeped in through the silted window on the far wall, giving the room a dim ambiance. He jumped into bed and began stroking himself to stay ready while he waited. As the minutes passed, he had to stop, the early stirrings of ejaculation arriving far too soon.

How long does one broad need to take a leak? he thought.

He laced his fingers behind his head, forcing himself to resist the temptation to continue jerking off. Had he allowed himself to finish, he'd have nothing left for the whore.

He lay back in all his glory as the blonde entered the room. She stopped at the foot of the bed backlit by the window—her skirt short, her feet wide, her posture inviting.

"It stinks in here," she said.

"That fat bitch I live with," he said. "Sweats like a pig. Ain't changed the sheets in a month, I bet."

"Where's my money?" she said. "I get paid up front."

"On the bureau. Why you still dressed?"

"Get out of bed."

"Why?"

"I wanna do you on my knees. Gets me off."

Simon flashed back to the bar and the holes in the knees of her designer hose.

"I thought you said straight fuck."

"You turnin' down a blow job?"

He grinned. "Noooo, ma'am!"

180

He fairly bounced off the mattress and stood naked beside the bed, pale in the weak light from the street, stroking himself and grinning like the Cheshire Cat.

The blonde picked up the money and stuffed it in her bag.

Madeline began to wonder about the other steps that she heard with Simon. Maybe it *was* her mother. What if Simon told her to come back? Maybe he wanted more money. Maybe he wanted to hurt her again. She couldn't just stay here and listen to him beat her. She had to do something. She had to help.

Madeline sneaked out and crossed the hall into her apartment. The lights were on in the living room and her mother's bedroom door was closed, but not all the way. She heard voices coming from inside and she was scared, but she said a small prayer, faced her fear, and crept to the door to listen.

Simon stood naked, watching with anticipation as the blonde removed something from her bag. It was long and cylindrical, and in the dim light, Simon could only guess what it was. He thought it a sex toy; a vibrator maybe, something for her, and maybe even for him. But all that changed when it began emitting a crimson glow. A red dot appeared over his heart, and a look of bewilderment crossed his face.

"Wha ... what are you doing? What is that thing? Is that a *gun?*"

The red dot held rock steady, unwavering, as if inked on his skin like a tattoo. Then it began to travel, easing its way down across his chest to his abdomen, and his rapidly dwindling erection where it stopped.

"I understand you like raping little girls, Simon."

"*WHA?*" Simon yelled. "Who the hell *are* you? How do you know my *name?*" He didn't wait for an answer before lunging at her. He advanced one-half of one step before a flash lit the room. Something akin to a loud click halted his attack and searing pain raced through his genitals. A heartbeat later, blood splattered over him. Another flash, another click, and a knee exploded. He screamed and collapsed, cradling his shredded manhood with one hand, his fractured knee with the other.

"Shut up, Simon, or I'll take out the other knee. I can make this very painful before it's over."

Simon clamped his mouth shut to muffle his cries. "Ummmf! Wha ..." He pushed down a scream and began to hyperventilate. "Why ... are you doing this ... to me?"

"You hurt that little girl, Simon. Raped her. She'll never be the same."

"She *asked* for it. She *wanted* me to do it to 'er."

"Is that what your sick mind told you? She was *eight years old!* The only thing she wanted was a normal childhood. You stole that from her, you piece of shit."

"I ... I did my time. I *changed.* I told her I ain't gonna hurt her no more."

"You did three of ten. A joke."

"I'll go back! I'll go back an' do all the time!"

"Sorry Simon, twenty wouldn't be enough. The system can't rehabilitate scum like you. You're rabid. You need to be put down."

A creak from the bedroom door came from her right, spinning Hanna around in a flash, the red dot of the laser searching for a threat. It found Madeline's forehead as she peered into the room, and Hanna was quick to jerk the weapon skyward.

Shit.

Madeline gazed at the Amazonian figure in the short skirt and knee-high boots. Without fear, she peered deeper into the room. There lay Simon Hoffer, naked as the day he was born and writhing in pain. There was a lot of blood. Unaffected by the sight, she wrinkled her nose and sniffed the air, then turned back and gazed upon Hanna, blue eyes fixed on blue eyes.

"Is this what angels smell like?"

Cordite, Hanna thought. *She smells the gunpowder.*

"Are *you* my Guardian Angel?"

"Am I what?"

Madeline lunged forward and wrapped her arms around Hanna's waist and held her tight. "My *Angel!* I prayed to God for my Guardian Angel to protect me from Simon and now *you're* here." Madeline found Hanna's eyes once more. "Can you *fly?*"

"No, Madeline, I can't fly. And I'm not an angel."

"You know my *name*. You know where I *live*. You *must* be my Angel."

Hanna removed Madeline's arms from her waist and dropped to one knee. Because of her recent falling out with God, the last thing she wanted was to be perceived as an angel, guardian or otherwise.

"What are you doing here, Maddie? Where did you come from?"

"Rona's 'partment ... 'cross the hall."

"Who's there with you?"

"Rona an' her grams."

"Shit."

"Angels ain't suppos' to cuss."

"I'm not an angel and I don't cuss."

"Angels ain't suppos' to lie, either."

Hanna heaved a resigned sigh. "I want you to go back to Rona's, okay?"

"Are you here to kill Simon?"

Hanna gazed at the girl, gauging how to answer.

Angels ain't suppos' to lie.

"Yes, Maddie. I am. Now go."

Madeline sighed and stepped backward through the door as Hanna set her Ruger on the bureau. She retrieved Simon's cash from her bag and dropped it next to her weapon. Next came a dark sweatshirt, a pair of loose-fitting bell-bottom jeans, and a Navy watch cap. Without removing her boots, she began pulling on the clothes over what she was wearing. Fully distracted, she stepped into the bell-bottoms, and while her hands were busy, Madeline rushed back into the room, snatched the Ruger from the bureau, and put the red dot in the middle of Simon's forehead.

Simon's begging caught Hanna's attention and she cried out for Madeline to stop, but before she could reach her, Madeline gripped the weapon with both hands and pulled the trigger twice. A pair of red dots appeared just above Simon's left eye and blood trickled down his forehead. A thin smile crept onto Madeline's lips as her eyes glazed over.

"You hurt me," she whispered.

Hanna grabbed the Ruger from Madeline and stood in horror. Never did she think an eleven-year-old would commit murder, but as the room succumbed to the quiet of the moment, gunshots rang out from the city streets nearby.

Gangs, Hanna thought. *Killing each other. Some of them are only eleven or twelve.* It's a new world, where children kill. She looked to Madeline.

"C'mon, Maddie. We're leaving."

"You're not gonna kill my Mommy?"

"*NO!* ... God no ..."

"Want *me* to do it?"

INFLUENCE

BY MARTIN ZEIGLER

State Senator Amory Turniken sat in the corner booth of one of those watering holes favored by the ambitious. All polished wood, brass, and marble tile. Wait staff in black and white, neither friendly nor rude but somewhere in between. And somewhat better service in return for a somewhat better tip.

Turniken was nursing his fourth whiskey sour when a shadow crossed his ice and he looked up to see a stranger standing at his table.

The joint was dark anyway, at least this end of it. The late afternoon light from the street-side windows barely reached this far. And yet the stranger standing here, with his fingertips poised on the table as if he were about to call a meeting to order, managed to look even darker in his black suit, black shirt, and black tie. His complexion alone, deep gray and slightly crimson in tone, suggested that something else, something unseen, was diminishing the light to his face.

"Senator," he said, with an acknowledging nod.

Turniken was still working on who to blame for his poor performance earlier today and did not wish to be bothered. "What do you want?" he asked brusquely.

"Looks like the debate didn't go too well," the stranger said.

"Why do you say that?"

"Because otherwise you'd be at a larger table with lots more people."

"Let me try this again," Turniken said. "What do you want?"

"Mind if I sit? The rest of the drinks are on me."

Turniken had no desire for company, not today. Even the free drinks didn't sound all that enticing. But he respected the offer. And in due course he would probably respect the drinks. So he tilted a hand toward the bench opposite—which the stranger accepted.

"Name's Bernard Ashland," he said. "But you can call me Bernie."

"Ashman?" Turniken asked. "You're a chimney sweep?"

"Too confined a space," Bernie said. "I prefer Ash*land*, as in *land* of the free, home of the brave."

Before Turniken could signal his understanding, a waiter—in black and white, of course—appeared from out of nowhere. Bernie ordered a scotch on the rocks, while the senator tapped the rim of his near-empty glass for a repeat.

Folding his hands on the smooth, varnished tabletop, Bernie said, "You probably want me to get to the point, senator, so here it is. You have one debate remaining, and it's crucial. You screw this one up the way you screwed up today's and last week's, and you might still win the governorship, but then pigs might fly come November too."

"Thanks for the vote of confidence."

"Face it. There's a general consensus that Halloran has been doing a standup job as governor. The feeling is that he's honest, listens to the people, and is pretty much a straight shooter. So why change horses? And you know what? I'm inclined to agree."

Turniken bristled. "This isn't even worth free drinks."

"Meanwhile there are a lot of folks who consider you a mediocre senator at best, a two-bit pol, not to mention a phony, a windbag, and little more than a self-serving opportunist. And I have to say that I concur with that assessment, as well."

Turniken leveled a baleful glare at the dark-suited stranger. "Get the hell out of my sight."

"All right, all right," Bernard Ashland said, his hands up in surrender. He slid out of the bench and stood up. "Then I guess it's Halloran in the governor's mansion for another four."

He reached into his pocket, pulled out a money roll, and peeled off a few bills. "But if it's Amory Turniken you want in office, I'm telling you it can be guaranteed." He slapped the bills on the table.

"One hundred percent."

As Bernie turned to leave, Turniken rapped his glass on the table a couple of times like a gavel. "Hold on, hold on," he said. "Sit down."

Bernie again slid into the opposite bench.

"What game are you playing?" Turniken asked.

"No game," Bernie said, adjusting his lapels. "Games are for dice rollers, for bleary-eyed wretches at the slots, for poor saps stepping out of 7-Elevens with their fists full of lottery tickets. No, what I'm talking about is a sure thing. Based on solid principle."

"And what principle is that?"

The waiter appeared again, tray balanced on his upturned fingers, and distributed the drinks. Bernie slid over the bills that he had slapped on the table and sent him on his way.

"A simple principle, really. It's that people never seem to know what they want, but they always know what they don't want. Especially come election time, when it's not 'may the best man win' so much as 'may the worst one tank.' Joe Voter, faced with two candidates, one who smells like roses and the other who smells like shit, will obviously pick the former, even though he would much prefer the sweet scent of carnations, and roses make him itch."

"Let's suppose that's true. How does—"

"It is true. And you know it is."

"Okay, it's true. How does it apply to me?"

"Right now, today, if we applied this principle to you, we would have to conclude that your goose is cooked. Compared to you, senator, anyone would look good. And Halloran cuts a pretty impressive figure on his own, but next to you he comes across as our Lord and Savior. You don't stand a chance."

"Now listen here, Ass Gland, or whatever your last name is—"

"Ass Gland. Very good. I'll have to try to remember that one. In fact, I definitely will remember it."

"Good for you. Do you definitely remember mentioning a one-hundred-percent guarantee? Because I didn't ask you to sit back down just so you could continue to insult me."

"No insult intended, senator. You are what you are, and that's just fine. I wouldn't dream of changing you, even for a second. In fact, it wouldn't be worthwhile. Why waste the effort building you up when the time would be better spent tearing Halloran down? Not just tarnishing his image and making him look bad in the public eye, but destroying him, completely and utterly."

To Turniken's ears, every word out of the stranger's mouth up to this point had been either a bald insult or so much dime-store political analysis. But this last line on Bernie's part—about destroying completely and utterly—was something he could wrap his arms around. "And how do you propose to do that?" he asked.

"Character assassination—with a twist."

Turniken took a sip from his sour and placed the drink carefully back down on the napkin. "You mean tell lies about him? I tried that. It doesn't work."

Bernie nodded in agreement. "Yes, I noticed. That's why we'll rely on the truth."

"But there's no dirt on the guy. One parking ticket back when he was in college. That's it."

"Yes, it's unfortunate," Bernie said with a resigned smile. "And that's why we'll need to create our own truth."

"Can we do that?" Turniken asked, imagining the possibilities.

"Certainly. After all, what is truth?"

"You got me."

"It's what leaves no doubt. It's what people see with their own eyes and hear with their own ears. It's what I'll demonstrate in a moment or two if you'll just bear with me."

It took but a few minutes for the waiter to show up again to see how they were doing.

"Still working on them," Ashland said, lifting his own glass and speaking for Turniken.

As the waiter headed back to the bar, Bernie plucked something out of his own shirt pocket—a thin, cylindrical device that looked almost like a dog whistle except for a small cone at the end of it. He now lifted the thing to his mouth and mumbled something into the cone that sounded vaguely like the word "halt."

Immediately, the waiter froze in midstride, like a child playing red light, green light. He held the circular tray out in front of him like a discus thrower and remained absolutely still.

"I'll be darned," Turniken said. "How did you do that?"

Bernie pulled the whistle thing away from his mouth. "Don't ask me. I didn't invent it. I just stole it. I believe the real inventor mentioned something about converting vocal commands to mental waves, but of course there's no way to get him to elaborate now."

Turniken understood, or thought he did.

"It needs improvement, though," Bernie admitted. "It only works over short distances. And you can't force anyone to do anything in the future but only in the here and now. But, hey, you work with what you're given."

Turniken nodded and continued to stare in fascination at the statue in black and white.

"Now, senator, I invite you to sit back and watch as this fellow does a few exercises, a trick with his tray, and lets us in on what he really thinks of his job."

Bernie again mumbled something into the cylinder, and the waiter broke free of his motionless thrall and turned to face the table. Another mumble, and the waiter let go of his tray. A third, and the poor guy began doing jumping jacks. Legs apart, hands together. Legs together, hands to his side. Repeating this over and over, counting out loud—"One-two-three ONE! One-two-three TWO! One-two-three THREE!"—like a student in phys ed, except in heavy black slacks instead of gym shorts.

Turniken and Bernie continued to watch and occasionally sip from their cocktails as if this were a nightclub act. "One-two-three TWENTY-NINE! One-two-three THIRTY! One-two-three THIRTY-ONE!"

By now, ripples of sweat were pouring out of the waiter's sopping hair and down the sides of his face, his words becoming more labored with each cycle. "One-two-three FIFTY-FOUR!"

"Poor guy needs to work out more," Ashland observed.

"Does he even know what he's doing?"

"Oh, yes, absolutely. But he can't help himself. He's inwardly cursing the day I was born, I bet, but that's about all the resistance he's allowed. That old saw about never having to do anything against your will under hypnosis might be true, but this isn't hypnosis. It's almost total mind-control."

"Amazing," Turniken said.

"One-two-three SEVENTY-SEVEN! One-two-three SEVENTY-EIGHT!"

"Okay," Bernie said. "I guess that's enough."

Another command from Ashland, and the waiter stopped immediately, but the next command allowed no rest. Drenching sweat, the waiter picked the tray up off the floor, aimed it, and sent it spinning like a Frisbee.

Turniken leaned out of his booth and watched the tray fly across the room, sail over a table where a lone diner sat, and shatter the window next to her, sending shards of glass everywhere. Turniken even spotted a spray of blood as the lone diner screamed and shot a hand to her eyes.

"Oops," Bernie remarked, peering around the edge of the booth. "Didn't see that coming."

Pandemonium ensued as patrons ducked out of booths and away from tables and dived to the floor. Screams and cries echoed everywhere, and the blatant din of the city came rushing through the shattered window.

Bernie mumbled into his cone, something that sounded to Turniken like "So leave if you don't like it." The waiter strode toward the injured woman who was now cowering in a corner with her hand still to her eye, blood seeping through her fingers. "So leave if you don't like it!" he yelled, his face in hers like a drill sergeant. "I don't like it either! I hate it! This place sucks! The food here sucks and the work here sucks! Go someplace else if you don't like it! Do you hear me?"

"A bit of a rambling tirade, I admit," Bernie said with a shrug.

From somewhere, who knows where, a man in a suit appeared, along with a burly fellow in black and white, and together they rushed the waiter, forcing back his arms and shoving him to the floor.

Ashland smiled, now looking at the senator and merely listening to the commotion behind him. "Sounds as if our waiter friend might be out of a job. My guess is that once news of this gets around, he'll never find work anywhere else in town, either. Such a shame. He seemed to be a good worker."

Turniken nodded appreciatively. "I think I see where this is going, Bernie."

"And I *know* where this is going, senator. Just make sure I get a seat close to the front. And once the debate starts, be yourself. Don't try to be someone you're not. Just give the same inane double-talk and long-winded answers you always give. And leave the rest to me."

"I'll do my best," Senator Amory Turniken said. He saw the waiter being dragged away along the marble floor just as Bernie was dropping his mind control whistle back into his pocket. "Amazing," he said again. "Simply amazing."

Bernard Ashland laughed. "Yes, it is amazing what a human being can accomplish once someone else puts his mind to it."

Turniken was sunk, and he knew it. The debate was nearing an end, and he had nothing to show for it. With each of the moderator's questions—the moderator, this evening, being Sally Baggers of Channel 4 NewsAndMoreNews News—Turniken had harbored the hope that this would be where Bernie pointed his whistle thingy at Halloran and got him to spout something monumentally stupid. Instead, the incumbent governor fielded each question with confidence and aplomb, while Turniken, even to his own ears, sounded increasingly like a rambling, incoherent blowhard.

Even before the first question, as the two candidates situated themselves at their respective podiums and Sally Baggers laid down the ground rules—about the debating format, about the need for the audience to remain quiet—Turniken had spotted Bernie in the second row. He had half expected the dark-suited guy to pull out his whistle right then and there and get the ball rolling, but Ashland just sat in his seat, upright and polite, like the rest of the convention hall audience.

And throughout the debate, Turniken kept hoping that now would be the time, now would be the time for Bernie to do his magic. But a glance out to the audience now and then revealed Bernie still sitting there, with his back straight and his hands in his lap, like some nauseatingly obedient third-grader, doing absolutely nothing! The result being that, for Turniken, certainly not for Halloran, the debate was turning into a hopeless fiasco.

By now Turniken had begun to suspect that the entire business at the restaurant had been a huge prank. That the waiter and the injured patron and Bernard Ashland himself had been part of a colossal joke perpetrated by the opposition. After all, what's one broken window in the realm of campaign expenses?

Mind control—how could he have ever fallen for such nonsense?

He saw his dreams dissipate as if he had suddenly been jostled awake—the dream of possessing the title governor, the dream of having his enlarged photograph displayed in schools and government offices throughout the state, the dream of living in a mansion, the dream of riding in a limo emblazoned with the state seal, and on and on.

"And now for closing statements."

Still, he couldn't admit defeat, not at this late stage. He had to be governor, he simply had to be, if only for the free breakfasts, luncheons, and dinners, which would far outnumber the free meals he had ever received as senator.

"Senator Turniken, from a previous coin toss, you were selected to speak first. You have two minutes."

Turniken looked at the camera with what he hoped was sincerity. He had never felt sincere about anything in his life but, since entering politics, he had made a careful study of sincerity, or, at least, had seen it portrayed in the movies. So he believed he was somewhat knowledgeable about what a sincere expression entailed—the angle of the brow, the turn of the lips—and he now drew on his experience to display that look as best as he was able.

"Thank you, Sally," he said. "Thanks, also, to the members of the audience and to those of you watching on television, and thanks to my wife, Penny, and to my two children, Nicki and Marshall. And thanks, as well, to everyone from the great state of—"

And he was off.

He reminded everyone of his solid record as state senator without citing a single achievement. He emphasized the importance of values without listing any. And he stressed the need for fairness and equality without elaborating, figuring the words packed plenty of punch on their own.

In no uncertain terms, he stated that he was a fighter and that he would fight for the people. Not only fight, but fight every step of the way. Not only every step of the way, but each and every day. And not only each and every day, but tooth and nail and with every fiber of his being.

And he promised to make things better. He promised a better

economy, first and foremost. He promised better housing and better schools. He promised better wages, healthcare, roads, bridges, and schools. And when he realized he had mentioned schools twice, he informed everyone that it bore repeating. And then he listed a slew of other things, things that came to him off the top of his head, and he promised to make each and every one of them better.

But most of all, he promised to fight for a better direction.

"You know ..." he said, with his forearm resting on the podium as if this were just you and him chatting, "as senator, I receive emails from the people of this great state all the time voicing their concerns. And I remember one email in particular from a Charlie Jones. He said—and I hope I get the wording right because it was quite eloquent—he said, 'Senator, this may not be my place, but I believe that what this state needs is a better direction.'"

Now, still maintaining that look of cinematic sincerity, Senator Amory Turniken concluded with these words, and just slightly over the two-minute limit:

"And so that's what I intend on fighting for. A better direction. And to that end, I ask you for your support in November. Together we will face the challenges of tomorrow and meet them head on, as we journey toward that better direction. Thank you."

Turniken hadn't the slightest idea what he had said over the past two minutes and change. Lofty-sounding bullshit was his gut feeling, but it might have been even worse. And what on earth had made him dream up a tired old name like Charlie Jones?

There was some applause, perhaps a smattering, certainly nothing raucous. But Turniken couldn't have cared less. All he knew was that he was doomed. And as the lights and camera and moderator focused on his opponent, Turniken leveled daggers with his eyes at the dark-suited stranger in the second row.

But Bernie didn't meet his gaze, apparently. He just sat in his chair staring off into the distance, inert and impotent.

Then, just as Governor Halloran began to speak, Turniken saw Bernie pluck the mind whistle from his shirt pocket and put it to his mouth. Turniken couldn't believe it. He shook his head ever so slightly and thought to himself, "It's a little late for that now, don't you think, Ass Gland?"

"... and, as you may know," the incumbent governor was saying,

"I'm the sort of person who prefers specifics to generalities. And with that in mind, I'd like to lay out three specific goals for my next term, should you choose to elect me. First ..."

An odd look suddenly came over Halloran as if he were struggling with his very own mouth, fighting against the next word it was forming, but it was a fleeting look. It came and went so quickly, Turniken wondered if he'd imagined it. Indeed, he must have, he figured, because Halloran kept speaking as if nothing unusual had happened. "Yes, first, what I'd really like to do first, is take that luscious thing in the blue dress sitting there in the first row and bonk the living daylights out of her."

Turniken detected a slight gasp from the audience and a confused look in Sally Baggers' eyes, but Halloran went on.

"And when I say *bonk*, I mean right now, right here in front of all of you. That means you, Sally, and you in the audience, and all of you from the great state of whatever state this is. Who cares? As long as it's a state of bliss, eh, sugar? Just let me slip off that pretty blue dress of yours, undo your bra, and pull down your panties. How's that sound? Huh?"

A host of murmurs passed through the audience, and Sally raised a hand to quell them. "Everyone ... please. Uh, Governor, is this really necessary?"

"Uhh, yeah, it's necessary!"

Halloran stepped out from behind the podium and approached the front of the stage. He looked down at the woman in the blue dress and proceeded to thrust his hips forward over and over, pulling his elbows back with each thrust. "Oh, baby! Oh, baby, baby, baby! You stay right there, honeybunch! Just open 'em up and lift 'em, and I'll be right down!"

"Governor!"

"What?" Halloran shouted back. "Are my two minutes up already?" He flashed his hand three times. "Fifteen seconds! That's all we need! Just fifteen seconds! Right, baby doll?"

Baggers pounded the table furiously with her fist. "Governor! Stop this right now!"

The sandbags of imposed silence gave way to a torrent of rage and anger from the audience. There was no silencing anyone now, and the moderator didn't even try. Here and there in the crowd, men and women shot to their feet, cupped their hands to their mouths, and screamed up at the stage.

"Someone get him out of here!"

"Halloran, you're a disgrace!"

"Impeach the bastard! This instant!"

Turniken observed the uproar with an inner delight—at least he hoped it was inner—as everyone now got up and rushed to the nearest exits as if someone had shouted fire.

Well, not everyone was leaving. A certain gentleman was still sitting down, calm as can be, with a whistle still to his lips.

"Wait a minute!" Halloran was now yelling. "No one wants to stay and watch? I demand equal time!"

The moderator from Channel 4 NewsAndMoreNews News was beside herself, struggling to regain control. "Shut off the cameras," she said finally. "Just shut off the damn cameras."

Down in the first row, someone else was not moving—the woman in the blue dress slumped over with her head in her hands, heaving sobs. A couple of people now helped her to her feet, spoke to her, consoled her, and together tried to spirit her up the aisle and out the back exit.

"Hey, where you going, you sexy thang?" Halloran cried out. "Come back here! The three of us—you, me, and the wife—in the governor's bed every day for the next four years! Can you picture that?"

Turniken didn't know for sure, but he sensed that the look of sincerity was slowly vacating his face.

Governor Amory Turniken sat back in his big governor's chair behind his big governor's desk and savored his good fortune. He had been savoring his good fortune every day since his swearing in three months ago, and only now did it dawn on him that someday he had better get down to business.

But not today.

He took in the immense desk at a glance and rested his head on it, feeling its cool smoothness against his cheek. He spread his arms wide, reveling in the desk's vast emptiness, and resolved to put something on top of it—a measure, a memo, a fountain pen—within the week.

Just then, the telephone on the nearby table buzzed, and, reluctantly, Turniken sat back up in his big governor's chair and answered it.

It was his personal secretary. "Governor, your appointment's here.

"My what? Who?"

"He says you know him. A—er—Burning Asshand?"

Turniken was certain he had not scheduled any appointments only because he was certain he had not done a stitch of work since getting elected, but no matter. "By all means, send him in," he said.

Turniken suspected he would have to learn his personal secretary's name at some point, but he had four years for that.

The door to his office swung open, and in marched Bernard Ashland in what looked like the same suit he had worn at the restaurant. The governor's office was much, much brighter than that place had been, what with the noonday light pouring in through the huge window behind the desk, but Ashland still looked as if he were standing in the bleak darkness of some deeply buried cellar.

Turniken managed the long trek around the desk, met his visitor mid-carpet, and clapped a big governor's hand on his shoulder.

"Bernie! Bernie! Bernie!" he gushed. "I owe you big time! I see a humongous steak dinner in your future."

Ashland took a step back and, with a tilt of his head, considered his host. "Really? I hand you the highest office in the state on a platter, and all you have for me is a dish of prime rib?"

"Well, there'll be a baked potato, of course. And some sort of vegetable. Salad, if you want it."

Bernie looked as if he was about to say something, but dismissed it. "We'll get back to this in a moment. In the meantime, did you hear the news?"

"No. What happened?"

Without ceremony, Bernie went over to the TV cabinet in the corner and grabbed the remote, aimed it at the screen, and clicked.

"I hope it isn't a flood," Turniken said. "That's all I need to begin my term—a goddamn state of emergency."

One or two seconds of warm-up, and Sally Baggers was up on the screen, her features etched with news-anchor grimness. Behind her: a

196

Channel 4 NewsAndMoreNews News video of the former governor.

Bernie immediately muted the sound and looked over at the current governor. "I'll try to summarize this in the most sensitive way I know how. Halloran just snuffed himself."

Turniken gasped—because that's what people did under these circumstances. "Oh, my God!"

"Couldn't have been more than a half hour ago. Didn't you hear the sirens?"

"No, I was busy."

"Listening to the people is your thing, not to their ambulances, eh?"

Turniken laughed. "Something like that."

"Anyway, he—Halloran—was out on the Capitol Plaza earlier—you probably could have seen him right here from your window—delivering his long overdue mea culpa to members of the press.

"It was quite the sob fest, from what I understand. He explained all about how, right after the debate, he realized what he'd done and immediately went into seclusion. He described how he'd shrunk into himself from shame and embarrassment over these past months, refusing to see or talk to anyone. How he began blaming outside forces for his behavior, as if it had been someone else making those lewd comments during the debate, not him.

"And then at some point, according to him, he realized that he couldn't blame anyone but himself, and that he had to get back out in public and face the music. And, oh, how he apologized. It's right there on the screen if you want to listen to it. A big 'Boohoo, I'm so sorry' to family, to friends, to the girl in the blue dress, to her family, to her friends. To the people of the state for letting them down—and to their family and friends. It must have been very moving.

"He promised to seek treatment and to devote the rest of his life to helping others with similar mental issues. He thanked everyone for coming. And then, inexplicably, he suddenly turned away from the reporters, dashed out toward the busy street, and hurled himself directly into the path of an oncoming truck."

"My God," Turniken said, again.

"They didn't show the aftermath on the news, obviously, but from what I gather, it wouldn't have qualified as a scenic wonder."

Turniken nodded solemnly. "I suppose I'll be expected to say a few words."

"Well, he was your predecessor, after all. And it might be the appropriate thing to do. On the other hand, it's Friday. Maybe by the time Monday rolls around, people will have forgotten all about it, and you'll be off the hook."

"I hope so. I'm not very good at this sort of thing."

"Yes, I know. Plus, it will only distract you from the work you really need to get done."

The word sent a cold chill down Turniken's spine. "Work? What work?"

Bernie reached into his jacket and whisked out a folded sheet of paper—and in doing so sent something else flying out of his pocket, which he caught in time. "Whoops," he said, holding up the cylindrical mind device. "Can't lose this baby."

He unfolded the paper and held it out to Turniken, who shied away from it as if Bernie were handing over a dead fish. "It's a complete list of tasks I expect you to accomplish during your first term."

Turniken gingerly took the list and perused the first couple of paragraphs, skimmed the next three or four, then glanced at the rest. "Bernie, I can't do this," he said and handed the list right back.

Bernie waved it off. "You keep it. I have a copy."

"You expect me to pass a law legalizing hit-and-run? You want me to raise the state's blood-alcohol level for drivers to one-hundred-percent?"

"If it's listed there, that's what I want," Bernie said, smiling. "As I said before, I didn't put you here for a taste of T-bone."

Turniken slapped the sheet with the back of his hand. "Do you even know what you've written? Somewhere here you tell me to ... where is it? Yes, here it is ... 'You, as governor, will issue pardons to every inmate currently being held in the state prison system, making sure to release the most serious offenders first.' I can't do that! I can't release rapists and killers!"

"There you go again with that word 'can't.' Think positive, my friend."

"But why? What do you hope to accomplish?"

Bernard Ashland held out his hands in an "it's obvious" gesture. "Why, complete havoc, of course. Rampant fear, anxiety, panic. The breakdown of social norms and the beginnings of complete anarchy. And, when all is said and done, the eventual victory of evil over good. Isn't that enough?"

"But it's wrong. It's all wrong."

"You got elected by completely ruining an innocent man's future, and now, suddenly, you've got religion?"

"This is different."

"Oh? How so?"

"I might be the lowlife politico you think I am, but if I allowed any of these to become law, I'd be no better than a murderer."

"You say that as if it's a bad thing."

"I won't do it. Any of it. Plain and simple. You're going to have to point that mind control gadget of yours at me and make me do this stuff, because there won't be any other way."

Bernie stood silently for a minute. "You know that's impossible," he admitted. "First of all, as I said back at the restaurant, I can't force you to do something days or weeks from now. I'd have to do it right this minute, and I wouldn't even know how to issue a command. I know nothing about the workings of government—the policies, the procedures—Robert's Rules of Order, for Christ's sake. That's your bailiwick. Plus, even if I were up on the lingo, the device works over such a short range, I'd have to be by your side twenty-four, seven, and I certainly don't intend on baby-sitting you four straight years. I mean, that's why we have a representative democracy, isn't it?"

"You're damn right."

Turniken knew he had won. He was free.

He strode over to his big governor's chair and confidently took a seat. He rolled up the list of demands and tossed it onto his desk, watching it flutter and slide along the surface. He crossed his arms, crossed his legs, and looked over at his visitor. "My offer for a free dinner still holds, Bernie. So what'll it be—a hamburger patty or chicken nuggets?"

"Why that's almost as witty as your Ass Gland remark. But in the end, you will do as I wish."

"The hell you say." Turniken sat back, triumphant, and wondered why he couldn't have performed this decisively at the debates. "On second thought, Bernie, skip the free meal. I want you out of my office right now."

Bernie smiled, walked slowly over to the desk, and rested his fingertips on it, much as he had done at Turniken's booth several months earlier. "Penny. Is that your wife's name?"

"Yes. So?"

"And your kids? Nicki and Mark, right? No, Marshall. That's your boy's name, isn't it?

"What are you getting at?"

"Oh, nothing. Oh, by the way did I tell you the news about Halloran?"

"Yes, you did," Turniken said, "Now please leave."

"I just want to let you know that I didn't really hear about it from Sally Baggers on Channel 4 NewsAndMoreNews News. I happened to be right there on the Capitol Plaza when the whole thing went down."

"Good for you. The door's behind you. You just remember how you came in and reverse the process."

"The reason I mention your family is that they're scheduled to make an appearance at that very same Capitol Plaza in a few weeks, isn't that right? For a rally? Arts in education, or something like that?"

"I wouldn't know."

"That's right. That would require you to consult an agenda. But anyway, trust me. They'll be there. And, in fact, so will I."

"I see where this is going, Bernie. But it won't work. What do you plan to do? Use your whistle to make my wife come on to some smelly, tenured history teacher who should have retired ages ago? Make my kids do leg thrusts on the concrete? And that's supposed to get me to free every prisoner in the state? Please."

"You're close, Governor," Bernie said. "But let's start small, shall we? I was hoping that by the time that rally takes place, you can maybe see to it that every con whose last name begins with the letter L gets sprung. That isn't asking for too much, is it?"

"And why would I do that?"

"Because if you don't, I'm sure I can get either Marshall or little Nicki to play out in traffic the same way I did Halloran."

As the words sank in, Turniken felt all hope drain from him as if he were being bled dry. He looked up at the man in his dark suit and perpetual shadow and said, "You're evil."

Ashland took the compliment with good grace.

"And I sold you my soul to get here, didn't I?"

200

"Oh, Governor, you sold it to me a long time ago—and for a pittance. And now, if you don't mind, I'll bid you a good day. But I'll keep in touch."

Governor Amory Turniken slumped in his big governor's chair under a leaden cloud of doom and despondency. In an instant it became clear to him what his life would be like from here on in. He stared ahead at the discarded list for the longest time and gradually permitted himself a smile. At least he had fulfilled his vow to put something on his desk by week's end.

AGNUS DEI

BY JEZZY WOLFE

October 30th

Randolph pulls the sheet back, revealing the body underneath, skin leather stiff and tinged blue. The man's brown hair is touched with silver at his temples, his hands smartened with the polished manicure of someone who never picked up anything heavier than an ink pen in his lifetime. There are no birthmarks, no scars, except for a small pale line bisecting one eyebrow. His eyes, clouded by the lack of oxygen, are flattening in their orifices. His tongue reminds Randolph of a slug stuck in the cracks of a sidewalk.

Perry Richards met an unexpected end, but at least he went well-groomed. Randolph makes an initial assessment: one massive, fatal heart attack. Also known as The Widow Maker.

"Dr. Brown, here is a copy of the official police report, and the photos." Eric Hayes, assistant to the head coroner, hands Randolph the manila folder.

"Thank you, Eric." He opens the file and scans the yellow page on top, his brow creasing. "Let's get him ready for X-ray, please. I need a moment to look this over."

Eric, brandishing a small camera, nods and begins photographing Mr. Richards' body. Dr. Randolph Brown carries the file to his office to review the police information.

Turns out his initial assessment is very wrong.

October 10th

"May her soul, and the souls of all the faithful departed, through the mercy of God rest in peace. *Amen*."

Flicking drops of tepid water across the mahogany veneer of the casket, Father Moore completes the last rites of the burial and watches, stone-faced, as attendants lower the coffin to its final occupation. He turns to the small sea of black-clothed mourners, sobbing politely at the loss of their dear mom, aunt, and friend. Their sorrow barely touches him. He hardly knew Delores.

Still, he forces empathy as her friends and family depart the graveside service. A few stop to inquire if he'll be attending the following wake. He smiles thinly, assuring them all that he will be along shortly, and watches as they trudge weary-footed to the parked sedans along the cemetery drive—a procession of wheeled sarcophaguses waiting to escort them to their next destination.

He doesn't notice him, not at first. He's watching the gravediggers heap clumsy mounds of crumbling earth on top of Delores's well-appointed casket. An insistent cough alerts him to the bespectacled man in the generic tan trench coat and black hat standing behind the rows of folding chairs.

"Father Moore?" His voice is crisp, unaffected by the afternoon's chill. Puffs of condensation punctuate his words.

The gravediggers, busy with their shovels, never look up.

October 30th

In his office, Randolph reviews the contents of Perry Richards' file. A diagram demonstrates the position of Perry's body when he was found. An order for the toxicology screen has been included. He gives the papers a cursory glance before settling on the official report, which includes notes from the questioning of the deceased's wife.

On Monday afternoon at 4:27 p.m., Mrs. Diane Richards found her husband unresponsive and slumped over his desk. Authorities arrived at the scene to find a tearful, albeit calm, wife and a very dead husband. They searched the office for any signs of struggles, attacks, or suspicious behavior, but encountered nothing out of the usual.

Being the one to find him, Diane was taken in and questioned as a formality. She called their attorney prior to the interview with the investigators, which raised dubious questions about her innocence. But no evidence was found in the home to contradict the information she gave the police.

At a quarter to one, Diane left Perry Richards in his home office so she could go shopping. New drapes, she explained. And a fresh French manicure, which she proudly displayed to the interrogators. When she returned almost four hours later, he sat dead in his chair. She called 911, and they instructed her not to move him. There were no obvious signs of pain or injuries. He didn't have preexisting conditions that might've precipitated a sudden death. But she did mention his complaint about a throat irritation that started at church the day before. She said he refused to eat anything, and swallowing food became difficult. So instead, he drank glass after glass of water. He insisted it felt like something was lodged in his throat, but did not think he needed to visit his doctor.

Dr. Randolph Brown closes the file, sitting back in his chair. No evidence of suspicious chemicals in the house. Poison hasn't been ruled out, but the events don't point to it, either. Samples of spittle around his mouth were taken at the house, but the tox screens haven't returned. An esophageal laceration might cause discomfort ... enough discomfort to put Perry off his food, even.

But that wouldn't kill a man.

A soft knock at the door startles him. Eric steps in halfway, silhouetted by the lights in the hall. His posture is too stiff, his scrubs too baggy for his thin frame. He looks awkward and uncomfortable right now. Much more than usual.

"I'm sorry to disturb you, Dr. Brown. But there's something you need to see ..."

October 12th

The air is too cold for October.

Father Moore pulls his jacket tighter across his shoulders and waits for the street vendor to hand him the cup of black coffee he orders daily. Picking up the day's newspaper and scanning the headlines, his mouth twists. It's a joke so bad, even he has to laugh.

These are dark times, indeed.

As a vessel, he can only offer forgiveness and love. His parishioners seek him out for absolution and guidance, whispering their vile secrets from the shadows of an archaic confessional booth planted in the church's vestibule. He won't allow them in his office as his contemporaries often do, where their indiscretions stain the air like nicotine. Administering penances from a textbook rubric, he provides the community their peace of mind ... but at the cost of his. No amount of *Hail Marys* can instill sincere conviction into the hearts of modern abominations. True change will only follow cataclysm.

He finishes his coffee and heads back to the church. Eight a.m., and his appointment is waiting by the rectory gates. "Good morning, Father Moore," says the man in the black hat.

October 30th

Large films clipped to illuminator panels reveal the immaculate skeleton of a fifty-four-year-old male in perfect health. No injuries, either past or present, appear on the screens. While the films show no obvious evidence of a stroke or heart attack, the next step of the autopsy will give them a better idea of what possible event concluded Perry Richards' life.

"We need to get started. Call the investigator," Randolph says, drawing each syllable out slowly, still staring at the films, his brow furrowed. He spots something unusual, a vague abnormality. It is so slight, he could well be imagining it. "Wait a second, Eric ..."

"Yes, Doctor?"

"Do you see that?" He points at a light cloud in the film.

Eric steps close to the screen, investigating the area beyond Randolph's finger.

Randolph feels pinpricks race up his arms and down his back. His intuition is kicking in. He always experiences chills right before—

"Check the ETA on the toxicology screen, please."

October 14th

Elections loom less than a month off, the fight for the 13th Congressional District heating the region faster than a waking volcano. The state, traditionally blood-red, turned a putrid shade of purple over the past term ... the color of rancid meat. Father Moore reads his evening news with a glass of scotch, but the sharp sting in his throat does little to calm the trepidation tying his gut in violent knots. He barely recognizes the world around him now. American society is flailing in a pool of hedonism and iniquity. Surely they will sink under waves of depravity so deep, they'll have to rename their country Gomorrah.

He pours another scotch and takes it to his office. The light from a small lamp casts the room in shadows as it spotlights the desk blotter's sole occupant. Settling in his office chair, he drinks the scotch in ambitious gulps. Resolve bolstered, he picks up the unmarked legal-sized envelope, turning it slowly in his hands.

I should throw this in the fire.

He doesn't. He's not going to. He just spent two days trying to convince himself that he is above the vile proposition offered to him. If he didn't need the money so badly, he would've flatly refused the offer. But recent circumstances have thrust him into a predicament that prayer has not absolved.

Recently, the diocese paid him a visit to discuss closing his parish and moving him elsewhere. The parish has struggled financially for years. The congregation that fills the benches every week are tight-fisted heathens who demand their faith with a discount. Seems the parish in the next county was more stable, and could use another lay minister. The long and the short—he needs money if he wants to keep his church.

Almost thirty years serving these people, gently prodding them toward salvation ... and they would let me be dismissed to work as a lowly assistant elsewhere. Where is the just reward in that?

The envelope contains only a single photograph. A glossy 8x10 black and white. The man in the photo is standing behind a podium, smiling at his audience. He wears a tailored suit and a generous smile. He is groomed to be magazine ready.

According to his recent caller ... a gentleman who only identified himself as Mr. Brimm ... the man is a parishioner in Father Moore's church. He doesn't remember seeing him at any of the services, but his face *does* seem familiar. He studies the photograph, the wide, oily smile dissecting a chiseled face, the classy suit that undoubtedly sported an Armani label. Bitter bubbles of bile rise in his throat. *Of course he smiles. He wears the church's money.*

Budget cutbacks were emasculating. The crew that maintains the church grounds has been downsized to one elderly man who cuts the grass twice a month. The ladies who keep the inside of the church pristine shrunk from five to two. The toiletries in the vestibule bathrooms are cheap bulk knock-offs purchased from a restaurant outlet supplier.

And the social services provided to the community disappeared completely. No food pantry. No homeless outreach. The only counseling he can afford to offer is to the young couples that want to get married in the church. Not that he charges for the counseling ... he just doesn't have the time now. He's too busy doing the menial chores he cannot pay others to do for him.

In addition to a dangerous drop in tithes, the other avenues of church income have also dwindled. Reserving the church for a wedding is now so cost prohibitive, wedding requests have dropped considerably. Organized fundraisers stopped a few years ago. Part of it resulted from the recession, of course. But much of it is simply the growing absence of God in the lives of his congregation.

Do I no longer inspire my flock to live holy? Are the words failing to reach them? Perhaps it is better I step down and let holier vessels lead the way?

This sudden lack of confidence angers him. At himself, sure, but mostly at the parishioners. They have put him in this position.

He has put him in this position.

Whoever this mark may be, he is, undoubtedly, a wicked soul. That someone else would plaintively seek for the destruction of one so vile ... certainly the world will not mourn such a decrepit person.

Maybe this is the answer to his prayers. Mr. Brimm's parting words resonate in his head.

"Consider this a mission of mercy, if it helps you sleep. You do not yet know the righteousness you are doing." He put on his hat. "But you will."

God placed me on this road. He will provide the transportation.

Father Moore picks up the telephone.

October 15th

He plans the services accordingly, executing each as per the usual. He offers Mass four nights a week, as well as two services on Sundays, but as he searches the faces of his flock, he does not spot his man among the throngs. *Perhaps Brimm is mistaken ... maybe this man is not a parishioner.*

He tries at first to identify the familiar stranger, without success. It must be God's plan that it remains a mystery. Would he still be able to follow through if he knew who he was after? He put the questions of the man's identity out of his mind ... ultimately, this is a sacramental lamb. His death will save them all. He no longer exists in Father Moore's mind as an innocent member of his congregation. It is him, or everyone else will suffer. He is a modern day Abraham preparing to sacrifice his son.

The Father's conscience only balks at the modus operandi. At first, the questions of "how" and "when" kept him awake at night. He refused to acquire a firearm. Any manner of poison would be easily detected and immediately presentable. A public crucifixion would be poetic, but hardly feasible.

Too bad, as he favors that method most.

He needs a miracle. An event so perfectly sculpted, not one who witnesses it will ever dare question why it happened. Something that could even be used to bring his faithful back into the fold. Something beautiful and reverent ... if death could ever be reverent.

By the following morning his sister has come to visit the parish, with his two nieces in tow. She comes to help with cleaning and preparation for the grand Liturgy of the Eucharist that he holds on the last Sunday of the month. Parishioners who do not attend weekly Mass services rarely ever miss the large once-a-month ceremony, complete with all the bells and whistles he usually leaves out. Another cutback due to poor finances. *Soon this will be a bad memory ... nothing more.*

He attempts to focus on his work, despite the chaos that disorders the rectory as the children are settled in for their visit. A cacophony erupts the silence of his office. The squeals of excited little girls interrupts his brevity as they rush to his desk to show him the trinket toys his secretary gave them when they arrived. Fashion dolls, plastic beaded necklaces, sopping wet sponges shaped like various zoo creatures the size of their fists ... he chuckles and teases, feigning interest for their benefit. One string of beads breaks and scatters across the floor, and a doll loses her head, casualties of their childish exuberance.

He engages them for a while, before their mom comes to his rescue. She chides the lively girls and apologizes as she shuffles them from the room, leaving a trail of water droplets in their wake. He smiles, shakes his head.

It is late at night and he is in bed when the answer comes. Divine intervention, some might say. In the dark of his room, he laughs out loud, his chest constricted with joy, thanking God for his newfound wisdom.

Every good gift is from above ...

October 18th

Father Moore preaches creationism, but harbors a secret fascination in science. In fact, one of his oldest friends is a professor at the state university. At first, he worried the professor would refuse his unusual request, but like yet another gift from God, he instinctively knew what spin to put on it.

"So you plan to sell these to the children?"

"It's perfect. Of course, their parents will be happy to buy these ... the little ones love them. Both simple and godly. And I can use the profits to bolster the church's coffers."

Professor Mark Taylor appears unconvinced.

"I got the idea from my nieces, truth be told," Father Moore continues. "Out of the mouth of babes."

"I know things have been rough for a while. That parish means everything to you, I get that." He sighs, rubbing his hand across his eyes. "Tell you what ... let me work up a prototype. Give me a few days. Then you can test it for yourself to see if it is what you had in mind."

"Can you give me two?"

"Uh, sure. I guess two are just as easy as one."

Father Moore shakes his friend's hand a bit too enthusiastically. "You've no idea the good you're about to do ... but you will."

Four days later, Professor Taylor delivers. The prototype works perfectly. Father Moore begins his planning. The end of the month approaches.

It is time.

October 30th

The toxicology report indicates Perry Richards was not an avid pill popper, unless those pills were vitamins and fish oil. There's no alcohol in his system, no traces of prescription medications. He might be the healthiest dead man Randolph has ever examined. Which makes death by stroke or heart attack less likely. Blood work shows the chemistry of someone who took his doctor's advice to heart.

More important, there are no traces of foreign substances. Arsenic, botulinum, cyanide, dimethyl mercury ... Randolph considers the possibility of a more antiquarian method. Perhaps aconite, which is typically untraceable, but causes arrhythmia and asphyxiation.

Yes. Definitely a possibility.

211

He studies the report intensely, looking for the smoking gun. The usual suspects are nowhere to be found. He starts pondering the question of an allergic reaction to something previously undetected.

A piercing throb above his brows interrupts his hypothesis, demanding his attention. Pressing his fingers deep into the corners of his eyes, he groans. He could use some hydrocodone.

Returning his attention to the toxicology screen, his bleary vision readjusts to the smeared typeface on the page, courtesy of an archaic fax machine.

Wait a minute ...

And there it is. Out of place, though not a usual red flag. An unassuming brown spider lurking on a bookshelf.

Hydrogel.

October 28th

Ten a.m., Sunday Mass.

The congregation mumbles The Lord's Prayer and observes in faux reverence as Father Moore recites the Agnus Dei, holding a round crisp above his head. He halves it, and then halves those pieces, repeating the steps until he has eight wedges in his hands. Distributing them among eight chalices, he says, "Lamb of God, you take away the sins of the world: grant us peace." He raises a chalice, and brings it to his lips.

After issuing communion to his attendants, the congregation lines up to receive the Eucharist. They approach him solemnly, eyes appropriately supplicant. Holding skyward a small communion wafer, he softly says to each person, "The Body of Christ." As they whisper their *amens*, he places the host on their tongues. The wafers dissolve just enough on contact that they can be swallowed without chewing. The supplicant then shuffles to the left where an assistant offers them a chalice of watered down wine. As parishioners receive the communion, they return to their seats to reflect and pray.

Administering Holy Communion to so many people dulls his reflexes, and his motions and words quickly become robotic. The faces are blurring together before him as he sets paper-thin, white disks on

212

fat, impatient tongues. On days such as this, the Lord's Work is tedious, and unsanitary. He resists rolling his eyes at some of the lesser-refined recipients who still manage to drop their hosts on the floor, or genuflect incorrectly as they approach. One lady drools on his sleeve. *Clumsy cows,* he scoffs.

He glances up, gauging the approximate number of people still in line to receive, when his eyes collide with a familiar face. Three people back. His hands remain steady, but his palms begin to sweat. His mark is waiting to receive.

It is time.

October 30th

"I'm not sure I understand, doctor." Eric hands the report back to Dr. Brown. "Hydrogel? He didn't have so much as a paper cut on him, and outside of a bandage, I don't see why that would come up in a tox screen."

Pointing again to the X-ray image, Dr. Brown says, "We need to see what *that* is all about."

October 28th

"Father?"

He stands before Father Moore, his suit impeccable, shoes polished to a mirror's sheen, hair perfectly coiffed ... probably with designer mousse. His aftershave overpowers the holy incense that fragrances the sanctuary. Even his only flaw—that slight scar cutting through his eyebrow—is pretentious. He has the whitest teeth Father Moore has ever seen, and he's getting an eyeful of those artificially brightened pearly whites. His heart pounds louder than the choir singing *"Ave Verum Corpus"* at his back.

"Father?" The mark seeks his attention, genuflects correctly—of course he does—and opens his mouth to receive the host.

Father Moore lifts a host from the silver bowl, before remembering his mission. With a jerk of his wrist, too subtle to be noticed by the man with eyes fixed skyward, he pushes the wafers aside and plucks up the one sitting on the very bottom of the bowl. It is slightly sticky to the touch, just barely shinier than the rest of the bowl's contents. He holds the wafer up and repeats, "The Body of Christ," then places it on the man's tongue.

The man swallows, a little slower than his counterparts, and replies, "Amen." Clearing his throat, he follows the procession of people to an assistant waiting with a wine chalice.

Father Moore forces his attention back to the task at hand, portioning out hosts until the communion line has passed through and all the patrons are back in their seats.

During prayer, he searches the crowd, but he has no idea where his mark is seated. He hears a soft cough from the left of the sanctuary. The congregation rises as he begins the concluding rite.

"The Lord be with you."

Cough, cough

In unison, the congregation replies, "And also with you."

Cough, cough, cough, cough

"May almighty God bless you ... The Father, and the Son—"

Cough, cough, cough

"And the Holy Spirit."

He sees him then, slipping out of a pew and quickly heading down the aisle toward the vestibule. A blonde woman attired in a conservative suit follows him out. He watches the door close behind them as the congregation ends the service with "Amen."

As parishioners file out of the doors, he can hear faint coughing drifting in from the outer hall.

October 30th

Dr. Brown hovers over the prostrate form of Perry Richards, while Eric takes notes. A small voice recorder placed at the corpse's head is running as Randolph rattles off the subject's name, age, weight, and other pertinent information. Officer Thomas North, the crime scene investigator, has joined them to take his own notes. This is standard procedure during a criminal investigation, everything done by the book. So even though Randolph knows where the answers he seeks will be found, he prepares to examine Mr. Richards' chest, abdomen, and head. Being the protocol for the industry-preferred *Virchow* method that most pathologists use, Randolph adheres to it closely.

He studies the face through a magnifying lens, and lifts each eyelid back. "Presence of *cyanosis* on the skin. *Petechiae* in both eyes." He motions Officer North to his side so he can see. "Cyanosis is the purple you see in his skin. And petechiae is hemorrhaging that appears in the eyes commonly due to suffocation. See those red specks?" He lifts the eyelids again to show the officer.

"So we are looking at a probable homicide by strangulation?" Officer North is furiously writing as Dr. Brown continues his examination.

"No bruises on the neck. X-rays did not reveal a broken hyoid bone. So far my guess *is* asphyxiation, but probably not by strangulation. Not enough physical evidence to support that."

Brandishing a scalpel, Randolph begins an incision at the right shoulder and pulls it toward the sternum, then makes another cut from the left shoulder in. He runs the blade down from the incision juncture to the pubic area. An additional assistant steps in to help him open the large, Y-shaped incision to investigate the chest cavity and organs. Each organ is removed carefully and weighed. Eric records the stats as Randolph relays them. As he'd already surmised, all are in perfect condition.

Richards could have lived to one hundred.

After removing the skull cap with an oscillating saw, Dr. Brown repeats the process of weighing, measuring, and examining the brain. Once again, a flawless organ. Eric and Officer North continue note taking as Randolph makes another incision along the jawbone. Very carefully, he traces the curve with his knife, extending it from ear to ear. The skin is carefully pulled back to reveal the musculature of the neck.

His gloved fingers run the length of the throat. *Yes. Right there.* He uses a smaller scalpel to make a shallow, vertical incision. As the cut separates, he slides three fingers into the cavity that should have been empty ... but isn't. He pulls the foreign body free.

Eric curses. The officer gasps.

Randolph is too shocked to speak.

October 29th

The soft drone of the television accompanies Father Moore's dinner. Alone in his small kitchen, he savors the stew that simmered in a crock pot for most of the afternoon. It tastes incredible. Another blessing from God. He is surprisingly calm, considering his machinations the previous morning. But there is no fear. No concern. He has done the Lord's work. Soon his parish will be saved.

He eschews the dire headlines of the evening paper for a lighthearted situational sitcom on television. He laughs like it's the first time. His spirits are so high, he indulges in a second bowl of dinner.

The program on the television is interrupted by a breaking news bulletin. He turns up the volume when the face of his mark appears on the screen.

"Republican Perry Richards was found dead at 4:37 this afternoon. He was discovered by his wife in their home. Authorities have not released a cause of death, but it is being ruled as suspicious. Richards was running for state representative of the thirteenth district against Democrat Aaron Grant, and with elections just weeks away, it is unclear at this time who will run on the Republican ticket in Richards' place. We will bring you more details as they are given to us."

Father Moore's stomach lurches as the stew threatens to make a comeback. He switches off the television and reaches for the bottle of scotch. He'd been instructed not to ask questions, and he didn't. The money was worth more than his curiosity. He didn't consider that the mark might be someone important.

But why not? Who offers that much money for the head of an average nobody, really? A politician, better yet, a *conservative* politician ... he never would have agreed, had he known. He told himself the man must be inherently evil. A thief stealing from helpless women and children. A pedophile. A rapist. An investment banker, maybe.

And a member of his parish. He should be flattered that such a public figure graced his services. But he disconnected from his flock years ago when they stopped providing. Was this God's punishment on him for being so bitter and detached?

He finishes the bottle quickly and heads for his bedroom. He has a hell of a lot of Hail Marys to say tonight.

Oh Lord, have mercy.

October 30th

"Jesus Christ!"

Randolph almost laughed at Eric's exclamation, despite the chill that snaked over him. "Yes. You are absolutely correct."

The mysterious intruder has to be carefully cleaned, it is covered in blood, saliva, and bile. A closer evaluation reveals that Richards vomited while he suffocated—normal during asphyxiation—but with the item lodged in his throat, the bile was trapped. It stained the bottom of the object, soaking into the porous foam.

But that is what sponges are supposed to do.

Eric whispers, "What is that thing?"

"It's ... *Jesus.*"

Randolph squeezes the figurine gently around the middle, and the head and feet bulge around his fist. It is five inches tall and roughly two and a half inches around.

And it *is* Jesus. Hands open at his sides. Broad smile on the bearded face. Halo on his head, sandals on his feet. Randolph could even make out dimples in the palms of his hands to signify nail holes. A miniature statue of Jesus Christ, sculpted in white rubbery foam.

"I don't understand," Eric says. "Why would anyone swallow a sponge?"

October 30th

His morning coffee scalds his tongue, numbing his taste buds. No matter. His appetite is gone anyway. He meets with his secretary, the parish treasurer, and oversees the choir rehearsal, throwing himself at his priestly duties in an effort to forget the dark shadow that looms behind him.

The news that morning offers no new developments, except to announce that Richards' body was now at the county coroner's office. He is anxious, trapped in a surreal daydream. He needs to separate himself from the pall of death trailing him. He smiles at the old ladies that trail in to light candles and say their prayers. Old-school Catholics. Just the distraction he needs.

He listens to a grandmother's lament over her wayward grandson, who recently joined band of punk rockers and now worships Satan. He pats her shoulder and assures her that her grandson most likely is just going through a phase, and probably really doesn't worship Satan at all. The black fingernails are a fashion statement, not evidence of a rotting soul. She smiles at the priest like he is the Savior. He starts to feel more relaxed.

A movement in his peripheral distracts him. A man in the vestibule is shuffling past the sanctuary doors. His drab coat droops off his hunched shoulders as he uses a cane to hobble in the direction of the confessional booth. After giving grandma another word of encouragement, Father Moore excuses himself.

The door to the confessional has just latched shut, so Father Moore steps into his cubby and slides open the partition. The screen obscures the occupant's profile, but he can just make out a head of gray unruly hair.

"Do you seek to confess, my son?"

The response is soft. Muffled. Father Moore cannot hear anything more than a murmur. He leans closer to the screen.

"I'm terribly sorry. I'm afraid I can't understand what you are saying. Would you mind repeating that for me?"

"I said, thank you." The voice is raspy, and doesn't sound particularly grateful.

"Thank you?"

A sudden zing, followed by a fiery punch to his abdomen, startles Father Moore. He is thrown against the side of the booth, disorientated. A small hole under the partition screen is smoking. He reaches for it, but his arm is suddenly too heavy to move from his side. He runs hot, feverish, but then abruptly feels cold. Weakly, he presses his side and feels hot, sticky wetness soaking through his robes. His hand comes away covered in copper-scented wine. Fresh, warm blood is pooling in his lap.

The booth fades to black.

October 30th

"He didn't swallow this on purpose. The police report indicates the wife mentioned he'd been feeling ill at church the day before."

"Guilty conscience?" Eric snickers.

"It would be funny, under other circumstances," Randolph says. "He's Catholic, right?"

Officer North replies, "Yes. I believe his wife said they are members of Holy Trinity."

"Who is the priest?"

"Father Peter Moore." Officer North is reviewing the reports. "Yesterday was communion, in fact."

Randolph's mind races, staring at the squishy Jesus in his hand. "Do you know what this is?"

"It's Jesus," Eric says.

"Not who. *What.*" Randolph's eyes mirror his excitement, but his mouth is a grim line. "This is an ultra-absorbent polymer foam. Same material as those funny toy dinosaurs that grow from eggs. You submerge them in water, and a day later, the egg is a Tyrannosaurus Rex the size of your hand. It is a novelty toy."

"I don't think you should be saying that Jesus Christ is a novelty toy, Doctor ..."

"I bet this Jesus didn't look like Jesus originally. Look at the color. Ivory white. You know what else is this color, don't you?"

Eric clears his throat, shifting uneasily. "Truth be told, I'm not much of a churchgoer."

Officer North, on the other hand, is. "Communion wafers."

The three men stare in horror at the toy Jesus in Randolph's hand.

"I think I'm going to visit Father Moore," Officer North says. "Maybe he has a sin of his own to confess."

219

Father Moore is discovered by his secretary. The police arrived to question him concerning Mr. Richards' death, but his secretary doesn't understand why it would be the Father's fault if a man chokes on a communion wafer. Seems to her, God metes out His own judgment on unrepentants who partake lightly in Holy Communion with sin on their souls.

After all, the Body of Christ is nothing to toy around with.

LABYRINTH

BY JAMES S. DORR

It was the Frenchwoman, Ariane, who taught him to know ghosts. He had been less than a week on Crete, still getting to know his way around the streets of Iraklion, when he came across a taverna off Odos 1866 that looked less a tourist trap than most, and decided to go in.

Even though it was early for dinner, the place was crowded. He looked around, blinking his eyes to adjust to the dimness, and finally spotted an empty chair.

"You mind if I join you?" he asked the woman who sat across from it drinking wine.

She looked up and smiled, then put her finger to her lips.

"Shhh," she said, but at the same time gestured for him to sit down. She smiled again, blonde, with long braided hair, wearing a summer dress, possibly, like him, a college student on summer vacation. Then, after a moment, she took another sip of her wine.

"You are an American?" she asked, her voice faintly accented.

"Yes," he said. "My name's Carey." She raised an eyebrow at that and he added, "My father was English. English-Welsh really, although he never lived in England. In fact, he grew up on the island here."

"Ah," she said. "Then you are visiting on his account?"

"Well, sort of," he said. He really wasn't, he wanted to tell himself, but his mother had insisted that, while he was here, he look up the

221

places his father had told about. "He was an aeronautical engineer," he said, "until he retired. He married late, after he came to the United States, so"—he smiled—"in spite of my British sounding first name, I'm American, born and bred."

"Ah," she said again. "Have you eaten yet? You must try the kakavia—the seafood chowder—it's the house specialty. They make it here with baby octopus."

"*Really?*" he asked. He started laughing.

"Really," she said. She started to laugh too. "I know it sounds awful, even for someone who grew up in France, but it *is* quite good." She called the waiter and ordered for both of them, then introduced herself while they waited. "But you," she added, "you say your family lived in Crete. Did your grandfather die here?"

Carey nodded. "He was with British Intelligence in World War II, stationed on Crete when the Germans invaded. My grandmother and my father were with him."

"Have you seen his ghost yet?"

"What?" he said. He opened his mouth again, not knowing quite what else to say, when their chowder arrived in two huge, steaming bowls. Glad to be off the hook for the moment, he stared down at the thick, rich liquid set before him, stirring it tentatively with his spoon. He saw the octopus—it was whole! Its tentacles radiated outward.

Ariane laughed. "It's thick enough to use a knife and fork," she said. "It's really more like a stew than a soup."

He nodded. He followed her lead and sawed off a small piece of tentacle. Cooked in a wine and tomato broth, with celery and onions, it really *was* good, he found. Then, when the waiter came back with a bottle, he filled both their glasses.

They ate in silence, drinking the wine, he gazing again from time to time at the bowl's swirling liquid, the tentacles spiraling almost hypnotically—almost beautifully—toward the bowl's center. And then he would look at her, beautiful too. Her hair swirling, also, around her face where her thick braid had loosened.

She ordered another bottle of wine later, when they had finished. "Have you seen the ruin yet?" she asked.

"No," he said. "I've seen the model at the museum, but ..."

"Shhh," she said suddenly, putting her finger to her lips the way she had before. He listened with her, thinking he heard what sounded like gunshots, far in the distance.

"Earlier," she whispered, "I asked you about seeing ghosts. Oh, I saw they way you looked at me. But Crete *is* haunted. Do you know its history?"

"You mean like the Greek myths?"

She frowned when he said that. "Not Greek myths. *Cretan* myths. Yes, those too, but I mean more recent. The street outside, for instance, named for the 1866 Revolution against the Turks. And then the reprisals that followed after. Other streets, like Martyron 25 Avgoustou, named for the people massacred that day in 1898, also by the Turks. And, before them, there were the Venetians. Before that, the Saracens."

Carey nodded. "Before them, the Romans. Yes," he said. "But afterward too, with Crete a part of Greece, there were the Germans."

"And now," Ariane said, "there are those who see Greek rule as an occupation too. But the thing is, throughout her history, Crete has known bloodshed. So much blood that the land is soaked with it. You heard the gunshots?"

Carey nodded.

"You hear them at night, if you know how to listen. Those who die stay here—as well as the ones who follow after. Perhaps *those* were Germans."

Carey laughed. He felt uncomfortable. "Maybe," he said. "But also they might have just been a taxicab backfiring. I've never seen a city with cars so dilapidated."

To his relief, she started to laugh too. "Maybe," she said. "One doesn't know, does one? But anyway, you say you haven't been to Knossos. Maybe tomorrow we could take the bus there."

Carey didn't see ghosts that night, but he dreamed of his grandfather. His father's stories, about the German paratroopers drifting down like a whirlwind of feathers. Like flakes of snow. Even his father, a ten-year-old boy then, armed with a rifle, trying to stop them. But there were too many.

His mother had insisted he come here, in part a reward for finishing college and agreeing to graduate school, to follow in his father's footsteps. To be an engineer. But now he wondered, now that he'd come here. The sun, the beaches, the baking heat seemed to turn his thoughts inward.

What was it *he* wanted?

And now, too, Ariane, dressed in jeans and a front-tied blouse when he met her at the taverna that morning. As he approached, he saw she was arguing, first with a young man, blond-headed, tall and thin, who looked much like her—*her boyfriend?* he wondered—then with the owner of the taverna. From the first she had taken a package, the second a basket.

"Hello," he shouted. The blond had already left.

"Hello," she called back. "I was just getting some things for our lunch. Do you want the wine *aretsino*—without resin, like we had it last night—or do you want to drink as the Cretans do?"

Carey shrugged. "I'll leave the choice to you."

Ariane nodded. "*Demestica* then," she said. "You'll be surprised, Carey. It's very good here." She paid for it and added it to her basket. "And now for the bus. The ruin is only five kilometers—three miles—from here, but it's through a working class section of town."

Carey nodded. He saw what she meant as they walked to the waterfront, then rode the bus out on a highway lined with factories, both within and outside the city. The ugliness passed, though, as they approached the site, dominating the hill it was built on.

"Jesus," he whispered as they got off the bus. Tiers of partially reconstructed ruins rose above them, layer on layer. They went through the main gate to the site proper, then up the ramped path to the palace's West Court.

"*Much* older than Jesus," she whispered back. "Most of what's here dates back to at least 1700 B.C.—what's called the New Palace—but it, in turn, was built on the foundations of the Old Palace. We'll see parts of that too. But even before that"—she gestured with her head to the left, to three circular pits in the courtyard below them—"they found even more ancient ruins at the bottoms of those cisterns."

"Jesus," he said again. Then he laughed. "Perhaps I should say Zeus?"

"Closer," she said. "He's buried, you know, on the mountain peak south of here. Mount Iouktas. The palace was built on this hill, in fact, so that the mountain would overlook it. But here is where my namesake grew up, Ariadne. The one who gave the thread to Theseus to find his way out of the Minotaur's labyrinth. You know the legend—how he and the other youths from Athens were going to be sacrificed, except Ariadne saw him when they arrived and she fell in love with him?"

"I can believe it," Carey said. By now they had entered through the West Porch and threaded their own way down the Corridor of the Procession, turning left to the South Propylaeum, then left again up the twelve stone steps to the upper level marked on the map Ariane had brought as the Piano Nobile. "That blond man I saw you with this morning, though. At the taverna. Is he *your* Theseus?"

Ariane laughed. She kissed him, suddenly, on the lips. "You mean my *lover?*"

Carey blushed. "I ... uh ... I guess it's none of my business. I ..."

Ariane laughed again. "His name is Georges. And he's my brother. We have a villa outside of Amnissos—you know, where the beach is. And anyway this Ariadne had many lovers. One of the legends says she even seduced Daedelus, the one who built the labyrinth—not *this* palace, but the first one, even older than the ruins beneath the pits we saw—even though he was a very old man. He gave her the thread that she then gave to Theseus, and, when the king found out, he got so angry he threw Daedelus and his son, Icarus, into the labyrinth and had it sealed up."

Carey nodded. "I think I remember. That's when Daedelus built wings so they could escape too?"

"Yes," she said. "Out of feathers and wax, except Icarus died flying too near the sun. But Ariadne didn't have a good time of it either, because the first chance Theseus got, he dumped her on the island of Naxos."

Carey laughed too now. "Talk about 'labyrinthian' stories. Plots within plots—and everyone loses. And so—remember what you said last night? Are *their* ghosts in this palace?"

"Shhh," Ariane said. "Can't you *feel* them? Look." She took him by the hand and led him down a long, narrow corridor, then to the right to a descending staircase. "Underneath us, just to our left, is what the restorers think was the throne room. And ahead of us, the Central Courtyard. Squint your eyes—like this."

He looked down the stairs to a huge, open area, gleaming beneath the late morning sun. Squinting his eyes he thought he saw ... figures? Drifting in long, stiff robes, the women with their breasts bared and their hair curled in tight rolls. He blinked. He saw—tourists. A small knot of people he recognized now from the ride on the bus.

"You did for a moment, didn't you see them?" Ariane said. "My namesake—she was a princess, you know. Her handmaids around her?"

"I ..." Carey laughed again. He *had* seen them. Or thought he had seen them. A trick of the light ...

Ariane kissed him, this time on the cheek. "Come on," she said, leading him down the staircase. "I think they're afraid of you. Anyway they're avoiding us now. And, in the meantime"—she found a shaded spot in the courtyard and put her basket down, showing him, inside, bread and cheese and cold, steamed mussels, stuffed with rice pilaf. She took out the wine bottle, wrapped in a damp cloth to keep it cool, and handed it to him along with two glasses.

"And in the meantime," he finished for her, "this exploring of the past makes a person hungry."

He slept with her that night, playing Theseus to her Ariadne. Or was it Daedelus? He wasn't old, though, he thought when he woke up in his hotel room with her beside him, her hair in swirled tangles across both their pillows.

He thought of the afternoon after their picnic. Crossing the Courtyard to the Grand Staircase, then descending flight after flight to the Hall of Colonnades, deep in the hillside, the King's and Queen's Quarters, the Queen's Bath, the Shrine of the Double Axes, the mazes of workshops. Finally they had gone out through the north, crossing the Theatral Area to the northwest, then back to the east to explore other ruins that surrounded the palace. It was there, to the east, that they found a shaded grove of trees to finish their picnic.

That was when she had brought out the packet that Georges had given her at the taverna. She handed him a hand-rolled cigarette.

226

"Only a little," she said when she lit it, then lit her own. "Georges and I had a fight about this—the penalties for having hashish can be very strict—but I said we could trust you. I hope I was right, Carey."

"Yes," he said. He breathed in the harsh smoke. "That is, I mean I don't use this stuff much. But, back in college ..."

"I know," she said. She kissed him—the sweetest kiss he could remember ever receiving. "But only a little bit for now. It's high quality."

"And will we see ghosts?" He started to giggle.

"Perhaps," she said. "But there really *are* ghosts here. And ghosts within us, too. We're part of the past, you know, whether we wish it to be so or not."

"The past within us." He giggled again and kissed her back, then helped her clean up and put their picnic things back in her basket.

And then they'd ridden the bus together, not yet lovers, she planning to transfer to another bus back to Amnissos, when they heard gunshots. The driver had hit the brakes—these weren't ghost gunshots—and started cursing.

"What the hell?" Carey said.

Ariane clutched his arm. "The Free Crete Movement," she whispered. "Last night, remember, I cautioned you to distinguish between Cretan myths and Greek ones? Because who knows who might have been listening. And then I said there are some who see being part of Greece as a foreign occupation as well? These are mostly idealists—intellectuals who only talk about revolution. But there are others, young, angry people. And with the heat we're having this summer ..."

He put his arm gently around her as the bus finally continued its way. "It's okay, Ariane," he murmured, not knowing what else to tell her.

"I-I'm frightened," she said. "Those shots last night. I thought they were ghosts, but ..."

And then, when they got off, they both thought it best she not take a second bus that evening. They found a restaurant near the Plateia Eleftherios—a brightly lit, tourist kind of restaurant—then went together back to his hotel where they had more hashish, then made love together.

But now, when she woke too, her spirits were higher. "I must take you with me tonight to our villa," she said as they got dressed. "And have you meet Georges. But first, you say you've already been to the Archaeological Museum and seen the model of Knossos there? I think, this afternoon, we should see it again together."

She smiled and kissed him, then added softly. "To review our journey."

That evening she found a little waterfront cafe where they had a light supper, no longer concerned about here-and-now gunshots, then took him out on the breakwater to the Venetian fort that guarded the harbor. "Look," she said as they watched the sky turn gold in the sunset. "Can you see the galleys coming in, fresh from a pirate expedition? These are ghosts too, the sailors and merchants who ruled Crete until 1669, when the Turks took over. They called the island Candia then."

"Oh?" he said. He squinted the way she had shown him at Knossos—he almost *could* see the Venetian galleys, their sails a deep purple, could hear the creak of their long, sweeping oars. "I know, in England, they once called Crete 'Candy.' My father told me that, but now I know why." He kissed her gently. "Because it's sweet, like you."

"Look," she said, her arms around him. "There, in the harbor!"

"Another ghost?"

"No. Right below us. Remember our supper the night before last? Our first meal together?"

He looked down at the harbor's swirling waters and then he saw it, its arms radiating out in a spiral. A half-grown octopus.

"According to legend," Ariane said, "the original labyrinth—the one the Minotaur was in—wasn't a maze like you see on the puzzle page of a newspaper, but rather a spiral, with all paths leading into the center. That's why it's easy to get in to it, but hard to get out. And the octopus is considered its symbol."

He thought, he didn't know why, of the tangles of her hair on his pillow that morning, then kissed her again. "You know, if we're going to get to your villa ..."

"Yes," she said. "It's not much farther away than Knossos—just down the coast about eight kilometers—and we can get the bus in the same place. In fact, in ancient times, the town was the seaport of Knossos."

"More ghosts?" he laughed.

She looked around her and, seeing the fort was nearly deserted, she pulled a cigarette out of her handbag. "Would you settle for more hash?" she asked. "Just one for the two of us, though, since we do have to get to the bus. To heighten the sunset?"

"Mm-hmmm," he said.

They smoked together for a few minutes and then she said, "May I ask you a favor? Monday—the afternoon plane to Athens. Could you take it for me? Then come back, of course, on Tuesday morning. I want you to take a package for me."

He looked at the cigarette they were smoking. "You mean ... ?"

She laughed. "No. Not drug smuggling—in fact, it's easier to get on the mainland." She brought her voice down to a mock whisper. "Actually, it's something worse."

"Oh?" he said. He was curious now.

"I'll show you when we get to the villa. It's a small vase, for an aunt in Paris. Nothing rare either, but you know how they are about artifacts. That's why I'm sort of *persona non grata* with the airline myself right now—otherwise I wouldn't even ask you. But if you *could* mail it for me on the mainland, it would get to my aunt that much faster."

He hesitated a moment, then nodded. She was right about the drugs anyway—although he didn't consider himself to be part of the culture, he'd seen them practically openly sold on the streets of Athens. And as for artifacts—he laughed—he could just see his father's face if he were caught. Not that he would be ... or, if he were, he couldn't claim ignorance on a first offense.

"Thank you," she said. She kissed him hard. "Now we've got to run." He followed after her down the jetty and back to the harbor streets, then to the bus where they sat, holding hands, on the trip to Amnissos.

When they arrived at Ariane's villa, her brother wasn't there. "He comes and goes on his own," she explained as she showed him around. "Perhaps he'll come later, but first, a swim?"

He nodded. "I'd like that."

She found him a pair of Georges's swim trunks that fit him well enough, then changed, herself, into a bikini. She led him down to a moonlit beach, her basket filled again from the kitchen, and had him make a driftwood fire. Afterward they made love on the beach, and then, again, later in her bedroom. And after that, when he woke the next morning, Georges was in bed with them.

"It's how the Greeks do it," Georges said when Carey pulled away, shocked.

"You don't have to," Ariane said as she woke too. But then she kissed him, and Georges did as well, and, perhaps because of the hashish he'd smoked the previous night, Carey suddenly thought it was not that unpleasant.

"I still don't know, though," he tried to protest once, even though he made no move to stop Ariane's brother. Nor did he object when Georges fondled Ariane too.

"We're a close family," Ariane finally said when it was over. Then she giggled. "But, if you wish, it'll be the last time—I mean with Georges. It'll just be you and I."

Carey shook his head, trying to clear it. Suddenly thinking of his father—what *he* would say if he knew what had happened.

"No, Ariane, he's one of us now," Georges said. "Isn't that right? Carey—is that your name?"

"Yes," Carey muttered, still clearing his head. It *wasn't* unpleasant and—he suddenly laughed at the thought—after all, Georges and Ariane were French.

The others laughed with him as they got out of bed and got dressed, but then Georges's voice turned suddenly serious. "Sister," he said, "I want you to know I'll be gone for a few days. Something's come up that I have to attend to."

"Oh?" she said.

"Yes," he said, putting on his shoes. "So it looks like you'll have your new friend to yourself after all for awhile."

Carey waited until he was gone, then asked Ariane, "What was that all about? I mean—you know—and then he suddenly leaves?"

Ariane laughed. "Probably he'd just come to announce that he's got a new girlfriend. Maybe somebody from the inland—he rather likes farm girls, although, as you see, he's not entirely prejudiced that way. But, like I say, he comes and goes."

She paused, then kissed him softly on the cheek. "You don't mind, do you?"

After that morning he began to see ghosts in earnest, at least in his dreams. That night back in his hotel, he dreamed that he had returned to Knossos, but that the palace he found now was new. An old man guided him, bent and bearded, and somehow he knew that this was Daedelus, even though the man never spoke.

He led him through workshops, through caves filled with feathers—the rookeries of the nobility's falcons—and yet other caves that were filled with beehives. Through hallways with walls lined with huge jars of honey. Some of these rooms Carey recognized from the ruins he and Ariane had explored, while others were new to him. Others still, on lower levels, had apparently not yet even been uncovered by the palace's restorers.

And, as they walked, he realized their path was a series of spirals, always leading back to the Grand Staircase, yet always lower with each new passage. Always more ancient.

And, as they walked, his silent guide wept.

When morning came, he rented a car. Ariane had told him the night before that she, too, would have to leave for a day. That perhaps it would be a good time for him to drive out to the places his father had lived, as his mother had asked him, so that, if he wished, he could be by himself with his family's memories. Except, on the road outside of Potamies, his car had had a flat—the rental people had warned him the roads were in ill repair—and, after he'd fixed it, it was nearly evening by the time he finally climbed to the Lasithi Plateau just below Mount Dhikti.

The Valley of Windmills! He gasped at the sight of scores of windmills surrounding a vast field, their sails slowly turning in the mountain breeze. Pink in the sunset. Spirals within spirals, circling the valley, with its tiny villages, up to the base of the mountain itself where, according to local myth, Zeus had his birthplace.

But also this was where the Germans had landed—the ones his father had met when he was ten. And, as Carey looked to the sky, he heard the ghosts of airplanes approaching, followed by the near-silent *swish* of the Nazis' gliders.

He looked up. He squinted. Now he could see them against the rapidly darkening sky—gliders so huge it took three planes to tow one—disgorging their contents. Parachutes unfolding like snowflakes, blizzarding toward him.

He looked for his father. He heard the rifle shots of the defenders—so pitifully few. And yet his father was nowhere to be seen.

Until after. Time slipped. Now it was full dark and the Germans, securing the field, had passed on to towns like Kera and Krasi. And now, one German parachutist lay still half unconscious, his left leg broken from a bad landing. A boy stood over him.

Carey's father.

Time slipped again. They were now in a shed, the boy and the German, the shed Carey's father had hidden in until the attack of the Germans was over. The boy had brought bread and cheese for his captive and didn't resist when the soldier reached to him.

"*No!*" Carey shouted. He watched them caressing—they didn't hear him—the boy's hand finally reaching to his belt. Slowly easing his trousers down ...

"No!" Carey screamed again as he fled to the field outside, not wanting to know more. He sat for a long time in the darkness, hearing occasional murmurs from inside. He thought of himself and Georges and Ariane. But not like this!

Except he hadn't minded when Georges had lain with the two of them, even if it was clear it was Ariane that he still *wanted*. "When in Rome," he had thought—or in Crete. And now he thought, too, of the words Ariane had used in the wooded grove outside of Knossos, that he and she were part of the past, bound to the past of the island itself as well as their own lives. Whether they wished it to be so or not. And he hadn't minded.

He thought of the present, forced the past from him, on the long drive back to Iraklion. He concentrated on the afternoon after Georges left them—on Ariane in the villa's kitchen, wearing an apron over her shorts but with her breasts bare.

She had been cooking octopus.

The following morning when Ariane met him she gave him a package. "The vase," she said. "For you to mail in Athens on Monday. You can open it if you want, as long as you promise to wrap it back neatly."

He took the shoebox-sized package from her and placed it on his hotel room desk. "Perhaps it's best that I don't," he said, his voice still tired from the previous night.

"Perhaps," she said. "That way, if you *should* be stopped for any reason—and you shouldn't be if it's packed in your checked-through luggage—all you'll need to say is it's a present. But, in the meantime ..."

She stopped and gazed in his eyes, then kissed him.

He kissed her back as they sank to his bed, fumbling with each other's clothing. Afterward they slept for a time—she was tired too, she told him later—then went sightseeing most of the afternoon. When the sun went down, they found themselves in an alley off Odos 1866 where, in front of them, stood the taverna. *Their* taverna.

"Shall we?" Ariane asked, pointing toward the open entrance. "I have some friends who may be here too—I'd like you to meet them. In any event, it's time we ate something."

Carey kissed her. "I'd like to," he said. He let her lead him to a large table surrounded by drinking men, one of whom stood and pulled out chairs for them. He helped her sit, then was about to sit down himself when, through the taverna's plate glass window, he saw an old man beckoning to him.

He squinted. The man outside was Daedelus.

"Are you all right, Carey?" Ariane asked as he hesitated, then squeezed her hand.

"I think so," he said. "Uh ... just a moment, though. I thought I saw something in the alley. I'll be right back, okay?"

Ariane nodded as he threaded his way out through the crowded restaurant into the street. He looked up and down—the old man had

233

vanished. Then, as he was about to turn to go back inside, he felt a force lift him and thrust him forward.

The taverna exploded. Behind him fire swirled through its shattered front window, engulfing the building. He stood up, unhurt himself, tried to rush back in to find Ariane, in spite of the searing flames, to save her somehow. When hands gripped his shoulders.

"You are an American tourist?" a voice asked.

Numbly he answered, "Yes," then looked up to see a policeman, surrounded by others. Some had their guns out.

"There is nothing in there for you," the first, English-speaking policeman said. Shadows danced in the alley around them, tinged with orange, as fire sirens sounded. As other men rushed up.

"*Why?*" he demanded.

"Bastards," the policeman muttered, then went on more loudly. "There's no one left in there. No one alive, anyway. You wouldn't understand—you are a tourist—but there's a group called the Free Crete Movement. This was one of their meeting places. Fortunately, though, they have their own traitors."

Carey twisted out of the man's grasp and ran to the lighted street beyond. Odos 1866—the street itself named for a revolution. He ran through light and dark, through squares and alleys, out of the city until, half staggering from exhaustion, he found himself climbing the hill of Knossos.

He entered the West Porch, pushing past guards staring out at the night sky. Almost touching their stiff leather armor. He threaded his way through the Procession Corridor, meeting few people—by this time most of the palace was sleeping—and knowing, somehow, that even those few who *were* up couldn't see him either. He crossed the Central Court to the Grand Staircase and counted the steps he went down in the darkness. Fours and threes. One story, two stories, deeper than he had gone even in his dream, until he came to a torchlit landing.

"This way," a voice whispered. Daedelus led him now, no longer silent, through rough stone passages spiraling inward, taking the weight of the palace above them. Until they came to a simple well.

"The Center," the ghost of Daedelus said. "This is where all the labyrinths lead to." He bent behind the well's raised lip and brought out a pair of wings, shimmering with wax and the feathers of hunting birds. Ospreys and sea eagles.

"These are for you," he said, holding them out for Carey to see them.

"I-I don't understand," Carey said.

"Ariadne," the old man said. "She never seduced *me*. It was you, Icarus. I only did what I did to help her for love of you, my son. But she betrayed us."

"I know," he answered. "But she was betrayed too—after, by Theseus." It started to make sense. Icarus. Carey. A kind of a sense, in its own bizarre way. He hesitated, then reached to take the wings, thinking of Ariane.

"But I still love her."

"Then do what you must," the old man said. They knelt side by side, rolling the wings up into a package small enough to fit under Carey's arm. Then the old man led him back through the passages, back through the Court and the workrooms and corridors, into the night air beyond the palace.

There Daedelus kissed him, clasping him in his arms not as a lover, but, rather, a father.

"Beware the sun, Icarus."

Carey never knew how he got back to his hotel that night, nor how he got through the following Sunday. He just packed his luggage. He took the whole day. He had his ticket for Monday afternoon's flight off the island, but, rather than just his overnight bag as he had planned, he packed everything to leave for good.

He packed in a daze, placing Ariane's vase in his largest suitcase along with his best clothes. It was the least he could do for her memory. Then he saw the wings.

He stuffed them in too, as a kind of padding. He didn't know why he did—he'd half expected to find them melted away in the sunlight, as ghost wings *should* be. But, straining, he got the suitcase closed, and his other bags packed, and, as soon as he could the following morning, he took a taxi out to the airport.

"You're lucky you bought your ticket early," the man at the counter said when he'd checked in.

"Oh?" Carey asked. He didn't really care, but, since he had hours before his plane took off, he might as well find out why.

"Yes," the man said. "Didn't you know? The Prime Minister's speech? He's in Iraklion this morning. He's scheduled to go back to Athens on the same flight you're on, so it's bound to be crowded."

"I guess I haven't been reading the papers," Carey said. He glanced around him, seeing now the men in dark business suits who could only be Government Service, keeping an eye on things. Then, squinting slightly, he saw from the corner of his own eye—a flash of long, blonde hair.

And then he understood, part of it anyway. Why Ariane had died. "Uh, just a minute," he said. He looked again. This time what he saw was Ariane's brother across the waiting room, flight bag in hand, heading toward the departure gate.

"Just a minute," he said again. He was curious now. "I, uh, really don't care much for crowds myself. You don't suppose there might be a seat on an earlier flight?"

The counterman shuffled through his schedules. "There is one," he said. "On the next flight out—it's starting to board now. If you want, there's just enough time to transfer your luggage ..."

Carey nodded and had his ticket stamped for the new flight. At the last moment he boarded himself—the plane, in fact, was practically empty—and sat in the back. Then, once it had taken off and started its climb, he moved forward and sat next to Georges.

"What are you doing here?" Georges demanded. "I—you're supposed to be on the afternoon flight."

"I know," Carey said. "But there's nothing to hold me here. Not anymore. So I came to the airport early, and then when I saw you ..."

Georges suddenly looked ill. "You idiot!" he whispered. He lunged for the flight bag under his seat and clutched it to him. The plane was still climbing.

And Carey stared at Ariane's brother, long and hard, as one more piece of the puzzle fell in place.

"Theseus?" he asked.

"*What?*" Georges answered. Then Georges's eyes widened as he slowly realized. Slowly understood.

Theseus.

Betrayer.

As, in Carey's luggage, the pressure-sensitive molded *plastique* that was Ariane's vase exploded into a miniature sun. As it ripped the plane in a shower of feathers. Feathers and boiling wax. Shredded drachma notes, mixed with bone and flesh.

Whirlwinding downward ...

... until Carey/Icarus opened his arms wide, no longer needing the wings of a Daedelus to glide out over the blood-dark ocean, searching in ever increasing spirals for his Ariadne.

BLENDERS

BY J. GREGORY SMITH

GenenHealth Office Building, Southern California

Carson Brooks rechecked the bug sweeper and confirmed the small conference room was clean while he awaited the signal from the guard downstairs. He stared at the wireless commbox that appeared to hover in space atop the near-invisible Lexan table. The white walls and floor of the egg-shaped room gave no place to hide for any listening device, no matter how small.

The room always gave Brooks a headache but the security gave him peace of mind that made his pounding skull a trivial matter.

When the intercom trilled he jabbed at the talk button. "Brooks."

"They're here, Sir." Lopez.

"Send Hayden, alone." He waited through the expected pause.

"Sir, they say they can't let him out of their sight."

"Anything that happens is on me."

"Mr. Parker says he needs to hear that from you directly, Sir." Lopez spoke in his usual patient tone of voice.

"Fine." Turnkey hacks never changed. "Put him on."

A new voice came on the line. "Brooks, do you understand what you're asking?"

"Shut up, Parker. What I'm *asking* is none of your damn business. What I'm *telling* is that you send him up and wait for me to return him

239

when I'm good and ready. Got that? You make me call Governor
Davis on this and you're on the street. That's a promise."

Delicious silence.

The elevator chimed and Brooks watched the lights indicate the
approaching car. The wall cracked open to reveal the small stainless
steel elevator with its precious cargo.

The slim man in faded coveralls blinked at the white interior of the
room. He'd lost weight since the photos Brooks saw from his file on
the guy. Not a real surprise. He also noticed some gray sprinkled in
among the cropped blonde hair.

"Welcome, Mr. Hayden, please step inside and take a seat. May I
call you Brian?" Brooks gestured to a clear Lucite chair that matched
the one he was using. The elevator doors closed without a sound
behind the man, and the seam vanished.

"You can call me Stinger." He raised arms Brooks saw were
shackled. "You'll forgive me for not shaking hands." He dropped into
the seat.

Brooks wrinkled his nose in distaste. "I am sorry. I should have
insisted those be removed."

Stinger shrugged. "I doubt they'd have let me come up here
without them. I'm still surprised they did. You seem to have more juice
than I thought."

Brooks let the remark pass. He pulled out a folder from a brown
leather satchel leaning against his chair. "How are you finding your
time?"

"What do you mean?" Stinger's eyes narrowed in suspicion. He
glanced around the barren room. "And did you hire your decorator
from the prison system?"

"Privacy can be a casualty of this age of technical marvels, but
we've gone to great lengths to ensure that we may speak freely."
Brooks said. "But back to my question. How do you enjoy ...
captivity?"

"My life sentence? It's everything I thought it would be."

Brooks saw the façade crack for an instant when Stinger shifted in
his seat. He glanced at the folder for effect. He'd long since memorized
the contents. "Four consecutive life terms total for the murders of half
a dozen men over a fifteen-year span."

"I got sloppy."

"You were betrayed by your client."

"Most of my clients knew better than to try. Like I said, I got sloppy."

Brooks pretended to read some more. "That client, Mr. Silver, 'passed away' before he could bring testimony that might have meant double the number of convictions."

"Bad luck for him." Stinger smiled.

"Or good for you. It says here it weakened the case enough to spare you the death penalty."

Stinger's shoulders sagged. "That's where your intel is wrong. It *was* a death sentence, it just gets carried out day by day. Execution by tedium."

"And we arrive at the point."

"Which is?"

Brooks put the papers down. "You were said to be one of the best."

"Don't believe everything you read. I was caught."

"What if you had a chance to expunge your record and leave a free man?" Brooks saw the man tense up.

"I don't buy bridges."

Brooks took out a document and slid it across the table.

Stinger looked at and laughed. "A death certificate? You went to all this trouble to take me out? You people can do that any time of day or night. What is this?"

"Just as you said. The end of Brian 'Stinger' Hayden, gone from this earth and never lamented." Brooks took another paper out. "Say hello to Roger Wilson. Or whatever name you like."

Stinger let out a long breath. "Who do I have to kill?"

"Make them comfortable. Mr. Hayden has chosen to hear me out. And don't interrupt me again." Brooks switched off the commbox and confirmed the interlocks on the elevator controls.

Stinger leaned back in his chair. The food and drink he'd eaten had taken off the edge and Brooks thought he'd be more receptive.

"How much do you know about GenenHealth?"

"Besides that you guys make a fortune on drugs and medical procedures? Not much. My stock portfolio is kind of thin these days."

"You're talking to one of the founders," Brooks said.

"Congratulations."

"I have a background in the life sciences but my real gift it turned out was on the business end. Much as I hate to admit it my partner, Wallace MacLean, is the genius behind the company." Brooks held up a screenshot of *Lifeline* magazine with MacLean on the cover.

"I recognize him." Stinger gazed at the shot.

Brooks was pleased to see the man studying the picture.

"He's the public persona of GenenHealth. His creations have driven the company to where we are today."

"So what's the problem?"

"The problem is that he's sitting on the greatest discovery in a lifetime. Maybe several lifetimes—and with what we could make on it, the entire net worth of GenenHealth is pocket change in comparison."

"So you want me to take this guy out?"

"It's not that simple."

"That's not *no*. Go ahead."

"In experimenting with animal genetics, Wally made a fundamental breakthrough. He was able to infuse certain traits into a human. At the genetic level."

"You want to corner the market on freak shows?"

Brooks tamped down his irritation. "He was looking for way to adapt healing and other benefits that our bodies can't manage on their own."

"And that's bad?"

"No. Stay with me, here." Brooks ran his hand through his hair. "He succeeded. He wasn't looking to create human animal hybrids from birth. He wanted to add certain genetic traits into an established subject. He called them 'Blenders.'"

"I see."

"Not yet. The process requires a precise insertion of DNA strand segments. Without the exact codes, what Wally calls *recipes*, the combinations killed the hosts." Brooks paused, recalling some of the grotesque early failures.

"Why would anyone agree to go through such a thing?"

"Everyone has a price," Brooks said. "Wally also managed to model some of the effects to minimize the need for live human testing."

"Again, what's this got to do with me?"

Brooks took a sip of the amber liquor that sat on the table in front of him. Mellow warmth crept down his throat. "We made remarkable strides in so many areas. Strength enhancement, adaptability, endurance. The bio-boys at the Pentagon were drooling."

"Good for you." Stinger looked impatient.

Funny reaction for a man with nothing better to do than return to rot in prison.

"Then Wally lost his wife and nearly his daughter from complications with her pregnancy. Despite the finest care, Death got the last word. But not for little Brenda."

"The daughter?"

"Right. She was born with a heart defect and not given much chance to survive a month."

"Too bad."

"Wally couldn't accept the grim prognosis. Baby Brenda became a test subject at barely a week old. Wally and some of the most loyal people we had took the baby to a secret location."

"I can imagine some people were looking for him."

"They were. But, as you'll see, he's rather good at staying secluded. Wally and his team gambled on what they thought was a lost cause."

"And?"

"By the time the police caught up to him more than a month later they were braced to file kidnapping and wrongful death charges."

"But he bought his way out?"

"No. There was no death. Brenda was alive and well. Completely well."

"What do you mean?"

"The hole in her heart? Healed. Not repaired, regrown. The hospital and police changed their minds on the kidnapping, and yes, I'm sure some funds changed hands. But I really think the hospital was eager to find out how he'd cured the defect."

Now Stinger was paying attention again. Good.

"How did he do it?"

"They used the blending process on the baby and gave her the attributes of a creature with regenerative powers."

"What creature?"

"A starfish."

"But there were complications."

"Life is funny that way."

"I find nothing funny about the need to keep a tiny girl isolated because part of the process completely suppressed her immune system."

"Why would they do that?"

"In order to get the body to accept the foreign DNA we had to suppress the natural defense systems. In the early days it was an all-or-nothing prospect. As such, the changes blended in with the host but sadly the subject was highly susceptible to infections and disease."

"Not a great trade."

"Agreed, however we've made massive improvements to the process."

"How is this girl Brenda doing?"

Brooks looked away. "That's the problem. When Wally acted we hadn't perfected the process. He got the healing effects as I mentioned but ... the changes didn't stop at regeneration."

"No?" Stinger stared at Brooks.

"It started at the fingers and toes. At first they thought it was a rash or some other illness but it was the new normal for her. The skin mutated to look identical to regular pebbly starfish skin."

"And then?"

"We worked night and day. Everything at our disposal to slow the runaway reaction."

"But you failed?"

"No! We created a drug that halts the reaction while enabling the immune system to function normally. The blended capabilities are essentially invisible to the body so the immune system won't attack them. We call it Haltizol." Brooks spoke with undisguised pride.

"And Brenda?"

"Fast wasn't fast enough."

"That's too bad."

"Wally was so blinded in his grief he turned against the entire program. Just when we were so close."

"Why not run the program without him?"

"We tried. And the team here made enormous strides in all areas but one."

"Yes?"

"The recipes. We don't know how many strains of animal he has, but despite our best effort we can't isolate a single new recipe. Wally is the only one with the catalogues, and after what happened to Brenda, he's secured the data and gone into hiding."

"Why such an extreme reaction?"

"Do you have any children?" Brooks knew the answer.

Stinger shrugged. "I'll take your word. I think I see where I come in. You need him out of the way to get the data and resume your monster factory, is that about right?"

"Almost. But I need your full agreement, in writing, if we're to proceed."

"And if I say yes and deliver on my end?"

"I call downstairs and send Parker and the guards away." Brooks saw the glint in the man's eye. "After, you are a free man. And a rich one."

The Next Day

Brooks entered the egg room to find Stinger poring over the building schematics. He'd slept in his clothes, if he slept at all.

Stinger looked up at the sound of the door hissing open. He waited until the egg resealed itself before speaking. "Looks like you're going to have to send me back to prison."

Brooks took a seat. "Sorry to hear that."

"Sorry to say it. But if this is his house and the drawings and reports are correct, there's nothing I can do and I really don't understand the point of even asking."

"Tell me what you see."

"Walls, security teams, cameras, and dogs for starters. And that's not even the biggest concern."

"No?"

"This," Stinger held up a manual. "You say this describes the vault where he keeps the data stick?"

"Correct. I expect he's added some customization as well."

"But why me? I know I got into some tight spaces and the Feds never did figure out how I penetrated security for several of my targets, but this is past state of the art."

"Agreed."

"So when does he come out? He might be vulnerable then."

Brooks held up a hand. We've thought of that. He hasn't been seen in public in over two years and rarely even videoconferences."

"Let's get clear. You do want him gone, right?"

"We do."

"We?"

"Confine your questions to the mission." Brooks forced a smile. "Please."

"The only good intel you've given me is that you know where he is."

"But we can't reach him."

"Of course you could. You're the co-founder, aren't you?"

"I meant in a more permanent fashion."

"You could drone strike him, raid the place, concoct bogus charges and arrest him, start a fire and smoke him out, any number of things. I'm sure 'We' has vast resources, am I right?"

"On every point. But obliterating MacLean and the data with him serves no purpose and would land some of us in prison."

"Perish the thought." Stinger smirked at him.

"We need him removed as an obstacle. And we need the data that permits us to utilize the asset he is hoarding. His death must look like an accident."

"That means getting close, and getting out."

"With the data stick."

"Right. Don't you think it will be missed?" Stinger shook his head. "Assuming I could get it out in the first place?"

Despite the pessimism in his tone, Brooks could see Stinger's interest sharpening. "I applaud your honesty. Under current conditions

I don't think you could penetrate the security. But, even if you could, the vault he's built is a monument to his paranoid genius."

"All safes can be cracked."

"I've seen it. Yes in some ways you're right, it's essentially a sturdy metal box subject to the laws of physics, as any safe is. The problem is that any breach of the safe walls or locks without MacLean will cause the data to scramble, becoming worthless to us."

"MacLean runs a risk with a system that's so touchy, doesn't he?" Stinger said. "Sounds like one wrong entry and he loses it all."

"Not quite. We're certain MacLean could reconstruct the data from other hidden sources, but the nature of the lock itself is advanced biometric. Only MacLean can open it."

Stinger folded his arms across his chest. "Why not get in there and compel him to open it? I can get the wet work done but coercive torture isn't my specialty."

Brooks shook his head. "He wouldn't cooperate."

"Come on. You know better, everybody breaks."

"No. He has to be relaxed. Stress will ruin his signature. And we need his death to appear natural. Besides, he doesn't deserve to suffer."

"You're a true friend."

Brooks let that one go. "You see what we're up against."

"You didn't bring me here just to tell me what I couldn't do, did you?"

"In a way, yes. But we needed you to understand the task and accept that you'll need help to accomplish the mission."

"What did you have in mind?"

"Cuttlefish."

One Month Later

"How do you feel?"

"Like someone came in overnight and unbolted every joint in my body." Stinger sat up in the bed. The IVs continued their feed. Stinger reminded Brooks of old-style cancer patients, right down to the hair loss.

One big difference—those chemo patients didn't add thick muscle to their frames.

"You'll compensate with your strength. How are your arms?"

"They itch where that linear rash started but I feel like I could crush an oil drum."

"Hang in there. We'll switch to the Haltizol after this session. Give you a chance to catch up."

"Will that chop my strength?" Stinger asked.

"No. All the changes, they'll hold where they are."

"The reversal is another process altogether, right? For after?"

"That's right."

Stinger glanced around to confirm the techs weren't listening. "Can I keep some of the changes?"

Brooks kept his expression in check but felt the elation surge in his chest. They might have a winner here after all.

"We'll talk about that later." Brooks pointed to the IVs. "Do you feel up to matching some color sheets after we get you unhooked?"

"Tell the lab boys to bring plaid!" Stinger's laugh accentuated the change to the sound of his voice.

Three Months Later, Alamo, California

Brooks watched the camera feed from inside the van. They'd cleared the main gate for the house and he could see Stinger sitting on a canister of cleaning chemicals. The other cameras, all on encrypted feeds that went to the "office" of Infinity Pool Service, showed the massive pool where the van would perform routine service, with one notable exception.

"You can hear me?" Brooks whispered into the microphone. He stared at the screen. Stinger nodded toward the camera. During the last phase of his transformation, he'd begun speaking less and less. The lab doctors explained that the vocal cords were getting pressured to make room for the internal gills.

Amazing application of the blend. Brooks still recalled the astonishment when they realized Stinger wasn't holding his breath for superhuman periods of time but that he was actually breathing under water. The discovery led to a moment of panic when they thought Stinger had evolved into a full-time water breather. No, he'd developed parallel respiration. Incredible.

"You're oriented and know where the extraction point is?"

Brooks noted that Stinger's skin flashed a bright red for an instant and he recognized that the man was becoming irritated.

Fine. This would work or it wouldn't, no sense coaching at this point. Since Stinger had become so quiet the whole crew had lost sleep wondering if the changes had affected Stinger's mind.

"Okay. Sorry. Wait for Lopez to open the doors. You should have enough space under the door to reach the pool. After that it is all you. Good luck."

Stinger took off the uniform and felt the pulse ripple across his flesh as it mimicked the just-shed clothing.

Best dressed nudist in Alamo.

He heard Lopez speaking to someone outside the van. "... should be done in under an hour."

Five minutes later the van backed up near the pool and Lopez opened the rear door. At the sound of the handle, Stinger pressed himself against the wall and let the texture flow to his body and skin.

Lopez glanced around the van and his face flinched when he looked where Stinger slouched.

"Oh shit," Lopez whispered. "Almost missed you. Can't get used to that. Slide out and get in quiet. Watch out when I use the vacuum."

"Right." Stinger could see a twitch of disgust in the man's mouth at the sound of his voice.

Who cared? No time for talking anyway.

Stinger imagined he was water and crept along the van floor and off the back to the stamped concrete. His stomach felt the pattern and his back mimicked it. He knew without looking that the rest of the skin was matching the colors, as if his eyes were cameras capturing every nuance and shade.

Not long ago, he remembered the frustration when trying to match colors for the lab boy and he looked like someone holding their breath too long. Once he started to let his body take over, the changes came naturally. Lately it was more of an effort to suppress the changes and appear normal.

Just a few feet to the pool, a huge free-form work of art complete with a faux boulder waterfall and waterslide snaking around the feature.

He was tempted to give the slide a try but too much was at stake here. Instead, he made for the edge and crossed a patch of grass that tickled the top of his back as much as his belly—the skin sprouted green shafts to mimic the manicured section of lawn.

He extended one arm until it touched the water's edge. Already he could feel the "grass" on his shoulders giving way to the sandy, rough concrete. He poured himself into the water using the discs now growing on his palms to slow his entry and avoid a splash.

Even if someone was staring right at him when he pulled the move, he doubted they'd comprehend what they'd just seen. His arms blended perfectly, even to his own eyes, and only up close might they appear to be a thick patch of cement.

Once in the water, he flattened his body against the pool wall and tipped his head up to slowly exhale the air from his lungs.

Above he heard the compressor start up and Lopez stomping around, trying to be as big a distraction as possible. Stinger also knew that the changes throughout his body heightened his senses.

He put his head under water, ignored the vestigial urge to hold his breath, and drew the water in. Still a strange sensation, but he was shocked by how comfortable it felt to have the water pass over his sore vocal cords. It never reached deep into his lungs, but at the same time he felt a sensation that he was breathing fresh, albeit thick, air. Oxygen spread through his body.

When Lopez inserted the pool vacuum it sounded deafening, but his earlier caution was unnecessary. He slid around it with ease and soon enough the man was done. The saltwater pool taste gave Stinger a sense of déjà vu, like he was home.

He could see through the refraction of the surface the walls of the mansion framing the courtyard. Columns and windows.

He guessed from the angle of the sun he had another hour or two to wait before making his move.

He thought he'd be bored, but the quiet and caress of the water filled him with a sense of peace and his mind felt unburdened. Strange, considering where he was and the state of his once-ordinary frame.

250

And yet there was a certain familiarity to it all. He was still a hunter waiting for prey, wasn't he?

He sensed vibration. He flattened out along the bottom and slowed his breathing. Stinger imagined that he was soaking into the cement, becoming part of it.

The splash sounded like an explosion. Stinger faced the surface and saw the swimmer twelve feet above him.

It was him.

MacLean swam along the surface and a wisp of what looked like smoke drifted in front of Stinger's eyes. He didn't understand until he realized it was a few drops of ink, and that it had come from him.

Time for more Haltizol?

MacLean took no notice and Stinger felt his confidence return. He'd been startled was all.

His target splashed above him. Stinger felt strength ripple through his muscles. Brooks never said he might have a chance at him here. Why not? A quick push off the bottom and wrap him up.

The thought rushed to Stinger's limbs in an instinctive response to the prey dangling above him.

No! That's not the mission. Not like this.

Stinger remained on the bottom of the pool and watched MacLean swim until the lights bathed the courtyard.

Strong swimmer. MacLean finally left the pool and Stinger waited for nighttime to take hold. He crept up the pool side rather than swim to the surface. The courtyard lights gave no relief but he was smooth and silent while he slithered over the edge and crawled to the ground-level basement window.

He knew from the diagrams that this part of the home contained the heating and plumbing equipment. He also knew there weren't alarms on the tiny window too small for a person to pass through.

The night was turning chilly partly due to the fact that, appearances aside, he was naked and wet. He did hold a small waterproof kit in a fold of flesh. He took it out and used the tiny pry tool to work loose the one-foot-square glass block. He returned the bar to his kit and concentrated on the next phase. He relaxed, cleared his mind, and then pushed his skull through the opening.

He had no problem until he reached his shoulders. Just the way the architects intended, he supposed.

Stinger remembered the training and, though this skill was one of the newest, he was able to get the bones dislocated without too much pain. First the left shoulder. He twisted it slowly and, when it came out of the socket, the collarbone moved down and gave him all the clearance he required. He wriggled through and lowered himself to the floor. He knew this room lacked the motion sensors and pressure pads that littered the upstairs.

The door was wired, of course, but that wasn't important. He replaced the window block. He recalled the schematic. The furnace and air-conditioners sat to the left. There.

He saw the duct like a silver pipeline to his quarry. He'd need to access the furnace ductwork, which looked large enough, though the supply vent looked tiny by comparison.

He adjusted the control on the furnace to ensure it would not kick on unless the night went from cool to cold.

Stinger let his one shoulder stay dislocated. He removed the cover to the main vent. He was able to fit inside but the duct leading up would have been a tight squeeze for a child.

A grown man would never be able to attempt what he was about to try.

Stay calm. That's the key.

He slipped the dislocated left arm up into the vent. The movement should have caused a flare of agony but the adjustment had settled into his body, which seemed to understand what was being asked of it. He felt the discs in his palms gain adhesion and the muscles filled with strength. He pulled himself up and wriggled until the bones of his skull shifted along with the other shoulder. His rib cage seemed to telescope until the rest of him was narrow enough to work himself along the shaft.

Despite the bizarre sensation of pressure along his organs and the way he was able to move his body up the smooth vent walls, Stinger felt at home in the enclosed place. More and more it was being out in the wide open that caused him to feel uncomfortable.

252

Back to work. He recalled the turns from the schematic and moved slowly, making much less sound than he'd expected.

The office was dark but Stinger found there was plenty of light for his eyes to see. Funny, before all this he'd been scheduled to see the prison optometrist. He wriggled a finger through the vent slot and managed to work the vent cover free. He was careful not to let it fall. That would have been disastrous, as the intel told him the motion sensors would detect anything moving inside the room. Luckily, they weren't calibrated to pick up movement inside the vent.

Part of him wanted to get out of the confining vent near the ceiling. He held the cover in place and waited. Brooks had told him that MacLean never went to bed before getting in a couple more hours of work.

Stinger looked around the room. He was positioned above a huge mahogany desk but, true to form, MacLean left the workspace immaculate, free of any interesting reading to digest before the main event. There were wood bookshelves that stretched near to the ceiling and a fine wooden library ladder. He didn't see the vault but knew which book to pull to expose the lock interface.

Stinger felt vibrations through the sheet-metal walls of the vent. Stronger than earlier times. Now he heard soft tones from a keypad and the distinctive click of a lock. The lights snapped on before the door even opened and Stinger was sure the sensors were now dormant, silent at the arrival of their master.

The thick wood paneled door, which Stinger knew from Brooks was steel-cored and bulletproof, opened. MacLean strolled in wearing a silk bathrobe. He was alone. He moved across the room to the desk and pressed a thumb to a pad, which responded by activating his computer.

Stinger held his breath. From the angle where MacLean stood, the vent would be just inside his field of vision. He wanted to slide backward but didn't dare risk dropping the vent cover. His flesh mimicked the vent and smooth metal, but MacLean never glanced his way.

Soon the man took a seat and became lost in the glowing display. Stinger could hear him breathing through his nose amid the clicking of the keyboard.

Time.

Stinger pushed the vent out and held the cover with one finger. He poured the rest of his body over the edge and used his arm first, then his leg, to slow his descent until he must have resembled a crushed heap on the floor.

MacLean stopped typing and sniffed the air. "Bleh."

Stinger rose and felt his bones click back into place, while new muscles lifted his frame ever higher.

"What *is* that?" MacLean muttered, and now Stinger had reached his full height. He flexed his arms and enjoyed the power infusing the limbs. He noticed that, without thinking, his skin had adopted the royal-blue silk robe MacLean wore. He concentrated on showing his real face. Brooks had assured him there weren't any cameras inside the sanctuary.

Stinger took a step forward and cast a shadow over the desk.

MacLean had already begun to turn and he whipped around at the sight of the shadow.

Stinger tried to laugh at MacLean's expression, but didn't recognize the sound that came out of his own mouth.

"How did you get in here?" MacLean backed up into his desk and faced Stinger while fumbling near the top drawer. Stinger watched carefully and saw the man's fingers near a panic button.

"No." Stinger lashed out one hand and seized MacLean's wrist. He felt strong enough to crush the bones and made sure not to apply too much pressure. "Sit."

Stinger eased MacLean into the leather chair.

"Who the hell are you?" MacLean stared at Stinger. "Why are you wearing one of my robes?" He jabbed Stinger in the chest.

His expression!

What looked like robe must have felt like rough, warm flesh.

"I didn't take your robe." Stinger's voice sounded raspy and it required more effort than he recalled to enunciate the words. Getting crowded around his vocal cords, he supposed. "And it doesn't matter who I am, just who you are."

254

Now it was Stinger's turn to stare at MacLean. He felt the impression sink in and his body responded.

"Like looking in a mirror?" Stinger rasped. He was impressed how fast MacLean recovered his wits.

"Brooks. He sent you, didn't he?"

"Why do you say that?"

"You're a blender. He's improved his process." MacLean looked Stinger up and down. Then he glanced over his shoulder and must have seen the open vent. "Chromatophores, phenomenal elasticity ... squid DNA?"

"Cuttlefish."

MacLean nodded. "Makes sense. For some reason, the adaptation took faster. But they weren't stable."

"Haltizol works well. And he can reverse."

MacLean looked startled, then smiled. "He told you that? He would, wouldn't he?" Now MacLean shook his head. "Sorry. Brooks used you, my friend."

"He said you'd lie." Stinger felt fear and anger combine. He checked his temper. Can't leave a mark on the man—but the fear lingered.

"You didn't come here to impress me. What do you want?"

Stinger rolled the chair with MacLean in it over to the library shelf. The heavy brass casters dug into the carpet but it didn't slow Stinger. He pulled on the book, *The Island of Dr. Moreau* by H.G. Wells. "Brooks didn't mention your sense of humor."

A section of the shelf slid aside and a biometric reader extended from the metal door of the hidden safe.

"The joke's on you. I won't open it. If you try to force me, the stress will ruin the read." MacLean said.

Stinger took MacLean's hand in his left and placed his right fingertips into the reader while putting his eye against the iris reader.

A harsh buzz confirmed his failure.

"Told you."

Stress.

Stinger practiced his breathing and imagined himself back in the pool.

The reader beeped and flashed green and then the door opened with a hiss.

"No! Don't do this. Brooks wants to sell blenders to the military."

Stinger took the memory stick out and added it to his pouch. He replaced it with one Brooks had provided. Perfect match.

"He's lying about the reversal. You're stuck the way you are, or worse. And think of the others."

"I'm not paid to think." Stinger didn't usually converse with his targets but this one *was* making him think.

"Do you believe if Brooks had a reversal process developed he wouldn't have approached me? I invented the technology. I didn't mean for it to fail."

"I'm proof you didn't."

"You'll be proof I *did* soon enough." MacLean sighed. "The Haltizol only slows the change, it doesn't stop it."

Stinger recalled the urgency for developing the drug in the first place. "How do you know?"

"My daughter."

"I know about her. Brooks said it was too late."

"He didn't tell you she lived, did he?"

"No." Stinger knew he shouldn't be listening. He had what he needed, finish the job and go.

But he didn't.

"I'll show you pictures. Back at my desk." MacLean pointed across the room.

Despite red flags that a rank amateur would notice, Stinger set aside his caution and allowed the man to stand, keeping one hand on MacLean's shoulder while they walked across the room to the desk.

"Careful."

"Her transformation was advanced by the time we had an experimental serum to test. One of the last things she said out loud was that she didn't want anyone to see her like she was. I told Brooks we lost her. It wasn't far from the truth."

Stinger felt the man shudder.

"We ran experiments on other subjects, but all the while I was giving Brenda the same infusions. For a moment, we hoped it would reverse the effects, give the body a chance to reassert its genetic dominance."

"No?"

"You've felt for yourself what happens without the Haltizol. The changes roar ahead. Not so with the drug, but the body develops a resistance to it and added concentrations don't work."

"So what happened to Brenda?" Stinger disliked how the need to know felt like a craving.

"May I?" MacLean pointed to a right-hand side drawer.

Stinger watched the hand. "Slowly."

"Of course." MacLean pulled open the drawer with two fingers and withdrew a folder he placed it on the desk. "These are the last pictures of what she became."

Stinger opened the folder and noticed the edges were finger-oil stained from frequent handling. His body grew cold and he saw the flashing colors across his skin before he regained his composure. For an instant he didn't know what he was seeing. It looked like a human shape covered in pebbly orange skin. Where the head should have been he saw a crude star-shaped mass with only a mouth visible.

"In the end, we let her make the choice. The hell of it was that she was healthy, but she wasn't Brenda. Not even close. You can still see the spot where she died over there." MacLean pointed to a section of parquet floor.

Stinger tore his gaze from the image and all he noticed was a polished floor. A flash of movement caught his eye.

He turned and saw the MacLean's hand dart forward.

And hit the panic button.

He heard no sound but was certain security forces did and were now charging to the room. "That was a mistake," Stinger said.

MacLean looked grim. "Was it? You felt sorry for me and were going to spare me? I know Brooks."

Stinger grabbed MacLean, wrapped his now-disjointed left arm around the man, and carried him across the room, where he closed the safe and dropped MacLean in the chair. He pulled out the pouch and removed the tiny strip.

MacLean saw what he was doing and began to struggle.

It didn't matter. Stinger hoisted MacLean and the chair up together and ran back to the desk. He also covered the man's nose and mouth, noticing that when MacLean tried to bite him, his teeth slipped over the adapted skin.

The man tried to yell, but Stinger's stretched arms muffled the sound. At the desk, he held MacLean's nose and, as soon as the man tried to breathe through his mouth, took the tiny gel strip, jammed it inside, and held it against MacLean's tongue.

It dissolved in an instant and Stinger knew it was safe to let go. He hoped the bruising was minimal.

MacLean looked like he was going through a seizure—the main target was to cause cardiac arrest and then break down into unremarkable metabaloids. Now Stinger felt vibrations in his feet that told him the cavalry was on the way. He raced to the door and locked it from the inside. It would buy just a moment or two, but it would be enough.

He heard a gargling sound and saw MacLean pointing at the open folder. He managed to utter a few words Stinger wished he hadn't understood.

"How. Will. You. Look."

They were at the door. Knocking first. Then shouting.

Stinger snatched the vent cover and surged up the wall.

It was close. If they hadn't been staring at MacLean, who sat wide-eyed and drooling, they might have noticed the last of what looked like a royal blue robe pull the vent into place.

Seventy-Two Hours Later: The Egg Office

Brooks sat at the table and plugged in the memory stick. Stinger ignored the pounding in his head and tingling sensation throughout his lower body.

"Good, good, good! Yeeees!" Brooks sounded like he was chanting. All it meant to Stinger was that he must like what was on the stick.

"Your crew got to the house first?" Stinger forced out the words. It hurt more than ever to speak.

Brooks looked up. "Oh, yes. There will be a 'full investigation,' of course, but I have it on good authority that the report will show a brilliant man passed away at his desk, thinking of his long lost daughter."

"Then I get paid. When do we start the reversal?"

"You were incredible. Are you certain you want to give it up? You are without a doubt the most unique assassin on the planet."

Stinger pointed at the memory stick. "Not for long." The skin flickered red and blue then settled to what he thought was a normal flesh tone.

"That's not your concern. But if you are sure ..."

"Don't feel right." He reached out and dropped several teeth onto the Lexan table. "They fell out last night. Look." Stinger opened his mouth to reveal the hard upper and lower single beak-like structures that had crowded out his other teeth.

Brooks failed to hide his disgust. "Fair enough. You were able to use the autoinjectors for the Haltizol?"

Stinger nodded.

Brooks reached into a satchel. He held up a kit with a row of spring-loaded syringes in plastic sheaths. "These work the same way. They are phase one. Use them in place of any leftover Haltizol. Do this for three weeks."

"Then?"

"Come back to see me. Not here. At my house. Contact information in the kit."

"All right." Stinger took the kit. He was careful not to crush them. His fingers felt numb more and more lately.

"These will prepare your body to revert to normal so don't expect to feel better just yet. That's part of the process. Just lay low, take it easy and let the meds go to work."

Stinger nodded. His throat burned from the talking.

"See you soon."

Three Weeks Later

"Maybe he won't show." Lopez checked the clock on his phone.

"He called, he'll be here. But he sounded like a mess." Brooks laid out the equipment. He stared at the tropical fish in the large aquarium that dominated one wall of his living room. Their colors and movements never failed to lower his stress.

259

Ten minutes later the doorbell rang.

"I didn't hear a car." Lopez peeked out at the driveway. Brooks glanced at a screen and dialed up the security cameras. Nobody in the driveway. Or at the door, for that matter.

"Huh?" Check it out, would you?" he said.

Lopez opened the door and the light shone on an empty stoop. Then a shadow shimmered and materialized. Lopez jumped backward.

"Stinger? Get in here. Don't let anyone see you doing that."

The man, if that word still applied, shambled in and Brooks wasn't sure where the legs stopped and the feet began. Even the shoes seemed to change and he realized all of it was illusion.

"Why didn't you wear something? You're flashing and shifting." Brooks motioned to the living room.

He could hear a wheezy whistling noise and realized it was Stinger breathing. It sounded like he was sucking air through a soggy paper tube.

"You sound awful. Can you speak?"

Stinger was standing by the men, but the top of his head rose and fell as if he were truly boneless and could stand only through efforts of his muscles. Almost like he could only imitate a man on his feet.

Stinger drew in a rattling breath. "Barely."

"Did you take all the drugs?"

"Liar."

"Excuse me?" Brooks said.

Lopez took several steps back.

Brooks felt sweat dance down his rib cage.

More horrible wheezing. "Tested. Water. Salt. Sugar. Mostly bullshit!" Stinger lunged at Brooks. The arms flopped forward like wet noodles, but one caught him by the neck and stuck like glue. The arm felt like a python with thorns.

Brooks started to yell when the muffled reports cut him off. Lopez stood nearby and pumped shot after shot from a large handgun into Stinger's torso. The suppressor kept it from being deafening, and several rounds penetrated clear through Stinger's body and peppered Brooks's kitchen.

He didn't care. Stinger released Brooks and fell in a heap to the ground. He thrashed on the floor and his skin flickered like a living strobe light. The wheezing ratcheted up, then fell silent. Brooks stepped away and put out an arm to tell Lopez to quit shooting. No need to tear up the floor on top of the kitchen cabinets.

"I thought you said he'd take his medicine." Lopez flicked on the safety and reholstered his weapon.

"I guess he got what he needed. I never saw anyone this far along and still alive. Usually the changes are so radical by this point that they die on their own."

"You're cut." Lopez pointed toward Brooks' neck. Now that he was starting to calm down, he felt where that arm had snaked around him. His fingers came back red and wet.

"Damn. Let me clean these up. Can you get the bag from the car? We need to get rid of this carcass." Brooks watched Lopez walk out the front door. The cuts on his neck began to throb.

He hurried to the bathroom and turned on the water. He let it heat up and could see the streaks alongside his throat. More than scratches, those barbs on the arm hadn't cut deep, but they might've become serious given a bit more time.

Just don't let them get infected.

He opened the medicine cabinet and took out a bottle of antiseptic. He closed the mirror and wadded up some toilet tissue. He doused the paper with the antiseptic and swabbed the wounds.

He clenched his jaw at the stinging pain. The burn meant the stuff must be working, but it hurt like hell. Despite the pain he felt better. Once they got the body out and cleaned up, he'd pour a tall glass of bourbon and *then* he'd be just fine.

He heard Lopez come back in and shout something in surprise.

Now what?

Brooks stepped out of the steamy room into the hallway.

"What?"

Lopez held a black body bag folded over his arm and stared. "Why do you want to cut him up here? That was fast, you got a surgical saw?"

"I was in the bathroom, what the hell are you talking—" Brooks reached the end on the hall where he could see past just Stinger's feet. "Where's his head?"

"That's what I was asking you." Lopez looked as confused as Brooks felt.

It wasn't where he left it. In what looked to be a clean and surprisingly neat cut, the only thing that remained was a slack torso.

261

The whole body looked like it was melting, but that could have been an illusion due to the soft or absent bones.

He saw a smear along the floor that reminded him of a slug trail. The body at their feet began to ooze from the neck.

Disgusting.

"I think I'm losing my mind. Maybe the head collapsed into the frame," Brooks said.

"You going to autopsy him here?"

"Funny. Scoop him in the bag and let's get him out of here."

Lopez shook his head. "Weirdest shit I ever saw."

"Take him to the car. I'll be right there. I want to wash this crap off my hands. Smells like fish guts." Brooks needed to make sure this thing got dumped where it would never be found. Lopez was a good man, but Brooks worried he might offload the body somewhere just to be rid of it.

Brooks heard something in the bathroom and his heart jumped. A second later, he recognized the sound and realized he'd left the hot water running in the sink. The small powder room was steamed up like a bathroom after a shower. He turned off the water and checked his cuts in the partially fogged mirror.

At first he didn't see them in the distorted reflection. He canted his head and the cuts appeared, almost glowing red. He saw his puzzled expression reflected and reached out to clear the fogged glass.

Why did the mirror feel rough?

Now he saw his reflection contort with rage and the eyes glowed bright yellow.

Brooks tried to back away, but tentacles lashed out from the sides of the frame. The last thing he saw was a bulbous shape, with a sharp, snapping beak at the center, detach from the real mirror and pull itself toward his face, smothering his scream.

ONE OF US

BY AUSTIN S. CAMACHO

I like to set meetings out on one of the long piers at the National Harbor, especially when I'm meeting one of us. For one thing, it's almost impossible for somebody to film you without you knowing it. The breeze would play hell with any recording device. It's public, but not too public. Nobody's going to sneak up on you. And best of all, you get to take a good long look at anybody headed your way before you have to talk to them.

Marty C was styling today in the three-piece suit, gators on his feet, and the hat dipped over one eye like Ne-Yo. He's wide and solid, but still moves like a dancer. I expected the two big guys hanging back behind him. I didn't expect the sister on his arm. She'd be tall even if she kicked off those six-inch Christian Louboutins. Soft features and perfect skin under a three-hundred-dollar weave. Bigger tits than mine, but that was okay. I had the nicer ass.

She stopped six yards out. I held her gaze while Marty continued, hoping the eye contact made it clear I was not competition. He stopped just outside arm's reach and nodded hello.

"I don't get introduced?"

"In a minute," Marty said. "Business first, if that's okay."

I smiled. "She's not business?"

"Well, sort of," Marty said. "There's a reason she's here, but really, she's just a friend I'm trying to help out." Her body language said it was true. His eyes told me he wished it wasn't.

"I see. She's got a problem you want me to solve."

"Yeah, but not the usual way. Carmen's brother disappeared. With all that's going on he's low priority to the DC cops. I thought you'd help. For your usual fee, of course."

I slipped my hands into my leather jacket pockets. "Me? I ain't no detective, Marty. I'm ..."

"I know," Marty said, palms forward. "You're one of us. But you're real good at finding people. I remember that dude who was in witness protection. And you might even know Yemmi."

"Yemmi the rapper? The guy who's starting to make a noise in the clubs?"

"See?" Marty grinned like he had won something. "You travel in some of the same circles. I'm betting you can find out what happened to him before some private eye could even get started. What do you say?"

I stared into the low afternoon clouds. It would be just like locating any mark, only I didn't have to do the actual job, and I got paid the same. I shrugged.

"What the hell. I'm between gigs." We shook on it. "I'm going to need some information to go on. Time for that introduction."

Marty waved the amazon toward us. We faced each other like fighters in a ring. He said, "Carmen, this is Skye, that friend I told you about."

Instead of touching gloves I turned to Marty and said, "Stay here." To Carmen I said, "Let's talk," and moved off. She fell into step beside me. I knew the guys would follow, but at a discreet distance. She ran her eyes up and down me, gathering that my black tights, calfskin boots, and leather jacket only looked cheap. And she would have noticed the absence of jewelry, unless you counted the silver-star belt buckle, and that my shoulder-length jet-black hair was all my own.

"So, Marty says you need help finding your brother Yemmi."

"He offered to help," she said in a smooth accent. "Opeyemi performed Saturday night and no one has seen him since. He calls me every day. He would not go a week without so much as a text message. Marty said you might be able to help. I would be very grateful."

264

She sounded as if that last sentence hurt to say. "Opeyemi? What is that, some kind of African name?"

"We are Nigerian. Family is important to us." She made it sound haughty. I wondered what Carmen might be short for.

"So what do you think is going on with Yemmi?"

"If I knew ..."

I stopped short and stared up into her soft brown eyes. "Look, people don't just disappear. There's only a few possibilities, right? Either he took off on his own and don't want to be found, or somebody grabbed him, or he's dead. Where would you place your bet?"

She clenched her eyes tight, then opened them. "I talk to or text with Yemmi every day. He would not just leave."

"Okay, so who hates him?"

"What? No one. Everybody loves Yemmi."

Of course. Loved ones always said that. Of course, if no one had any enemies I'd be out of business.

"Then you've got nothing to worry about. Who would have seen him last? Who are his closest friends?"

"I'm afraid he still associates with gangsters," Carmen said, looking a little embarrassed. "There's Jimmy, he's bad news. And Bobby who goes by Smuggla. Maybe his best friend is his DJ, Scratch Daddy. He sells their CDs all over the city."

I found Scratch Daddy on Wisconsin Avenue leaning up against a maroon van. When he saw me approaching he reached into the open back door, pulled a disk out of a box and handed it to me. He opened his mouth but I cut him off.

"Save the sales pitch. Yemmi's sister Carmen sent me. She needs to know where he is."

"Me too," he said, glancing at the heavy gold Rolex on his ebony wrist. "We got business to take care of. But I ain't seen the brother since Sunday when he asked me to make that delivery."

"Delivery? To who?"

He cut me a glance. "Why's it any of your business?"

"Didn't I just tell you his sister sent me? Look I ain't trying to spend all day chasing this dude."

He puffed up and leaned in on me. "And I ain't trying to give up my boy, so maybe you better ..."

Stiffened fingers into his solar plexus backed him up while I dropped the blade down out of my right sleeve. When I pressed the point against the notch of his collarbone he backed against the van and froze.

"You could bleed out right here and people would step over you for hours," I said, just loud enough for him to hear. "Or, you can tell me what Yemmi told you to take where on the day he went missing."

I don't think it was the dagger at his throat that opened his mouth. But Scratch Daddy looked into my eyes and could see I was for real.

"Look, it was just one of his CDs. Seriously, he scribbled a note on the label and told me to take it over to Flex, sort of like a calling card before he went over there, and when I got back he was gone and I ain't seen him since."

"Now, was that so hard?" I asked, backing off and pushing the blade back into its ejection holder in my right sleeve. "Now you don't have to see me again ... unless you're lying. And you know what? Give me one of those CDs."

I popped the disk into the Miata's CD player and was bobbing my head while I piloted the little red Mazda across town toward Georgetown where I knew Flex, born Noah Allen, lived. Yemmi had the kind of flow that helped you get through the midday traffic. It wasn't long before I was parking half a block away and listening to my boots click on the brick sidewalk toward the big square brick house. A white boy dressed in full livery opened the door and escorted me to the back where Flex sat by the pool. Three cell phones sat by his elbow and a Shaquille O'Neil look-alike stood six feet away. I greeted him, keeping my hands in plain sight. The bodyguard did too. Signs of mutual respect.

Flex's skin was the color of a walnut shell and beneath the smoothly shaved head his face was lined with deep wrinkles. He poured Remy into a glass and pointed to an empty one for me, but I waved it off. Everything he wore—golf shirt, jeans, tennis shoes—bore a designer label. His smile was dazzling. I could see he took the shift from performer to promoter and producer very seriously.

"You're easier to see than I expected, Flex."

"What, you think just because a nigga lives in a ten-million-dollar house he got to turn away company? I ain't like that. Besides, Junior here said he knew your name. He says if you was looking for me for the usual reasons you wouldn't be ringing the doorbell."

"He's right," I said. "I'm actually looking for Yemmi. And not for the usual reasons. His sister is worried. She's tight with Marty C so he asked me to help her out. Yemmi has gone missing." Like my own brother, I didn't say out loud.

Flex grinned. "Marty C? Can't believe that weasel helping somebody out. But, yeah, Yemmi stopped by here Sunday morning and stayed for lunch. He's a standup dude and him and me, we go back a long ways. He came by to see if I might front him some cash to produce his next disk."

"Yemmi your homeboy? Did you take care of him? "

"Of course. Like I said, we go back a long ways. Ran the streets together when we was kids. Look, he brought me his latest joint."

He tossed me the CD with its black marker inscription:

We got to pop the cork,
You had to mad kervork,
Words spun, we won,
Now we take New York.

"If he's rhyming at you I guess he is your boy. What's this about New York?"

Flex sipped his cognac. "Yeah, we was talking about setting up a tour up there. Guess if he don't turn up that ain't happening."

I was thinking maybe Yemmi took off to New York on his own, and what a pain it would be to track him there, when my phone rang. I turned to face the pool as I pulled it out. It was Marty.

"Hey, Skye, I wanted to tell you, you can stop looking for Yemmi. They just found him in a stall at Union Station with a knife sticking out of his ribs. No money on him, looks like he was mugged. Wherever he was heading, he won't never get there."

It was the flip opposite of the last time I saw her. I stood in the shadow of the Ferris wheel at National Harbor, but Carmen approached while Marty hung back. When she was close enough to talk without shouting she got right to the point.

'It was Marty, wasn't it? He killed my brother, didn't he?"

"How the hell should I know?" And if she thought that, I wondered, why was she still hanging with him?

"But he's capable of it, isn't he?"

I shrugged. "Wouldn't be the first nigga Marty capped. But why would he go after Yemmi?"

"Because," Carmen said through clenched teeth, "Yemmi disapproved of Marty. And Marty knew I'd never stay with a man Yemmi didn't think was good enough."

I had to admit I could see where Yemmi was coming from. "What does Marty say?"

"It wasn't me," Marty said, stepping closer. "I swear to God it wasn't me."

I turned to Carmen. "So what do you expect me to do? This is police business now. Go lean on Metro PD to find out who did Yemmi."

Marty stepped forward, getting uncomfortably close to me, and lowered his voice. "Look, you know that's bull. If them clowns was any good you and me wouldn't be standing here. I got people inside feeding me all they got, which ain't much. But look, Skye, Carmen won't hardly talk to me until she's a hundred percent sure I didn't whack Yemmi."

"Look, like I told her ..."

"No, you look," Marty said. "I trust you. More important, she trusts you. And you may not know for sure who done this, but you know how I work and you could prove it wasn't me. It's worth a lot of money to me ..."

"Double my usual fee?"

Marty hesitated, but only for a couple seconds. "Sure. Sure. Damn, you some expensive help."

"Okay. It's clear Yemmi was into something that got him taken out. Maybe if I can find out what that was I can track back to who.

Meanwhile, you get me everything you can from the cops in your pocket."

It was pushing toward midnight: no moon, overcast, cool with a bit of a breeze to make nearby trees rustle for cover noise. In other words, my kind of night.

I had talked to Scratch Daddy and saw he wasn't really a player. But Yemmi's other two friends, Jimmy and Smuggla, they were serious Gs. I knew Jimmy was a pretty good shot. Smuggla was a well-known blade man like Mack the Knife, a heartless killer they made a song about. If Yemmi made a bad enemy it would be through his association with them.

That's why I was slipping in through the narrow street-level window. Jimmy and Smuggla stayed in the basement of one of the row houses in South East DC, just off New Jersey Avenue. I dropped to the floor of their backroom, quiet as a rat pissing on cotton, just a shadow among shadows. I moved across the darkened room with my little .32 auto in my right fist. Stepping in the next room I found the boys watching TV with their backs to me. Jimmy sat on a beat-up sofa. Smuggla was in a leather recliner to my left. I took two steps to the right so they were both easy targets without moving my arm much.

"Evening, boys," I said in what I hoped was a nonthreatening tone.

Smuggla's hand whipped toward his pocket but froze when he saw my pistol. Jimmy had his hand on the gun at his back before he realized who I was. He knew that at that distance I'd have no trouble putting one of those lead pellets in his eye. His face flashed surprise, rage, and finally grim acceptance. He really was a G.

"Okay," he said. "Just ... be nice to know who sent you."

I smiled and moved closer. "I'm not here for you guys. Just want to conversate a bit. How 'bout it?"

In response, Jimmy pulled his piece out with two fingers and dropped it behind the couch. "It's your world, Skye. I don't want no shit with you." Smuggla nodded, resting his hands on the arm of the chair.

269

"Good. You don't start no S-H, won't be no I-T. I just figure y'all two the most likely to know why somebody thought Yemmi should be dead. What was he into?"

"I got nothing, Skye," Jimmy said. "Honest to God."

"Maybe he just got mugged," Smuggla said. "He liked to carry a lot of cash ..."

"Like any of us," Jimmy put in. "But these days he been pretty broke."

That got my attention. "You mean he wasn't burning it up rapping?"

"Well ... there's a lot of expenses," Jimmy said.

"You his posse. You must know if he was doing something shady to pick up some ..."

Both men froze when the knock came at the door. I crossed the room to look through the peephole. When I turned to my hosts, I was grinning.

"Well this is interesting. You guys gonna be good?" When they both nodded I slipped my piston into the paddle holster at my back in my waistband and pulled the door open. Junior stepped in, looked around, nodded toward me, and moved to the side. Flex walked in and took in the room in one wide-angled glance. When his eyes settled on me he was still trying to decide what he should think.

"Based on your rep, I didn't think this was your kind of thing. But I brought the cash. You send the text?"

I glanced at Jimmy and he looked downright embarrassed. "Text? I didn't send you any text, Flex. What did it say?"

Flex whipped out a phone and held it up for me to see the screen. *We know what he knew. Be here by midnight. Same amount.* Then there was an address. The one I was standing in. Watching Flex, in his two-thousand-dollar suit and shoes that probably cost more, the tumblers began to fall, as if my brain was an old-fashioned combination lock.

"Well, damn. Yemmi was hustling you. Blackmail."

"Where the hell did you get that?" Flex asked.

I hooked my thumbs in my belt. "First of all, the note on your CD. He sent it ahead to make sure you'd let him in when he got to the door. You took somebody out, back when you used to run with Yemmi. Maybe he was the only one who knew."

"What?" Smuggla asked. "Flex was a killer?"

270

"Must have been, back in the day," I said. "In the rhyme. 'You had to mad kervork' he said. Like that crazy doctor Kevorkian, right? You helped somebody die. At the time it probably gave you street cred. But you a legit businessman now."

"That's right, "Flex said, pulling a fat envelope out of his inside jacket pocket. "And I ain't trying to do no time. So take the ten K, same as I gave Yemmi, and let's all just go on about our business."

"You saying you paid him off? Or was it cheaper to just kill him?"

"Are you serious?" Flex looked honestly hurt by my accusation. "The brother was broke and needed operating capital for a video, studio time, and promotion to make a splash at some New York gigs. He only asked for ten large. That ain't the kind of cash I'd kill somebody for. Hell, the sad thing is, I'd have fronted him the money without the whole blackmail bullshit. Yemmi was a good investment."

I was just shaking my damn head. "So I guess that means one of these chuckleheads sent you that text. And that means they knew what Yemmi was doing, even if they didn't know what he had on you." I gave Jimmy the evil eye and he crumbled. Then I turned to Smuggla and stared him down. He didn't even try.

"Alright, alright, can't a brother try to make some dough?"

"YOU tried to hustle me?" Flex said. Junior hovered over Smuggla like he was about to push his head down into his body.

"Hey, we was Yemmi's posse, his roadies and I scored dope for him. Of course we knew he was running a game on Flex. We all sort of got the idea together."

"You mean when you found out Yemmi had something on this brother whose wallet's fat, you talked him into taking advantage," I said. "And then you figured you'd go back to the well and tap him again."

"I'll cop to the first part," Jimmy said, "But I wasn't after no money. All I know is, we sent Yemmi to pull some cash out of Flex here, and we never saw him again. I wanted to get this nigger over here so we could maybe find out what he did to our boy."

"What I did?" Flex clenched his fists, trembling with rage. "Now I get it. You both knew Yemmi left my place with ten large in his pocket. And now I see how you niggas live, how do I know you didn't snatch him up, grab his stash, and leave him bleeding in a gutter somewhere?"

Junior, reading his boss' intent, reached under his jacket. Before things got out of hand I had my pistol out, knowing if I aimed at Flex, Junior would cool out.

"All right, let's all chill."

It seemed like an odd time for a knock on the door.

"Who the hell?" Flex shouted.

From the hall we heard, "It's Marty, bitch. Open the goddamn door!"

Keeping my front sight on Flex's heart, I slid to the door and pulled it open. A trim brother in a tailored suit with a bulge under his left arm walked in and stepped to the left. Another man pressed from the same mold came in behind him and stepped to the right. Marty followed, closed the door behind himself, and leaned back against it as if sealing the entrance.

I did a slow pan across the room. By my count, I was in there with six stone killers and one loudmouth producer known for keeping things popping. And the magazine in my little Beretta Tomcat only holds six rounds.

"Yep," I muttered under my breath. "Shit just got real."

Marty had been thinking it through too. When he finally spoke it was to me. "What the hell are you doing here?"

"I might ask you the same question," I replied.

Marty took a deep breath. "While you been checking around so have I, and I came up with something. We need to talk."

I nodded. "There's a backroom. If your boys can keep it cool in here."

Over his shoulder Marty said, "Anybody gets frisky, control the situation." Then he followed me into the back. I flipped the light on. The backroom turned out to be a small kitchen. I pushed my pistol into its holster, spun a chair around so its back faced the table, and dropped onto it. Marty sat down the usual way.

"I came by to question Yemmi's crew," I said, and pointed to Marty.

"You're ahead of me," Marty said, pulling a photo from an inside jacket pocket. "I'm here because of I got some good dope from my cop on the inside and just couldn't wait until morning to grab the guy who can clear my name with Carmen."

Marty laid a photo on the table and spread it out flat. It was an open folding knife with a four-inch blade, according to the ruler beside it.

"This is what they pulled out of Yemmi's ribs. You recognize it?"

It was a distinctive piece with a slim, sinuous outline. It's called a Laguiole, a folder with a narrow, tapered blade and a cutaway handle shaped kind of like a woman's leg. It was an artist's tool.

"Yeah, I recognize it. But we got to be sure."

"Of course. You need to be sure, because you're the one Carmen believe."

Returning to the front room I saw that Marty's two men were controlling the situation by displaying their nine-millimeter attention getters. It was time to decide who the danger man was. Smuggla and Jimmy were unarmed. Flex would be slow. His man didn't have any skin in the game. Having put the risks in order in my mind I walked straight over to Smuggla, who looked up as if he was expecting me.

"Okay, Smuggla, where's your knife? You know, that sweet little Laguiole you carry."

He turned his eyes away from mine. "I don't have it with me right now."

"No? I bet you know where it is, don't you?"

"Kind of. I gave it to Yemmi."

"What?"

"Look, he was scared," Smuggla said, warming to his story. "Guess I understand why, now. He knew he was going to try to hustle a known killer. Anyway he wanted to have something with him, just in case, so I loaned him my knife."

"Seriously?" Marty said. "That's what you're going with?"

I backed away, starting to circle the sofa. "So what happens now? You turn Smuggla over to your cop friend?"

Marty waved the comment away. "I could care less what happens with this idiot. All I care about is you telling Carmen that you know who killed her brother, and that it ain't me."

It was a tough spot. There was a best way to handle it, a smart way, but that just wasn't me. I looked back at Smuggla.

"So how long you been on Marty's payroll?"

"What you talking about now?" Marty asked, with an edge in his voice. I walked back toward Smuggla, keeping my focus on him.

"I know you, man. You one of us, a pro, and that's your signature blade. No way in hell you left it behind in a vic, knowing it would point right at you." Then I turned to Marty. "He gave you his knife, didn't he? You know, I might have went along with your silly-ass story if you hadn't tried to play me."

"What are you talking about?" Jimmy asked. "I mean, I know we didn't take Yemmi out, but how do you?"

"You mean aside from what I just said?" I hooked my thumbs into my belt. "Well, for one thing, I believe you that you wanted to get Flex here to tell you what happened to Yemmi. If you just wanted to hustle him, why wait until Yemmi's body turned up? I mean, if you killed Yemmi you would have already known he was dead, but you could have made Flex think he was being hustled by the same guy. And seriously, would you have tried to make his death look like a mugging? I don't think so. If you didn't have time to grab that knife, you sure as hell wouldn't have taken the time to go through his pockets to take his money."

"So we was right?" Jimmy asked.

"Oh yeah," I said, cutting my eyes toward Marty's gunmen. "Flex did it." The two guns swung toward him.

"You ain't putting this on me," Flex snapped. But Junior eased away from him.

"Like hell I ain't," I said, standing behind Jimmy on the couch. "And so would everybody else I know if not for all this static Marty was throwing up. You the only one who was all about what great friends you and Yemmi were. Nobody else really cared what I thought about that, but then, they wasn't trying to make me think they wouldn't hurt him. And just being the last one who saw him alive puts you at the top of the list. But most important, these boys confirmed the blackmail scheme, and that makes you the nigga with the only real motive."

"Then why'd Marty try to throw Smuggla under the bus?" Jimmy asked.

"Well, at first I figured he just wanted to clear his name with Carmen as fast as he could, and this was an easy story I could back up. But now I'm thinking how Flex told me he knew Marty, and knew he was a snake. Now I'm thinking Flex went to Marty after he killed Yemmi. He's not one of us, you know. He don't really know how to

274

cover up a murder, how to get himself clear. And Marty here, he sees a way to kill two birds with one stone."

"You on drugs or something?" Marty asked.

"Come on, Marty. You needed somebody to testify to Carmen for you. A cop or even a private eye would have dragged Smuggla to jail, and a real investigation might have turned up the truth. You knew I'd never get one of us arrested. But you could convince Smuggla that the evidence was against him. He'd think you were helping him if you got him out of the country. Then you just convince the cops it was Smuggla. Flex is in the clear, and you get the girl. It was a pretty slick setup. You just shouldn't have tried to play me."

"Easy, Skye," Marty said, stepping back between his two gunmen. "You don't want to be on my bad side."

"You know I won't lie for you," I said. "But there's still two ways this can go."

"No," Marty replied. "There's only one way this can go."

I took his word for it.

I maintained eye contact with Marty while my right hand yanked my silver belt buckle free and flipped the throwing star into Marty's throat. At the same time, my left yanked upward on Jimmy's belt, helping him flip over behind the sofa with me.

Marty's boys lost two tenths looking at their boss. By the time they were back on task I had dropped the dagger out of my right sleeve and thrown it into the gunman on my left. His mirror image managed to get off one poorly-aimed shot in my direction before Jimmy came up with his gun and double-tapped him up against the wall.

I wasn't thinking about him. After my throw my attention went to Junior. I had dropped low before he managed to decide where the threat to his boss would come from. He put two into the sofa before I brought my Beretta on line and shot him in his right bicep. He'd live, and might even stay in his line of work.

The action, from star toss to shooting Junior, had taken four seconds.

Flex, for once, was speechless. He stood in the middle of the floor looking lost while I retrieved my tools from two of the dead men—the one who tried to use me and the one who tried to protect him. When I turned to Flex I'm sure my weariness showed on my face. He raised his palms in surrender.

275

"I got no beef with you," he said. "And I heard you don't do this stuff unless you get paid or you protecting yourself."

"You heard right. For me killing is usually just business. And I don't care about whoever you killed back in the day. But I know you killed a man a couple days ago when you could have just paid him off. And when you did that, you took away another woman's brother. That's enough."

I didn't need to kill him. But he needed killing. I raised my pistol and shot him at the top of the bridge of his nose. Then I dropped the gun. I'd never use it again. Before he hit the ground my mind was already turned toward cleanup.

"You need to get moving," Jimmy said behind me.

I smiled. "I can take care of my own messes."

"No, we owe you," Jimmy said.

"Yeah, we got this," Smuggla said. "You go ahead."

On my way out the door I considered that I had judged Yemmi's posse correctly. Jimmy was a real G, old school. Smuggla was too, but he was also a killer. One of us.

Of course, I'm a bit more.

I am a true assassin.

THE ABSINTHE ASSASSIN

BY JM REINBOLD

Arnaud crept along in the darkness behind Rene. With only a bull's-eye lantern to light their way, he found himself clutching at the bookseller's coattails as Rene navigated the uneven limestone floor of a tunnel in the vast maze of passages and ossuaries beneath the streets of Paris. The maze held the bones of six million souls. The bones did not disturb him as much as the catacomb's narrow passages and low ceilings. Arnaud feared he would panic if forced to crouch any lower. Again his head brushed the ceiling. Rene's voice instructing him to drop to his knees added to his terror. Arnaud felt the bookseller's coat pulled from his fingers. Alone in the pitch-black, he cried out. The light appeared in front of him.

"Arnaud, you fool, where are you? Follow the light. Come through the hole."

The urge to bolt overwhelmed him. Arnaud dropped to his knees. Now he could see an opening, barely high and wide enough for a man to crawl through.

"Hurry," Rene hissed. "We'll be late."

An easy feat for the bookseller, skinny as a worm. Not so for Arnaud with his broad shoulders and barrel chest. He poked his head through the hole, twisting and turning to free his shoulders, then his chest. Finally, heart pounding, he wrenched his hips free. Rene grasped

Arnaud's jacket as he staggered to his feet. At least, the chamber they had entered allowed him to stand up straight. The walls were no longer closing in on him; he stretched his arms into empty space. He could hear water dripping. There was a damp chill in the air that took only seconds to pass through the thin fabric of his trousers and sink into his bones. Arnaud wondered how far underground they had come.

Rene moved as silently as a cat. In contrast, Arnaud's footfalls crunched and cracked as they crossed the bone-covered floor. Something gripped his ankle. With a cry he lunged forward.

"Something grabbed my leg!"

Rene made a gathering sound in his throat and spat into the dark. "Your imagination, Arnaud. No one is here."

"I know what I felt."

"You felt nothing."

"Give me the light then. Let us look."

Rene did not give Arnaud the light. Instead he walked on.

"The light."

Rene turned, his bony face made grotesque by the lantern. "You do not want to see."

Arnaud tensed, his muscles so knotted he feared cramp. "What are you saying?"

"I am saying we are almost there. Shut up and follow me."

Lit with oil lamps and candles, the crypt they entered was filled with bones stacked floor to ceiling. Skulls, hundreds of them, stared from niches in the walls. It was here the bohemian writers gathered, those who had become outlaws, those whose daring, unconventional books—many said scandalous—would not be published by any house that catered to the bourgeoisie. Arnaud knew who they were. The eroticist, Anaïs Nin; the Dadas with their upside down, inside out gibberish that simultaneously titillated and outraged an audience; the beast Miller, his French so butchered it made one's ears bleed; and the genius Didier who made slaves of his audience with his opium-like prose.

Arnaud loitered at the edges of the cafés and hotels in Montmartre and Montparnasse where the outlaws lived and wrote. He was one of them. He knew this in his soul. Had Didier himself not confirmed it? Arnaud, stinking of fear, sweating, his hands shaking like an old grandmother, had approached Didier as he took his midday meal. Arnaud had shown him his book, handwritten, and begged him to read it. No one, he swore, could claim a greater devotion to Didier's work. No author a greater inspiration to Arnaud than Didier himself. Didier, taken aback by Arnaud's fervor, embarrassed perhaps by Arnaud's adoration, had taken Arnaud's manuscript, promised to read it. He invited Arnaud to sit at his table, fed him soup and bread, cheese and wine. A whole bottle of wine. Arnaud felt the eyes of the outlaws on him. He, Arnaud, in the place they all wished to be.

It was rumored that Didier only wrote when he drank absinthe, that the green fairy was his muse. It was rumored that he would read tonight from his latest novel. Those invited had gathered in a circle around a makeshift dais. Some perched on portable camp chairs. Others sat on chunks of limestone, stretched out on picnic blankets, or leaned against the walls, living faces next to grinning skulls. Wine bottles passed from hand to hand. Arnaud scanned the audience—men, women, thirty, maybe forty of them. Young, reckless, fashionable, in their wide-legged pants and tight skirts. Intoxicated by the danger of secretly entering the under city. Arnaud had never understood that thrill. Where was Didier? Nauseous with anxiety, he could barely admit to himself the foolhardy thing he had done while caught up in the manic giddiness and bravado that had fueled his recent encounter with Didier. He had handed Didier his original manuscript, all of it. He had no copy. What had possessed him? He had convinced himself that Didier would read a few pages and, unable to contain his admiration, would summon him, shower him with praise, and offer him publication through the secret press that published his own words.

Arnaud had waited. A day. Then three. A week. No summons came. No word, good or bad. His anxiety had turned to fear. Why had Didier not contacted him? Arnaud had intended to read tonight. He must retrieve his manuscript. What if Didier were not here? Arnaud had lurked about the café for days and Didier had not appeared. No one had seen him. Writing, they said. He will not appear again until he is done his work. Even though this bone gallery was chilly and damp, sweat poured from Arnaud. When a bottle came by he grabbed it and swallowed half before relinquishing it, only to be reprimanded by the worm, Rene. Arnaud muttered a slur and turned his back. The bookseller jammed a knee between his shoulder blades. Arnaud snarled and moved away. The first reader had taken the stage, but Arnaud had no interest. Sick with worry, he snagged a full bottle from a couple's blanket as they listened intently to the reader and paid him no attention. Tearing the cork out with his teeth, he slid into a shadow behind the dais and nursed his prize.

Arnaud awoke with a start to the commotion that ensued with the arrival of Didier. He'd drunk most of the bottle and dozed off. Still bleary-eyed, Arnaud crawled through the crowd, larger now than when he and Rene had arrived, positioning himself as close to the front of the stage as he could. Didier looked like a decrepit lion, his massive head surrounded by an unkempt mane of grizzled hair. His drink-coarsened skin, reddened by spider webs of broken veins. His heavy, once-muscular body hobbled by old injuries. He limped to the stage. Arnaud relaxed. He would listen, let himself fall under Didier's spell, but not so much that he would forget his manuscript. He would accompany Didier when he left and retrieve his book. Even if he received no praise, Arnaud would not care. All that meant was that Didier was jealous. That was how it worked. If these bastards thought you were a hack, they would praise you until you shat gold. But if they thought you were better, their silence was absolute. No matter. Arnaud hugged the bottle.

Didier began to read. Arnaud closed his eyes, rested his head against the wall of bones. He let Didier's voice wash over him. He sighed and stretched. Didier wrote about the experiences most ordinary and transformed them into occasions of profound human revelation in language that sang and howled, his voice both base and exalted. The man was a genius. But something about Didier's reading made Arnaud uncomfortable, irritated his mind.

"Lost, alone in the impenetrable dark, those scattered, long-dead remnants of humanity cried out to my living bones, begging for flesh, bargaining for life. Five-hundred years could not silence them; they hungered for permanence. Who were they to savor eternity? Six-million souls starving for sunlight, warmth, breath. I tread upon hundreds, thousands, hundreds of thousands. I felt the memories of their hands clutching at my legs. Only a fool believes the dead rest in peace."

Arnaud bolted up, striking his head. His words! Didier was reading Arnaud's words! Fists at the ready, he stalked toward the dais. Then the little voice in his head, that had thus far been silent, whispered in his ear, told him to stay still, keep quiet. Remain hidden. Do not let Didier see you, know that you are here. Act, the voice whispered, as if you know nothing of what Didier has done. You are not in his clique. Not even supposed to be here. You can, the voice said, when the time is right, get your revenge and recover your manuscript. Arnaud slipped back into the shadows.

When Didier finished reading, Arnaud was shaking. For a long time he could not move. Inside his head a hurricane of chaos howled. Even if his little voice had not held him back, he could not have assaulted Didier. His rage, it seemed, had paralyzed him. Blinded him. When he came to himself, Didier was gone. Only a few stragglers remained. Arnaud looked around in alarm. Rene, the bookseller, had gone, left him. Arnaud had been in the catacombs before, true, but never here where the bookseller had brought him. He had no idea how to find his way out. He followed the stragglers, but they stared at him over their shoulders, gave him queer looks. He ran after them, but still they managed to elude him. Arnaud felt a trickle of sweat slide down his back. In danger of his nerves betraying him, he charged toward a tunnel where he thought he heard an echo of laughter. A few steps in the dark stopped him. He hurried back into the chamber. As he reached for one of the candles that had been left burning, a gruff voice halted his hand.

"You are lost, yes?"

Arnaud spun around. A decrepit old man stood there, his clothing old fashioned and much patched, white hair unkempt beneath a peaked leather cap, his thin beard long and stained. He gave off an unpleasant odor. Where had he come from? Surely, he had not attended the reading.

Arnaud eyed him suspiciously. "Who are you?"

The old man looked around and shrugged. "It appears that I am your salvation."

His salvation, indeed! The old man had not led Arnaud back to the streets above, but instead, despite Arnaud's protests, brought him to his encampment and deeper, or so it seemed, in the catacombs. It was there, huddled around a smoldering fire while the old man skinned and roasted rats, that Arnaud recounted the devastating events of the evening. He smacked a fist into the palm of his hand.

"I will destroy the thief, Didier!"

The old man leaned toward him, eager. "How will you do it?"

"Didier is an absinthe drinker. He cannot resist. I will poison his absinthe."

The old man frowned. "What if this Didier will not see you? Why should he? He has stolen your work. He will not speak to you again. If you accuse him he will deny your accusation."

"I will not accuse him."

"Bah. He will never let you near him. He is an absinthe drinker you say?"

Arnaud nodded.

"Then you must entice him; persuade him with something he cannot refuse. You must bring to him an absinthe that is legend, an absinthe no one has tasted in two hundred years."

Arnaud scoffed. The old wretch was mad. "And where would I get such a thing?"

"From me, you pompous fool." The old man glared at Arnaud with such blistering fierceness that Arnaud pissed himself.

"Who are you?" Arnaud whispered as he pushed himself away from the fire, distancing himself from the old man's angry gaze.

"Going somewhere?" the old man asked, mockery plain in his voice. "Unless I guide you, you will never find your way back to the streets."

Arnaud stayed still, wary. "What do I need with a fairytale when I can just as easily poison the cheap bottle he buys for himself?"

"Because you fool, you can bargain for your manuscript. What poison were you going to use? *Poudre de succession*, I imagine. So easily detected, the arsenic. You would be captured and guillotined because you are not only a murderer, but a stupid murderer."

"Murderer." Arnaud could hardly breathe.

The old man's laugh was nasty. "I know a woman. An alchemist she is. Some call her a witch. It is she who brings the Émèraude absinthe into being, and it is she who can make for you a poison untraceable."

Arnaud observed the smoke streaming horizontally across the small chamber. Fresh air entered the catacombs from somewhere above, filling the low-ceilinged room before the tunnels sucked it away, dragging the smoke from the fire with it. The old man had said only in chambers like this one could a fire be lit without consuming all the oxygen and suffocating the fool who lit it. Not much air down here, he cautioned. Go down into the lower passages and you'll get light-headed, start hearing things, seeing things.

Arnaud watched the smoke. What was the old man up to? Why should he care if Didier stole Arnaud's manuscript? Why would he offer to help Arnaud exact his revenge?

"Why would you help me?"

"There is a book," said the old man. "That rat-faced, bastard of a bookseller stole it. He keeps it locked up in a safe."

Arnaud sat up, eyes sharp. "I know this book," he declared. "Rene showed it to me once when he was giddy from wine."

The old man's eyes were bright, feral. "You live with him. You can get it."

The air around Arnaud suddenly felt much colder. He blew into his hands. "You don't know what you ask."

The old man's phlegmy laugh ended in a fit of coughing. Drops of mucus fell into the fire. The flames hissed.

"I know exactly what I ask, mon ami." He choked and spat out a blood-flecked gob.

Arnaud could not help himself. His mouth twisted in disgust. It seemed to him now that the old man's aroma had become even more malodorous, a stench that issued from his body and threatened to engulf Arnaud.

"What?" In the face of the old man's imminent decomposition, Arnaud had forgotten what they had been talking about.

"The book, you ninny, the one your bookseller keeps locked in his safe. It is one of a kind. He steals books, that one. How do you think he came by all those rare editions he has hidden away in his shop? He steals them and he sells to the highest bidder."

Arnaud had not moved. The look in the old man's eyes had paralyzed him.

"I want it back. If you have to kill him to get it, that is no more than what he deserves." Another glob of bloody phlegm hissed in the fire. "And, in return, I will get you the Émèraude absinthe and that tiny vial of death that will end this Didier." He smiled, revealing a nearly toothless mouth. "Are we in agreement?"

That night as they lay beside the fire, Arnaud heard sounds rising up from the deeper tunnels, shouting, and then a scream to freeze one's blood. They sat up, waiting. But there was nothing else. A prostitute, no doubt, the old man said, with a dissatisfied customer. Arnaud did not sleep. He lay awake, feeding the fire, listening to the old man snore like a broken bellows, wondering how he could sleep, worrying that the sound of his snores would attract whoever or whatever had caused the scream.

Arnaud followed the old man deeper into the catacombs. These passages were higher and Arnaud did not feel the terror of walls closing in on him. Still, his nerves were raw. The old man, like Rene the bookseller, had only a bull's-eye lantern and a map of the tunnels imprinted on his brain. If the old man were to abandon him, Arnaud could not find his way to the surface. He must be mad to follow this old derelict, but if he could give him the means to dispose of Didier and not be caught, then he must take the chance. Arnaud had heard of this Émèraude absinthe, but he had thought it a fairytale. The stories of its miraculous powers could not be true—to cure illness, defy old age, induce *la petite mort*, mesmerize with visons of ecstasy. The little voice in his head told him not to be too hasty in his judgment.

The old man stopped at the entrance to another chamber. He turned to Arnaud, held a finger to his lips, and mimed for him to wait. Arnaud nodded. The old man shimmied through the opening and shortly Arnaud heard a distant muttering of voices. A sliver of fear slid down his spine. The old devil could be in there with anyone, plotting to take his life. Ridiculous, his little voice whispered, you have nothing. What would they do with you except eat you? Then, out of the shadows the old man appeared. So quick was he that Arnaud did not have time to be startled before a gnarled hand gripped his arm like a vise and dragged him inside.

Dozens of candles lit the chamber. The sudden increase in light stung his eyes. Arnaud covered his face. Beeswax. He could smell it.

284

And now he could see mounds of wax on the floor. Cascades of wax dripping from niches cut into the walls. He could not believe his eyes. The place was furnished! He almost laughed out loud. Only a few pieces, of course. But what pieces! Old, elegant wood elaborately carved. And tapestries! The colors of the silk thread glowed like jewels.

Arnaud heard a soft, throaty chuckle. He peered further into the chamber. She was as pale as the candle wax. A sheen of phosphorescence on her skin. She had a wasp's nest of white blond hair. Her eyes were green and feral. A cruel mouth, despite her full, moist lips. She was dressed in a green satin wrapper that might slide off her shoulders at the slightest provocation. She was scrutinizing him, waiting, perhaps, for him to speak. Despite her appearance, was she not a lady, after all? He was not so sure of it, but he dared not take the chance of insulting her.

"*Mademoiselle*," he said making a little bow.

She came to him. Stood directly in front of him. Close enough he could smell her. She held out her hand. Arnaud took it and pressed his lips to her fingers. Her skin was cool, moist.

"*Monsieur* Arnaud, my father tells me you intend to kill a man and you wish me to assist you. That I will do. When you return with our book you will have your Émèraude absinthe and your poison. You will not be suspected, *Monsieur*, but you must make sure he drinks the Émèraude to the last drop."

"He will drink it all. I need not be there to know this."

"You are not understanding me, *Monsieur*. The Émèraude must be consumed all at once for the poison to work."

Arnaud gaped at her. "Impossible! He will be unconscious before the bottle is gone."

"It will take time. All night perhaps. But it must be done so."

Arnaud stared at her in consternation. "If I do not drink, he will be suspicious."

"It is simple enough. Drink wine."

"It will not do, *Mademoiselle*. At the green hour, no one drinks wine."

"Well then, you must drink with him."

"And poison myself!"

"Three glasses, *Monsieur*. I will make extra. Three will not kill you. And Didier will still have the full dose."

285

"The poison will not hurt me?"

"I did not say that. I said it will not kill you."

Arnaud's skin prickled. "What will it do to me?" Where was his little voice? He needed its counsel, and yet it had been strangely silent throughout this bizarre encounter.

"You will see things, hear things, feel things that may or may not be real. You are familiar with that, are you not, *Monsieur*?"

Arnaud shifted uneasily. They had been conversing for some time and this strange woman had not offered him a seat. Arnaud had also lost track of the old man. Her father, she'd said. Horrifying! His feet hurt, and all this talk of absinthe had given him the thirst.

"*Mademoiselle*, if you please, I must sit down."

"But of course." She clapped her hands once, twice. "Papa, bring *Monsieur* Arnaud a chair."

The old man materialized from the shadows of the room like a wraith. So, he'd been there all along listening to them. Now he scuttled about like a spider, dragging a chair for Arnaud.

"Now sit, *Monsieur*. We will speak of this no more." With a coy tilt of her head she said, "Perhaps you would like to join us in a little indulgence, yes? So you know what you are paying for."

Arnaud's heart skipped a beat. "The Émèraude absinthe?"

"*Oui*, the Émèraude absinthe." She laughed a sultry laugh, a knowing laugh that filled Arnaud's mind with fantasies of ostrich feather fans and naked skin the color of cocoa. The heat from the candles had become oppressive, coating his body in a glaze of sweat.

She reached beneath the tapestry-covered table and brought out a crystal bottle sculpted like a twist of smoke on an autumn evening. The liquid within was a startling, luminescent green.

"The Émèraude's color does not change even after you add the water. Nothing can dim this green jewel."

Arnaud watched intently as she withdrew three exquisitely etched glasses from a cache, poured the absinthe, set a silver filigree spoon on each. Tiny skulls, molded from sugar—some white, some black—were next. Then the water. "*Monsieur*." She handed him a glass.

Arnaud gazed into the green depths.

"Do not look too long, *Monsieur*. The Émèraude has other abilities ... it is an ancient formula created when men knew more of the world than what is easily seen."

Arnaud sipped. Green fire spread through his veins. If asked, he would swear he could see it. Pleasure spread through his loins, to his heart, then his head. He froze mid sip, staring, ecstatic.

Arnaud watched the greenish waters of the Seine. If one sat long enough under a bridge, one could see all manner of things float by. Bodies mostly, but other things, too, furniture, hatboxes, bottles. Tonight, under the light of a full moon, a boat had come drifting out of the mists that hung above the water, carrying a couple in full wedding dress. The bride's jewel-embroidered veil was thrown back, the groom's top hat rested in his lap. As they drew across from him, Arnaud saw they held hands and, with their free hands, lifted empty glasses to him. It was then he realized the antiquity and deterioration of their attire and saw their faces, as wizened as dried apples and as deeply wrinkled. The boat spun in a circle, steadied itself, then, pulled along by the current, sailed on out of Arnaud's sight.

Arnaud shook off the memory. The day was dawning, but what day? In the catacombs there was no time. He might have been there a day or a week, longer, for all he knew. The old man had finally brought him back to Monmartre. Had told him where to leave a message. Arnaud had no doubt now that he could dispose of Didier. With the Émèraude absinthe, the thief had no chance. He must get the book from Rene. But how? He did not know how to crack a safe. The old man had suggested he kill Rene. Preposterous! If Rene were dead, he still could not open the safe. What then?

Think, you idiot! He would have to return to the bookstore and go about his business as usual. He would have to wait for a chance. Who knew when Rene would open the safe again and for what reason? When he did, Arnaud would have to be ready. If stealing this book would give him the means to destroy the devil Didier, then he would get the book.

He, Arnaud was a clever man, one might even say cunning. And what was Rene to him, after all? Yes, he gave him a place to stay and asked no rent. But who would ask rent for a cot in a dusty corner of a storage room? Yes, Rene fed him. But Arnaud barely survived on a breakfast of one coffee, a crumb of cheese and a slice of unbuttered bread for lunch, then a single hard-boiled egg and glass of wine for his supper. The few francs Rene paid Arnaud hardly allowed him to live. A few cigarettes was all he could afford on his pittance. Rene published the works of outlaws, but refused Arnaud's book. To hell with Rene.

Arnaud peered through the shelves of books. One of Rene's customers had just paid for a rare volume with cognac. Rene walked the old gentleman out and locked the door. Cognac was the bookseller's weakness. Soon he was drinking and bragging. "That book is medieval," he said, "written by the Templars. It reveals all the secrets of Chartres. This cognac," Rene held the bottle aloft, "is two hundred years old."

"And you do not offer even one glass to your old friend, Arnaud?"

Rene sputtered. "Old friend! I found you nearly frozen to death in my doorway. Another would have kicked you into the gutter. I am a Christian; I took you in, brought you back to life. You have a place to sleep; you eat; I even pay you for the little you do. I do not see you for weeks and then you return. When the sun shines and the birds sing, you are in the streets day and night. When the north wind blows, you begin to cast about for someone to take you in. The least you could do is write well, but you will not do even that."

Arnaud was beginning to feel quite sour. He thought of punching Rene. Instead, he said. "The book you just sold, where did you get it?"

The bookseller's eyes narrowed. He sat up straight in his chair. "What are you babbling about?"

"It is said that these books," Arnaud waved his arm at the stacks, "are stolen."

"Who says this?" a red-faced Rene demanded of Arnaud. "They are liars."

"Envious gossips," Arnaud said, enjoying his pretense of placating the bookseller. "Troublemakers. I did not believe them. I said so to the others." Arnaud chuckled to himself. Rene would be beside himself for days, fuming over the affront.

Rene poured himself another cognac, swallowed it in one gulp, and poured another. But this time he poured cognac for Arnaud.

Together they moved closer to the fire, warming their hands and their glasses.

Arnaud awoke in darkness on his cot. He did not remember going to his bed. He lay on his back listening to the moonlight that entered through the window high up in the wall. He tried to hum along, but the tune eluded him. In the shaft of light, specks of dust floated and sparkled. They made a whispering sound when they moved, a louder tick when they collided. There, too, the sound of mice scrabbling through the walls and doves cooing in the rafters. These noises were a comfort to him, made it possible for him to stay in his bed, but now he heard another sound—creaking, something moving over the ancient floorboards. Arnaud sat up, rubbed himself against the chill, and then slipped out of the storeroom. He stood in the doorway, listening. They'd had intruders before. As he tiptoed past the fireplace, he took the poker with him. Arnaud peered through a shelf of books; the light of a single candle illuminated the back of the bookseller, crouching in the closet he called his office and picking out the combination to his safe.

Arnaud clutched the book concealed beneath his coat. It was a slim volume, bound in gray cloth with a single black stripe, frayed at the corners. Its ink-smudged, stained pages were covered with numbers and ciphers written in a cramped script. Arnaud could make no sense of it; a code of some sort. He did not fear walking openly on the street. Rene had friends, yes, but none who would inform the *gendarmes*. The bookseller did not even have a legal shop. His business squatted in a condemned building in an all-but-abandoned street. Who, Arnaud asked himself, would discover the bookseller's body? The rats. Only the rats. He had nothing to fear from rats. The old man was another matter.

They were to meet beneath the Pont Neuf. Arnaud did not like having to wait. He watched the piles of rags half hidden in shadows. Thus far they had remained still.

"Where is the book?"

A bolt of fear nearly stopped Arnaud's heart. Where had the old man come from?

"Waiting for you," the old man said as if reading Arnaud's mind. "Show it to me!"

Arnaud slid the book from beneath his coat. The old man reached for it, his claw-like fingers flexing in anticipation. Arnaud retreated to the river's edge. He held the book over the water.

"What are you doing?" the old man snarled.

"You will have this when I have the Émèraude."

The old man's mocking smile unsettled Arnaud, but he did not allow himself to show his unease. The old man turned and disappeared in the shadows. Arnaud's heart raced. The faster he concluded this transaction and got away from this place the better. For all he knew the old man had thugs waiting out of sight to take the book from him. He saw the old man returning. He was alone and carried a small cardboard box. He stopped where he'd been standing before and stared malevolently at Arnaud. Arnaud did not withdraw his arm.

The old man placed the box on the ground and shoved it with his foot.

"Closer."

The old man walked to the box and shoved it again until it slid within inches of Arnaud. Arnaud squatted beside the box without taking his eyes off the old man. He lifted the bottle.

"This bottle is sealed," he said angrily. "How do I know it is not just green water?"

"Does green water glow?" The old man's sarcasm scalded Arnaud like acid. He flushed. When he held the bottle in the moonlight it glowed with a green luminescence that seemed to pulsate. Arnaud could barely stand to look at it.

"It cannot be unsealed until you are prepared to drink every drop. If you have forgotten her instructions, then I pity you."

Arnaud ignored him. There was a jar of sugar skulls in the box, but he saw nothing else.

"Where is the poison?" he cried. "You think you can cheat me?"

The old man gave Arnaud a pitying look. "There is one drop of evil on each skull."

Arnaud stood up.

The old man took a step toward him. "Listen to me, you must ..."

Arnaud flung the book at the old man's head. It struck him between the eyes. The man shouted and stumbled backward, falling hard on his ass. Arnaud snatched the box and ran as if the devil were on his heels.

Arnaud stood in shadows that grew deeper and darker as the sun proceeded in its descent. Already the street lamps were lit. He had been waiting nearly an hour for the arrival of Didier. It was the green hour at the Café Lumière, and those who courted the green fairy had already filled the booths. Where was Didier? If he did not come soon, the cold would force Arnaud off the street. He heard a sound, distant, but coming nearer. The hair on the back of his neck prickled. He could not see who or what approached; he didn't need to. He could hear the sound more clearly now—a flat, tuneless whistling that grated on the ear. The dry, cold air amplified the noise. Arnaud waited. Moments later, Didier came into view, muffled to the ears in his winter coat and scarf, his cap pulled down. Arnaud stamped his feet. Didier strolled down the center of the boulevard, whistling. From time to time, he stared openmouthed at the sky as if he had never before seen stars. A black, low-slung Avions Voisin, its silver wings flashing, tooted at him to clear the road. The driver lowered the window and shouted, revved the powerful engine, forcing him onto the sidewalk. Didier dismissed him with a wave of his hand. Finally, he drew near. Arnaud stepped from the shadows.

"*Bon soir, Monsieur* Didier."

Didier stopped abruptly. Arnaud saw panic in his eyes an instant before Didier realized who he was.

Didier's eyes narrowed. "What do you want, Arnaud?"

"My manuscript, *Monsieur.*"

"Have some patience, man."

Bile rose bitter and scalding in Arnaud's throat. Didier lied through his teeth. At the reading in the catacombs he'd said the book would soon be published. Did he think Arnaud would not find out? That he could do nothing? Was Arnaud nothing? No better than trash blowing about in the streets? Who would believe him anyway in the face of Didier's lies? Arnaud knew better. Didier was a slave to the green fairy. Maybe his words were gold and diamonds at one time, but no more. Perhaps they had never been. Had Didier stolen all his books? Arnaud forced a smile. He must ingratiate himself yet again with this monster. He bowed his head a little as if in deference. He must make this turd believe him an innocent, ignorant scribbler begging for crumbs of praise at his feet.

"No, no, *Monsieur*. Forgive me, I do not wish to take advantage. It is too much to ask of you. In the heat of the moment. My excitement in your presence. I did not consider. Please, *Monsieur* Didier, allow me relieve you of this burden." Arnaud crossed his fingers behind his back. Had he been subservient enough? It was all he could do to keep his rancor concealed. Arnaud was struck dumb when Didier patted his shoulder as if he were a child.

With a wave of his hand Didier dismissed Arnaud's request. "Nonsense! It is not so much. It will give me a good laugh no doubt. I am in need of a laugh." He turned and made for the Café Lumière.

Arnaud snatched at Didier's sleeve and caught it. Didier turned abruptly and shook him off. He raised his arm as if to strike. Arnaud cringed and held up his hands in supplication.

"Please, *Monsieur*, I mean you no harm. I am in your debt. I had thought to give you this gift in apology, but now it is in gratitude for what you do for me." Arnaud slid the bottle of Émèraude from inside his coat.

"It is the fabled Émèraude," Arnaud whispered. He moved closer to the café so the bottle caught the light. The absinthe glowed like a green star.

Didier took a step back. He stared with the awestruck look of a simpleton. "It cannot be."

Arnaud laughed to himself. Didier knew! He knew! "I tell you it is. I know the woman—some say she is a witch—who makes this elixir."

Didier reached for the Émèraude. "Give it to me."

Arnaud slid the bottle inside his jacket. "Let us go inside. There is a special way it must be prepared. I will show you." He could sense Didier's reluctance. "It is important that it is prepared just so. You have heard of its powers?"

Didier nodded. "Tell me."

Arnaud shook his head. "It must be shown."

Didier snatched Arnaud by his jacket. "Come, then, before I freeze to death."

Arnaud allowed Didier to hustle him along. He felt Didier's fingers plucking at the buttons of his jacket. He kept a tight grip on the absinthe.

"Keep that bottle in your coat," Didier said before opening the door of the Café Lumière. Once inside, he called to the man at the bar. "Henri!"

Wrapped in a long, wide apron, Henri held a bottle of cheap wine, ready to fill the glasses of a pack of young men lounging at the bar. They resembled the Apaches of years past with their striped shirts, fancy jackets, and shiny, sharp-toed boots. Henri set aside the wine, wiped his hands on his apron, ran thick fingers through his thinning hair, then hurried from behind the counter amid protests from the young men who shouted and pounded empty glasses on the bar. Henri cast them a contemptuous look.

"*Monsieur* Didier, it is an honor as always. Your room is prepared. What may I bring you?"

"My usual meal, *s'il te plait.*"

"And your bottle?"

"Not tonight. *Monsieur* Arnaud has brought me a special bottle."

Henri smiled. "As you wish, *Monsieur.*"

When he turned to Arnaud the smile disappeared. "And for your ... friend?"

"Nothing. He will not be staying long."

Henri nodded and made a little bow. As he returned to the bar, the gang of young men, who had been watching them, began to shout again. Henri, now red-faced and fuming, threatened to throw them into the street. "Shut up!" He snatched up their money, slammed down a bottle, and told them to serve themselves.

"Solange!" Henri shouted. The waitress appeared to whistles and wolf calls from the bar. "Get out!" Henri shouted. "Out!" Howling with laughter, the boys grabbed their bottle and in a slow, dramatic pantomime slouched through door, crying out in mock horror at the icy blast. Solange flung the bar rag at them. "Shut the damn door!"

Laughing, Didier motioned for Arnaud to follow him.

He opened a door behind the bar that led to a flight of stairs. Arnaud followed him. Up they went to a second floor hall. There were doors to rooms on either side of the passage and one at the end. That one, Arnaud thought, that will be Didier's room.

Arnaud could not conceal his surprise. The room at the end of the hall was warm and inviting. Thick carpets on the floor, a feather bed, and lamps with painted globes that spread a golden radiance. Spare, but rich, so rich. The room smelled of violets. The luxury nearly caused him to weep. A knock at the door distracted him.

"Come," Didier called. The door opened and Solange entered bearing a covered tray. The savory aroma of rabbit stew and freshly baked bread invaded Arnaud's nostrils. His mouth began to water. He wiped saliva from his lips with his sleeve. The urge possessed him to snatch the crock that held the stew and flee with it. Surely, Didier and the girl could hear the racket his stomach was making. Solange set the tray on a table in an alcove. She went back into the hall and returned with another tray that held two glasses, slotted spoons, a dish of sugar, and a pitcher of water.

"*Merci*, Solange," Didier said.

As she turned to leave she winked at Didier.

"Later," he said. "When I am ready to sleep."

Solange pulled a face then laughed. "Didier never sleeps."

To Arnaud, her laughter sounded like tinkling bells. She passed close to him. He could smell her sweat, her odor. She poked her tongue out at him and shut the door in his face. Solange smelled of violets.

Behind him Didier laughed. "Don't get any ideas."

Arnaud ignored him. "Do you live in this place?"

"When it suits me."

Didier had begun to perspire. He took a towel from the wash stand and mopped his forehead and the back of his neck, before dropping into a chair at the table. "L'Émèraude." He stared at Arnaud with feverish eyes.

Arnaud would not have to convince Didier that they must finish the bottle. More likely he'd have to wrestle the bastard for even a drop. Arnaud smiled to himself. The witch had not said how Didier would die, but he hoped it would be painful and frightening. More than anything he wanted to see the terror in Didier's eyes when he told him he was a dead man. When Didier was deep in the grip of the absinthe,

Arnaud would beat him. He would beat him hard and long. He would make him pay for every word he had stolen.

Didier motioned for Arnaud to sit at the table. Arnaud sat. Impatient for him to prepare the absinthe, Didier shoved the crock of stew aside.

"I'm hungry," Arnaud said. He sat down and pulled the crock to him.

"Not now!"

"Now," Arnaud said. He set the bottle of Émèraude on the table. He shook a finger at Didier. "Do not touch it." Arnaud ate greedily, noisily. The thick gravy and tender shreds of meat, the fresh, firm vegetables filled him with emotion. He soaked up more of the gravy with buttered bread he had no doubt had been baked that morning.

Didier, murmuring to himself, appeared entranced by the absinthe's luminescence. His wonder-filled eyes met Arnaud's. "It glows as the legends say."

Arnaud nodded. He set two shallow glasses between them. He cracked the seal on the bottle and removed the cork. Then, placing two fingers first against the side of one glass then the other, he poured the absinthe. "Just so."

"You are drinking, too?" Didier asked. "You said the Émèraude was a gift for me."

"Do not be greedy, *Monsieur*. There is enough absinthe in this bottle for seven drinks. I will have three and you will have four."

Next he placed a slotted spoon atop each glass. Didier lifted two lumps of sugar from the bowl. Arnaud pushed Didier's hand away. "*Non!*" He pulled the bag of sugar skulls from his pocket. He held one up so Didier could see then placed a skull in each spoon.

Didier lifted his sugar skull and examined it. "What is this?"

Arnaud smiled. "The end of us."

Didier chuckled. "From that witch of yours, I suppose."

Arnaud, grinning now, nodded.

Didier put the sugar skull back in the spoon. Arnaud lifted the pitcher of water and began to pour it, one drop at a time, over the skull.

"You torture me."

Arnaud moved from one glass to the other, pouring drop by drop. "Look."

Didier sucked in his breath. "The color does not change! The green is even brighter."

"That is why," said Arnaud, "it is called L'Émèraude. Now, let us see if the rest of the legend is true."

He handed the glass to Didier. Didier took the glass and lifted it to his lips.

"Wait! We must have a toast."

Didier looked perplexed. "A toast?"

"To celebrate the Émèraude and, of course, your words."

Didier tutted. "I will celebrate the Émèraude; the rest is tempting fate."

"As you wish." Arnaud raised his glass, Didier raised his. "To the Émèraude and *la petite mort.*"

The absinthe felt hot on Arnaud's tongue. In fact, it burned. Arnaud swallowed. The absinthe slid down his throat leaving a trail of fire in its wake.

Didier waved a hand in front of his open mouth. "What in God's name have you done?" Didier started to say more, but ... Didier's eyes turned a brilliant green. Arnaud rocked back in his chair. Didier chortled and pointed at Arnaud.

"Your eyes! Look in the mirror!"

Arnaud rose slowly. He peered into the mirror above the bureau. He started at the sight. His eyes, too, shone a brilliant green.

The laughter caused Arnaud's skin to tingle as if a bolt of lightning had electrified the air and caused all the hairs on his body to vibrate. He spun around. The witch sat in Didier's seat. From beneath dark, arched brows she regarded him with eyes as pale green as the absinthe should have been. A petite emerald green hat of crushed satin with a green-and-yellow-feathered parakeet clinging to it perched atop her mass of teased white blonde hair. A green gloved hand clutched a fur-trimmed gold lamé wrap that had fallen away from her shoulder. Her skin was flawless and pale as wax. She might have escaped from the Grévin.

Arnaud's eyes darted around the small room. "Where is Didier?"

A slight smiled parted her lips. Her teeth were small, sharp. Had they been so when he first met her? He couldn't be sure. She had not smiled then and he wished she would not now.

"You would murder the genius Didier?" The sound of her voice made Arnaud nauseous.

"He is no genius. He is a thief."

"A thief? What has he stolen?" She lifted Didier's glass and swallowed the last mouthful of absinthe. She pushed the glass at Arnaud. "More."

"No more. It is for Didier, as you well know." Arnaud stopped himself. He had been so astonished by her appearance and the intensity of her presence that it had not occurred to him that this was still Didier with whom he spoke; that the Émèraude was the cause of this strange apparition. He must be careful. Didier was trying to trick him.

"You have not answered my question."

"My book."

Her forehead creased. "What book?"

Arnaud stroked the bottle. "*L'Empire de la Mort.*"

She threw back her head and laughed. The sound was like shattering glass to Arnaud's ears. When her laughter ceased, she fixed him with a fierce stare. "You claim to have written this masterpiece?"

Arnaud drew himself up and leaned across the table. She waved him away as if he were an annoying fly.

"I do not claim. I wrote it!"

"Words written by a genius, not a madman."

Arnaud bristled. He had to remind himself again that this creature was Didier. That he was seeing Didier through the glamour of the Émèraude. Absinthe had shown him things before, but not like this ... "You stole them from me."

"I stole nothing."

Arnaud lunged across the table. He grasped a fistful of her hair; straw that felt like silk in his hands. Again she laughed at him. Her sharp little teeth gleamed. She bit him. Hard. Her teeth sunk into the flesh below his thumb. Arnaud shrieked and shook her off, bits of his skin caught in her teeth. He knocked his chair to the floor as he fled the table. The derision in her laughter scalded him as if she had flung a pot of boiling water in his face.

Arnaud lay on the bed nursing his hand. An armoire and a section of wall blocked his view of the table. Thank God, she had not followed him. He examined the bite. It still bled. And the pain. He was near the door. He should leave. But what of his book? His revenge? How had this happened? He started to roll off the bed. No! He could not leave the Émèraude.

There was no question that Didier would drink the entire bottle. But he might not use the poisoned sugar. The Émèraude was more powerful than he remembered when the witch had given him a taste. Didier might succumb before he finished. Arnaud licked his lips. She said he could have three glasses and remain unharmed. The fourth glass would carry the fatal dose. The bottle held seven glasses. He'd had one glass and look what had happened. He looked around the room. There was nothing there that should not be there. Despite the initial euphoria and the following hallucination, his mind was clear. He should go. He must go. He heard the clink of metal on glass. Didier was preparing more absinthe. He should go. He heard the scrape of the stopper being pulled from the Émèraude. Arnaud stood up. He peered around the edge of the wall.

"Ah, there you are. I thought you'd run away."

Arnaud stood frozen in place. The creature that spoke to him now was neither Didier nor the witch. The man was skeletal. Skin stretched taut over bone. Hair of no particular color, a forgettable beige, long and ragged. He, too, had wax-like skin, paler even than the woman. His fingernails were stained. But it was his eyes that kept Arnaud pressed against the wall. One eye was the same iridescent green as the Émèraude; the other pure white, the pupil the size of a pinprick. For the first time it occurred to Arnaud that what he was seeing was real and not an absinthe-fueled hallucination. That somehow Didier had been spirited away by these devils.

The white eye unnerved him, but he could not move. The gaunt man smiled, revealing bloodstained teeth. He held up a glass of the glowing Émèraude. Arnaud glanced at the bowl of sugar skulls; three remained. The gaunt man tilted the glass gently from side to side. Something within the absinthe seemed to gather itself into a form of sorts, then dispersed into a cloud of gold within the green.

"I don't like to drink alone."

Every nerve urged Arnaud to flee. The white eye blinked slowly. Arnaud stepped away from the wall, the door. He approached the table cautiously. He hovered just out of reach of the glass. Through a slender gap in the heavy velvet curtains shone the lights of the dance hall across the street. The gaunt man pulled the velvet curtains away from the window just enough that Arnaud could peer down at a corner of the street. Illuminated by a streetlight, a figure passed and was gone. *Don't be a fool*, Arnaud told himself, *that is still Paris out there, still Montmartre. I am still Arnaud.*

"Sit down." The gaunt man tipped the glass at Arnaud's chair, which, Arnaud saw, he had righted. "I don't bite." Pleased with his little joke, he laughed, a girl's high-pitched giggle. He set the absinthe at Arnaud's place. Cautiously, Arnaud slid into the chair.

Arnaud held the glass in both hands, held it beneath his nose. Wormwood, anise, fennel. All familiar. He smelled it again. A memory. How could he smell a memory? Of what? Arnaud touched the surface of the liquid with his tongue. It burned. Glimpses of the memory teased him.

"What have you done with Didier?"

"You are here to murder him, yes?"

Arnaud set his glass down. He looked warily at the gaunt man.

"How do you know that?" he asked before he could stop himself. This was Didier he was talking to.

"If you plan to poison him with this elixir, he will die a happy man." The gaunt man smiled. The white eye held Arnaud captive. "Is this what you want?"

"No."

"Do you not want him to suffer for what he has done to you?"

Arnaud nodded.

"He has condemned you to obscurity, my friend. Your name will never be known. Never be spoken. If you are remembered at all, it will be as a traitor to your master. A pretender whose arrogance blotted out his reason, who was so great a fool he thought he could steal fire from a god."

Arnaud was on his feet in an instant. He seized the bottle of Émèraude, ready to crush the gaunt man's head. It was all he could do to return it to the table.

The gaunt man smiled. If a corpse could grimace. "Another glass?" Arnaud looked away. He poured the absinthe.

"If you want him to suffer, cut off his fingers." The gaunt man laid a butcher's cleaver on the table between them. The edge of the blade shone. There was no mistaking its sharpness. "If he has no fingers, he cannot write."

299

Arnaud looked into the white eye. For a split second the gaunt man was gone and Didier sat there grinning at him. Arnaud seized the cleaver with one hand and Didier's wrist with the other. He brought the knife down hard on Didier's hand. He severed four fingers, the little finger hung by a shred of skin. Blood everywhere. And then the pain. Arnaud screamed. It was his hand from which the fingers were cut. His hand that bled like a river on the damask tablecloth. He ripped the cloth from the table. The tray and Émèraude crashed to the floor. Arnaud wadded the cloth around his hand. The pain was excruciating. He retrieved the absinthe and one-handed removed the stopper, upended the bottle, and poured the liquor down his throat. Immediately, the pain disappeared. It was then that he realized the gaunt man had gone. He let the Émèraude fall, and watched as the last of the absinthe trickled out. Like a genie escaping its bottle, a green mist formed and hovered over him. Arnaud gasped. The undulating cloud drew itself over him like a quilt, warming him, numbing him. He could not escape it now, nor did he want to.

The sun rose bright above the fields, bathing all of Paris in an early spring light. He stood over the coffin of his friend, who had more than once declared that when he died he wanted no priest mumbling over him. So the job had fallen to Rene. "Friends," he said, to the crowd that huddled around the grave in the chill air. "I beg you to remember Arnaud Didier as the genius he was, and not the madman he became."

SLAY IT FORWARD

BY ADRIAN LUDENS

Next Week

The professional assassin known as By the Books crouches with his gloved finger on the trigger. A trickle of perspiration tickles the small of his back, but he ignores any urge to move or react. He's waiting for his target to leave her townhouse and step out onto the sidewalk. When the woman makes her appearance, just as she's done at this time every day this week, he squeezes the trigger. Through the scope he sees what looks like a poppy blossom on her kneecap. She staggers and collapses. People instinctively clear away from her. They know who she is, what she has done. Already they realize what's happening.

The woman turns and begins to crawl—painfully, he hopes—up the steps toward her townhouse. He gives her time, allows her a glimmer of hope. Then he centers the crosshairs on the back of her rotten melon head. He clears his mind of past jobs. Forgets all the other lives he's claimed. The slate is wiped clean. By the Books conjures up a single image: a baby.

He's never met this innocent. But he knows its story. This baby's drunken mother put the baby in her oven and cooked her like one would a roast turkey, only with less care and preparation. This woman, according to prosecutors, wanted to get back at her estranged husband for saying he would take her to court for custody of their child. Her defense in the courtroom came down to blackout drunkenness. She had no recollection of the events of that evening. Reasonable doubt, her attorney said. Someone else could have broken in to her townhouse and done the deed. This woman's attorney told the jury there was no indisputable proof, and certainly no mother would do that to her child. His client went free just in time for happy hour.

This same woman now reaches for her doorknob.

The passersby have mostly stopped, but no one steps forward to help. A faint breeze carries the tantalizing odor of curried beef to his nostrils. By the Books decides he'll have Indian for dinner at the same moment he squeezes the trigger again. The woman who cooked her baby collapses in a puddle of her own tainted brain matter. Her shooter sees fragments of bone, blood, and hair slide down her still-closed door. He hears fragments of scattered applause as he disassembles his charcoal-colored tool of justice.

He knows the police and paramedics won't break any records with their arrival time. This movement that he is a part of has spread like wildfire. By the Books will be at least three miles away by the time the first paramedic kneels at the dead woman's side. A police officer will ask questions, seek witnesses. No one will speak.

By the Books has received payment for more hits than he'd care to remember, but he won't see a penny for this job. It's a freebie, a service in the interest of the public. *Bless the Idea Man*, By the Books thinks.

Four Weeks Ago

"You look like James Garner. Anybody ever tell you that?" The Wild Card mixes himself another whiskey sour and flops back down in his hardwood deck chair.

"Quite often, but that was decades ago." His host's lips twitch into a smile, perhaps remembering happier days. "And what may have happened between me and any of the women who thought this is certainly none of your business and not the topic we're here to discuss." The Idea Man mixes himself a gin and tonic and turns back to his guest. "Have you given my proposal any further consideration?"

The Wild Card runs his fingers through the thicket of hair on the top of his head. He wants to play it cool with The Idea Man. The spirits are top-shelf. The furniture is top of the line. The house is perched at the top of the hill. He looks west and ponders the Spaghetti Western sunset.

The Idea Man wasn't always referred to as such. In fact, only a precious few recently started using that moniker. The Idea Man is a retired crime lord. A kingpin, one might say. He'd amassed his fortune outside the law. Never a cruel man, if the stories were true, but he was not one to be bothered by niceties either. He'd used the services of killers-for-hire on a number of occasions. There were casualties, but it was never personal.

Then one ill-fated evening about six months ago, his daughter and granddaughter were struck and killed four feet into the crosswalk of an intersection. The driver who hit them told police his portable music player had jostled loose of its dock and had fallen. He'd been leaning over, trying to retrieve the device from the floor mat. He didn't even see them. *There were casualties, but it wasn't personal.*

The Idea Man took it hard. But he also knew he'd be a hypocrite to kill the driver of the pickup truck. Instead, he read the papers—an array of local and national rags—with a keen eye.

A suitable replacement for his vengeance presented himself when, just two states away, a sobbing woman burst into a police station to report the death of her kindergarten-age daughter. It had been, according to her, at the hands of the little girl's grandfather, who'd been visiting. She couldn't understand it, she said; when her father came into *her* bedroom when she was a girl, it hurt sometimes, but she'd never bled as much as her daughter had. The newspapers carried all the sordid, horrifying allegations. But allegations were all they amounted to. The man was questioned, but never arrested. It seemed no physical evidence or DNA samples implicated him. Instead, the man's daughter was arrested and charged for the crime. The Idea Man didn't like how this was playing out at all. He had looked at their pictures and had known instantly the older man was guilty. The Idea Man had seen all sorts during his career. He'd gotten to know the different faces of evil and could read people just by looking in their eyes. He recognized guilt the way other folks recognized mold on rotten fruit. And this guy, The Idea Man knew, was rotten to the core.

The Idea Man had a thought. It germinated into the grand initiative that gave him his fitting epithet. He thought to himself, *Justice is not being served. Why sit idly by, when I have the capability and resources to right this wrong?*

So he booked a flight.

Three days later, just past three o'clock in the afternoon, the Idea Man strolled up the sidewalk in front of the rotten man's home. He noticed the unmarked police car parked halfway down the block on the opposite side of the street, and decided the local authorities felt justice wasn't being served either. But the Idea Man didn't have the patience to wait for the wheels of justice to grind; slow, fine, or otherwise. He rounded the corner and then cut back through the alley, crunching across the gravel toward the rear of his intended target's house. The Idea Man noted that no children played in the adjacent yards. He heard no girlish laughter, no shouts of boyish excitement. He wasn't surprised. In their hearts, the people in this community knew the truth.

The Idea Man pulled on a pair of gloves and opened the gate. He strode up the sidewalk to the man's back door. Forty five seconds of work with a torsion wrench and hook pick and he was past the lock.

Once inside, The Idea Man slipped from room to room. He paused in a kitchen that smelled of burnt coffee and selected two straight-edge knives from the cutlery block on the counter. Before long, he found his target lounging like Caesar in a leather recliner, one hand down his pants, eyes glued to a scantily clad pop princess grinding her hips and lip-synching on the 51-inch flat screen affixed to the opposite wall.

The Idea Man was practical. He harbored no delusions of being an action hero or costumed vigilante. He was just a guy with an idea. So he eased up behind the child-murderer and visualized the young girl he'd seen pictured in the paper. The little moppet with auburn curls and outrageous dimples, who would never see another sunny day, would never again jump in a puddle, or blow out candles on a birthday cake. Images of the atrocities she'd endured at the hands of a man she

304

loved and trusted loomed in the Idea Man's mind. He reached over the back of the recliner and crossed the knives in front of the man's throat. When the murderer lunged from his seat in surprise, he did most of the damage himself.

The Idea Man watched his prey stagger around the living room. Now it was a dying room. The rotten man tottered forward and, amazingly, fumbled with the power button on the side of the television. The Idea Man watched the pop music Lolita blink out of existence, and then returned his gaze to his victim. He looked on with quiet excitement as the other man collapsed and bled out.

"Not just anyone can do this, of course," The Idea Man says, resuming his pitch. "This is a task for professionals. It's a new calling."

"What about public perception? What about law enforcement?"

"We and the latter will continue to coexist as we always have. And public opinion, whether actually expressed publicly or not, will side with us." The Idea Man leans forward in his chair. "These are trying times. We are divided as a nation. Why not choose a tangible target for our growing discontent? Why not champion a cause we can all agree upon?"

"That was quite the speech." The Wild Card says dryly.

"You and I both know there's truth in what I've said."

"So you contacted me, invited me here, to pitch me. Are you asking me to join your band of merry men?" The Wild Card grins at his silver-haired host. He hopes he doesn't look too sardonic.

"I prefer to think of it as recruiting a small, select group of men and women to 'give something back', as the saying goes. I've been extremely selective, contacting only a handful of others on the Deep Web. It's the best course of action. Thanks to the layers of encryption in the TOR software, I can use the same method people use to hire our services to post potential candidates for elimination. As with a regular job, our identities aren't divulged to any Web servers or routers. Our aliases remain intact, our bases of operations unknown. Bear in mind, these are not hits to pad our wallets. These hits would make the world a better place. I don't expect everyone to be on board. I'm sure only a few will ever consider it. I hope you will take all the time you need to give the matter careful consideration."

"Count me in," The Wild Card says after only a moment's pause.

Three Weeks Ago

The Introvert keeps his head down and hurries across the street. A motorist—apparently angered at having to wait the eight seconds this takes—honks and flips him the bird. The Introvert hunches his shoulders, but does not respond.

Inside the prison, The Introvert produces his identification at the guest check-in desk and waits to be escorted to his client. He perches on the edge of a dirty plastic chair and adjusts his metal frame glasses. The Introvert smiles at the prisoner as he is brought into the room. The prisoner is shackled and clad in a bright orange jumper. The Introvert knows this designates the severity of his client's crimes. The newcomer throws his weight onto the chair as if he wants to crush it. "You ain't my lawyer. Where's Blackberg?"

"He's fallen ill. Not to worry; he should be fine in a day or two. I'm here in his place."

The prisoner scowls. "You know what's going on? What I want?"

The Introvert waits for the guard to leave the room before he speaks.

"I strongly advise against making the request you contacted Blackberg regarding."

"Of course you would, but I don't care." The prisoner sneers. "You tell the judge we want to play the videos. Right there in court."

The Introvert shakes his head, adjusts his glasses again. He's not used to them and they pinch his nose. "If it's self-recorded camcorder footage of you raping those women, we definitely do not want that shown to the jury."

"But I wanna watch the videos." The prisoner leans forward to make his point. "This might be the last time I get to see them. I want those broads to have to watch themselves. I want their families to watch what I did. I want the jury, the judge, every damn person in that courtroom to watch me—"

The Introvert, pretending to nervously fiddle with his glasses, withdraws the four inch needle from its hiding place against the arm piece and his arm flies across the table. For a fraction of a second, it looks as if The Introvert might slap his client. Instead he plunges the needle into the convict's brain through his ear.

The prisoner gapes. The Introvert sees a fine red mist darken the white of the other man's left eye. He extracts the needle and deftly returns it to its hiding place. He waits out a slow mental ten count as the serial rapist shudders and tumbles from his chair. While he counts, he thinks about rock climbing, playing guitar, and all the other innocuous activities he engages in to keep his hands strong.

Not many people can do what I do, The Introvert thinks. He stands.

"Guard? Hey, guard! There's something wrong with my client. I think he's having a stroke or something."

After he gives a statement, The Introvert pauses on the prison steps long enough to check his current prepaid cell phone. One missed call. He dials the number and listens.

Someone has a lucrative job for him. The Introvert flushes with pleasure. *Instant karma.*

At the same time, The Wild Card strolls along a street in a city that he is only passing through. He is anonymous, instantly forgettable. And yet, for one terrifying moment, something in a shop window draws him back to his past. His stomach tightens at the sight of fishing tackle in the display window of a sporting goods store. For one terrible moment, The Wild Card is a helpless kid again.

"I'll tell you the secret," his father said. He leaned closer, as if fish lurking nearby might overhear. "Soak each piece of corn in vanilla extract before you slide it onto the hook." His father drew back and pick up his own rod again. "Fish like the taste so much they get a case of the stupids. Can't help themselves. They know they should leave it be, but they go for it anyway."

The boy who was not yet The Wild Card watched his father for some sign the older man was joshing him but saw none. His father made his cast and then settled back. Frogs sang their bellicose song from the reeds. A pair of ducks paddled together at the far end of the pond.

The boy baited his own hook and cast his lure into the calm green-black water. Father sat nearer the bow facing the port side of the little dinghy, son sat near the tiller, facing the starboard side. Far overhead the contrails of a jet intersected the sky and dissipated at roughly the same speed that grass grew or paint dried; the perfect pace for an afternoon spent fishing.

His father fidgeted in his seat. Coughed. Just as the boy turned to look at his father, the older man's hand shot out, knocking his rod and reel into the water. The boy, not understanding what was happening, stood, lurched, and reached over the gunwale for the gear but it drifted out of his reach and sank from view into the murky depths below.

His father writhed on the bottom boards like a fish deprived of oxygen. The boy knew the Heimlich maneuver but his father hadn't been eating anything. He didn't think it was heatstroke. Was it a real stroke? A heart attack? The boy found himself at a complete loss, utterly helpless. He cried for help but there was no one nearby. This was in the days before cell phones. The boy watched as a silent, invisible assassin took his father's life.

It took him thirty-three minutes two row to shore and load his father—now dead though the boy would not admit as much—into their pickup truck. He was one year shy of getting his learner's permit but he drove to the nearest town like a seasoned race car driver. In the end it didn't matter. A doctor determined the cause of death, a "massive coronary failure."

This marked an ending and a new beginning for the boy who would become The Wild Card. The event planted a seed that eventually bloomed into his present career. Arms burning, oars churning, the boy vowed never to be helpless in the face of death again. He would control it, make it work for him. If Death rode on a pale horse, The Wild Card wanted to be the stagecoach driver cracking the whip and telling it where to go.

Two Weeks Ago

Lady Justice takes less than ten seconds to get past the catch on the motel room door. She pockets a pliable rectangle of plastic—one of many tools of her trade—and closes the door behind her. She scans the dingy interior, missing nothing. Her jaw and stomach tighten at the sight of the laptop lying atop the stained, gray mattress. She knows what types of photos and videos are contained in encrypted folders on the computer's hard drive.

Lady Justice walks silently to a bathroom that is two decades overdue for new fixtures and stands in semidarkness behind the warped door. She keeps her knees slightly bent, staying loose. Her arms hang relaxed at her sides. She closes her eyes and thinks about the motel room's temporary resident.

According to the information she received in an email from The Idea Man on her encrypted Deep Web account, her target runs a mobile roofing business. He travels from town to town, chasing hailstorms, passing out fliers. He gets jobs putting new shingles on houses by undercutting the local guys. But it's all a front.

The man currently possessing a key to this room also peddles child porn. What started as a vice had escalated into a full-time career once he got in with the right circle of like-minded individuals on the Deep Web. Now it's all he can do to insure that the supply keeps up with the demand. He's made a fortune in Bitcoin. Lady Justice has read all the notes The Idea Man emailed her. She verified all the information supplied and then made arrangements.

Now she smiles. Her keen ears have picked up the sound of approaching footfalls. She hears a key being inserted in the flimsy lock. The door squeaks as it is opened and the latch clicks when the door closes. Lady Justice slows her breathing and remains still, a poisonous spider patiently awaiting prey. The fly has returned, unaware that a newcomer has converted the bathroom into the proverbial parlor. The squeaking floorboards beneath the threadbare carpet betray his approach. The light switch clicks on, and the man's trousers drop with a swish around his ankles. He empties his bladder into the toilet bowl.

Lady Justice finally opens her eyes and takes advantage of the sound of the stream hitting the water to ease out from behind the door.

As he's shaking the last drops from his member, she speaks: "Umm, excuse me mister ..."

The man with a hard drive full of graphic depravity turns, gaping at her. With his pants still dropped around his ankles—and pants of a different sort escaping his open maw—he takes in her petite frame and schoolgirl skirt and blouse and his eyes glaze. He undergoes an immediate transformation into a leering beast.

"Can you help me? I'm lost."

She looks down between his legs and eases into a crouch. A quick glance back up at his eyes shows that he's mistaking her intentions. She knows he believes—irrational as it may be—that she's about to pleasure him. Her target is nearly a foot taller and outweighs her by at least one hundred pounds; she's simply creating leverage and momentum for her first strike.

Lady Justice drives her body upward, leading with her closed left fist. Every muscle in her body uncoils, pushing the punch, increasing its force. When her blow connects under the man's chin, his teeth clack together like exploding firecrackers. His head jerks back and he staggers. Lady Justice drives her right fist into his solar plexus, and follows it up with a chop across his windpipe to silence him. His face reddens and he tries to rush her, his enormous hands pawing the air on either side of her. Lady Justice drops again, visualizing a rattlesnake about to strike. She drives the meat of her palm into the glaring man's nose, and bone and cartilage retreat straight into his brain. He crumples, a fleshy pinball ricocheting off the sink, toilet, and tub in the small confines of the room.

Lady Justice leaves the motel room and strolls the four blocks to her waiting rental car. An R&B classic by Jean Knight greets her from the radio speakers when she turns the ignition. She guides her so-nondescript-it-is-invisible rental into traffic and sings along with the deliciously appropriate chorus. Lady Justice rides her endorphin high for as long as she can.

This method of operation is new to her. Her previous hit had been a small-town mayor who'd threatened to blow the whistle on a corrupt city councilman. Ending the mayor's life hadn't been personal. None of her jobs ever were. But when The Idea Man had contacted her, she'd felt intrigued by his proposition. It made sense on multiple levels. She knew of another contract killer who volunteered at homeless shelters and retirement homes to alleviate his mounting guilt. Lady Justice wasn't that softhearted. But the opportunity to make a positive impact while staying in practice appealed to her a great deal. Inspired by the concept of balancing the scales, she changed her name and her outlook. The rechristened Lady Justice responded to the Idea Man mere hours after he first initiated contact.

"Make every tenth hit a freebie and insure that it's one that makes the world a better place," The Idea Man had said. "Or perhaps, every fifth hit, if you feel inclined."

Lady Justice bites her bottom lip as she changes lanes. She wonders if The Idea Man might scold her for being *too* active. To balance the scales, Lady Justice has decided to make every other hit a public service assassination. She wonders if they'll all feel as good as this one.

The man who refers to himself as TapTap on the message boards of the Deep Web jogs along a sidewalk that skirts a municipal park in a midsize city on the Great Plains. There's still a chilly bite to the early morning air and, for the moment, he's alone. He contemplates the message he received from The Idea Man the previous evening.

The Idea Man is a stranger to TapTap, and yet he somehow knew about TapTap's past, because he introduced his idea of charity assassinations as a way to atone for past mistakes. People didn't understand how grueling life as a cop could be. It had quickly become apparent to TapTap that fighting the good fight would be a never-ending—and all-too-often losing—battle. It wasn't long before he was on the take, turning a blind eye to certain activities and transactions. Sometimes not all the evidence seized at crime scenes made its way to the evidence room. He made extra cash on the side with the resale of these items. And he'd been smart enough to leave the force the moment he felt the noose tightening around his neck. He relocated and now supplemented his income by drawing on skills from his past. He'd received several commendation bars for his marksmanship, and kept the same cool detachment he had at target practice when the targets were moving and shooting back.

Hits paid well, or well enough, for him to live comfortably despite his minimum wage job. The Idea Man wanted pros to assume the added travel expenses and additional time needed to plan a hit. And for what? To satisfy the bloodthirsty unwashed masses? To quell their own guilty consciences?

Another man rounded the bend and came jogging toward him. TapTap did not slow his pace, but only glanced back as they neared. The sidewalk remained clear. TapTap and the approaching man had crossed paths jogging three consecutive mornings now.

When fifteen feet separated the men, TapTap reached behind his back with his left hand. He drew his .22 and emptied the clip into the other jogger's chest at point-blank range. Then he increased his pace, leaving both the dead man and any further consideration of The Idea Man's plan behind.

Across the nation, other professional killers, a few master hit men whom The Idea Man had reached out to directly—and the journeymen who read his message board proposal—came to the same conclusion. This idealistic and unworkable idea was not for them.

Last Week

"Have you given my proposal any further consideration?"

The Wild Card shakes off a feeling of déjà vu and swallows the last of the scotch in his tumbler. The liquid sears his throat and his stomach feels like a pit of writhing snakes. He runs his fingers through his tangled hair and ponders another sunset. This is a similar location, but a different situation.

The drinks are top-shelf. The furniture is immaculate. This house also perches at the top of a hill. But this is not The Idea Man; this is The Devil's Advocate. How he located The Wild Card has not been divulged. But he has contacted him to set up this clandestine meeting. Other professionals would be content to exchange information on the Deep Web, but The Devil's Advocate knows that The Wild Card insists on doing business face-to-face. He's contacted The Wild Card and he's offered a counterproposal.

"I'm torn. I see his side of it, and I see yours."

The Devil's Advocate leans forward, strong hands gripping the armrests of his Lodgepole Pine throne. "His idea is idiotic; a pipe dream. Contract killers doing charity work? Conscience plays no part of this! Who's he trying to fool?"

The Wild Card says nothing. He fingers the rim of his tumbler and waits for his host to continue. "Anyone misguided enough to follow through on his crazy notions risks exposing themselves to law enforcement, and worse, public scrutiny. They draw back the veil. We're all exposed." The Devil's Advocate stabs the air between them with a meaty finger as if picking his guest out of a lineup.

The Wild Card takes this as his cue. "He's only spoken to a few of us. Maybe his idea will fail to gain any traction and the movement will fizzle."

The Devil's Advocate bares his teeth in a snarl. "The fact that you just referred to it as a 'movement' tells me that we need to nip this in the bud. And we need to do it now."

"Are you putting a price on his head?"

"I am."

"How many zeros are we talking about for the hit? No Bitcoin in an escrow account either; I only take cash."

The Devil's Advocate gives him a number. The Wild Card decides it is enough.

By the Books squeezes the trigger from his rooftop perch. The cannibalistic old man who'd been found not guilty by reason of insanity drops to the sidewalk like a sack of rotten produce. By the Books knows everyone in the city will sleep better tonight.

Three hundred eighty miles south, Lady Justice snaps the neck of a celebrity who had been accused of beheading his live-in girlfriend. In a case that divided the nation, the celebrity went free. Now, at last, justice has been served.

The next day, in Los Angeles, The Introvert serves a hazelnut and strychnine Café Latte to an aspiring actress who has delivered her junkie roommate into the hands of a producer of snuff films.

The Wild Card knocks on the door of his intended victim. His heart hammers in his chest while he waits. The Idea Man opens the door and The Wild Card shoots him five times; one slug through each eye socket and three more slugs into his heart.

This Week

It is nightfall.

"I see you took care of our mutual problem. Quick and effective, but headline-grabbing," The Devil's Advocate frowns. "You risked too much publicity."

"I carried out a hit." The Wild Card says, gazing at his host. "You never specified what method I should use. The subject you wanted eliminated is out of the equation, and I appreciate your prompt payment."

The Devil's Advocate sighs. "It was reckless, but it's done. Still, I think it would be for the best if we were to never meet again."

"I agree." The Wild Card draws his weapon and once again pulls the trigger. This time it's a single shot to the temple. He wipes his prints from the gun, and places it in the other man's hand. He leaves The Devil's Advocate in a growing puddle of blood.

The Wild Card hopes the right people find out about The Idea Man's murder. He hopes they will spread the word about his idea with the fervent zeal of religious converts. If the average citizen, fed up with all the injustices and loopholes of the legal system, begins to condone these public service assassinations, the entire justice system could change.

"Let the revolution begin," The Wild Card whispers, and disappears into the darkness.

TANTSE SO SMERT'YU
(DANCING WITH DEATH)

BY ERNESTUS JIMINY CHALD

A tall Kazakhstani man enters the doorway of a sumptuous penthouse suite on the top floor of the Fairmont Hotel in downtown Chicago, dressed in black and carrying a large tactical briefcase. He walks purposefully toward a set of large casement windows overlooking Grant Park, and sets his briefcase on a nearby table. A fly on the wall could tell that this room's mysterious occupant is enacting something rehearsed—something he's plotted and played out in his mind in great detail leading up to this moment. There is a look of total detachment in his eyes, which peer out coldly from behind a pair of lightly tinted spectacles.

With methodical precision, he opens his briefcase, revealing the unassembled components of a .50 caliber Windrunner M96 sniper rifle. He removes each of the rifle's five pieces individually from the briefcase's thermal-lined interior, and, in a matter of moments, holds in his hands a fully assembled long-distance implement of murder. He then retrieves two pillows from the suite's impeccably made king-sized bed and places them on the carpet to rest his knees upon as he perches himself in front of his window of choice, one that affords him an unimpeded view of the bustling park below. Once he's completed building his nest, the assassin draws a cigarillo out of a crumpled pack

315

in his hoxter and waits. He shifts his gaze periodically from the digital interface of his wristwatch to his scope's eyepiece, which he's focused at a podium on a large stage that's been erected in the park below. A massive crowd of spectators has gathered around this stage, and continues to grow as the clock inches its way toward six p.m.

Emblazoned across the front of the podium his scope is locked upon is the Presidential Seal. The assassin occupies himself by counting the arrows and stars depicted on the seal while softly whistling the melody of "Hail to the Chief." At half past six, a group of political figures emerges and ascends the stage flanked by Secret Service agents wearing dark suits, black sunglasses, and impassive expressions. The crowd cheers uproariously as the President approaches the podium and begins to address them—all smiles and assertive hand gestures—utterly oblivious of the high-powered, magazine-fed rifle currently aimed directly at his forehead. The Kazakhstani's breathing grows shallow and focused as he wraps his index finger gently around his M96's trigger and braces himself for the powerful recoil his body's about to absorb.

He inhales his pre-squeeze breath slowly and deeply, deriving a warped sense of satisfaction in knowing that, the moment he begins to expel this very breath, his finger will exert a slight flicker of pressure against his trigger, and he will see the President's face explode instantaneously. Just as his finger begins to flex, the tip of a carbon-steel broadhead arrow, having made a precise trajectory from the back of his skull and through his brain, pierces through the sniper's squinting left eye, and he slumps over dead instantly. Hovering above the Kazakhstani's lifeless body is the silhouette of a dark, fearsome figure wearing a hooded cloak of charcoal gray and brandishing a massive arbalest. As this specter emerges further into the light to inspect its kill, its ballistic face mask—molded to resemble the face of a stylized ghost—peers out vacantly from beneath the hood of its heavy cloak.

With great precision and speed, the specter's gloved hands open a large trolley case and remove a folded triage tarp, which is quickly unfolded and spread across the suite's plush carpeting. The sniper's corpse is then dragged into the center of the tarp, the fatal arrow still lodged firmly in its skull. The hooded figure splays the sniper's arms and legs apart before retrieving a pneumatic surgical saw from a suitcase and attaching the saw's pressurized fluid inlet to a small helium gas compressor. The saw emits a soft whine as its blade begins to spin, tearing through the corpse's clothing, flesh, and bone like lunch meat. Blood begins to pool on the tarp as the sniper's extremities are removed one by one and placed inside the arbalester's suitcase, which is lined with heavy-duty polyethylene plastic.

When the body has been separated into eleven pieces and each of these pieces has been stuffed inside the suitcase, the Kazakhstani's M96 is field-stripped and situated neatly back in the dead man's briefcase, which is then stuffed on top of his dismembered remains. The masked specter quickly refolds the gore-splattered triage tarp and places it inside a separate compartment of the suitcase before field-stripping the arbalest and situating it alongside its broadhead quiver in the luggage's anterior compartment. With the crime scene thoroughly stripped of evidence, the specter begins to undress.

Beneath its hooded cloak, the arbalester is clad in black from head to toe—a black, Kevlar-reinforced ballistic bodysuit, black carbon fiber gloves, black tactical boots, black utility belt, and, most strikingly, that menacing black facial helmet. When the specter unbuckles and removes its helmet, the face of a beautiful young woman is revealed—a woman with dark Slavic eyes and long auburn hair that spills out of her helmet and cascades down her shoulders. She stands five foot six, and her body is a fine-tuned specimen of impeccably toned musculature and curves. At first sight, one might even mistake her for a professional dancer; few would peg her as the merciless killing machine that she actually is.

Her name is Ogrifina Voronina, but those enmeshed in the insidious underworld of murderers-for-hire know only her nom de guerre—Prizrak ("The Wraith"). She is one of only a small handful of what are known in her native tongue as Ubitsayedi—assassins that specialize in assassinating other assassins—in the world. She is the sole surviving member of the legendary Hishniki clan, an assassin sect whose lineage can be traced back more than two-hundred fifty years to Grigory Lagunov, the assassin who exterminated Peter III in 1762. Although the Hishniki are no more, their dynasty of dominance in the assassin underworld lives on through Ogrifina, who has earned her position at the top of the Ubitsayed food chain under the Prizrak guise by successfully executing one contract after another for more than a decade now. The name alone—Prizrak—is enough to cause even the world's most hardened assassins to shudder. This fear-inciting name, for them, is synonymous with death ... for wherever Prizrak goes, death follows.

Ogrifina peels off her tactical gear one shred at a time until she's down to bare flesh, then begins retrieving fresh articles of clothing—a high-necked floral sundress, whale-net stockings, red pumps, a wide-brimmed hat, and a pair of oversized sunglasses with heart-shaped frames—from her suitcase's anterior compartment and dresses herself. She then folds her Prizrak gear, places it in her suitcase's clean anterior compartment, and gives the suite a final once-over before exiting the room, suitcase in tow, looking much like a tourist as she strolls casually down the hall to a nearby elevator. In a matter of moments, she finds herself ambling down the street, blending in perfectly with passersby as she makes her way toward the lakefront where a docked boat awaits her. A muscular Russian man with grizzled hair and a bushy mustache stands on deck, his arms folded. A look of relief comes across his face when he sees Ogrifina approaching.

He doesn't ask her any questions or even greet her verbally. He simply smiles and waves her on board. As the boat sails away, Ogrifina watches the monumental Chicago skyline shrink slowly away from view, disappearing in the night. Once the city is only scarcely visible, she opens her suitcase and begins to scatter its contents in the deep, murky waters of Lake Michigan. When the suitcase has been emptied, she casts it overboard and watches it sink slowly away.

To some, the events that transpired on this day in the life of Ogrifina Voronina might seem grisly and traumatic. To Ogrifina, it was just another day on the job.

Ogrifina often finds herself lying awake at night reminiscing about her past. As a child, when most girls her age were busy playing with dolls and studying ballet, she was performing complex assassination drills underground in the Hishniki hive, which was located in Uliuiu Cherkechekh—"The Valley of Death" in western Yakutia. Her father, Vasily Voronin, was a fifth-generation Hishnik and the clan's elected leader. A legendary and formidable figure in the ubitsa underworld, Vasily could trace his own lineage with the clan back to its origins.

318

At the time of Ogrifina's birth, there were sixteen Hishniki living in the clan's subterranean hive. Each of them had received the same highly specialized training as Ogrifina herself. Being a Voronin entitled her to no special treatment. She was Vasily's daughter—his blood—and he expected her performance to reflect that. Rather than teaching her social etiquette, or instilling in her a sense of conventional morality, he taught his daughter ubitsa etiquette—the etiquette of death. He honed her awareness and acceptance of the fragility of life—the fact that it may be taken from anyone in a single calculated instant. Strong and weak alike—anyone can die in the blink of an eye.

By the age of thirteen, Ogrifina was being jobbed out to several of Vasily's most notable contractors. As a child—and somewhat of an assassination prodigy—it was easy for her to complete many contracts, as nobody expected a lovable little girl to be a highly trained murderess in disguise. Initially, most of her targets were low-level grifters, hitmen, and extortionists. But, as her skills advanced, her father promoted her to higher-profile assignments—high-ranking clergymen, politicians, and, ultimately, other assassins. The need for Ubitsayedi was greater than ever. Assassins tend to be a duplicitous lot. Many will default on jobs abruptly without warning (take-the-money-and-runners), leaving their contractors, who are often mere middlemen themselves, to face whatever ramifications may come as a result of their failed or botched jobs. Unscrupulous and self-motivated, many assassins are also easily bribed. All it often takes is a better offer from their target to make an assassin train the old crosshairs back around on the original contractor.

Of course, these sorts of actions are frowned upon by the contractors themselves. To let an assassin take advantage of them without facing grievous repercussions would make the contractors look unwary and impotent. Therefore, when an assassin defaults on a job—for whatever reason—the contractors find themselves in the unenviable position of having to hire another assassin to eliminate the assassin who screwed them over. This is where Ubitsayedi come into play. As assassins themselves, they know how their peers think. They know all the tricks and tools of the trade—how to disappear when shit needs to blow over, and how to track down those who've already disappeared.

As she reclines in her bed at night reminiscing, certain memories tend to be recalled more vividly and with greater frequency in

319

Ogrifina's mind than others. She can barely remember her mother's face, for example—it has been lost with the passage of time. Yet she can remember as if it had occurred just yesterday the face of the first man she assassinated at the age of thirteen (an unsavory swindler and art forger who swindled the wrong person and found himself choking on a bowl of borscht Ogrifina had covertly sprinkled with cyanide). Most vividly of all, Ogrifina remembers her father and the countless hours of brutal, intensive training she'd spent under his strict tutelage—the same sort of training he'd received himself from his own father before him. Manufacturing human killing machines was what the Hishniki clan had done since its inception, and nobody has ever done it better.

Each member of the sect followed the same strict code of ethics— a code that was as legendary among those in the ubitsa underworld as the clan itself. The "Kredo Krovi" consisted of a series of secret commandments that clan members were forbidden from violating, lest they bring shame upon their entire sect and tarnish the reputation of fidelity and unfaltering success their forefathers had established centuries before. The creed itself was memorized verbatim by each Hishnik, and an inability to recite any or all of its tenets on command invariably resulted in severe punishment (which might include anything from flagellation to waterboarding). To actually break any of the commandments would automatically condemn the offending Hishnik to death. Only once in the clan's history did a Hishnik break one of the Kredo Krovi's commandments. An assassin named Nestor Travkin defaulted on a contract in 1897 and was subsequently castrated and forced to devour his own sautéed genitals before being drawn and quartered. A fellow Hishnik promptly completed Travkin's unfinished contract, thus keeping the sect's unblemished track record intact. Assassins and contractors alike from around the world knew without question that anybody the Hishniki were contracted to eliminate would die one way or another. The clan's reputation spoke for itself.

The end of the Hishniki clan's dominance in the ubitsa underworld came abruptly during Ogrifina's twenty-first year. She returned to the Hishniki hive after having successfully completed a difficult contract to eliminate a legendary assassin known as Rezchik Trup—"The Corpse Carver." He was known to collect different body parts from each of his victims, which he would subsequently plastinate and assemble into grotesque statues of discrepant anatomy for his own personal collection of macabre art. Ogrifina approached the hive's secret entrance hatch (which was indistinguishable from countless other strange metallic objects jutting from the area's uninhabited landscape), eager to share with her father the harrowing details of her completion of this contract. Rezchik Trup had nearly escaped when a powerful gust of wind caused her arbalest's arrow to strike a wall mere millimeters above her target's forehead, alerting the doomed man, who scrambled to his feet and attempted to take flight. Her second broadhead's aim was true, however, and he collapsed like a broken marionette. But it was immediately evident to Ogrifina, as she entered the hive, that something was horribly wrong.

The entry hatch itself had been wrenched from its hinges, and a faint trail of smoke rose from the uncovered opening. She rushed down the ladder leading into the hive's main entry corridor and gasped at the sight she beheld. Strewn about the floor in every direction were the smoldering remains of her Hishniki brethren, burnt to near unrecognition and stacked in blackened piles. Frantically, Ogrifina rushed to her father's quarters. There she found the charred remains of Vasily Voronin, his still-smoldering left hand reaching for his beloved Kalashnikov RPK. She reached down to cradle his head, searing her hands against his sizzling flesh but refusing to let go. A war had indubitably been waged in the Hishniki hive—the only home Ogrifina Voronina had ever known—and not a single survivor had been left in its wake. She was now the sole remaining member of her clan.

There was no question who, in one fell swoop, had eliminated the entire sect: Kliment Fakel ("The Torch") Krasnomyrdin, a former Hishnik himself who'd been trained alongside Vasily Voronin. He'd gone rogue after years of clashing over what he considered to be the sect's antiquated bureaucracy. Krasnomyrdin alone, familiar as he was with the clan's subterranean hive, could've overridden its security systems and penetrated its walls. Most damning of all, he'd left behind his calling card in the form of the flames themselves, which continued to burn dimly around Ogrifina as she sat on the blackened carpet, cradling the head of her dead father in her lap.

She'd been trained her whole life to purge herself of emotions, which only hinder one in the field when the success of any given contract—and the weight of the Hishniki legacy—is on the line. She'd

321

learned not to smile as a child; not to speak unless necessary; not to cry when she fell and scraped her knees; not to feel anger, jealousy, or envy when a fellow Hishnik-in-training bested her in tests of skill; not to harbor love for human life; not to grow attached to worldly possessions or pleasures. All the training she'd undergone to suppress her emotions was not enough to prevent her from weeping that night as she sat there surrounded by the carbonized remains of her fallen comrades. She remembered her father's words: "Hishniki do not cry, sol'nishka, nor are we moved by the tears of others." And yet Ogrifina wept that night until she could weep no more.

She knew where to go. They had drilled hive-breaching scenarios—what to do in the event of the hive being compromised or annihilated entirely—countless times before. Yet the weight of what had befallen her clan made it physically difficult for Ogrifina to move. When she finally mustered the will to rise and disembark, she moved in a detached, enervated manner. In later years, she couldn't even recall collecting the few personal items she left the hive with that night—her arbalest, broadhead quiver, and a drag bag filled with light artillery, clothing, and other basic provisions. But she left the hive, knowing deep in her heart that she would never return, consumed with an unquenchable thirst for unbridled retribution.

After abandoning the decimated hive, Ogrifina followed the protocols her father had established for such a scenario, and made her way to the secluded safe house of a man named Evgeny Klebakhin. Although not a Hishnik himself, Evgeny had served the clan unfalteringly for decades as both a faithful comrade and a liaison between the Hishniki themselves and their powerful contractors. Most high-level assassins rarely deal directly with the contractors who employ them (for the safety of both parties involved in the event that either is apprehended and interrogated). For a fee, provodniki, or "inbetweeners," like Evgeny negotiate contracts on behalf of the assassins who employ them. Evgeny was more than just the Hishniki's provodnik, however. He also performed perilous reconnaissance missions for the clan to obtain critical intel (which can often mean the difference between life and death for those in the field), and also served as their primary supplier of weapons and other specialty equipment required for any given contract.

Devastated by the news of what had befallen the hive, and fearful for Ogrifina's safety as the last surviving member of a clan clearly targeted for extinction, Evgeny followed his own emergency protocols. He secured safe passage for himself and Ogrifina to America, where he maintained an extensive network of underbelly contacts who could ensure their safety. Before long, the émigrés were set up in a remote cabin in the wilderness of southern Utah with expertly forged identities. Though Evgeny hoped that Ogrifina would take advantage of her opportunity to lead a less treacherous life, he knew that this would never be possible for her. She was born a Hishnik and she would die a Hishnik. Assassination was in her blood, and had been for ten generations. Evgeny also realized that he would never be able to leave his own life as a provodnik behind—it was the only line of work he'd ever been any good at—so he agreed to continue serving Ogrifina just as he'd served her clan for over thirty years.

Taking advantage of his vast network of underworld connections, Evgeny soon began securing contracts for Ogrifina. Word had already spread throughout the ubitsa underworld that the Hishniki were no more—that Fakel and a small team of cohorts had eradicated them all. But whispers had also begun to circulate that at least one Hishnik remained, and that this solitary predator was yearning for a reckoning. There was scarcely an assassin alive who dared to even utter the name of this raptorial specter who quickly became known simply as Prizrak. Some actually believed that it was the vengeful ghost of Vasily Voronin himself, exacting his revenge upon the entire ubitsa community by executing them all—one assassin at a time.

Ogrifina learned how to lead a double life—something she'd never been forced to do before the extinction of her clan. She learned how to blend in seamlessly with the city dwellers she encountered while walking the streets of Salt Lake City, wearing a hooded sweatshirt and sunglasses. The pedestrians she walked amongst were utterly oblivious of the fact that a legendary assassin was in their midst. Evgeny, meanwhile, made extensive modifications to the cabin in which they lived, adding nondescript wall panels in the cellar that opened to reveal secret stashes of military-grade weapons and sophisticated surveillance equipment. An outsider looking in would've noticed nothing unusual about this unobtrusive cabin. Yet life was far from ordinary for its unlikely occupants.

The extinction of the Hishniki clan had shattered Ogrifina psychologically. Her thirst for retaliatory blood became her life's sole fixation. She would replay her father's words on emotion over and over again in her mind—words she knew had been intended to desensitize her and enable her to remain functional as she carried on with her grisly work. "Feelings are your enemies, sol'nishka," he used to say. "Feelings will only get you killed." She understood what her father had meant when he uttered those words. The more one grows attached to earthly things—people, possessions, life itself—the more one stands to lose when the inevitable day arrives that the things they hold so dear are taken from them.

This is why the Hishniki believed it was so critical to cultivate a sense of total detachment from their emotions. All it may take at times is a moment's hesitation—or an emotional jumping of the gun—for a target to get the drop on you. Ogrifina ruminated deeply on this principle of emotional detachment. Yet, as much as she wished to believe that her emotions were held in check, she could never soothe the burning desire for vengeance that surged within her heart, threatening to consume her and everything in her path. She knew that, as a Hishnik, her sole purpose was to take the lives of others remorselessly, and that every life she took represented a tragic loss in the heart of someone somewhere. Every contract she'd ever completed left behind grieving widows and fatherless children. Realizing the dichotomous hypocrisy of her emotions, however—being hell-bent on revenge against Fakel for causing her the same sorrow she caused countless others—did little to alleviate her retaliatory bloodlust. And, as the years progressed, she only grew increasingly volatile and sadistic when it came to the elimination of her targets.

Before the extinction of her clan, she had remained calm and detached in the field. But, over the years that have subsequently elapsed, she became utterly merciless. No longer would a simple broadhead through the forehead or strychnine in a bowl of kasha suffice. She began making it a habit to eliminate the bodies of her targets entirely so that, once her work was done, there no longer remained even a trace of the person she'd just clipped. The simple utensils of her trade grew increasingly complex as she began to add power tools and sophisticated surgical implements to her lethiferous arsenal.

Twelve years have now elapsed since the extermination of Ogrifina's sect. For the past six years, Evgeny has brokered most of her contracts through Kacper "The Polack" Kozłowski, a powerful Polish mafioso headquartered on the south side of Chicago but with a reach that stretches across the country and even overseas. The Polack usually functions as somewhat of an inbetweener himself, contracting Prizrak—via Evgeny—to eliminate targets on behalf of other high-ranking Polish mafiosi and associates from around the world. Ogrifina has amassed a considerable fortune during her career and established Prizrak as a legendary figure in the ubitsa underworld along the way. Yet she remains humble and true to her Hishniki roots, living by the Kredo Krovi and prepared to die by it at any moment. The money she makes is ultimately inconsequential to her. She kills because that is what she was bred to do.

Although she never shies away from eliminating targets who aren't assassins themselves, hunting the hunters is still Prizrak's bread and butter. Ogrifina continues to derive her greatest kicks from exterminating her peers, many of whom have enjoyed long, legendary careers themselves before their names wind up—for one reason or another—on Prizrak's hit list. Lately, it seems like assassins have been slipping up left and right, rubbing the wrong people the wrong way by defaulting on or otherwise botching contracts. Within the past year alone, Ogrifina has eliminated twelve of the world's deadliest assassins, including Vern "The Vulture" Gottlieb (who, perched upon his toilet in Reno, found himself staring down the business end of Prizrak's arbalest before having his body dissolved to oblivion in a vat of sodium hydroxide); Silvio "The Suppressor" Pesaro (who met his demise in an abandoned stone quarry in the small town of Garnetsville where he was holed up after assassinating a local politician before being tracked down by Prizrak, who derived sadistic gratification from crushing him beneath a forty-ton block of granite dropped from an overhead crane); and Percy "The Mortician" Pendergrass, an assassin who'd amassed nearly two-hundred kills during his illustrious forty-year career before falling prey to Prizrak (who eviscerated him on his own private yacht off the coast of Tahiti and used his intestines to chum the water, which was quickly swarming with voracious mako sharks that tore his body to shreds).

Evgeny continues to trawl his extensive network of contacts on Ogrifina's behalf for any intel that might lead to the whereabouts of Fakel and his associates. Ogrifina knows that Fakel would've been unable to eliminate her entire clan single-handedly, and she's determined to uncover the identities of his accomplices. Intel over the years has been spotty. Vague, mostly unsubstantiated reports have occasionally surfaced that Fakel was headquartered in one continent or another, but nothing concrete. Nevertheless, she continues to harbor hope that she will ultimately be able to pinpoint her archenemy's precise location. If anybody knows, they are unwilling to sing, fearful of the retribution they'd face from ratting out an alpha-assassin like Krasnomyrdin. Tracking him down will take as long as it takes. Every predator has its day.

Evgeny sits fidgeting impatiently in the back room of a dingy sausage shop in Chicago's Back of the Yards neighborhood. He stares expressionlessly at two Polish brutes, both wearing matching pinstriped suits and mirrored aviator sunglasses, while fiddling with his bushy mustache. It's difficult to fathom a hard-ass like Evgeny feeling intimidated by the presence of others, but he can't help but feel small with two of The Polack's most gargantuan goons staring him down. He glances down at his pocket watch nervously, awaiting his scheduled meeting with The Polack to collect the second half of Prizrak's payment for eliminating the Kazakhstani, and also to discuss a new contract The Polack has assured him is tailor-made for his client.

When he's finally ushered through the doorway by The Polack's goons, he breathes a sigh of relief at no longer having to see his own uncharacteristically sheepish reflection in their mirrored lenses. He finds The Polack himself seated at a small table in a room that was clearly once used as a meat locker but has subsequently been converted into a makeshift office. The Polack is a corpulent middle-aged man with thinning black hair slicked back with brilliantine and a bulbous nose from which wiry little gray hairs protrude wildly. It's suppertime and The Polack is in the midst of stuffing his face with pierogi and sausages, his stubby fingers lousy with gaudy rings and coated with kiełbasa grease.

"Evgeny Klebakhin, just the kacap bastard I was looking to see," the Polack mumbles, his cheeks stuffed with partially masticated bits of sausage. "Have a seat."

Evgeny seats himself at the opposite end of the table as the Polack licks the grease from his fingertips. "Evgeny, my friend," the Polack says, "my associates and I are very pleased with the bang-up job Prizrak did on this one. Exemplary service, as always." He reaches beneath the table and retrieves a briefcase. "If I had to gripe with something, I'd say it's a shame Prizrak didn't wait to clip the Kazakhstani off 'til after he'd clipped off the President."

"You know that Prizrak is utterly unconcerned with matters of politics," Evgeny retorts. "But if the President is a target you'd like my client to eliminate, that can, of course, be arranged for a fee."

The Polack erupts in a fit of laughter and slides the briefcase across the table. "This is why I love this guy," he says to one of his goons, "A real mądrala!" The goon forces an affected chuckle, but quickly resumes looking dour. "So let's get back down to business," the Polack continues. "That briefcase squares us up for that Kazakhstani job. Since my associates and I were so pleased with Prizrak's performance, we've included a little bonus loot for you both. Now on to our next transaction. Does the name Marcin Kalinowski mean anything to you?"

Drawing a blank, Evgeny shakes his head. "I can't say it rings a bell."

"Good," the Polack says, "it shouldn't. Marcin is the nephew of an associate of mine. *Was*, I should say—his body turned up in a dumpster near Altgeld Gardens a few weeks ago. Turns out the people who wanted him dead wanted him *real* dead. The man was gassed, mauled by a tiger—I shit you not!—and burnt to a crisp."

Evgeny screws up his eyes with hesitant recognition.

"Does the name Warrington Linwood ring a bell?" the Polack asks.

Evgeny nods. "Yes ... the so-called 'Mad Gasser.' A living legend whose actual deeds are far grislier than the urban lore that surrounds him suggests. Used to work the freelance circuit in the '40s and '50s— creeping into people's bedrooms at night and gassing them with a modified Flit gun as they slept. Last I heard, the Gasser had retired due to age and infirmity—he must be in his nineties by now—and disappeared from the map."

"Very good, Evgeny. Get this man a Bozo button, will ya'?" the Poloack says jokingly to his goons. "The only bit you were off on there was the bit about his retirement. The bastard's ancient but he's definitely still in the game, as Marcin Kalinowski would attest if—if he could. How about this one: Finbar Freiling. Mean anything to you?"

Evgeny nods again. "'The Animal Trainer'. Another legendary—and eccentric—assassin. Uses trained animals and insects to carry out his hits, making it difficult for authorities to charge him with murder since he rarely kills anyone directly."

"You're on a roll here, Evgeny," the Polack says. "I sort of like this Animal Trainer guy. Never met the bastard myself but he's got panache. Uwagi zdobywające! You hear about the hit he pulled off last year at La Sabaneta, right? Took out the entire prison block his target was pent up in by filling the joint with scorpions, didn't he?"

"Phoneutria, actually," Evgeny replies. Sensing the Polack's confusion, he elaborates, "He took out the prisoners by unleashing thousands of Brazilian wandering spiders into the prison's ventilation system."

"Ah yes, that's what it was then," the Polack says. "You're two for two here, Evgeny. The last potential bell-ringer is ..."

"Kliment 'Fakel' Krasnomyrdin," Evgeny interrupts. "The Torch."

"Look at this kacap bastard here," the Polack marvels, gesturing his hands toward Evgeny. "Quick on the draw and accurate to boot! Clearly your intel is on point as usual. What do you know about this Torch guy?"

Evgeny takes a deep breath before responding, "One of the deadliest assassins in recorded history. An ex-Hishnik turned rogue mercenary after falling out with the clan's higher-ups. Fakel was responsible for the extinction of this once indomitable faction. Flamethrowers are his signature weapons of choice. A very dangerous man."

"That's three for three, Evgeny! You see where I'm going with this?" the Polack says.

"Unfortunately I do," Evgeny responds, his brow furrowing deeply.

"These are the pajace that clipped off Marcin Kalinowski. The less you know about that the better. But my people have been receiving chatter that these knobs are holed up in a fortified cathedral in the Czech Republic. They're trying to assemble an entire hive of legends to put the assassination game on lockdown," the Polack says. "But here's the thing that's going to make this job tricky. There's all sorts of underground politics involved here, but my associates and I need Prizrak to rub out the Mad Gasser and the Animal Trainer ... but the Torch can't be touched—not even in self-defense. I can't stress the importance of this stipulation enough."

A look of abject confuzzlement worms its way across Evgeny's face. "But Fakel torched your associate's nephew, did he not?" he says. "How could you wish to eliminate the other two yet let him walk away unscathed?"

"Well," the Polack begins, "that's where we get into the realm of underground politics and the poop of the matter. It turns out Fakel's done a lot of big favors for a lot of big people—including some of my closest associates ... so if I were to put a hit on him, I'm liable to be ventilated myself. Plus, let's be frank here. Marcin was dead before The Torch lit his ass up ... if the poisonous gas didn't do it, I'm sure the tiger tearing his throat out did. My associates are willing to let Fakel slide for desecrating the corpse, but the other two pajace ain't fortunate enough to have such important benefactors, and my associates want them both taken off the shelf, see?"

The Polack senses hesitation in Evgeny that he's never detected before in all their years of negotiating hits. He reaches below the table, retrieves another briefcase, and slides it over to Evgeny. "Look," he says, "I know this job ain't a cinch by any means. Infiltrating a hive of legendary killers is a good way to get popped—especially when you're forbidden from even dumping off at their leader. I get that. But I'm offering this job to you because Prizrak's the best. If anybody could pull off this contract ..."

"It's a suicide mission, Kozłowski, and you know it," Evgeny snarls. "Do you really expect Fakel to sit by idly while his comrades are liquidated?"

"It very well may be. I certainly can't expect Prizrak to infiltrate this hive without getting stung. I can offer a few of my own men to go in there with your client as back-up. But I know how adamant you've been in the past about Prizrak not playing well with others," the Polack says, wiping a thin layer of perspiration and sausage grease from his upper lip with an embroidered silk handkerchief. "There's a lot of dough in that briefcase, Evgeny ... and you know that's only the first installment."

Evgeny sits silently, staring vacantly at the two briefcases before him. He knows that the likelihood of Ogrifina walking out of that cathedral alive is miniscule. As gifted as she is, she stands little chance against an entire hive of legendary assassins—a hive whose population is unknown. Declining the contract, however, would strip Ogrifina of her first—and perhaps only—concrete opportunity to confront the man responsible for the extinction of her clan. And yet the stipulations of the contract itself forbid Ogrifina from eliminating her archrival. How would she be able to reconcile her lifelong adherence to the Kredo Krovi—which forces her to abide by these stipulations—with her compulsion to exact revenge?

After ruminating deeply, Evgeny exhales plosively, unfurrows his brow and rises, lifting both briefcases from the table. "Where can we obtain the dossier for this job?" he asks.

The Polack grins gleefully. "It's in that briefcase. GPS coordinates, blueprints of the cathedral—the whole nine yards. I know this one's a herculean task, but Prizrak's never failed me before."

"You'll hear from me after the job's completed," Evgeny says as he exits the room, briefcases in tow.

Ogrifina is summoned by Evgeny to a run-down warehouse in K-Town that's occupied by one of his most dependable weapons suppliers. He fills her in on the details of the contract, and is astonished by how calmly she reacts as he divulges the identities of her targets and the particularities of the mission. Below the surface, she can feel her lust for vengeance throbbing more powerfully than ever before, yet she remains composed as Evgeny breaks the mission down for her. The hive is located in Moravia. It will be heavily fortified and even more heavily guarded. Ogrifina's targets know that they have prices on their heads and will be ready to defend themselves against anyone who comes to collect their bounties.

Ogrifina has the pick of the litter in this warehouse when it comes to weaponry. Virtually every weapon imaginable is in stock and at her disposal. But, aside from a few specialty items she requests (flash grenades, explosive broadheads, a rebreather mechanism for her facial helmet, and canisters of flame-retardant barrier gel), she opts to keep her arsenal simple and lightweight. While Ogrifina inspects the warehouse's collection of submachine guns, Evgeny unfolds a set of architectural blueprints from the mission's dossier folder. After selecting a pair of Kashtan AEK-919Ks, she joins Evgeny in reviewing these blueprints. They pinpoint an entry point through which she may be able to infiltrate the hive undetected—a large ossuary in a nearby cemetery that connects to the cathedral's undercroft via a network of underground tunnels. Not knowing exactly how many assassins are stationed in the hive, stealth is of critical importance. She knows that, once her presence has been detected, she's liable to be swarmed by assassins, and, confident as she may be in her ability to neutralize multiple assailants simultaneously, this will only make her job more difficult.

Within a matter of hours, Evgeny has arranged for a private plane to transport Ogrifina to Moravia. As she is preparing to board, examining her gear one final time to ensure that everything's in proper working order, Evgeny's heart grows heavy. He can't help but worry that this might be the last time he ever sees her—this lethiferous killing machine he's come to love like a daughter. Yet he knows that he cannot stop her from attempting to sate her retributive bloodlust. There are no teary-eyed goodbyes or lingering hugs. He maintains his composure and simply winks at Ogrifina as she boards the plane. After the plane has taken off, however, Evgeny Klebakhin breaks down and weeps.

Suited up in full Prizrak regalia, her abalest slung across her back and carrying a small drag bag filled with her gear, Ogrifina makes her way through the small cemetery adjacent to the Moravian cathedral her nemesis has reportedly established as his hive. Cloaked by the darkness of night, she is soon able to locate the ossuary she'd pinpointed as her point of entry. The cathedral's undercroft is accessible via a secret passageway connected to one of the ossuary's dank tunnels. She switches on her helmet's night vision optical system and begins her descent into the ossuary. Slipping through the catacomb's narrow tunnels, which are lined on either side with unlit torches and the intricately arranged bones of long-dead villagers, Ogrifina blends seamlessly with the darkness surrounding her.

"The Hishniki have no greater friend than the shadows, sol'nishka," her father used to say. "Under the veil of darkness, you may move imperceptibly both before and after your job is completed. To succeed as a Hishnik is to seek out and embrace the darkness—to become one with it. An assassin who embraces the light of day is an assassin whose career will be short-lived. Therefore, you must eschew the light and find the darkness—let it engirdle you in its acherontic embrace. *Become* the darkness."

Ogrifina Voronina has become the darkness. With each silent step taken as she advances, she can feel her bloodthirst intensify. Though she struggled internally during her flight to Moravia with how she would handle this job's contractual restrictions, her mind is now firmly decided. She will kill everything that stirs once she enters the cathedral—especially the one individual she is forbidden from eliminating. Her clan is extinct. The Kredo Krovi is now no more than a series of memorized words to her—a meaningless mantra. Her wrath is alive and beckoning to be sated. Tonight she will have her reckoning. Tonight her saga ends.

She soon finds herself standing before a large wrought-iron door leading directly into the cathedral's undercroft, and makes short work of the door's decorative lock. The fact that this doorway is not heavily guarded raises an immediate red flag. Her instincts tell her that something isn't right—that this mission isn't quite what she was led to believe it would be. Yet she presses on undeterred, making her way down a long corridor and into the undercroft itself, where torches burn brightly along the walls. She flicks her helmet's night-vision optical device off and steps silently through the doorway, hugging the undercroft's tenebrous walls cautiously as she sidesteps behind a large marble column to scan the room for activity.

ERNESTUS JIMINY CHALD

All is deafeningly silent—too silent for an active hive. She reaches inside her cloak and softly grips one of her Kashtan's handles. Suddenly, she hears a distant high-pitched chattering sound. Her eyes dart along the undercroft's ceiling attempting to pinpoint the source of these strange squeaking sounds, which grow louder by the second. She soon spots something in the distance—small and black—flying toward her, the high-pitched squeaks growing louder as it approaches. When Ogrifina realizes what it is—a large bat with a small explosive device strapped to its body—she's barely able to dive aside before the bat detonates mere feet away. The explosion sends chunks of the nearby limestone wall hurtling in every direction. Before the dust has fully settled, another bat-bomb swoops down, forcing Ogrifina to roll out of its path as it explodes, leaving a massive crater in the stone floor. She leaps to her feet, seeing several more bat-bombs hovering in the distance, and, withdrawing her Kashtans, opens fire on these bats, causing them to detonate on impact amidst a shower of exploded bat matter and shrapnel.

Suddenly, a deep voice rises above the ringing silence left in the wake of these explosions. "Welcome to our humble home, Prizrak. We've been eagerly awaiting your arrival." Ogrifina remains silent, taking cover behind another marble column to holster the Kashtans and load her arbalest. "Aww, it's impolite to ignore your hosts, Wraith," the voice sneers. "Perhaps you were expecting a warmer welcome? Well, fear not—your formal welcoming party will arrive to greet you shortly."

A large wooden door on the opposite end of the undercroft creaks open slowly. Ogrifina peers around the column, fixing her gaze on the open doorway and resting her index finger on her arbalest's trigger, ready to squeeze at the first sign of movement. A deep roar is suddenly emitted from behind her. She jerks her body around just in time to see the orange-and-black blur of a massive Bengal tiger barreling toward her. Before she's able to squeeze, the tiger leaps at her and sinks its fangs deep into her left shoulder, crushing her clavicle and tearing out a huge chunk of flesh and muscle. She screams out in agony as blood gushes profusely from her shoulder.

"Don't mind Mr. Nibbles," the voice shouts—a voice she now knows belongs to Finbar "The Animal Trainer" Freiling. "He's just so excited to have company."

Acting quickly and instinctively, Ogrifina yanks a flash bomb from her utility belt, squeezes her eyes tightly shut, and hurls it at the tiger's feet. Blinded by the flash bomb's detonation, Mr. Nibbles, whose chops are stained red with Ogrifina's blood, growls menacingly and stumbles into a nearby wall.

"No!" the Animal Trainer screams in protest as he rushes out from behind a statue of Saint Lazarus, brandishing an UZI. Ogrifina rolls behind a nearby pillar just as Freiling begins to spray the room wildly with bullets. Once he's run out of ammo, he reaches into his boot and withdraws a stiletto switchblade, then charges recklessly toward Ogrifina. Before he's within striking distance, Mr. Nibbles, still disoriented from the flash bomb's detonation, lunges blindly through the air in another orange-and-black blur, knocking Freiling to the ground. The Animal Trainer lets out a bloodcurdling shriek as Mr. Nibbles begins to maul him mistakenly.

With great difficulty, Ogrifina rises to her feet and watches the tiger tear its own master to shreds. A faint rattling sound can be heard emanating from Freiling's throat as Mr. Nibbles devours his trainer's flesh. Her first target effectively eliminated, she tears a swatch of cloth from her cloak and fashions a makeshift tourniquet around her damaged shoulder. She then goes through the open doorway on the undercroft's opposite end and ascends a long set of winding stone steps that lead into the cathedral's nave. She moves cautiously, her arbalest and drag bag slung across her back and a Kashtan at the ready in each hand.

The cathedral is brightly illuminated with lit torches situated along its walls beneath grimy stained glass windows depicting the Via Dolorosa. Candles burn brightly around the altar. As Ogrifina steps through the nave's entryway, she can see the back of a figure hunched slightly forward upon one of the center pews—the bald contour of a pale, liver-spotted head. She raises both Kashtans, aiming directly at the figure's head, and approaches it cautiously from behind. The figure remains motionless as Ogrifina glides silently through the cathedral's center aisle to inspect it. She hears the door she'd entered through suddenly slam shut behind her and ducks down beneath the pews.

Crawling closer to the figure seated in the center pew, she realizes that it's merely a waxen effigy of an elderly man. Strapped to its chest is a small black box upon which a red light flashes. Before she can leap to safety, the effigy erupts in a violent explosion, obliterating the pews around it in a cloud of splintering wood and unsettled dust. The body armor Ogrifina wears beneath her cloak takes the brunt of the impact, but tiny bits of shrapnel from the explosive device are able to pierce through her bodysuit's ballistic nylon material. Ogrifina winces at the sharp, stinging sensations in her torso and legs where the shrapnel has penetrated deep into her flesh.

Her helmet has also sustained substantial damage from the blast. She can feel the warm sensation of her own blood trickling down her left cheek where the helmet has fractured, and her ears, suffering from minor acoustic trauma, are filled with a deafening ring. A thick green fog of poisonous gas now begins to fill the cathedral. Disoriented yet vigilant, Ogrifina retrieves her Kashtans from the floor and rises unsteadily to her feet, ready to dance with target number two—The Mad Gasser. Fortunately, her helmet's rebreather mechanism remains intact and appears to function despite the damage it sustained in the blast, enabling Ogrifina to shield her lungs from the chemical gas being pumped into the room.

A figure emerges from a doorway beside the altar—a tall, thin man heavily clad in ballistic body armor, his face obscured by an antiquated gas mask. In his left hand, the Gasser clutches his signature Flit gun. A quavery nonagenarian voices issues from behind his mask.

"Welcome, child, to my holy tabernacle of death," the Gasser says as the cloud of chemical fog grows denser, making it impossible for Ogrifina to pinpoint her target's position. She fires her Kashtans at random, blindly spraying lead in every direction amidst a cacophony of metallic clacking. When both magazines are empty, Ogrifina takes cover behind a pew to reload. But the Gasser advances on her through the fog with startling agility for his advanced age, wrapping a garrote around her neck from behind and twisting it tightly against her throat. With Ogrifina subdued, he reaches down with his right hand, unbuckling the straps of her helmet, and tears if from her head, cackling maniacally while his garrote constricts ever tighter around her throat.

Just as Ogrifina can feel herself losing consciousness, the Gasser abruptly releases his garrote's grip around her throat and begins to taunt her, "Breathe, child. Just a few deep breaths and this will all be over."

Ogrifina recalls how she felt on the night she knelt on the floor of the Hishniki hive, cradling her father's immolated body, and is filled with a sudden cocktail burst of adrenaline and enmity. Without consciously sensing it, her body shifts into autopilot mode, opening a small pouch on her utility belt and retrieving an octagonal shuriken. She quickly reaches back and severs the Gasser's right Achilles tendon, forcing him to stumble backward into a pile of splintered pew debris. Still holding her breath, she seizes this opportunity to grab her helmet and secure its rebreather mechanism over her mouth, enabling her to safely gasp for air. The Mad Gasser struggles to his feet and lunges toward her. But Ogrifina, reaching into her cloak and unholstering a Ruger Super Redhawk double-action revolver, has the drop on him, and empties six rounds into her opponent's chest.

The Mad Gasser topples over the pew debris behind him. Mortally wounded, he attempts to crawl away, clutching uselessly at his Flit gun. Ogrifina goes in for the kill, pistol-whipping his face and shattering his mask's glass lenses. His mask fills immediately with poisonous gas, and, eyes reddened and watering profusely, he begins to cough violently. She reaches down and yanks the broken mask from his face, and watches the liver-spotted nonagenarian choke on his final breath. A frothy white liquid tinged pink with blood drips from his lips and his pupils dilate fixedly—bereft of life. Not one to take any chances, Ogrifina produces a short-handled sickle from her drag bag and deftly decapitates the Gasser's corpse.

With her mission technically completed, Ogrifina faces a choice. She can honor her contract and return to the states to collect her payment ... or she can venture further into the cathedral in pursuit of vengeance. Her attention turns to a large, ornately carved door beside the sanctuary's altar. Without hesitation, she makes her way to the doorway and begins a long ascent up a set of winding limestone steps into what she knows to be the cathedral's belfry. Massive bronze bells are bolted along the ceiling, illuminated by moonlight pouring in through openings on all four sides of the bell tower's walls.

In a dark pool of shadows cast by the bells, Ogrifina can barely make out the figure of a tall man gazing at her, arms folded impassively and apparently unarmed. She knows immediately from this figure's size and the silhouette of his wiry hair that, for the first time since the destruction of her hive, she is within near striking distance of her archenemy.

"So this is the legendary Prizrak," Fakel says, his arms folded casually as he steps forward into the moonlight. "Or should I call you Ogrifina Voronina?"

Ogrifina advances toward her nemesis slowly, stopping mere feet away. She unbuckles her helmet and tosses it to the ground, enabling her to clearly perceive the features of Fakel's face, features she could never forget.

"Your reputation precedes you, Ogrifina," Fakel says. "You are even more beautiful than I remembered. I was so disappointed that you were away when I came to your hive and eradicated your people. I'd been so eagerly looking forward to killing you!" He takes a step toward her before continuing, "You know, there are no kills a man ever cherishes as much as when he kills a beautiful woman."

Ogrifina tears her tattered cloak off and casts it on top of her helmet, her battle-damaged bodysuit glistening with blood.

"I've been hailed as a God among assassins ever since I vanquished that insufferable clan of yours," Fakel continues, advancing another step closer to Ogrifina. "Finbar and Warrington assisted me, of course, but the glory was all mine. Yet I always knew that, as long as you were out there breathing somewhere, I never truly deserved the veneration I received from my peers. But now I have been granted a second chance to finish the Hishniki genocide I initiated twelve years ago." He steps forward again, placing both assassins within striking distance of one another. "As you can see," he says, "I am completely unarmed ... but as you know I am far from defenseless, for I was once a Hishnik myself. I received the same rigid training in the art of murder as you—my entire body is a weapon. So why don't you drop that useless arbalest of yours and we shall see how evenly matched we are?"

Fakel uncrosses his arms and adopts a forward-weighted Hishniki battle stance as Ogrifina drops her arbalest behind her and removes her utility belt. "Do your worst, Prizrak!" Fakel shouts as Ogrifina advances upon him with lightning speed, her fists raining down upon her adversary like a meteor shower of pent up malice. He backs away slowly, expertly deflecting Ogrifina's blows. A crooked grin forms in the corner of his mouth. "Very impressive," he says scoffingly as he continues to parry her blows. Ogrifina connects against his Adam's apple with a hard open palm strike, catching him off guard and causing him to fall to his knees clutching his throat.

Seizing her upper hand, she lunges at her opponent, but Fakel overpowers her with a devastating backhand. He then rises to his feet and continues to mock her, "You really know how to turn a man on, Ogrifina. However, I believe it's time we put an end to this foreplay and move on to the main event."

Backing away from Ogrifina with his eyes glued to her, Fakel reaches behind him and begins to hoist his signature weapon—a customized LPO-50 flamethrower. But Ogrifina bears down on him before he's able to strap on his fuel pack. She executes a devastating helicopter kick to his face, sending him hurtling through the air. "You're a feisty little twat," he says, spitting out several teeth, and visibly frustrated as he struggles to regain his footing. Ogrifina rushes at her foe again, her closed fist thrust at his face. But Fakel quickly sidesteps and latches onto her, digging his fingers deeply into the throbbing wound in her shoulder and yanking at the exposed muscle. Ogrifina is on the verge of passing out when Krasnomyrdin tosses her to the ground like a broken toy. He then returns to his flamethrower and begins strapping on its fuel pack. Ogrifina, meanwhile, has discreetly removed a canister of flame-retardant gel from her nearby utility belt and is applying it to her face.

"You put up a good fight, Prizrak," Fakel says as he lurches toward her, "... but unfortunately this is where the Hishniki saga truly ends." He squeezes his flamethrower's trigger, blasting Ogrifina's body with a massive stream of ignited flammable liquid. With her eyes clenched tightly shut, Ogrifina's bodysuit and flame-retardant gel temporarily shield her from being incinerated, but she can soon feel the flames searing through to her skin. The belfry is quickly filled with the stench of her burning hair and flesh. Krasnomyrdin releases his igniparous trigger and glares down at Ogrifina's smoldering body. Though she can feel her flesh bubbling away, she remains deathly still.

"Spokonoi Nochi, Prizrak," he says, crouching down to inspect his kill. When she can sense that her foe is within reach, Ogrifina's eyes pop open and she clutches Fakel's throat, her gloved hand still ablaze. She rolls to a crouched position, leaps on her prey, and showers his face with a devastating flurry of flaming-fisted punches. He loses consciousness after a few blows, but Ogrifina continues to drive her fists into his face, which is soon swollen and bedrabbled with gore. She can feel her knuckles shattering with each merciless blow, yet, in a murderous daze, she continues to pound her enemy's face until it caves in completely and she can see deep inside his exposed skull cavity.

Mortally wounded and burned beyond recognition, Ogrifina rises to her feet and retrieves her loaded arbalest. She gazes at the mangled face of Kliment Krasnomyrdin one last time before firing an explosive broadhead directly into his fuel pack, causing his remains to detonate on impact in an explosive shower of gore.

It takes considerable time and effort for Ogrifina to make her way back down the belfry's winding steps and into the sanctuary below. The Mad Gasser's gas has now cleared. Ogrifina saunters weakly past his corpse toward the church's main entrance. When she's mustered the strength to pull the large wooden door before her open, the entryway is immediate flooded with light from the rising sun. Her legs give way and she stumbles onto the stone steps beneath her. Resting her back against these steps, she gazes up into the clear blue sky above. Though her injuries are direful, Ogrifina Voronina can feel an involuntary smile worming its way across her scorch-marked face.

The realization dawns on her that, having spent her entire life embracing the darkness—"Dancing with Death," as her father used to put it—she never actually had an opportunity to enjoy the sunlight or embrace life. How wonderfully incongruous it is then, she thinks to herself, that this is how she will spend her final moments—embracing the light. A cool breeze caresses her welmish flesh, soothing the pain from her grievous wounds, and causing her smile to grow even broader. She struggles to remember the last time she's smiled like this. Perhaps she's never actually smiled before at all.

She knows what she has to do. By killing Fakel, she defaulted on her contract, breaking the inviolability of the Kredo Krovi, and marring her own unblemished track record irreparably. Even if she were to survive her devastating injuries, the balance of her days would be spent on the run and in hiding—constantly looking over her shoulder for other Ubitsayedi who would indubitably be sent to eliminate her. Ogrifina would rather not give anyone else the honor of saying that they were the one to eliminate the legendary Prizrak. She won't allow herself to become a notch on some other assassin's belt.

As the sun shines down upon her, Ogrifina Voronina loads an explosive broadhead into her trusty arbalest. A broad smile remains on her face as she rests the butt-end of her weapon on a stone step between her feet and places her thumb against its trigger. The smile remains on her face as she lowers her forehead and feels the broadhead's razor-sharp tip pressing against her flesh. The smile remains on her face when she squeezes her thumb willfully against her arbalest's trigger, launching the broadhead into her skull—obliterating her head in a grisly explosion of fragmented brain matter, flesh, and bone.

The smile remained on Ogrifina Voronina's face until her face was no more.

WHAT THE BLENDER SAW

BY L.L. SOARES

This elevator is small enough to be a coffin.

The metaphor wasn't lost on Jeff Gangler as he slipped inside. There was just one other person there, a man in a suit who had been working late. For all he knew, they were the last two people left in the building—except for the security guard, of course. But the guard hadn't seen Jeff come in.

"Working late?" Jeff asked.

The man, whose name was Howard Saxon—it had said so on the manila folder—stared straight ahead and did not respond. Either he was too tired or just didn't want to be bothered. Jeff found this rude and it made his job all the easier.

The ancient elevator groaned as they moved down.

Despite the fact that the man tried to avoid eye contact, Jeff slid right in front of him, making it impossible for him to be avoided. He stared straight into Saxon's eyes. All he needed was a connection.

"What's the big idea?" the businessman asked, clearly annoyed that Jeff was invading his personal space. But in such a small elevator, was there really such a thing as personal space?

Jeff did not say a word, he just maintained eye contact, and then he saw the look on the guy's face that told him:

He's feeling it.

Before Saxon had any real physical reaction, Jeff stepped back and to the side of the elevator. "I'm sorry," he said. "I just thought you were someone else. Someone I used to know. My eyesight's not that good."

The businessman muttered something under his breath and tried to ignore him.

"It's pretty late," Jeff said, trying to sound empathetic. "Do you usually work so late?"

Saxon said nothing as they reached the lobby and the door slid open. Jeff gave the man a wide berth and let him leave first.

Not even a thank you, Jeff thought.

The security guard wasn't at his desk. He must have been making the rounds of the building. This time of night, his job was probably pretty lonely.

Saxon looked over his shoulder, as if suddenly paranoid that Jeff was following him to his car. So, to put his mind at ease, Jeff went in the opposite direction.

All he needed to do was establish an imprint. He never had to lay a finger on anyone.

As the businessman got out his keychain and shut off the alarm electronically, Jeff went down the street and got into his own car. He watched the man in his rearview mirror.

Saxon moved forward to open his car door, but suddenly stumbled back, as if he had been punched in the stomach.

There was violent activity throughout the man's body, especially his stomach and upper torso. Jeff could see it even as far away as he was: a series of violent spasms. The street was so quiet, Jeff was sure that if he was a little closer, he could even hear the sounds of the man's insides struggling to get out.

The spasms, the jerking about, the whole process made Saxon look like some kind of giant marionette, being jerked around by an angry child. Then, just as suddenly as it began, it stopped, and the man dropped to the asphalt. Blood began to drain out of his mouth and ears, creating a puddle on the street.

Jeff waited a few minutes before he started his engine.

Fucker didn't see that *coming,* he thought as he drove away.

I met Jeff Gangler when he was in seventh grade and I was in eighth. My family had just moved to the neighborhood, and Jeff lived next door. I'd seen him come and go a few times. He never seemed to have any friends to play with, and went off by himself a lot. One day I got curious and I followed him without him seeing me. He went out to this clearing in the woods behind our houses. There was an old toolshed there. I had no clue whose property it was on, but it looked like no one had used it for eons.

I looked in the window, and that's when I saw what he was doing to the cat. It was a white cat that lived with an old woman down our street. She had put up a few flyers with a picture of him and the offer of a twenty-dollar reward if anyone found him.

I remember thinking that twenty dollars wasn't much of a reward, even back then. She mustn't really want her little friend back, I had thought at the time.

But, watching Jeff in that shed, I quickly learned two things. First, Jeff was a sadistic fuck who was probably going to grow up to be some kind of serial killer. And second, he had no respect for animals.

It became my mission to befriend him, to channel his impulses elsewhere.

You see, no matter what I may have done in my life, I've never stooped so low as to hurt a defenseless animal.

"I've got to get to work," she said, sliding off the bed. "I'm going to be late."

Jeff didn't say a word as she retrieved her clothes from the floor.

"I'm just going to use your bathroom first," she said. "Where do you keep your towels?"

He told her and rolled over to watch, but she grabbed some spare towels out of the closet and then shut the door of the bathroom after her. He heard the shower running.

They had met at the bar of a TGI Fridays. He usually went there for dinner on Wednesday nights. He liked the food and the surroundings just seemed so Middle American and normal. After dinner, he went to the bar to get a couple of beers and pretend to

343

watch whatever everyone else was watching on the television, usually sports. He made the effort to be social.

Linda was already half in the bag when he offered to buy her a drink. She was there with work friends. It sounded like she was having an especially rough week on the job and had come for the margaritas. At first her friends, older women who introduced themselves but he didn't remember their names, were protective of her. As it got later, and he and Linda drifted to a booth and started making out, her friends left to go back to their own families, and she was on her own.

The sex had been good, but the morning had come too quickly. He liked having someone else in bed with him, but she was getting ready to leave. Just once, he wished one of them would call in sick and take the day off to spend with him. But they all seemed in a hurry to go.

The bathroom door opened and Linda was dressed, and she had done her best not to look too disheveled.

"Sorry I've got to run," she said. "I'll be late as it is. See you around."

But he knew he probably wouldn't see her again. The next time she had the urge to drink too much and have a one-night stand, she'd probably go to Ruby Tuesday's instead.

This annoyed him, the way they always left in a hurry. And he could have done something to her, but he controlled himself because control was important. He kept telling himself how important it was. So instead of giving her an aneurysm or stopping her heart, like he could have done quite easily, he watched her go.

On the stairs, she would have a nosebleed. It would be messy and aggravating, since she was in a hurry and all. But it wouldn't be fatal.

The telekinesis thing came as a total surprise. One day we were shooting BB guns in the woods when he put up a hand and told me to stop.

"I've got something to show you, Gus," he said.

There was a bird sitting on a fence, and he looked at it. He looked at it so hard, I thought he must think it was the most fascinating thing in the world. And then, suddenly, it jerked violently off its perch and

344

dropped to the ground, bleeding. It struggled for a moment on the ground, trying to get up again, and then it stopped moving completely.

"I did that," Jeff said. "I did it with my mind."

I pretended to be impressed. I had a good idea what he was capable of before we even became friends. You can sense when someone else is like you. It was what had changed my mind when, at first, I seriously considered getting rid of him. For what he did to that cat. It would do the animals of the neighborhood a favor to exterminate him. But two things stopped me. One was the awareness that he could do things with his mind, that he had latent abilities that could be mentored and even exploited. The other thing that stopped me was that we had more than one thing in common. We also shared the desire to hurt, to kill. And I was determined to get him to leave animals alone and move up a level.

It was time for him to start practicing on humans.

But first, before we shared any secrets, we were just kids, hanging out. Riding bikes and shooting BB guns. I took it slowly. I studied his patterns. How often he needed to exercise his cruelty. How much control he had over what he could do.

Slowly, I learned everything I needed to know about Jeff Gangler.

And then, just as slowly, I began revealing the things that made us alike. But I only showed him what I wanted him to know.

"I wanted to talk to you about a special job," Gus said, sitting across from Jeff. "It's a big one, and it will need both of us."

They had just finished lunch. Every other Sunday, Gus made a large meal and Jeff came over and spent the afternoon. Neither of them had any family that lived nearby, and the two of them had grown up together. It was just a habit they got into. Even when there had been women in their lives, they had kept the Sunday meal habit. It had outlasted a lot of relationships.

"Sure," Jeff said. "This is out of the ordinary, isn't it? Usually we get instructions from someone else."

"I know," Gus said. "Basically, this was a job I said I'd take care of. But then I realized I needed help. It's involves multiple targets. I just think I'd feel better with backup. And, frankly, you're the only person I trust."

"Okay," Jeff said.

Gus got a map and spread it out on the kitchen table. Jeff could not remember the last time he had used an actual map. Everything was GPS and Google Earth these days.

"I wanted to go over the logistics with you," Gus said.

He indicated an area with his hand. "This is where the first target will be."

Gus wondered if Jeff's abilities had progressed at all in the last few years. As far as he could tell, they hadn't. Still no signs of telepathy. Not that it was crucial to the job, but it didn't hurt. Gus read Jeff's mind now, and didn't find much of interest. Just the same old things that Jeff thought about, and the things he was pointing out on the map. Still no awareness he was in there, no attempt to communicate nonverbally.

"It all happens on Friday, at eleven a.m.," Gus said. "Meet me at seven o'clock. And we should probably meet a couple more times between now and then, to iron out any possible problems."

Jeff nodded. Just another job.

Gus hated to take in a partner. He normally liked to work alone. But there wasn't much room for error with this one, and he knew he could subtly control Jeff and make sure nothing went wrong.

I hadn't been nervous about a job in years, but then again I normally do it all myself and don't have to rely on someone else. Jeff and I don't work together very often. Maybe three times in the last ten years, but it's gone smoothly enough in the past. He takes direction well. And he never hesitates to get things done.

This time, though, I found myself a little anxious the night before and didn't get much sleep. We'd gone over it all enough to anticipate any eventualities. Nothing could go wrong. But still, I guess I just don't play well with others. At least, if I have to rely on someone, it's someone who is just as much of a professional as I am.

I have a nickname for him. *The Blender.* Because that's how he does it, he gets inside someone, grabs onto their internal organs, and grinds

346

it all up like the inside of a blender. It's become his signature move, his calling card if you will, and it tells anyone in the know, right away, that he's been there. No routine executions for us. Sure, the old way of doing it inspired fear in people, kept them in line. But the way we do it is even scarier. They never see us coming.

And no one has a clue who did it or how it was done. Well, the bosses know who did it, the people who hire us. But even they don't really know when it's going to happen. And they're just as wary about it happening to them. Who knows when a rival will pay to eliminate the competition? Keeps them on their toes.

Needless to say, we provide a very specific service, and we get paid extremely well for it.

We don't even have to be near the intended targets. We just have to see them. And Jeff told me he doesn't even have to do that anymore. He meets them beforehand, puts some kind of "imprint" on them, and he can kill them from afar. I can't say I totally understand it, but it seems to work for him.

I guess maybe his abilities have been evolving after all. Just differently than mine.

He still enjoys his work. I remember the last time we teamed up, my telepathy had just started to get strong, and I could feel the adrenaline pumping inside him as he did his part of the job. Could feel the pure ecstasy he took in hurting another person. Ripping them apart internally. It was almost like a sexual release. It was so intense, it kind of scared me.

I wonder if I'll feel anything like that this time. We'd be pretty far apart—we wouldn't be able to see each other. We'd arranged to meet at a coffee shop later on, after it's done. So I wouldn't be close by.

They secretly called it a "Dealey Plaza" job. Not that they were anywhere near Dallas. They were in New York, not Texas. But it was like hitting points in a parade route, except this one wasn't supposed to be public knowledge. And there weren't any grassy knolls around. Just lots of big buildings.

Jeff and Gus were on different rooftops, at different points along the route. Gus couldn't see his partner, but he could faintly *feel* him.

Once you got into someone's head, especially someone with the abilities Jeff had, a definite impression was made. A strange sort of connection, even if they didn't feel it too. Gus guessed that must be what Jeff meant when he talked about "imprints," something like that.

Gus saw his target below. A man in an overcoat, trying to blend in with the crowd. He waited until the man was about to cross the street, then orchestrated an elaborate tableau that would appear to all witnesses to be a car accident. They wouldn't find much of his subject.

Meanwhile, he could feel the adrenaline as Jeff took out his target further down the street. There was more commotion down that end, signaling another job completed. Gus pictured the scenario in his mind. A man stumbling to the ground, bleeding from the mouth. A crowd of concerned citizens either gathering around him, assuming he had had some kind of heart attack, or, once they saw the blood coming from the man's mouth, aggressively avoiding him. (Was it some kind of illness? People usually didn't take chances to find out.)

Nobody would even think to look for *them*. No one would have a clue that these two seemingly unrelated incidents had anything to do with outside forces. At least until autopsies were performed. And if they were, it would be way too late for answers. It wasn't like they left fingerprints or DNA behind.

It all went smoothly, until, suddenly, there was the crack of a rifle being fired, and a wave of panic coming from Jeff's direction.

Gus did not hesitate to get moving. He had to get to Jeff.

When I got there, I saw a stranger sprawled on the rooftop not far from Jeff, clearly dead, a puddle of blood growing around the unmoving body. A rifle nearby, one of the man's fingers still touching it. Jeff was also on the ground, unconscious. I instantly checked for a pulse. Jeff was alive, but barely.

I put on my gloves and checked the other body for ID. There wasn't any. No wallet, no papers. Just a half packet of chewing gum and some spare ammunition. The face was not familiar. Who was this person? Another assassin hired to make sure this job went off successfully, who had orders to kill us both when it was done? It seemed possible. Maybe the guy even thought Jeff was me. No one else knew I had hired him as my backup.

If this guy had orders, then there was a short list of possibilities. Not many people knew about this job, or how it would be handled. Few people knew what I or Jeff could do. I never went into any kind of detail when people asked me how I did my job. All that mattered to them was that things got done.

I pinpointed where the bullet was, but I was no surgeon. I was a cudgel. To save Jeff, I'd have to get him out of here. People had heard the gunshot.

I left the dead man in his puddle and lifted Jeff up from the ground. My telekinesis gave me the extra muscle it took to get Jeff downstairs. We got the elevator to ourselves. I didn't want to have to eliminate anyone else. Down at street level, I used telepathic signals to confuse and distract any onlookers, as I got Jeff to my car.

On my cell, I dialed the number of a doc I knew. Jeff was stretched out on the backseat. I did what I could to slow the bleeding, but I had a lot of balls to juggle.

It was hours later before Jeff came to. He found himself in a bed in a backroom somewhere. Or maybe a cellar. From what he could feel, his upper body was naked and bandaged. The lights weren't on and the room was dark.

He thought about calling out, then felt a twinge of pain and decided against it. He didn't want to draw any attention to himself until he knew exactly where he was.

He laid back down, staring up at the ceiling, obscured by the darkness, and waited.

What seemed like an hour later, the doc came in. An older guy who had probably lost his license to practice years before. Gus was with him. Jeff felt it was okay to move a bit, and let them know he was awake.

"How are you feeling?" Gus asked.

"Alive," Jeff said. "What the hell happened up there?"

"A double-cross," Gus said, but didn't elaborate. "It looked like you took care of him good."

349

"Too little too late," Jeff said. "When I crushed his heart he had already shot me. Came out of nowhere."

"He knew where one of us would be, and was probably sent to keep us quiet," Gus said. "Or rather keep *me* quiet. I find it hard to believe anyone else knew I'd hired you. You didn't say a word to anyone, did you?"

"What do you think?" Jeff said. "I'm a professional. Besides, who am I going to tell?"

That was true. Jeff didn't have much of a personal life to speak of. Killing was all he had.

"You died," Gus said. "The doc said we almost lost you forever. You're lucky to be up so soon."

Jeff nodded.

"So what did you see when you died?" Gus asked. "Did you see a tunnel with a light at the end?"

"No," Jeff said. "Not that. But I saw Jesus."

Jesus? Do you believe that shit? We're talking about one of the most hardcore stone hearts I knew, a man who wouldn't hesitate to pull the arms off babies if he had to. And here he is, looking earnest as hell and telling me he just saw Jesus.

I have to admit, I had no clue how to respond to that. It wasn't the kind of conversation I normally had with people, especially not someone like Jeff. That was the last thing I thought he'd ever say to me.

He must have seen the skepticism in my eyes, because he reached out and touched my arm.

"No, I'm serious," he said. "He was right next to me, just like you are now, and he spoke to me."

"Spoke to you?" I asked.

"He told me to stop. But I knew what he meant. He wanted me to stop killing."

I forced a laugh. "Fucking useless thing to say," I said. "To someone like you. It's in your blood."

"No," he said. "I'm serious. He told me to stop. And I will."

He looked really shaken up, so I just nodded and tried to calm him down. Then the doc gave him a shot of something to knock him out again. The doc said the best possible thing he could do was rest, now that we knew he was out of the woods. Rest up and heal a bit before I took him home again.

"Come in," Jeff said as he opened the door wide for Gus. "It's good to see you."

"Same here," Gus said, looking around. It had been a long time since he had been in Jeff's apartment.

They walked out onto the patio, and Jeff sat down on a lawn chair. He beckoned for Gus to do the same.

"I haven't heard from you in a while," Gus said.

"Yeah," Jeff said. "It's always good to see old friends."

"People have been trying to reach you," Gus said. "But they told me you keep turning them down."

"I told you already," Jeff said. "I'm done with that life."

"So you were serious?"

"Of course I was serious," Jeff said.

"So what are you doing now?"

"I've made enough money to give me a nice nest egg. I've been taking it easy. "

"So it seems. So you don't miss it at all?"

"I thought I would, but I don't."

"It's been a long time," Gus said. "We were kids when we started with all this stuff. It's a lot to throw away."

"Not really," Jeff said. "I had no idea what to expect. How long I'd be able to stay away from it, but I'm very peaceful now. No more need for violence."

"So you don't use your skills anymore?"

"No reason to," Jeff said. "That part of my life is over."

"So how did you do it?" Gus said. "How were you able to stop something that was such a part of your very nature?"

"I told you. He came to me and told me to stop. That's all I needed."

"You do realize that you lost a lot of blood? That people do hallucinate in times like that?"

"Well, if it was a hallucination, it was a pretty vivid one. It seemed real enough to me. And I don't have any regrets since I listened to him."

"I see," Gus said. "So I'll tell them you've retired for good. You're not doing jobs anymore."

"I'd appreciate if you did. I hate having to screen my calls all the time. I only answered it when you called, because I knew I could be honest with you."

"Sure."

"Would you like something to drink?" Jeff asked.

"You got any bourbon?" Gus asked.

"There must be a bottle around somewhere," Jeff said. "Although I haven't touched a drop in weeks now."

"You've really changed, huh?" Gus asked. "You weren't joking around about turning over a new leaf."

"When did you know me to be such a comedian?" Jeff said. "I've always been pretty serious, but now you make it sound like I'm playing some kind of practical joke on you."

"And there's nothing I can do to change your mind?" Gus said. "Not money or anything?"

"I've got all I need, Gus. You should really consider it, too. We've both been in that world much too long. If I got out of it, so can you."

"I'll think about it."

"I wish you would."

"Can I use your bathroom?" Gus asked.

"Sure, you know where it is," Jeff said, not getting up.

Gus got up and went to the bathroom. When he closed the door, there was a picture of Jesus hanging on the wall, baring his sacred heart.

Gus took a piss and then went out to the living room. He stood in the opening that led out to the patio.

"I think I'll leave now."

"Leave? You just got here."

"I know. But I was here to ask you to do a job, and I can tell I'm just wasting my time. You're done with all that."

"Yes, I am," Jeff said. "I don't know what else I can say to convince you. But I appreciate your respecting my wishes."

"Oh, you've convinced me. Don't worry about that."

"Good."

I don't know who was sitting out on that patio, but it wasn't the Jeff I knew. The Jeff I grew up with. That guy didn't have an ounce of compassion in him. Didn't even know what peace felt like. And definitely would never retire from what he loved best.

I thought he'd try to talk me into joining him in this new peace of his, but he didn't try very hard. He wasn't judging me. He was only judging himself, and had found an answer.

Even though we knew each other since we were kids, and he would come over to my place every other Sunday afternoon, I found that I really didn't have any strong emotions either way when it came to Jeff. I really thought that I'd feel sentimental, standing here in his apartment, maybe seeing him for the last time. We weren't living in the same world anymore.

And the people who ran that *other* world, the one he had left, weren't too crazy about leaving witnesses behind. People who had suddenly decided that violence wasn't for them anymore. Who had found religion and suddenly wanted to do good things with their lives. It made no sense to them.

The people I worked for didn't trust people like that.

I was surprised we didn't have a stronger bond. But in another way, I wasn't that surprised. We were both men who had made our livings by not getting attached to much in life. To not baring our hearts to anyone. Even all those Sunday dinners at my house. It was our way of killing time between jobs, but it hadn't made us that much closer.

I remember I used to watch him when he was around my dogs, Fritz and Thurston, two mutts I got from an animal shelter. I wanted to make sure he didn't have a thing for hurting animals anymore. I could read his mind if he even thought about hurting the animals. He had thoughts like that, once or twice, but never acted on them. And those were rare occasions. I was glad I had changed the direction of his cruelty all those years before. At least I had done that much.

353

He hadn't been over to my house for dinner in a long time. Not since he got shot.

I looked right at Jeff as he sat there on his lawn chair, and it only took a moment. It was like something big and heavy fell on top of him, except—and this was the fun part—I got to see it all, the way his body squeezed in on itself, the way his flesh flattened, the way his crushed intestines found their way out of his mouth. And then there was a second pounding, with even more force than the first, and I could feel every bone inside him snap.

When the third invisible fist came down on him, there wasn't much that was still recognizable.

You see, Jeff's nickname was the Blender, because he could blend up someone's guts right inside of them, reducing them liquid. But I have a nickname, too, in the biz. And I've grown proud of it over the years.

They called me the *Pulper*.

CODE NAME TRINE

BY MARTIN ROSE

Go to Paris, they said. *Your target is known only through his code name: Trine.*

They give me targets and I send them on to the undiscovered country. I do it with quiet and discretion. From the equator to the poles and through tropical heat to frozen deserts, I belong to the globe. My citizenship and my identity become fuzzy with the card shuffle of passports and false papers until even my real name seems an empty prop. I awaken in strange bedrooms and drug dens, unable to remember my location or the year. I mark the passage of time by whom I kill and each job completed; then I am on to the other. My vitality is financed by death.

I learned how to kill from my father.

He gave me a glass jar and a cotton ball soaked with ethyl alcohol; that summer, I collected butterflies and sent them to their deaths in the thin and toxic air of my Mason jar. I was not an angry child or a disaffected youth. It turns out you have to be taught compassion, and my father was not interested in those lessons.

I moved on from butterfly collecting to stripping at a gentleman's club in the outskirts of DC. I was giving a government spook from Langley a lap dance and writing out my mental grocery list when he leaned forward to whisper hotly in my ear:

You look cold in the eyes, darlin'. That's the kind of cold I look for and like. You wanna kill for the government?

In those three seconds of fraught silence, I could smell nothing but ethyl alcohol before I said yes.

They sent me to Paris through bleached streets and in designer shoes with my hourglass body drawing stares from a three-mile radius—but this is my magician's trick. The big distraction so they don't notice the abracadabra when I pull a snub-nosed gun out of my hat. I bleached my hair for the last kill, but it needs redoing. I started out as Marilyn Monroe and but now it looks like Elvira is trying to escape through my black roots.

Now, I watched this man I was sent to kill, who had no name but Code Name Trine.

Trine walked with the same jaguar ease of any predator. I ghosted him by not being invisible at all. The art of my camouflage relied on kitsch; my too-loud clothes and my carnival sway. I flirted with men and women alike. Bumped elbows with fruit sellers and ate an apple half moaning while people stared in my passage and the only one who did not stare was Trine. I tapped in my heels behind him, like a doe down a used game trail, following the jaguar ahead of me, with fruit juice dripping down my throat. A doe with wolf's teeth.

I tracked him the next day and the one after that. I would assume his habits and visit the stores he liked. I would stare through the glass of a bookshop and wonder what tome he chose among the many; pick out his discarded newspaper from the trash and discover the headlines were in Italian. Pick up his cigarette butts out of the trash and smoke what was left with my fingertips bright red at the ends as the talons of a hawk. Tasted his residual saliva from the cigarette like I could kiss him through the smoke, and count down the minutes to killing him.

I loved him the way customers in a strip club used to love me, for just this moment in the throbbing dark they could be anyone or any fantasy affixed to the blank face.

In passing he was handsome, but older; gray through the sides of his temples and wrinkles dusted around his eyes. A pleasing bone structure, a detachment in his eyes. I caught his reflection in a shop window.

Between his eyes and set in the center of his forehead carved a deep vertical slash—some raw and half-healed scar like a seam in his face, stopped me dead on the concrete. Even in the summer heat, it made me cold from the beginning of my toes to the top of my spine. And though he walked on, I did not follow him farther.

In the hotel room, I stayed swaddled in blankets. Sleepy in the summer heat from too much French champagne and smoking myself into oblivion, pouring smoke into the ceiling. I wondered if he had been tortured. If they had held him down and cut that seam into his forehead. Anointed him with the sharp end of a knife. Wondered if he was an escaped prisoner, or a POW from some distant war, a retired spook, a mob boss or a master thief.

He'd escaped someone else's Mason jar once before; he would not be so lucky once I closed the lid.

I inhaled tobacco and stubbed out the smoke. I pulled my pants up and kicked away the clothes in the twilight dark. Then I grabbed the end of the sniper rifle where it swiveled on the tripod and aimed the telescopic sight across the blue atmosphere of the Paris dawn—the city giving herself to me unendingly. But I didn't want the city. All I wanted was this thin millimeter of laser red, aimed at the bull's-eye of Trine's scar, turning the slit into a cross, the scar into a benediction.

Trine stayed in the hotel across from my own, a strip of air space and glass separating us. Through the lens I had watched him for days now. Seen him traverse his apartment. He spent hours reading in the uncomfortable hotel chair. I was used to seeing man in his every undressed state and humble transition. Beating off, picking their noses, tweezing their pubic hair.

But Trine's life revolved around intellectual pursuits. He forgot to eat. He turned page after page and the five o'clock shadow became a ten o'clock beard. He undressed once and I watched with dispassionate curiosity as the shape of him emerged from his rumpled and unwashed suit. One evening, he returned with blood on his button down and he bleached it in the tub, fastidiously hung it to dry in the closet with the fan turned on high.

Our time together had been short but interesting, and he unlike any other subject; I was sorry to see him go.

357

I aimed the rifle and let the crosshairs descend. A flicker of red across his face trembled and then steadied.

He snapped his book shut. I imagined the paper *snap!* Heard his footsteps as he got up and in one motion queered my whole shot. I could only track him with the lens, hoping to catch him at rest again.

Trine opened a drawer and withdrew a length of rope.

I considered secondary options. Other weapons, other sites for disposal, when I realized he was not leaving.

He was staying in the room and unwinding the rope. He reached up into a ventilation grate in the ceiling above his bed. Fixing the rope through the rungs and tugging on it hard, testing it with his weight by leaning on it.

Pleased with the effect, he pulled the bed away from the swinging rope, and then I saw it was not a rope at all, but a noose.

My finger fell away from the trigger.

He was going to kill himself.

Trine examined his two hotel room chairs and considered which to aid him, testing the construction of one with his polished shoe. All thoughts cleared my head and left a wasteland of crumpled butterflies on the floor of memory. Ethyl alcohol rank in the air, wings beating against glass.

I dropped my rifle, it clattered to the floor.

I scooped up my shirt and slid into my heels and tapped down the hall, my footfalls like the second hand of a clock turning seconds faster than time should allow. Breath burning fast over my beating heart. Into the elevator and then out into the sun again. When I couldn't go fast enough in my heels, I took them off and ran barefoot into the street into the broiling summer and didn't give a damn. Crossed the street and slid into the hotel and past the screaming concierge.

Up the stairs. Launching upward like I could rocket skyward into flight and counting the levels because I didn't know the room number but I knew the layout, knew where he would be.

Down the hall. I stopped at the room and rapped my knuckles like a garage band drummer. Nothing, no answer. I rapped the door beside it. An older woman answered with a brusque "no room service" and I pushed her aside. She yowled. Tinted hair in curlers, a billowing nightgown as big as a shower curtain.

358

I ran for the back, to her balcony. Lifted my feet into empty space with my hands on the railing, and swung around to the room adjacent. I dangled several stories up and heard the honks of taxicabs desecrating the ancient city and, leg over leg like a dancer, landed into his suite.

I found him.

Too late.

He dangled from the vent. The rope creaked and groaned over the old woman arguing with thin air and then she slammed her balcony window closed. His corpse cast a shadow over the plush carpeting. I took the other chair and cut him down, I hauled him over my shoulders like an oxen and tottered to the bathroom. I slid him into the tub. He looked tall but weighed nothing. All those days of reading and forgetting to eat had wasted him. Lying in the tub with his mouth half-open and his hair haphazard, he could have been sleeping. Lips tinged purple. I untethered him from the noose. A purple line around his throat and the skin striated with red lines and burst blood vessels.

I closed his eyes. My fingers passed over his skin, and his skin was still hot; his scar livid in the bathroom light. I inched my thumb to the center and the rest of my fingers followed and I touched the seam. It looked as a scar looks, but deeper.

I rubbed it, pressing it apart like I could force a flower to open.

It split open and bloomed.

I cried out, jumped back and tripped into the toilet, fell upon the seat still staring at him in the tub. He was not alive, and he did not move. I listened for sounds. We were alone. If anyone knew I was in here or cared, they had forgotten; or they had better things to do.

I leaned forward and touched the scar again. I pressed it and it peeled open.

And when it did, I saw it was not a scar at all—but one gray eye in the center of his face.

"Code name Trine," I whispered.

Tiny eyelashes bent outward around his third eye and after staring at it like the jewel of a sacred crown, I closed his final eye at last. I would never know his story now. The job was done.

I pulled the shower curtain around him and left the door cracked. I made a pass over his possessions. The book on the coffee table he used to read beside, face-down. I turned it over: *The Tibetan Book of the Dead.* I turned it back the way I'd found it, intending to leave it there.

I took it at the last second, and left his body in that room in Paris.

Back in the United States, I had to meet with the in-between man, because deals like this aren't done face-to-face with the guy who wants it done, but with the middle guy. I came back through Russia, then Asia, then across the Bering to Alaska, and down through Canada.

I can't say why I took my time, because there was a payday waiting for me. I could have worked all my life as a stripper and never seen money like that. I could retire and do whatever spinsters like me do when they don't bother with marriage and kids. And friends.

I couldn't forget his eye, his third eye. I wondered if he was born like that or if someone set it into his face, altered him like I'd altered my tits, set it there like a jeweler putting a diamond into a ring setting.

In my dreams, he opens his eyes in the bathtub and our eyes meet. I can't tell if he's angry, if he's dead, disappointed to see only me there, or looking at me the way johns in the strip joint look, hungry and electric. He's a cross among all three.

When I wasn't dreaming him, I thought I saw him sometimes in passing traffic or riding in the driver's seat of other cars. I googled "third eye" and only ever came up with new-age malarkey and crystal gazers trying to attain ultimate enlightenment.

I searched the news for the day he died and the name of the hotel. Nothing hit a blip; if it did, it was in French and I couldn't read it anyway. I never found his picture. All I had as proof of his existence was *The Tibetan Book of the Dead* in my back pocket, and the memory that left me sweating when I woke up from dreaming him. In one nightmare I was giving him a lap dance in the tub, but there was little sexual about it.

Every time I moved my hips, explosions went off in the distance. When I snapped my fingers, civilizations rose and fell. The hotel windows were filled with fire in the outside world and mushroom clouds. I looked down and blood rained from between my legs, and turning his suit scarlet. He opened his eyes and wore a Buddha smile. Stole it right off Mona Lisa's face. The blood became roses. He stuffed pages of *The Tibetan Book of the Dead* into my g-string and paid for my dance in philosophy. It was a nightmare, and I loved it.

I wound my way down south into the States. Farther and farther until the land was tropical with humidity far beneath the Mason-Dixon line. And from there I took coordinates to a hotel in a southern city, where they still had plantations built on pain from centuries past; our rendezvous point.

From there, I was invited to a room. I kept *The Tibetan Book of the Dead* in my back pocket. I listened to an ancient grandfather clock tick away the seconds; turned off my cell phone and tucked it into my interior pocket. When I received my payment, I was going to get a room in this hotel and take a shower. Clean the humid grime off me and sleep on silk sheets. Sigh and drink champagne and go to sleep and forget about Paris and Trine and all this mess. I'd close the lid on tight and never open it again.

The in-between man entered. A scuzzy pale fellow with a cut from shaving on his face and a black eye. Strung out and nervous and his eyes ticking like the clock. He had a briefcase in his hand and I smiled and nodded.

He set down the case on the table between us and thumbed in the key code. A click, and he opened it up and stared down at the contents. I smoothed out my skirt and stood to face him, waiting for him to turn the briefcase.

He did. I stared.

There was no money in the briefcase. There was only a coiled rope formed as a noose.

"What the fuck is this?" I snarled through my red lipstick.

"This," In-Between said calmly, "is what happens when you don't do the job and the target ain't killed."

He pushed the briefcase with the noose inside in my direction and withdrew a gun. He rattled the case once and flicked the muzzle up and down to indicate that I should take the rope.

"What am I supposed to do with a noose? Cash it in at the bank?"

He smiled thin. It curved an 'S' beneath his black eye.

"Wear it."

He leveled the muzzle at me.

I looked down at the noose.

So this is what the inside of the Mason jar looks like.

A cold calculation of facts. Which held my greatest chance of survival? Getting shot wasn't like in the movies. And this close to me, he'd pulverize my heart. Even if he had bad aim. Even if a mountain lion severed his gun arm while he rode a Ferris wheel in hyperspeed, he'd hit me at this distance. Do you know what a bullet does to flesh at this proximity?

Strangling to death is no great send-off, but my odds of survival were greater.

I unlooped the rope, and taking his direction, began to sullenly set up the knot around the ceiling fan connection. If I was lucky, the ceiling fan wasn't anchored to a beam, and would yank right out. But I wasn't born lucky. I'd hang to death the way Trine had.

No one would close my eyes for me. No one would cut me down and lay me in a bathtub.

I climbed up on the table and waited. In-Between was packing up his briefcase and making for the door. The implication was clear. If I didn't do this on my own, he'd come back and finish the job.

It occurred to me this outcome would have been the same, no matter what I did. That there had never been a payday in my future.

I reached for the noose.

I took a deep breath and closed my eyes. I pulled it over my head so I could feel the rough and fraying edges and smell blood and dried saliva. Someone had used this noose before. A blast of cold air washed over me as though I had donned a hood instead. And taking another breath, I stepped off the edge and straight into the undiscovered country.

The rope cut into my neck. My windpipe folded over like a rolled newspaper and my eyes bulged open. I thought this was how I would be remembered. Purple eyes. Red face. Broken blood vessels as I swung on the empty air and kicked out even when I swore I wouldn't.

But when I opened my eyes, I realized I was not in that hotel room in the humid and sticky south.

I was in Paris.

I recognized this room. Someone swapped the Mason jar. Confusion married to my terror, my breath incendiary in my lungs.

This was the room Trine had died in, hanged himself in from the grate.

If I arched my spine with this fading strength, bucking like a bronco in a ring, I could see the grate above me, and this, this wasn't *my* rope, this was Trine's. *The Tibetan Book of the Dead* sat on the end table as though I had never been here, never cut Trine down and swiped it off the table.

I had heard that when people die and the oxygen cuts off from the brain, we swirl in a miasma of memory and illusion. We remember things that never happened and experience a future that may be wholly imaginary. Our dreams and reality merge and break apart. Our life flashes before our eyes. That old chestnut.

It gave me sudden peace to know I was dying, then—and in my last moments, dying through someone else. Dying by proxy. Going back to the past to be in Trine's shoes, even if only for a moment. The noose become a magic portal, a time machine.

Shouts outside. Through the raging blood rush in my ears, I heard to a tray knocked over with a clatter. The hotel room door slamming open and coming undone from the hinges.

My vision turned gray at the edges. My heart beat slammed my rib cage side to side like a wrecking ball. A figure appeared from fathoms away, a gray silhouette and three circles of light in his head, blazing fire from his skull, and then I was dead, and I didn't know anything anymore.

I woke up on a hotel bed.

A book set on the end table: *The Tibetan Book of the Dead.*

A voice spoke French and then shifted into Italian. "*No molto lira. Dollaro, por favore.*" I opened my mouth. Nothing came out but a dry husk of air. I looked away to feel a ring of fire around my throat, tearing and pulling at every muscle and vocal cord, it silenced me.

Trine turned away from the window, and closed off the cell phone. He set it on the table, took the chair and turned it backward to sit on it, facing me. Laced his hands over the back and set his chin on the end, staring.

Two eyes open. The third sealed shut.

Above us, the noose swung emptily. The rope creaked.

Through the opening in the noose, I believe I saw flashes of a hotel room in the south. Men arguing. In-Between man shouting. A portal shimmering, revealing the place I had come tumbling through like Alice in Wonderland.

I swallowed and tried to speak.

"If I put my head through that noose again," I croaked, "where will I end up? Or will I only die?"

He said nothing and looked at the book sitting on the table. Clock ticking, someone cleaning up a tray outside in the hall.

"I saw you die," I whisper.

He rested his head on the chair. Languid in the ancient hotel room. Car traffic drifting in from outside.

"That was real. Why am I not dead?"

"Your name is Portia Joyce. When you were eight, you were struck by a car. You almost died, but you had a good surgeon and they brought you into the operating room, just in time. When you were ten, you thought unicorns were real, and when no one bought you one for Christmas, you cried and cried. When you were thirteen, your mother died. When you were fifteen, you left. You waitressed some and lived in a van for a while. You send letters to your dad in Idaho, but you don't talk about how terrible you feel about all those butterflies you killed in the jar, and how angry you are that he taught you that. But you don't shed a tear for the people you kill."

He leaned forward then, putting a thumb beneath my eye. He swiped it in a semicircle, and the pad glistened in the light. He sucked it off the end of his thumb.

"Your father hired me," he said. He removed his thumb from his mouth with visible regret.

"Hired you?"

He didn't answer.

"Hired you for what?"

"You kill people, Portia," he whispered. "They hire me to bring them back to life. You close the jar. I open it back up."

"I don't deserve to live."

He held his hand out without judgment, embodied the archetypal scales.

"Do the people you kill deserve to die?"

"Why me?" I asked.

He smiled. "I have a job for you."

"A kill target?"

His smile widened and his third eye, opening in the pale light like a glowing coal.

"No. We're going to bring them back to life."

In Milan, I closed the bullet wound of a man assassinated for funneling money into a children's hospital, and made his heart beat again. Past the Rhine, I brought a child back to life caught in the crossfire of a bank robbery. In Argentina, I gave breath to a fallen bull brought down in an arena. The matador who loved him paid us handsomely.

Now, when I dream, Trine opens the lid of a Mason jar through which all the dead butterflies come pouring back out.

BEST-SELLERS GUARANTEED

BY JOE R. LANSDALE

Larry had a headache, as he often did. It was those all-night stints at the typewriter, along with his job and his boss, Fraggerty, yelling for him to fry the burgers faster, to dole them out lickity-split on mustard-covered sesame-seed buns.

Burgers and fries, typing paper and typewriter ribbons—the ribbons as gray and faded as the thirty-six years of his life. There really didn't seem to be any reason to keep on living. Another twenty to thirty years of this would be foolish. Then again, that seemed the only alternative. He was too cowardly to take his own life.

Washing his face in the bathroom sink, Larry jerked a rough paper towel from the rack and dried off, looking at himself in the mirror. He was starting to look like all those hacks of writer mythology. The little guys who turned out the drek copy. The ones with the blue-veined, alcoholic noses and eyes like volcanic eruptions.

"My God," he thought, "I look forty easy. Maybe even forty-five."

"You gonna stay in the can all day?" a voice yelled through the door. It was Fraggerty, waiting to send him back to the grill and the burgers. The guy treated him like a bum.

A sly smile formed on Larry's face as he thought: "I am a bum. I've been through three marriages, sixteen jobs, eight typewriters, and all I've got to show for it are a dozen articles, all of them in obscure magazines that either paid in copies or pennies." He wasn't even as good as the hack he looked like. The hack could at least point to a substantial body of work, drek or not.

And I've been at this ... God, twelve years! An article a year. Some average. Not even enough to pay back his typing supplies.

He thought of his friend Mooney—or James T. Mooney, as he was known to his fans. Yearly, he wrote a best-seller. It was a best-seller before it hit the stands. And except for Mooney's first novel, THE GOODBYE REEL, a detective thriller, all of them had been dismal. In fact, dismal was too kind a word. But the public lapped them up.

What had gone wrong with his own career? He used to help Mooney with his plots. In fact, he had helped him work out his problems on THE GOODBYE REEL, back when they had both been scrounging their livings and existing out of a suitcase. Then Mooney had moved to Houston, and a year later THE GOODBYE REEL had hit the stands like an atomic bomb. Made record sales in hardback and paper, and gathered in a movie deal that boggled the imagination.

Being honest with himself, Larry felt certain that he could say he was a far better writer than Mooney. More commercial, even. So why had Mooney gathered the laurels while he bagged burgers and ended up in a dirty restroom contemplating the veins in his nose?

It was almost too much to bear. He would kill to have a best-seller. Just one. That's all he'd ask. Just one.

"Tear the damned crapper out of there and sit on it behind the grill!" Fraggerty called through the door. "But get out here. We got customers lined up down the block."

Larry doubted that, but he dried his hands, combed his hair, and stepped outside.

Fraggerty was waiting for him. Fraggerty was a big, fat man with bulldog jowls and perpetual blossoms of sweat beneath his meaty arms. Midsummer, dead of winter—he had them.

"Hey," Fraggerty said, "you work here or what?"

"Not anymore," Larry said. "Pay me up."

"What?"

"You heard me, fat ass. Pay up!"

"Hey, don't get tough about it. All right. Glad to see you hike."

Five minutes later, Larry was leaving the burger joint, a fifty-dollar check in his pocket.

He said aloud: "Job number seventeen."

The brainstorm had struck him right when he came out of the restroom. He'd go see Mooney. He and Mooney had been great friends once, before all that money and a new way of living had carried Mooney back and forth to Houston and numerous jet spots around the country and overseas.

Maybe Mooney could give him a connection, an *in*, as it was called in the business. Before, he'd been too proud to ask, but now he didn't give a damn if he had to crawl and lick boots. He had to sell his books; had to let the world know he existed.

Without letting the landlord know, as he owed considerable back rent, he cleaned out his apartment.

Like his life, there was little there. A typewriter, copies of his twelve articles, a few clothes and odds and ends. There weren't even any books. He'd had to sell them all to pay his rent three months back.

In less than twenty minutes, he snuck out without being seen, loaded the typewriter and his two suitcases in the trunk of his battered Chevy, and looked up at the window of his dingy apartment. He lifted his middle finger in salute, climbed in the car, and drove away.

Mooney was easy to find. His estate looked just the part for the residence of a best-selling author. A front lawn the size of a polo field, a fountain of marble out front, and a house that looked like a small English castle. All this near downtown Houston.

James T. Mooney looked the part, too. He answered the door in a maroon smoking jacket with matching pajamas. He had on a pair of glossy leather bedroom slippers that he could have worn with a suit and tie. His hair was well-groomed with just the right amount of gray at the temples. There was a bit of a strained look about his eyes, but other than that he was the picture of health and prosperity.

"Well, I'll be," Mooney said. "Larry Melford. Come in."

The interior of the house made the outside look like a barn. There were paintings and sculptures and shelves of first-edition books. On one wall, blown up to the size of movie posters and placed under glass and frame, were copies of the covers of his best-sellers. All twelve of them. A thirteenth glass and frame stood empty beside the others, waiting for the inevitable.

They chatted as they walked through the house, and Mooney said, "Let's drop off in the study. We can be comfortable there. I'll have the maid bring us some coffee or iced tea."

"I hope I'm not interrupting your writing," Larry said.

"No, not at all. I'm finished for the day. I usually just work a couple hours a day."

A couple hours a day? thought Larry. A serpent of envy crawled around in the pit of his stomach. For the last twelve years, he had worked a job all day and had written away most of the night, generally gathering no more than two to three hours' sleep. And here was Mooney writing these monstrous best-sellers and he only wrote a couple of hours in the mornings.

Mooney's study was about the size of Larry's abandoned apartment. And it looked a hell of a lot better. One side of the room was little more than a long desk covered with a state-of-the art computer station and a multifunctional printer. The rest of the room was taken up by a leather couch and rows of bookshelves containing nothing but Mooney's work. Various editions of foreign publications, special collectors' editions, the leather-bound Christmas set, the paperbacks, the bound galleys of all the novels. Mooney was surrounded by his success.

"Sit down. Take the couch," Mooney said, hauling around his desk chair. "Coffee or tea? I'll have the maid bring it."

"No, I'm fine."

"Well then, tell me about yourself."

Larry opened his mouth to start, and that's when it fell out. He just couldn't control himself. It was as if a dam had burst open and all the water of the world was flowing away. The anguish, the misery, the years of failure found expression.

When he had finished telling it all, his eyes were glistening. He was both relieved and embarrassed. "So you see, Mooney, I'm just about over the edge. I'm craving success like an addict craves a fix. I'd kill for a best-seller."

Mooney's face seemed to go lopsided. "Watch that kind of talk."

"I mean it. I'm feeling so small right now, I'd have to look up to see a snake's belly. I'd lie, cheat, steal, kill—anything to get published in a big way. I don't want to die and leave nothing of me behind."

"And you don't want to miss out on the good things either, right?"

"Damned right. You've got it."

"Look, Larry, worry less about the good things and just write your books. Ease up some, but do it your own way. You may never have a big best-seller, but you're a good writer, and eventually you'll crack and be able to make a decent living."

"Easy for you to say, Mooney."

"In time, with a little patience ..."

"I'm running out of time and patience. I'm emotionally drained, whipped. What I need is an *in*, Mooney, an *in*. A name. Anything that can give me a break."

"Talent is the name of the game, Larry, not an *in*," Mooney said softly.

"Don't give me that garbage. I've got talent and you know it. I used to help you with the plots of your short stories. And your first novel—remember the things I worked out for you there? I mean, come on, Mooney. You've read my writing. It's good. Damned good! I need help. An *in* can't hurt me. It may not help me much, but it's got to give me a damn sight better chance than I have now."

Larry looked at Mooney's face. Something seemed to be moving there behind the eyes and taut lips. He looked sad, and quite a bit older than his age. Well, okay. So he was offended by being asked right out to help a fellow writer.

That was too bad. Larry just didn't have the pride and patience anymore to beat around the bush.

"An *in*, huh?" Mooney finally said.

"That's right."

"You sure you wouldn't rather do it your way?"

"I've been doing it my way for twelve years. I want a break, Mooney."

Mooney nodded solemnly. He went over to his desk and opened a drawer. He took out a small, white business card and brought it over to Larry.

It read:

BEST-SELLERS GUARANTEED
Offices in New York, Texas, California,
and Overseas

The left-hand corner of the card had a drawing of an open book, and the right-hand corner had three phone numbers. One of them was a Houston number.

"I met a lady when I first moved here," Mooney said, "a big-name author in the romance field. I sort of got this thing going with her ... finally asked her for ... an *in*. And she gave me this card. We don't see each other anymore, Larry. We stopped seeing each other the day she gave it to me."

Larry wasn't listening. "This an editor?"

"No."

"An agent?"

"No."

"Publisher, book packager?"

"None of those things and a little of all, and a lot more."

"I'm not sure ..."

"You wanted your *in*, so there it is. You just call that number. And Larry, do me a favor. Never come here again."

The first thing Larry did when he left Mooney's was find a telephone booth. He dialed the Houston number and a crisp female voice answered: "Best-sellers Guaranteed."

"Are you the one in charge?"

"No, sir. Just hold on and I'll put you through to someone who can help you."

Larry tapped his finger on the phone shelf till a smooth-as-well-water male voice said: "B.G. here. May I be of assistance?"

"Uh ... yes, a friend of mine ... a Mr. James T. Mooney—"

"Of course, Mr. Mooney."

"He suggested ... he gave me a card. Well, I'm a writer. My name is Larry Melford. To be honest, I'm not exactly sure what Mooney had in mind for me. He just suggested I call you."

"All we need to know is that you were recommended by Mr. Mooney. Where are you now?"

Larry gave the address of the 7-Eleven phone booth.

"Why don't you wait there ... oh, say ... twenty minutes and we'll send a car to pick you up? That suit you?"

"Sure, but ..."

"I'll have an agent explain it to you when he gets there, okay?"

"Yes, yes, that'll be fine."

Larry hung up and stepped outside to lean on the hood of his car. By golly, he thought, that Mooney does have connections, and now after all these years, my thirteenth year of trying, maybe, just maybe, I'm going to get connected, too.

He lit a cigarette and watched the August heat waves bounce around the 7-Eleven lot, and twenty minutes later a tan, six-door limousine pulled up next to his Chevy.

The man driving the limo wore a chauffeur's hat and outfit. He got out of the car and walked around to the tinted, far backseat window and tapped gently on the glass. The window slid down with a short whoosh. A man dressed in black with black hair, a black mustache, and thick-rimmed black shades looked out at Larry. He said, "Mr. Melford?"

"Yes," Larry said.

"Would you like to go around to the other side? Herman will open the door for you."

After Larry had slid onto the seat and Herman had closed the door behind him, his eyes were drawn to the plush interior of the car. Encased in the seat in front of them were a phone, a television set, and a couple of panels that folded out. Larry felt certain one of them would be a small bar. Air-conditioning hummed softly. The car was nice enough and large enough to live in.

He looked across the seat at the man in black, who was extending his hand. They shook. The man in black said, "Just call me James, Mr. Melford."

"Fine. This is about ... writing? Mooney said he could give me a ... connection. I mean, I have work, plenty of it. Four novels, a couple of dozen short stories, a novella—of course I know that length is a dog to sell, but ..."

"None of that matters," James said.

"This *is* about writing?"

"This is about best-sellers, Mr. Melford. That is what you want, isn't it? To be a best-selling author?"

"More than anything."

"Then you're our man and we're your organization."

Herman had eased in behind the wheel. James leaned forward over the seat and said firmly, "Drive us around." Leaning back, James touched a button on the door panel and a thick glass rose out of the seat in front of them and clicked into place in a groove in the roof.

"Now," James said, "shall we talk?"

As they drove, James explained, "I'm the agent assigned to you, and it's up to me to see if I can convince you to join our little gallery. But, if you should sign on with us, we expect you to remain loyal. You must consider that we offer a service that is unique, unlike any offered anywhere. We can guarantee that you'll hit the best-seller list once a year, every year, as long as you're with us.

"Actually, Mr. Melford, we're not a real old organization, though I have a hard time remembering the exact year we were founded—it predated the Kennedy assassination by a year."

"That would be sixty-two," Larry said.

"Yes, yes, of course. I'm terrible at years. But it's only lately that we've come into our own. Consider the bad state of publishing right now, and then consider the fact that our clients have each had a best-seller this year—and they will next year, no matter how badly publishing may falter. Our clients may be the only ones with books, but each of their books will be a best-seller, and their success will, as it does every year, save the industry."

"You're a packager?"

"No. We don't actually read the books, Mr. Melford, we just make sure they're best-sellers. You can write a book about the Earth being invaded by giant tree toads from the moon, if you like, and we will guarantee it will be a best-seller."

"My God, you are connected."

"You wouldn't believe the connections we have."

"And what does your organization get out of this? How much of a percentage?"

"We don't take a dime."

"What?"

"Not a dime. For our help, for our guarantee that your books will be best-sellers, we ask only one thing. A favor. One favor a year. A favor for each best-seller."

"What's the favor?"

"We'll come to that in a moment. But before we do, let me make sure you understand what we have to offer. I mean, if you were successful—and I mean no offense by this—then you wouldn't be talking to me now. You need help. We can offer help. You're in your mid-thirties, correct? Yes, I thought so. Not really old, but a bit late to start a new career plan. People do it, but it's certainly no piece of cake, now, is it?"

Larry found that he was nodding in agreement.

"So," James continued, "what we want to do is give you success. We're talking money in the millions of dollars, Mr. Melford. Fame. Respect. Most anything you'd want would be at your command. Exotic foods and wines? A snap of the fingers. Books? Cars? Women? A snap of the fingers. Anything your heart desires, and it's yours."

"But I have to make a small, initial investment, right?"

"Ah, suspicious by nature, are you?"

"Wouldn't you be? My God, you're offering me the world."

"So I am. But no ... no investment. Picture this, Mr. Melford. You might get lucky and sell the work, might even have a best-seller. But the slots are getting smaller and smaller for new writers. And one reason for that is that our writers, our clients, are filling those slots, Mr. Melford. If it's between your book and one of our clients', and yours is ten times better written, our client will still win out. Every time."

"What you're saying is, the fix is in?"

"A crude way of putting it, but rather accurate. Yes."

"What about talent, craftsmanship?"

"I wouldn't know about any of that. I sell success, not books."

"But it's the public that puts out its money for these books. They make or break an author. How can you know what they'll buy?"

"Our advertising system is the best in the world. We know how to reach the public and how to convince. We also use subliminals, Mr.

Melford. We flash images on television programs, theater films; we hide them in the art of wine and cigarette ads. Little things below conscious perception, but images that lock tight to the subconscious mind. People who would not normally pick up a book will buy our best-sellers."

"Isn't that dishonest?"

"Who's to tell in this day and age what's right and wrong? It's relative, don't you think, Mr. Melford?"

Larry didn't say anything.

"Look. The public pictures writers as rich, all of them. They don't realize the average full-time writer barely makes a living. Most of them are out there starving, and for what? Get on the winning side for a change, Mr. Melford. Otherwise, spend the rest of your life living in roach motels and living off the crumbs tossed you by the publishing world. And believe me, Mr. Melford, if you fail to join up with us, crumbs are all you'll get. If you're lucky."

The limousine had returned to the 7-Eleven parking lot. They were parked next to Larry's car.

"I suppose," James said, "we've come to that point that the bullfighters call 'the moment of truth.' You sign on with us and you'll be on Easy Street for the rest of your life."

"But we haven't talked terms."

"No, we haven't. It's at this point that I must ask you to either accept or turn down our offer, Mr. Melford. Once I've outlined the terms, you must be in full agreement with us."

"Accept before I hear what this favor you've talked about is?"

"That's correct. Best-seller or Bohemian, Mr. Melford. Which is it? Tell me right now. My time is valuable."

Larry paused only a moment. "Very well. Count me in. In for a penny, in for a pound. What's the favor?"

"Each year, you assassinate someone for us."

Larry dove for the door handle, but it wouldn't open. It had been locked electronically. James grabbed him by the wrist and held him tightly, so tightly Larry thought his bones would shatter.

"I wouldn't," James said. "After what I've told you, you step out of this car and they'll find you in a ditch this afternoon, obviously the victim of some hit-and-run driver."

"That's ... that's murder."

"Yes, it is," James said. "Listen to me. You assassinate whomever we choose. We're not discriminating as far as sex, color, religion, or politics goes. Anyone who gets in our way dies. Simple as that. You see, Mr. Melford, we are a big organization. Our goal is world domination. You and all our clients are little helpers toward that goal. Who is more respected than a best-selling author? Who is allowed in places where others would not be allowed? Who is revered by public figures and the general public alike? An author—a best-selling author."

"But ... it's murder."

"There will be nothing personal in it. It'll just be your part of the contract. One assassination a year that we'll arrange."

"But if you're so connected ... why do it this way? Why not just hire a hit man?"

"In a sense, I have."

"I'm not an assassin. I've never even fired a gun."

"The amateur is in many ways better than the professional. He doesn't fall into a pattern. When the time comes, we will show you what you have to do. If you decide to be with us, that is."

"And if not?"

"I told you a moment ago. The ditch. The hit-and-run driver."

Suddenly, Herman was standing at the door, his hand poised to open it.

"Which is it, Mr. Melford? I'm becoming impatient. A ditch or a best-seller? And if you have any ideas about going to the police, don't. We have friends there, and you might accidentally meet one. Now, your decision."

"I'm in," Larry said, softly. "I'm in."

"Good," James said, taking Larry's hand. "Welcome aboard. You get one of those books of yours out, pick out a publisher, and mail it in. And don't bother with return postage. We'll take care of the rest. Congratulations."

James motioned to Herman. The door opened. Larry got out. And just before the door closed, James said, "If you should have trouble coming up with something, getting something finished, just let me know and we'll see that it gets written for you."

Larry stood on the sidewalk, nodding dumbly. Herman returned to the driver's seat, and a moment later the tan limo from Best-sellers Guaranteed whispered away.

James was as good as his word. Larry mailed off one of his shopworn novels, a thriller titled TEXAS BACKLASH, and a contract for a half-million dollars came back, almost by return mail.

Six months later, the book hit the best-seller list and rode there for a comfortable three months. It picked up a two-million-dollar paperback sale and a big-shot movie producer purchased it for twice that amount.

Larry now had a big mansion outside of Nacogdoches, Texas, with a maid, a cook, two secretaries, and a professional yard man. Any type of food he wanted was his for the asking. Once he had special seafood flown in from the East Coast to Houston and hauled from there to his door by refrigerated truck.

Any first-edition book he wanted was now within his price range. He owned four cars, two motorcycles, a private airplane, and a yacht.

He could own anything—even people. They hopped at his every word, his most casual suggestion. He had money, and people wanted to satisfy those with money. Who knows, maybe it would rub off on them.

And there were women. Beautiful women. There was even one he had grown to care for, and believed cared for him instead of his money and position. Lovely Luna Malone.

But in the midst of all this finery, there was the favor. The thought of it rested on the back of his mind like a waiting vulture. And when a year had gone by, the vulture swooped in.

On a hot August day, the tan limo from Best-sellers Guaranteed pulled up the long, scenic drive to Larry's mansion. A moment later, Larry and James were in Larry's study and Herman stood outside the closed door with his arms akimbo, doing what he did best. Waiting silently.

James was dressed in black again. He still wore the thick-framed sun shades. "You know what I've come for, don't you?"

Larry nodded. "The favor."

"On March fifteenth, Best-sellers Guaranteed will arrange for an autograph party in Austin for your new best-seller, whatever that may be. At eleven-fifteen, you will excuse yourself to go upstairs to the men's room. Next door to it is a janitor's lounge. It hasn't been used in years. It's locked but we will provide you with the key.

"At the rear of the lounge is a restroom. Lift off the back of the commode and you will discover eight small packages taped to the inside. Open these and fit them together and you'll have a very sophisticated air rifle. One of the packages will contain a canister of ice, and in the middle, dyed red, you will find a bullet-shaped projectile of ice. The air gun can send that projectile through three inches of steel without the ice shattering.

"You will load the gun, go to the window, and at exactly eleven-twenty-five, the Governor will drive by in an open car in the midst of the parade. A small hole has been cut in the restroom window. It will exactly accommodate the barrel of the rifle and the scope will fit snugly against the glass. You will take aim, and in a manner of seconds, your favor for this year will be done."

"Why the Governor?"

"That is our concern."

"I've never shot a rifle."

"We'll train you. You have until March. You won't need to know much more than how to put the rifle together and look through the scope. The weapon will do the rest."

"If I refuse?"

"The best-selling author of TEXAS BACKLASH will be found murdered in his home by a couple of burglars, and a couple of undesirables will be framed for the crime. Don't you think that has a nicer ring to it than the hit-and-run program I offered you before? Or perhaps, as a warning, we'll do something to your lady friend. What's her name, Luna?"

"You wouldn't!"

"If it would offer incentive or achieve our desired goals, Mr. Melford, we would do anything."

"You bastard!"

"That'll be quite enough, Mr. Melford. You've reaped the rewards of our services, and now we expect to be repaid.

379

"It seems a small thing to ask for your success—and certainly you wouldn't want to die at the hands of other best-selling authors, the ones who will ultimately be your assassins."

In spite of the air-conditioning, Larry had begun to sweat. "Just who are you guys, really?"

"I've told you. We're an organization with big plans. What we sponsor more than anything else, Mr. Melford, is moral corruption. We feed on those who thrive on greed and ego; put them in positions of power and influence. We belong to a group, to put it naively, who believe that once the silly concepts of morality and honor break down, then we, who really know how things work, can take control and make them work to our advantage. To put it even more simply, Mr. Melford, we will own it all."

"I ... I can't just cold-bloodedly murder someone."

"Oh, I think you can. I've got faith in you. Look around you, Mr. Melford. Look at all you've got. Think of what you've got to lose, then tell me if you can murder from a distance someone you don't even know. I'll wait outside with Herman for your answer. You have two minutes."

From the March fifteenth edition of *The Austin Statesman,* a front-page headline:

GOVERNOR ASSASSINATED, ASSASSIN SOUGHT

From the same issue, page 4B:

BEST-SELLING AUTHOR, LARRY MELFORD, SIGNS BOOKS

Six months later, in the master bedroom of Larry Melford's estate, Larry was sitting nude in front of the dresser mirror, clipping unruly nose hairs. On the bed behind him, nude, dark, luscious, lay Luna Malone. There was a healthy glow of sweat on her body as she lay with

380

two pillows propped under her head; her raven hair was like an explosion of ink against their whiteness.

"Larry," she said. "you know, I've been thinking ... I mean there's something I've been wanting to tell you, but haven't said anything about it because ... well, I was afraid you might get the wrong idea. But now that we've known each other a while, and things look solid ... Larry, I'm a writer."

Larry quit clipping his nose hairs. He put the clipper on the dresser and turned slowly. "You're what?"

"I mean, I want to be. And not just now, not just this minute. I've always wanted to be. I didn't tell you, because I was afraid you'd laugh, or worse, think I'd only got to know you so you could give me an *in*, but I've been writing for years and have sent book after book, story after story in, and just know I'm good, and well ..."

"You want me to look at it?"

"Yeah, but more than that, Larry. I need an *in*. It's what I've always wanted. To write a best-seller. I'd kill for ..."

"Get out! Get the hell out!"

"Larry, I didn't meet you for that reason ..."

"Get the hell out or I'll throw you out."

"Larry ..."

"Now!" He stood up from the chair, grabbed her dressing gown. "Just go. Leave everything. I'll have it sent to you. Get dressed and never let me see you again."

"Aren't you being a little silly about this? I mean ..."

Larry moved as fast as an eagle swooping down on a field mouse. He grabbed her shoulder and jerked her off the bed onto the floor.

"All right, you bastard, all right." Luna stood. She grabbed the robe and slipped into it. "So I did meet you for an *in*; what's wrong with that? I bet you had some help along the way. It sure couldn't have been because you're a great writer. I can hardly force myself through that garbage you write."

He slapped her across the cheek so hard she fell back on the bed.

Holding her face, she got up, gathered her clothes and walked stiffly to the bathroom. Less than a minute later, she came out dressed, the robe over her shoulder.

"I'm sorry about hitting you," Larry said. "But I meant what I said about never wanting to see you again."

"You're crazy, man. You know that? Crazy. All I asked you for was an *in,* just ..."

Luna stopped talking. Larry had lifted his head to look at her. His eyes looked as dark and flat as the twin barrels of a shotgun.

"Don't bother having Francis drive me home. I'll call a cab from downstairs, Mr. Bigshot Writer."

She went out, slamming the bedroom door. Larry got up and turned off the light, went back to the dresser chair and sat in the darkness for a long time.

Nearly a year and a half later, not long after completing a favor for Best-sellers Guaranteed and acquiring a somewhat rabid taste for alcoholic beverages, Larry was in the Houston airport. He was waiting to catch a plane for Hawaii for a long vacation when he saw a woman in the distance who looked familiar. She turned and he recognized her immediately. It was Luna Malone. Still beautiful, a bit more worldly looking, and dressed to the hilt.

She saw him before he could dart away. She waved. He smiled. She came over and shook hands with him. "Larry, you aren't still mad, are you?"

"No, I'm not mad. Good to see you. You look great."

"Thanks."

"Where're you going?"

"Italy. Rome."

"Pope country," Larry said with a smile. But at his words, Luna jumped.

"Yes ... Pope country."

The announcer called for the flight to Rome, Italy. Luna and Larry shook hands again and she went away.

To kill time. Larry went to the airport bookstores. He found he couldn't even look at the big cardboard display with his latest best-seller in it. He didn't like to look at best-sellers by anyone. But something did catch his eye. It was the display next to his. The book was called THE LITTLE STORM, and appeared to be one of those steamy romance novels. But what had caught his eye was the big, emblazoned name of the author—LUNA MALONE.

Larry felt like a python had uncoiled inside of him. He felt worse than he had ever felt in his life.

"*Italy. Rome*," she had said.

"*Pope country*," he had said, and she jumped.

Larry stumbled back against the rack of his book, and his clumsiness knocked it over. The books tumbled to the floor. One of them slid between his legs and when he looked down he saw that it had turned over to its back. There was his smiling face looking up at him. Larry Melford, big-name author, best-seller, a man whose books found their way into the homes of millions of readers.

Suddenly, Hawaii was forgotten and Larry was running, running to the nearest pay phone. What had James said about moral corruption? "We feed on those who thrive on greed and ego ... once silly concepts of morality and honor break down ... we will own it all."

The nightmare had to end. Best-sellers Guaranteed had to be exposed. He would wash his hands with blood and moral corruption no more. He would turn himself in.

With trembling hand, he picked up the phone, put in his change, and dialed the police.

From today's *Houston Chronicle*, front page headline:

POPE ASSASSINATED

From the same edition, the last page before the want ads, the last paragraph:

BEST-SELLING AUTHOR MURDERED IN HOME
Police suspect the brutal murder of author
Larry Melford occurred when he surprised
burglars in the act. Thus far, police have
been unable to . . .

For Anibal Martinez

THE WRITERS

MEGHAN ARCURI

Meghan Arcuri writes fiction and poetry. Her short stories can be found in various anthologies, including *Chiral Mad* and *Miseria's Chorale*. She lives with her family in New York's Hudson Valley. Please visit her at meghanarcuri.com or facebook.com/meg.arcuri.

JOSEPH BADAL

Joe worked for 38 years in the financial services industry, retiring in 2007 after six years as a director and senior executive of a New York stock exchange-listed company. Before he began his finance career, Joe was a decorated military officer, having served in the U.S. Army for six years, including tours of duty in Vietnam and Greece. He also served in the New Mexico House of Representatives.

Joe has had seven suspense novels published: *The Pythagorean Solution, Evil Deeds, Terror Cell, The Nostradamus Secret Shell Game, The Lone Wolf Agenda* (which was awarded First Prize in the fiction category in the NM/AZ Book Awards in 2013), and *Ultimate Betrayal,* which was released April 2014. His short story "Fire & Ice" was included in the Smart Rhino anthology *Uncommon Assassins,* and his short story "Ultimate Betrayal" was included in the *Someone Wicked* anthology. He is a member of International Thriller Writers and Southwest Writers Workshop, and was named one of the "50 Best Authors You Should Be Reading." Joe has written dozens of published articles about various business topics and is a frequent speaker at writers and business conferences and at civic organization meetings. He has extensive experience as an interviewee on radio and television. Visit his website at www.josephbadalbooks.com.

Joe's story, "Fire & Ice," was published in the Smart Rhino anthology *Uncommon Assassins*. His story, "Ultimate Betrayal," appeared in *Someone Wicked: A Written Remains Anthology*.

DOUG BLAKESLEE

Doug Blakeslee lives in the Pacific Northwest and spends his time writing, cooking, gaming, and following the local WHL hockey team. His interest in books and reading started early thanks to his parents, though his serious attempts at writing only started a few years ago. He often blogs about writing and other related topics at The Simms Project at http://thesimmsproject.blogspot.com/. Published works can be found in the anthologies *Uncommon Assassins* and *Zippered Flesh 2* from Smart Rhino and the upcoming anthologies: *ATTACK! of the B-Movie Monsters, Someone Wicked, Astrologica: Stories of the Zodiac*, and *A Chimerical World: Tales of the Unseelie Court*. His current project is an urban fantasy novella featuring a group of changelings in the modern world. He can be reached on Facebook or simms.doug@gmail.com.

Three of Doug's stories have been published in other Smart Rhino anthologies, including "Madame" in *Uncommon Assassins*, "Perfection" in *Zippered Flesh 2: More Tales of Body Enhancements Gone Bad*, and "The Flowering Princess of Dreams" in *Someone Wicked: A Written Remains Anthology*.

CARSON BUCKINGHAM

Carson Buckingham knew from childhood that she wanted to be a writer, and began, at age six, by writing books of her own, hand-drawing covers, and selling them to any family member who would pay (usually a gum ball) for what she referred to as "classic literature." When she ran out of relatives, she came to the conclusion that there was no real money to be made in self-publishing, so she studied writing and read voraciously for the next eighteen years, while simultaneously collecting enough rejection slips to re-paper her living room ... twice.

When her landlord chucked her out for, in his words, "making the apartment into one hell of a downer," she redoubled her efforts, and collected four times the rejection slips in half the time, single-handedly causing the first paper shortage in U.S. history. But she persevered, improved greatly over the years, and here we are.

Carson Buckingham has been a professional proofreader, editor, newspaper reporter, copywriter, technical writer, and comedy writer, and now a multi-published fiction author. Besides writing, she loves to read and work in her vegetable garden. She lives in Arizona, with her wonderful husband, in a house full of books, plants, and pets. Check out her blog at carsonbuckingham.blogspot.com.

Carson's story, "Skin Deep," was published in *Zippered Flesh 2: More Tales of Body Enhancements Gone Bad.* Her story, "The Plotnik Curse," was included in *Someone Wicked: A Written Remains Anthology.*

AUSTIN S. CAMACHO

Austin S. Camacho is the author of five novels in the Hannibal Jones Mystery Series, four in the Stark and O'Brien adventure series, and the new detective novel, *Beyond Blue.* His short stories have been featured in four anthologies from Wolfmont Press, including *Dying in a Winter Wonderland* (an Independent Mystery Booksellers Association Top Ten Bestseller for 2008) and he is featured in the Edgar nominated *African American Mystery Writers: A Historical and Thematic Study* by Frankie Y. Bailey.

Austin is deeply involved with the writing community. He is a past president of the Maryland Writers Association, past Vice President of the Virginia Writers Club, and is an active member of Mystery Writers of America, International Thriller Writers and Sisters in Crime.

Check out Austin's website at www.ascamacho.com and his blog at http://ascamacho.blogspot.com.

ERNESTUS JIMINY CHALD

Ernestus Jiminy Chald was born in Salt Lake City, Utah, but has spent the bulk of his existence in Chicago, Illinois. His published works include *The Rubbish Bin* (a polymorphic novel in the form of an actual trash can filled with crumpled pages of narrative prose, handwritten correspondences, and various forms of "garbage") and *Black Carnations* (a collection of elegiac poetry). He is also the author of *The Philosophy of*

Disenchantment; or The Ephemeral (mis)Adventures of Arthur Snowpenhauer (a comic book). Chald is the founder of Peisithanatos Press, an underground publishing enterprise.

His story, "The Tail of Fate," was published in *Someone Wicked: A Written Remains Anthology*.

DB COREY

DB Corey lives in Baltimore with his wife Maggie, an offish Chocolate Lab, and a Catahoula-Leopard Hound. After a stint in college, he joined the USNR flying aircrew aboard a Navy P-3 Orion chasing down Russian subs. During his time there, he began a career in I.T. He began writing in his mid-50s. His debut novel—*Chain of Evidence*—was released on August 1, 2013. He's currently working on a second crime thriller with a target release date in 2015.

Check out his website at www.dbcorey.com and his blog at bit.ly/DBCorey_BeyondtheNovel.

PATRICK DERRICKSON

Patrick Derrickson has been a fan of speculative fiction from the age of nine when he first read *The Stand* by Stephen King. Since then, he has been the majestic hero of kingdoms, galaxies, and unspoken horrors. A member of the Written Remains Writers Guild and the Written Remains Mixed Genre Critique Group, he has finally found the outlet for the bizarre thoughts that chase each other inside his head. Patrick is a soccer referee, follows technology obsessively, and listens to too many podcasts. He lives in Delaware.

Patrick's story, "The Next King," was published in *Someone Wicked: A Written Remains Anthology*.

JAMES S. DORR

James Dorr has two collections from Dark Regions Press, *Strange Mistresses: Tales of Wonder and Romance* and *Darker Loves: Tales of Mystery and Regret*, while his all-poetry *Vamps (A Retrospective)* came out last August (2011) from Sam's Dot Publishing. An active member of SFWA and HWA with nearly four hundred appearances in venues from *Alfred Hitchcock's Mystery Magazine* to *Xenophilia*, Dorr invites readers to visit his site at http://jamesdorrwriter.wordpress.com for the latest information. His story, "The Wellmaster's Daughter," was published in the *Uncommon Assassins* anthology.

JACK KETCHUM

No stranger to controversy, Jack Ketchum's first novel, *Off Season*, published in 1980, was a turning point in the field of horror fiction. Stephen King said of him, "Jack Ketchum is an archetype, no writer who has read him can help being influenced by him and no general reader that runs across his work can easily forget him, he has a dark streak of American genius."

Jack has received four Bram Stoker awards and three nominations. Many of his novels have been adapted for film, including *The Lost*, *The Girl Next Door*, *Red*, *Offspring*, and *The Woman*.

Visit Jack's website at http://www.thejackketchum.com for more about his latest releases, movie adaptations of his work, and other information.

JOE R. LANSDALE

Joe R. Lansdale is the author of over 40 novels and 400 short stories, essays, articles, reviews, and introductions. He has written screenplays, comic books, stage plays, and poetry. Lansdale has received many awards for his work, including The Edgar Award, nine Bram Stokers, and many others. He is a member of The Texas Literary Hall of Fame, Texas Institute of Literature, Writer in Residence at Stephen F. Austin State University. He is the founder of Shen Chuan Martial Science.

DENNIS LAWSON

Dennis Lawson received an Individual Artist Fellowship from the Delaware Division of the Arts as the 2014 Emerging Artist in Fiction. His crime fiction has recently appeared in the *Fox Chase Review* and the *Rehoboth Beach Reads* anthology series. Dennis is the Executive Director of the Newark Arts Alliance, a nonprofit art center and gallery located in Newark, Delaware.

ADRIAN LUDENS

Adrian Ludens is a dark fiction author and radio announcer living in Rapid City, South Dakota. His short stories have appeared in *Blood Lite 3: Aftertaste*, *Woman's World*, *Darker Edge of Desire*, *Shadows Over Main Street*, and *Surreal Worlds*. His collection, *Bedtime Stories for Carrion Beetles*, is available in multiple formats from Amazon and Smashwords. Also available is *Gruesome Faces, Ghastly Places*, a multi-author collaborative collection also featuring South Dakota horror authors Doug Murano and C.W. LaSart. For news and updates, visit adrianludens.com.

LISA MANNETTI

Lisa Mannetti's debut novel, *The Gentling Box*, garnered a Bram Stoker Award and she was nominated in 2010 both for her novella, "Dissolution," and a short story, "1925: A Fall River Halloween." She has also authored The *New Adventures of Tom Sawyer and Huck Finn* (now a Smart Rhino publication); *Deathwatch*, a compilation of novellas—including "Dissolution"; a macabre gag book, *51 Fiendish Ways to Leave Your Lover* (2010); two nonfiction books; and numerous articles and short stories in newspapers, magazines, and anthologies.

Her story "Everybody Wins," which was included in the *Uncommon Assassins* anthology, was made into a short film by director Paul Leyden, starring Malin Akerman and released under the title *Bye-Bye Sally*; the film has been posted on YouTube.

Two of Lisa's other stories have also be included in other Smart Rhino anthologies: "Paraphilia" in *Zippered Flesh: Tales of Body Enhancements Gone Bad* and "The Hunger Artist," which was nominated for a Bram Stoker Award, in *Zippered Flesh 2: More Tales of Body Enhancements Gone Bad.*

Lisa lives in New York. Visit her author Web site at www.lisamannetti.com, as well as her virtual haunted house at www.thechanceryhouse.com.

SHAUN MEEKS

Shaun Meeks lives in Toronto, Ontario with his partner, Mina LaFleur. Shaun's work has appeared in *Haunted Path, Dark Eclipse, Zombies Gone Wild,* and *A Feast of Frights* from the Horror Zine, as well as his own collection, *At the Gates of Madness.* He will also be featured in the anthologies *A Six Pack of Stories, The Horror Zine 4,* and *Fresh Grounds Volume 3,* and will be releasing a new collection with his brother called *Brother's Ilk* in late 2012 and his new novel, *Shutdown,* in early 2013. To find out more, visit him at www.shaunmeeks.com.

Shaun's story "Taut" appeared in *Zippered Flesh 2: More Tales of Body Enhancements Gone Bad,* and his story "Despair" was included in *Someone Wicked: A Written Remains Anthology.*

CHRISTINE MORGAN

Christine Morgan divides her writing time among many genres, from horror to historical, from superheroes to smut, anything in between and combinations thereof. She's a wife, a mom, a future crazy-cat-lady and a longtime gamer, who enjoys British television, cheesy action/disaster movies, cooking and crafts. Her stories have appeared in maby publications, including *The Book of All Flesh, The Book of Final Flesh, The Best of All Flesh, History is Dead, The World is Dead, Strange Stories of Sand and Sea, Fear of the Unknown, Hell Hath No Fury, Dreaded Pall, Path of the Bold, Cthulhu Sex Magazine* and its best-of volume *Horror Between the Sheets, Closet Desire IV,* and *Leather, Lace and Lust. She's also a contributor to The Horror Fiction Review, a former member* of the HWA, a regular at local conventions, and an ambitious self-publisher (six fantasy novels, four horror novels, six children's fantasy books, and two role-playing supplements). Her work has appeared in *Pyramid Magazine, GURPS Villains,* been nominated for Origins Awards, and given Honorable Mention in two volumes of Year's Best Fantasy and Horror. Her romantic suspense novel, *The Widows Walk*, was recently released from Lachesis Publishing; her horror novel, *The Horned Ones*, is due out from Belfire in 2012; and her thriller *Murder Girls* was just accepted by Skullvines. She's currently delving into steampunk, making progress on an urban paranormal series, and greatly enjoying her bloodthirsty Viking stories.

Christine's work has been published in a number of Smart Rhino anthos, including "Thyf's Tale" in *Uncommon Assassins*, "The Sun-Snake" in *Zippered Flesh 2: More Tales of Body Enhancements Gone Bad*, and "Sven Bloodhair" in *Someone Wicked: A Written Remains Anthology*.

BILLIE SUE MOSIMAN

Billie Sue Mosiman's *Night Cruise* was nominated for the Edgar Award and her novel, *Widow*, was nominated for the Bram Stoker Award for Superior Novel. She's the author of fourteen novels and has published more than 160 short stories in various magazines and anthologies. A suspense thriller novelist, she often writes horror short stories. Her latest works include *Frankenstein: Return From the Wastelands*, continuing the saga of Robert Morton from Mary Shelley's classic, and *Prison Planet*, a near-future dystopian novella. She's been a columnist, reviewer, and writing instructor. She lives in Texas where the sun is too hot for humankind. All of her available works are at Amazon.com. Check out her blog, "The Life of a Peculiar Writer," at www.peculiarwriter.blogspot.com.

Her story, "Second Amendment Solution," was published in *Uncommon Assassins*. Billie's story, "The Flenser," appears in *Someone Wicked: A Written Remains Anthology*.

JM REINBOLD

JM Reinbold is the Director of the Written Remains Writers Guild in Wilmington, Delaware. She is the author of the novella "Transfusions," published in the anthology *Stories from the Inkslingers* (Gryphonwood Press, 2008). "Transfusions" was nominated for a Washington Science Fiction Association Small Press Award. Her poetry has appeared in Red Fez Magazine, *Strange Love* (2010) and *A Beat Style Haiku* (2012). In 2011, she received an honorable mention from the Delaware Division of the Arts Individual Artist Fellowships for her novel *Prince of the Piedmont*. She has been selected twice (2008, 2012) by the Delaware Division of the Arts as a fiction fellow for the Cape Henlopen Poets & Writers Retreat. In 2009, her novel-in-progress, *Summer's End*, was a finalist in the Magic Carpet Ride Magical Realism Mentorship competition. She is currently working on a mystery/crime novel, a number of short stories, and haiku. You can visit her online at www.jmreinbold.com.

Her story "The Future of Flesh," was published in *Zippered Flesh 2: More Tales of Body Enhancements Gone Bad*. JM's story, "Missing," was included in *Someone Wicked: A Written Remains Anthology*.

DOUG RINALDI

Doug was born and raised in the bowels of Connecticut. Spending his younger years exploring the woods near home, Doug envisioned otherworldly scenarios that ignited his imagination. Art was life. Throughout adolescence, he created, inventing horrifying tales about devious lunch ladies and world-eating monsters. In 1995, he received his art degree in Computer Animation and Special Effects for stage and screen. However, writing dark fiction was his true calling. At the turn of the millennium, he joyously bid Connecticut a final farewell and relocated to Boston, Massachusetts where he's been continuing to hone his writing and artistic skills ever since.

MARTIN ROSE

Martin Rose writes a range of fiction from the fantastic to the macabre. His latest horror novel, *Bring Me Flesh, I'll Bring Hell,* is available from Talos, with short fiction appearing in *Handsome Devil* and *Urban Green Man* anthologies, and slated to appear in anthologies like *Death's Realm* from Grey Matter Press, and *Shrieks and Shivers* from the Horror Zine. More details are available at www.martinrose.org.

J. GREGORY SMITH

Greg Smith is the bestselling author of the thriller *A Noble Cause* and the Paul Chang Mystery series, including *Final Price*, *Legacy of the Dragon*, and *Send in the Clowns*. His latest novel is *The Flamekeepers*, a doomsday cult thriller. Prior to writing fiction full time, Greg worked in public relations in Washington, D.C., Philadelphia, and Wilmington, Delaware. He has an MBA from the College of William & Mary and a BA in English from Skidmore College. His debut novel, *Final Price*, was first released as a self-published work, and then signed to publisher AmazonEncore, and was rereleased November 2010. Since then Greg has been working with Thomas & Mercer. He has just completed a new thriller outside of the Chang series called *Darwin's Pause*. Greg currently lives in Wilmington, Delaware with his wife, son, and dog. You can reach him at gregsmithbooks@yahoo.com.

Greg's story, "Something Borrowed," was published in *Zippered Flesh, Tales of Body Enhancements Gone Bad*. His story, "The Pepper Tyrant," appears in *Uncommon Assassins*.

L.L. SOARES

L.L. Soares is the Bram Stoker Award-winning author of the novel *Life Rage*, which was published by Nightscape Books in the fall of 2012. His other books include the short story collection *In Sickness* (with Laura Cooney), published by Skullvines Press in 2010, and the novels *Rock 'N' Roll* (from Gallows Press, early 2013) and the upcoming novel *Hard*, coming from Novello-Blue in the fall of 2013. His fiction appeared in such magazines as *Cemetery Dance*, *Horror Garage*, *Bare Bone*, *Shroud*, and *Gothic.Net*, as well as the anthologies *The Best of Horrorfind 2*, *Right House on the Left*, *Traps*, and the one you're holding in your hands. He also co-writes the Bram Stoker-nominated horror movie review column *Cinema Knife Fight*, which now has a whole site built around it at cinemaknifefight.com. No matter how many times he forces radioactive arachnids to bite him, he just can't seem to get the amazing abilities of a spider. To keep up on his endeavors, go to www.llsoares.com.

L.L.'s story, "Sawbones," was published in *Zippered Flesh: Tales of Body Enhancements Gone Bad!* His story, "Seeds," appeared in *Zippered*

394

Flesh 2: More Tales of Body Enhancements Gone Bad! His psychological horror tale, "Sometimes the Good Witch Sings to Me," is included in *Someone Wicked: A Written Remains Anthology.* L.L.'s novella, *Green Tsunami,* written with his wife, Laura Cooney, has also been published by Smart Rhino.

JEZZY WOLFE

Jezzy Wolfe is an author of dark fiction, with a predilection for absurdity. A lifelong native of Virginia Beach, Jezzy lives with her family and quite a few ferrets. Her poems and stories have appeared in such ezines and magazines as *The World of Myth, The Odd Mind, Twisted Tongue, Support the Little Guy,* and *Morpheus Tales.* She has also been published in a variety of anthologies, such as Graveside Tales' *Harvest Hill, The Best of the World of Myth: Vol. II,* Library of the Dead's *Baconology,* Western Legends' *Unnatural Tales of the Jackalope,* and the Choate Road fun book, *Knock, Knock ... Who's There? Death!* She was a founding member of Choate Road.com and at one time cohosted the blogtalk radio shows "The Funky Werepig" and "Pairanormal." In addition to her brand of humor and horror fiction, she maintains both a blog and storefront for ferret owners and lovers, known as FuzzyFriskyFierce. You can visit Jezzy Wolfe on her author's blog at jezzywolfe.wordpress.com, or her ferret blog at FuzzyFriskyFierce.wordpress.com.

Jezzy's story, "Locks of Loathe," was published in *Zippered Flesh: Tales of Body Enhancements Gone Bad.* Her story, "Luscious," was included in *Zippered Flesh 2: More Tales of Body Enhancements Gone Bad!*

MARTIN ZEIGLER

A retired software developer, Martin (Marty) Zeigler spends a good deal of his time writing fiction—primarily mystery, science fiction, and horror. His stories can be found in small-press anthologies and journals as well as online. In addition to writing, he enjoys reading, watching movies, dabbling on the piano, and taking long walks around his hometown of Portland, Oregon.

THE ILLUSTRATOR

WHITNEY COOK

Whitney Cook is a self-taught, professional freelance artist currently residing in Florida where she spends most of her free time spoiling her cat, drawing, reading, and collecting comic books (her collection being Wolverine-saturated.) She also spends a great deal of time goofing off on the Internet with her fellow comic book enthusiasts. Whitney does not remember being able to draw the first moment she grasped a crayon, like many artists claim. Rather, she had an "Aha!" moment—or more accurately a "Holy crap, I can draw!" moment—during high school, which is when things got much more colorful and creative for the artist. She has worked for multiple comic book companies as a colorist, and often takes personalized commissions from fans on the side. To see more of her work, visit www.whitneycook.deviantart.com.

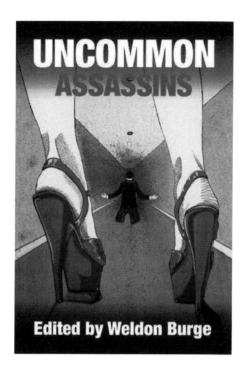

UNCOMMON ASSASSINS

Hired killers. Vigilantes. Executioners. Paid killers or assassins working from a moral or political motivation. You'll find them all in this thrilling anthology. But these are not ordinary killers, not your run-of-the-mill hit men. The emphasis is on the "uncommon" here—unusual characters, unusual situations, and especially unusual means of killing. Here are 23 tales by some of the best suspense/thriller writers today.

Stephen England * J. Gregory Smith * Lisa Mannetti * Ken Goldman * Christine Morgan *
Matt Hilton * Billie Sue Mosiman * Ken Bruen * Rob M. Miller * Monica J. O'Rourke *
F. Paul Wilson * Joseph Badal * Doug Blakeslee * Elliott Capon * Laura DiSilverio *
Michael Bailey * Jame S. Dorr * Jonathan Templar * J. Carson Black * Weldon Burge *
Al Boudreau * Charles Coyott * Lynn Mann

Available in paperback and Kindle eBook from Amazon.com.

Also visit smartrhino.com for the latest from Smart Rhino Publications.

ZIPPERED FLESH 2:
More Tales of Body Enhancements Gone Bad!

So, you loved the first **ZIPPERED FLESH** anthology? Well, here are yet more tales of body enhancements that have gone horribly wrong! Chilling tales by some of the best horror writers today, determined to keep you fearful all night (and maybe even a little skittish during the day).

Bryan Hall * Shaun Meeks * Lisa Mannetti * Carson Buckingham * Christine Morgan * Kate Monroe * Daniel I. Russell * M.L. Roos * Rick Hudson * J.M. Reinbold * E.A. Black * L.L. Soares * Doug Blakeslee * Kealan Patrick Burke * A.P. Sessler * David Benton & W.D. Gagliani * Jonathan Templar * Christian A. Larsen * Shaun Jeffrey * Jezzy Wolfe * Charles Colyott * Michael Bailey

Available in paperback and Kindle eBook from Amazon.com.

Also visit smartrhino.com for the latest from Smart Rhino Publications.

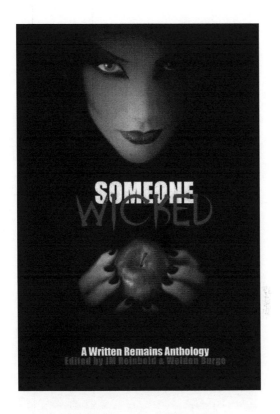
401

GREEN TSUNAMI
A Novella by Laura Cooney & L.L. Soares

Laura Cooney and L.L. Soares have created an apocalyptic novella that is disturbing, graphic, and provocative. A mysterious "green tsunami" has swept the planet—and nothing will be the same as both living and inanimate things begin to metamorphosize into a new horrifying reality. The story is told entirely via emails between a man and his wife, separated by the catastrophe, describing the terrors they must face as they strive to survive.

The cover illustration is by Dan Verkys, with a cover design by Ju Kim. Interior illustrations were created by Will Renfro, Justynn Tyme, and Ju Kim.

Available in paperback and Kindle eBook from Amazon.com.

Also visit smartrhino.com for the latest from Smart Rhino Publications.